ALTERNATE
PEACE

Other Anthologies Edited by:

Patricia Bray & Joshua Palmatier

After Hours: Tales from the Ur-bar
The Modern Fae's Guide to Surviving Humanity
Clockwork Universe: Steampunk vs Aliens
Temporally Out of Order
Alien Artifacts
Were-
All Hail Our Robot Conquerors!
Second Round: A Return to the Ur-bar

S.C. Butler & Joshua Palmatier

Submerged
Guilds & Glaives

Laura Anne Gilman & Kat Richardson

The Death of All Things

Troy Carrol Bucher & Joshua Palmatier

The Razor's Edge

Patricia Bray & S.C. Butler

Portals

David B. Coe & Joshua Palmatier

Temporally Deactivated

Steven H Silver & Joshua Palmatier

Alternate Peace

ALTERNATE PEACE

Edited by

Steven H Silver
&
Joshua Palmatier

Zombies Need Brains LLC
www.zombiesneedbrains.com

Interior Design (ebook): April Steenburgh
Interior Design (print): ZNB Design
Cover Design by ZNB Design
Cover Art "Alternate Peace" by Justin Adams

ZNB Book Collectors #15
All characters and events in this book are fictitious.
All resemblance to persons living or dead is coincidental.

Kickstarter Edition Printing, June 2019
First Printing, July 2019

Print ISBN-10: 1940709261
Print ISBN-13: 978-1940709260

Ebook ISBN-10: 194070927X
Ebook ISBN-13: 978-1940709277

Printed in the U.S.A.

COPYRIGHTS

Table of Contents

SIGNATURE PAGE

Steven H Silver, editor:

_____

Joshua Palmatier, editor:

_____

Elektra Hammond:

_____

Dale Cozort:

_____

Harry Turtledove:

_____

C.W. Briar:

_____

Rick Wilber:

_____

Juliet E. McKenna:

_____

Michael Robertson:

_____

Kat Otis:

_____

Kristine Kathryn Rusch:

_____

Brian Hugenbruch:

_____

Stephen Leigh:

_____

Elizabeth Kite:

_____

Ian R. MacLeod:

_____

Mike Barretta:

_____

Kari Sperring:

_____

Justin Adams, artist:

_____

INTRODUCTION

Steven H Silver

Like science fiction, alternate history is a game of "what if." While science fiction explores the ifs of science, alternate history explores the ifs of history, introducing points in time when the fictional history branches off from the established history of our own timeline to produce a new world, rife for exploration.

Sometimes it seems like the only historical branch points that are explored by authors are those that arise out of war. What would have happened if the Civil War had gone a different way? What if the Nazis had won World War II? What if the American Revolution had failed?

However, there are many more peaceful points of divergence which can be explored, some of which may impact world history just as much, while others may have more focused changes.

On June 5, 1858, a cub pilot on the steamboat *Pennsylvania* got into yet another argument with the pilot who was teaching him. The pilot, William Brown, put the cub pilot ashore and continued his journey. The cub pilot managed to continue his training under another pilot on a different steamship.

This incident can be used to explore how alternate history can work on a microscale. The cub pilot could have stayed on the *Pennsylvania* with Brown rather than the two men going their separate ways. If the cub pilot had stayed on board, surely nothing really would have changed. Except…

On June 13, 1858, the steamship *Pennsylvania* was cruising on the Mississippi near Memphis, Tennessee when its boiler exploded. The ship was destroyed and more than 250 of the 450 people on board were killed, with many more fatalities over the next few weeks, including the cub pilot's brother, who had recently been brought on board at his brother's urging.

The altercation between Brown and his cub had a major impact on the young man's life. Although he lived, when he otherwise may have died, he suffered the immense loss of his brother. Still, nothing really changed the world's history because he was put ashore. Except…

The cub pilot was a boy named Samuel L. Clemens, who would adopt the name Mark Twain. His writing, which included descriptions of the loss of the *Pennsylvania*, was often influenced by his training on the river and the tragic death of his brother Henry. Had William Brown not put Clemens ashore, the world would have missed out on the writings of Mark Twain, as well as all those he influenced over the years.

Many alternate histories can be written that trace the point of change to Mark Twain's death in the explosion on board the *Pennsylvania* in 1858. Others could explore how different Twain's writing might have been if Henry hadn't been injured in the explosion and died a week later, or if Twain had never found Henry a berth on the doomed ship in the first place.

Each branch point, whether in time of peace or time of war, can lead to a myriad of stories, limited only by the imagination of the author and the plausibility of the changes they introduce into the time stream.

There is a time for war and a time for peace. This is the time for peace. This volume offers the latter, with fifteen stories of alternate history that explore changes that occurred in a time of peace. Some of the stories take place immediately after the point where the timelines diverge and will present a world which is familiar to the one in which we live. Others are set many years after the divergence and may seem to be set in practically a different world.

—Wapakoneta, OH, March 31, 2019

O-RINGS

Elektra Hammond

Letter Steve to Christa, 1/23/1986

Darling—

The kids are good, but they miss you. It's hard for them. You've been gone so long it feels like forever.

Don't get me wrong—I'm the one who pushed you into applying to be the Teacher in Space, and I still think that NASA, and the whole world, are damn lucky to have you. I just wish there was some way that the kids and I didn't have to give you up for so long to make it happen.

I thanked Scott for spurring us to move to New Hampshire—it's been a godsend having family nearby. You should have seen the confused look on his face! I explained that we'd talked about raising our family in New Hampshire, but it wasn't until he was born that we really sat down and hashed it out. It made him feel really good to know that he played such an important role in our relocation, and it distracted him from missing you. I've really done well here, working in the AG's office, although I can't help but wonder sometimes what would have happened if I'd taken that position at Justice and we'd stayed in D.C. One thing's for sure—you wouldn't be where you are. I think you'd be a lawyer, not a teacher, maybe working with me at Justice. Maybe on civil rights? With your knack for organization you might be a judge already. But I wouldn't take going into space away from you, not for anything.

I still don't have the whole "running the household" thing down. I don't know how you do it. I've practically been living on cornflakes for the last nine months. If not for your parents and mine feeding the kids from time to time—and taking them off my hands once in a while so I can catch up—I don't know what I would do. There's not enough time to work and take care of the kids and cook and do laundry. And sleep. It has been the longest nine months of my life. I am so proud that you're doing this, but I don't know if I can keep it up.

I so miss our old life, when we did everything together. I miss you, space lady. This is my last letter before we see you in Florida—can't wait.

I love you, always.

—Steve a.k.a. the Cornflake Kid

MEMORANDUM

To: Jess Moore, Associate Administrator of the Office of Space Flight, NASA Mission Management Team

From: Allan J. McDonald, Senior Representative, Space Shuttle Solid Rocket Motor Project, Morton Thiokol

Subject: Shuttle Solid Rocket Boosters (SRBs)
Date: 27 January 1986

I cannot sign off on the launch of Challenger tomorrow, due to concerns about the ability of the SRBs to perform in extremely low temperatures. The Solid Rocket Boosters are only rated as low as 40 degrees—it could be as much as 20 degrees lower than that tomorrow. There have been some indications of trouble with temperatures as high as 53 degrees. This is a possible design flaw we need to investigate further.

Weather below freezing may also cause the formation of ice on the launch pad, a circumstance that we have not allowed for. It could cause unanticipated problems with the launch or, in the worst case, damage to the shuttle.

Additionally, I've been advised the shuttle recovery ships are experiencing rough seas. They need to check over their equipment and are currently too far out of position to support an early morning launch.

In my professional opinion, we should delay until more clement weather, ideally a minimum of 55 degrees.

[NASA News Logo]

National Aeronautics and
Space Administration

John F. Kennedy Space Center
Kennedy Space Center, Florida 32899
AC 305 867-2468

                                     For Release
Shirley M. Green   Immediate
Headquarters/Washington, D.C.
SHUTTLE MISSION 51-L LAUNCH POSTPONED

Shuttle mission 51-L, originally scheduled to launch on January 28, 1986 has been postponed until Monday, February 3rd, 1986, due to unseasonably cold weather at the Kennedy Space Center.

NOTE TO EDITORS: This release and other NASA information is available electronically through ITT DIALCOM. For access to NASA NEWS through this system, contact Jim Hawley, ITT Dialcom, Inc. At 202/488-0550.

[Transcript of audio communication from Challenger]

I love you, Steve! How're Scott and Caroline? We had a bit of excitement when we launched, made me realize how unprepared I really am, even after one hundred seventeen hours of training. One of the tool cabinets got knocked open and we ended up with some gear swinging through the cabin. The crew though is incredible. They locked it down before I could move. Ron and Judy somehow managed to grab the stuff and hang on to it, but one piece still smacked me in the arm. It could have been so much worse if they hadn't been on the ball.

As soon as we have a good TV signal, I've got to give my class in space. I love you, Sweetheart. See you soon!

[Note on bottle of champagne from Barbara Morgan to Christa]

Christa—

Congrats! You did it!

It was the look on your face when you landed. I've heard of the look of eagles—never thought I'd actually see it. You seem…more, somehow. I was on the fence about what to do, but talking to you gave me real clarity. I've decided to stay in the program, train to be a mission specialist.

I've never been second best at anything, but it's not jealousy. The joy you brought back—I want to follow the trail you blazed into space.

Your friend, forever,

Barbara

Concord Monitor, February 24, 1986

"Teacher in Space Returns Home" by Robert Hohler

Our newest celebrity is back. Concord High's Christa McAuliffe returned home today after spending 6 days in space aboard the shuttle Challenger, doing what she does best—teaching. Now the whole world knows why her classes are so popular. She's in town for a few days to spend time with her family before she goes on tour promoting NASA and the space program.

I had the opportunity to view her lessons from space, along with the students from Concord High, and the energy in the room was incredible. Her excitement about space exploration was evident in "Where We've Been, Where We're Going, and Why," the second of the transmissions from the Challenger. She looked so comfortable up there, weightless—a glimpse into our future. I could see that energy reflected on the faces of the students, as her fascination with history and science drew them into the lesson. I predict an awful lot of these kids are going to work hard on their science homework, with thoughts of being astronauts on their mind.

If only I were younger…

Letter Steve to Christa, 6/15/1986

Darling—

I'm okay, busier than usual. The kids are great—the usual end of the school year stuff is keeping them busy. Scott is doing great in all his classes, despite all the distractions. I'm afraid Caroline has been a little off—we might see some Cs on her report card this term. She's been talking about being a teacher, just like her mom. Scott wants to be an astronaut, like his mom. No lawyers to follow in their dad's footsteps.

I keep trying to set aside time every Sunday to write you, but I get distracted trying to catch up with the stuff I didn't do all week. Mundane stuff like laundry and cleaning.

I've also been under the gun at work. We've got a huge case that may end up being a class action suit against one of the utilities. It's keeping everyone occupied taking depositions and correlating information. If it's as big as I think it is, we might end up before the Supreme Court. Or they could settle. That would be better for the clients, I think.

I miss you very, very much. Not just because the house runs so much better when you're here. I mean, it does, but it's empty enough to echo when you're out of town. After the kids go to bed, I wish I could call you. But I never know the number. You're traveling all the time. I know it's exhausting for you, but holding down the fort is tiring, too.

I miss you more than I can adequately explain.

I love you,

—Steve a.k.a. chief holder down of Fort McAuliffe

Concord Monitor, January 20, 1987

President Reagan has announced he will nominate Steven J. McAuliffe to be Federal district judge for the District of New Hampshire. Mr. McAuliffe is currently in private practice in Concord, New Hampshire. Previously he served as an assistant attorney general in New Hampshire.

Letter Christa to Steve, 1/20/1987

Sweetheart—

It's so exciting that you're going to be a judge. I know it's something that you thought would happen one day, but not so soon. That class action suit you were lead on, and the great settlement you got the utility to give up, really put you in the public eye. I know this is just the start of great things for you!

I'll make sure that I'm in Washington for your confirmation hearing—it looks better if your spouse is there to support you. I'm sure my mom will take care of the kids. Maybe you could stay in Washington for a couple of days and we could have a weekend away, just the two of us?

Love you,
—Christa

Telegram Christa McAuliffe to Steven McAuliffe, 3/18/1987

STEVE, CONGRATULATIONS ON BEING CONFIRMED. SO SORRY I COULDN'T MAKE THE HEARING, EMERGENCY CAME UP. WILL CALL YOU WHEN YOU RETURN TO NEW HAMPSHIRE. LOVE, CHRISTA

Letter Steve to Christa, 10/18/1987

Darling—

The kids are starting to act out. They miss you. You need to call more often. Better yet, you need to visit. Sending them letters once in a while, and calling them once a week, just isn't enough. You've only been home once since Christmas!

This is really, really wearing on me. It's not that I mind taking care of the kids, but I've been doing this solo act almost nonstop 2 1/2 years. I'm starting to forget what you look like. The kids need their mother. Don't get me wrong— it's great that you're promoting the space program and you're writing a book, but don't forget that you have a family. We need you, too.

There was a time when we could talk about anything. We made it through college in different states—but back then you visited me all the time. Remember coming down to VMI every couple of weeks? We had it great back then. I didn't appreciate how lucky I was that you took the time to come visit when you had classes of your own back home. Troublemaker that I was, I was restricted to campus most weekends. And I was the only guy walking patrol whose girlfriend walked it with him, keeping him company. I set some sort of record for gaining rank and then losing it again. The high point of my entire college career was your visits.

From the time we started dating in high school, it's always been you. I never even looked at another girl. I never wanted to.

We can work this out—I just need to see you and talk to you. Please.

I love you,

—Steve a.k.a. that guy from VMI

Letter Christa to Steve, 12/12/1987

Sweetheart—

I'll be home from Christmas to New Year's and we can have a mini-vacation. I'm so looking forward to finally getting home. I'm sorry I had to cancel my last two trips back—but the book is finally done. And I have just one more speaking engagement, then I'm done until next year.

I've missed you and the kids so much. I bought the kids little gifts from everywhere I've been, and I've got a bunch of magnets to add to the refrigerator.

I'll set aside time to talk. And I'll cook a bunch of stuff for the freezer. It's not that much longer before I'll be home for good.

Love you,

—Christa

Letter Steve to Christa, 12/13/1987

Darling—

We're all fine here, eagerly waiting for you to get home for Christmas. I know you'll be home soon, but I wanted to tell you again how much we all miss you. I can't wait until you're home full time. After Christmas, it's just a few months and then you're done, right? We get to go back to our rather dull, ordinary life all together in New Hampshire.

The Christmas tree is ready, sitting in the living room waiting for you so we can decorate it as a family. I've done all the shopping, all we need to make things perfect here is you.

Whatever you do, please don't cancel this trip. I don't know how I would explain it to the kids. We really need the family time. And you and I need to spend some quality time together.

How do you feel about going away the weekend after Christmas, just the two of us? We could drive down to Boston and stay in a nice hotel, maybe get tickets for a show or the ballet.

Merry Christmas. I love you,

—Steve a.k.a. the holiday cookie maker

Letter Christa to Steve, 3/30/1988

Sweetheart—

I got a job offer. I know this NASA thing was winding down, and I was supposed to be coming home for good, but I have to consider this.

Do you remember when I applied for the assistant principal job? I wanted to do more—not just teach classes but organize, run things, make a difference on a larger scale. This job would let me do that. I would be in charge of Communications—for all of NASA—helping get the message out. Think how many people I could help, how much good I could do.

But we'd have to move back to Washington. That wouldn't be so bad—you've got contacts at Justice, and I know people, too. Or you could go into private practice— or work for congress. Your old boss Steny Hoyer is in the House of Representatives now, I bet he knows folks who need a good prosecutor.

Let's talk about this.

I love you so very much. Please understand.

All my love,

—Christa

Letter Steve to Christa, 4/5/1988

Christa—

Please don't take this job. You talked me into leaving Washington to go to New Hampshire—it was the right thing to do—but we can't uproot again and move back. The kids are still in school. Our families are here. My job as a federal judge is here. It's just not fair to the family. We've spent the last 3 years being the nonstop Christa show—is this ever going to end and go back to being the McAuliffe FAMILY?

I love you so very much, but for the sake of your children, think about this very hard.

Love,

—Steve

[NASA News Logo]

National Aeronautics and
Space Administration

John F. Kennedy Space Center
Kennedy Space Center, Florida 32899
AC 305   867-2468

For Release

Shirley M. Green   May 13, 1988

Headquarters/Washington, D.C.

MCAULIFFE NAMED ASSISTANT ADMINISTRATOR FOR
COMMUNICATIONS

S. Christa McAuliffe has been appointed
Assistant Administrator for Communications
at the National Aeronautics and Space
Administration. The appointment is effective
May 16, 1988.

McAuliffe first joined NASA when she was
selected for Shuttle Mission 51-L, beating
out thousands to be the first teacher-in-
space, charming the nation as she conducted
the ultimate field trip aboard the space
shuttle *Challenger*.

For the year following the launch, she
proved invaluable at promoting NASA and the
space program. Her book, *Space: The Ultimate
Field Trip*, based on her selection and
training for the 51-L mission, was the top
selling book of 1987.

Prior to working for NASA, McAuliffe was
a teacher at Concord High in Concord, New
Hampshire, where she developed a class called
The American Woman, showing history from the
perspective of ordinary people.

McAuliffe received a bachelor of arts
degree from Framingham State College and
a master's degree in education from Bowie
State University.

McAuliffe and her husband, Steve, have two
children.

NOTE TO EDITORS: This release and other NASA information is available electronically through ITT DIALCOM. For access to NASA NEWS through this system, contact Jim Hawley, ITT Dialcom, Inc. At 202/488-0550.

Letter Christa to Steve, 5/10/1988, delivered in person with a big box of chocolates and a dozen red roses

Steve, Sweetheart—

I'm so sorry—this is the kind of job I've been looking for all my life. It will allow me to make a difference. Once the school year is over next month we can find a place, in the right school district, and move the kids down here.

I will spend the rest of my life working to make this move up to you. I promise.

It'll be educational for the kids to live in Washington— they'll love the Smithsonian and all the monuments, especially now that they're old enough to really appreciate them. We'll make sure you find a terrific job, too, even if I have to go door-to-door through the halls of Congress asking who's looking for a prosecutor and telling them how great you would be.

I love you so very, very much,

—Christa

[NASA News Release ON LINE Logo]
JOHN F. KENNEDY SPACE CENTER

Barbara Selby
Headquarters, Washington, D.C.
February 2, 1994
(Phone: 202/358-1983)

RELEASE: 94-21

MCAULIFFE NAMED ASSOCIATE DEPUTY ADMINISTRATOR POLICY

S. Christa McAuliffe has been appointed the Associate Deputy Administrator for Policy at the National Aeronautics and Space Administration, starting February 3, 1994.

For the last five years, McAuliffe has been serving as the NASA Assistant Administrator for Communications. Almost exactly eight years ago she made history as the first civilian in space, as part of Shuttle Mission 51-L aboard the space shuttle *Challenger*.

The publicity surrounding her shuttle trip was a boon to NASA, helping justify our budget requests. She's been a part of the NASA family ever since, taking on growing responsibilities as she helped build NASA's image into something we're all proud of.

Prior to working for NASA, McAuliffe was a teacher at Concord High in Concord, New Hampshire.

McAuliffe has a bachelor of arts from Framingham State College, a master's in education from Bowie State University, and a master of business administration from Georgetown University.

McAuliffe and her husband, Steve, have two children.

-end-

Letter Christa to Steve, 4/5/1995

Steve—

The kids are done with school June 10th. There are some parties that weekend they'll want to attend.

Feel free to make arrangements for them to travel up to New Hampshire for the summer any time after that. They'll need to be back by August 20th for me to get them ready for the school year.

—Christa

[NASA News Release ON LINE Logo]
JOHN F. KENNEDY SPACE CENTER

Dwayne C. Brown
Headquarters, Washington, D.C.
April 8, 1999
(Phone: 202/358-1983)
RELEASE: 99-51

MCAULIFFE NAMED NASA ADMINISTRATOR

S. Christa McAuliffe has been appointed Administrator of the National Aeronautics and Space Administration, effective immediately.

McAuliffe began her NASA career as the "teacher-in-space" aboard the space shuttle *Challenger* in 1986. She combined working to promote NASA to the general public with improving internal communications and organization, moving steadily through the ranks until her current appointment.

McAuliffe has a strong commitment to education. She worked as a teacher at Concord High in Concord, New Hampshire prior to joining NASA, and she has a bachelor of arts from Framingham State College, a master's in education from Bowie State University, and a master of business administration from Georgetown University. She is currently working toward her doctor of philosophy in government from Georgetown.

    McAuliffe has two children.

    -end-

A DAD OUGHT TO HAVE NIGHTMARES

Dale Cozort

Raymond Oakes, Ray to his friends, paced in the waiting room at six in the morning on February 25, 1955, as his wife had their first son. The world remembers that day for a different sun, the brief one the Nazis created in a depopulated stretch of jungle in the German Kongo.

Ray didn't hear about the German-made sun—the first of three that blossomed within the next month—for several hours. The crowd around the TV caught his eye, but he ignored it, engaged in his own worries. He discovered what had happened when his pacing took him near the waiting room's bulky black and white TV. The TV showed the mushroom cloud and said President Dewey would address the nation in the evening.

Ray missed the speech because he finally got a chance to see his wife and his incredibly tiny, fragile son. Nobody offered to let him hold the little boy and he didn't feel any urge to do so. *I would drop it…him.*

The doctor told him to go home and get some sleep. He drove his three-year-old Studebaker sedan to an empty ranch-style house in the Misty Ridge subdivision, upper-middle class and recently torn from a cornfield. Ray hadn't thought much about the German atomic bomb blast at the hospital or on the way home. *Another piece of German bombast, like their satellites and space station and moon base.* The Führer was on TV when he got home, looking old and paunchy as he spoke, and an interpreter passed on the words, touting the new German weapons as a demonstration of German power, but also a symbol of the Reich's desire for peace.

How does that even make sense? Ray wished the fat German a massive coronary, but Herman Goering droned on. Douglas Edwards of CBS News came on. "This just in: British Prime Minister Eden has announced that the British Commonwealth has developed the same technology the Germans used for their super bomb and will be testing it in Australia within the month. French Premier Faure has announced a similar test. Neither Italy's King Vittorio Emanuele IV nor Josef Stalin, the increasingly reclusive General Secretary of the Soviet Union, have had any comments so far."

News anchor Douglas Edwards summarized President Dewey's speech. *A lot of nothing.* Blah blah concerned this new technology will escalate tensions in Europe. Blah blah confirms the wisdom of US policies of avoiding entangling European alliances. Blah blah our technology is the best in the world. *Except in ship-building, rockets, and now super bombs.* Blah blah the power of the new German bomb is unknown and may or may not represent a breakthrough in power. *Except it's obvious from the pictures that it does unless they managed to fake the size of the explosion.*

Ray's engineering mind did an order of magnitude calculation. He went back over his figures a couple of times, writing them down on the back of an ink-stained receipt, and finally figured he had to have misplaced a decimal point. He tossed the paper on his desk.

Nazis. A bunch of bloody-handed idiots. And now they ruin my son's special day. "Daniel Oakes." He said the name out loud. There was still some question as to whether that would be the little boy's final name. Ray liked the sound of it. Jenny, his wife, was less enthusiastic.

Ray didn't know what to make of the new German bomb. He worried about tensions in Europe but while Europe always seemed headed toward another Great War, it never quite got there, not since the Great War's guns fell silent.

The oceans isolated the US from Europe's squabbles, though not as much as they once did. German, French, British, and Italian satellites passed over the US daily, advertising their owners' global reach. The Dewey Administration mostly ignored space, leaving the field to private efforts by big aerospace and auto companies.

He didn't intend to fall asleep in front of the TV, but he did. The phone woke him late that evening. He heard a familiar voice. "Raymond, we have a job for you. "

"I have a job. And a son. Daniel Oakes." *I hope. I love that name.*

"Congratulations. You're doing well as a commercial pilot, too, I hear."

"Very well. I'm happy. I'm looking forward to time with my son and my wife. You aren't part of my plans."

"The Germans aren't part of my plans or your plans," the familiar voice said. "But there they are. Their rockets can send satellites over the United States. And now they have super bombs. I'm sure you calculated the power to weight ratio."

"The bomb is too heavy to fit on a rocket," Ray said. "We've stayed out of Europe's problems. The Germans don't worry me." His voice betrayed the uncertainty that lurked in the back of his mind. He felt a fierce surge of protectiveness toward his son, still untouched by his hands and only glimpsed for a few minutes. *Careful. That's what he wants. A decision made from fear.*

"It will certainly fit in one of their bombers. And are you sure they won't make it smaller? Maybe not in a month, but in a year or five years? You're in this for the long haul now. That's what having a kid is all about, isn't it?"

Ray leaned his head back, stared at the white-tiled ceiling, and thought about a little boy, *Daniel!* playing in a crib, taking his first steps, saying his first words, tossing a soft oversized ball to his dad, all in the shadow of Goering's rockets and the big German jet bombers coming over the North Pole, equipped with the new bomb.

"There isn't a lot I can do about it," Ray said. "They have this super bomb and we don't. It's a good thing we stay out of European politics."

"Except that we don't have any friends in Europe and if Germany decides to put battleships off Brazil or Mexico we'll have to keep those bombs and missiles in mind when we decide what to do about it. Or if Goering and company screw up the German economy beyond redemption, do you think they won't come to us and politely but firmly tell us that cut-rate loans will be necessary, with their super bombs sitting at the negotiating table, with the threat of burning US cities sitting in the back of everybody's minds?"

"What do want me to do?" That wasn't something he wanted to ask, not exhausted, not on this special day, not with Daniel's life just starting. He asked it anyway, his voice resigned.

The voice at the other end of the line, the voice from another life, one before wife or Daniel, didn't change. No hint of triumph. No relief. No emotion at all. "Meet me at Eagle Park. Nine tomorrow morning. Call in sick to work. You should be done in time for work Monday. Oh, and congratulations. I'll have a cigar for you tomorrow." Those last words sounded warm and sincere, an oddity given their source.

Ray sat staring at the receiver as the dial tone grew angry. Finally, he put it firmly back on its black base. Thoughts of Daniel and his wife clung to a corner of his brain as he shifted to a rusty but still solid set of habits. He pulled a box off the top shelf of his closet and extracted a semi-automatic 9 mm pistol, along with a magazine and a box of ammo. He checked the mechanism, then paused and stared at the weapon. He saw the nearly hairless, fragile face of his son—still red from the trauma of birth—in the air between him and the weapon. Finally, he filled the magazine. *For you, Daniel. I hope.*

He put the magazine in the weapon and held it with a mix of eagerness and revulsion. Revulsion won, temporarily. He popped the magazine out and put the unloaded weapon in the nightstand drawer.

The TV was still on. He walked over and turned the dial. All four channels were filled with news of the German bomb. CBS news was calling it an "atomic bomb," quickly shortened to A-bomb. Douglas Edwards mentioned the short time between the German test and the planned British and French ones and asked retired Air Force general Curtis LeMay if it was the result of a close-run arms race. The general shook his head. "If the British and French really do test A-bombs within a month, they have almost certainly had A-bombs for a while, but wisely, in my opinion, decided not to do a public test of them. The biggest secret about this type of bomb is that it is possible."

"Does the US have a secret program similar to the British and French ones?" Edwards asked.

"If we didn't yesterday, we do now," General LeMay said. "And if we didn't yesterday that's the biggest and darkest secret that our government has at this time."

The commentator went on to talk about Europe's bloody history, about the madness of the Thirty Years' War, the Napoleonic Wars, and the final horrible spasm of the Great War. He also talked about Europe's bloody conquest and colonization of most of the world, and ended with the "cleansing," the ironic term the Nazis used for their systematic deportation of black Africans from their Kongo colony to death camps deep in the interior or to be worked to death in the huge public works projects that the original Führer was so fond of.

The Nazis still denied the existence of the "cleansing," as did their apologists in the US. *Way too many of them burrowed into our society and this A-bomb will encourage them, just like the moon shots and the moon base did. They'll claim that it's German super-technology, from the master race, from the political and economic system of the future.* The fat comic-opera figure of the Führer on TV made a mockery of that carefully orchestrated propaganda, though not in the eyes of the true believers, the inevitable discontents of society, always looking for simple answers to unanswered problems in their own lives. *They aren't so much Nazis or Commies; they simply want convenient answers, a system of beliefs to embrace the way they would have embraced religion before that went out of style among intellectual types.*

Ray fell asleep with his clothes on. It was surprisingly untroubled, fueled by exhaustion. If he dreamed, those dreams faded before he woke.

* * *

The park was nearly deserted on Saturday morning, with the exception of a gray man standing by a teeter-totter, idly swinging the ends up and down. The gray man, in his gray suit, gray hat, and faintly gray complexion, turned as Ray approached him.

The men did not exchange pleasantries. The gray man said, "Are you still good at what you did?"

"I'm rusty. Why me?"

"The other side has been suspiciously successful at rolling up or turning our assets lately, enough so that we're in a mole hunt."

"Which other side? The Nazis or the Soviets?"

"The Nazis, which is part of the reason to suspect a mole. The *Abwehr* has historically not been that good. But suddenly they are."

Ray nodded. "And you haven't isolated the source of the problem."

"Not yet. And now we have a walk-in that may give us a break in the biggest mystery of the last two decades. I want him alive. I want him unintimidated. I don't want to give our mole any chance to tip off the *Abwehr*. So I know about this, and you. Nobody else. I called you last night from a random payphone after I made sure I wasn't being followed."

"How about this morning?"

"Are you trying to be insulting?"

Yeah, the thought had crossed my mind. "Everybody slips up sometime. Doesn't hurt to ask."

"The source checks out as far as I could tell without drawing attention to him, but you have the engineering background to know if he really has something useful. Debrief him, get the information and the source directly to me, and go home to your wife and your son. That's all."

Ray didn't ask what the mystery was. He didn't have to.

The gray man gave him the details of the mission, then forced an anomalous smile to his face and produced a pricey Cuban cigar. "Congratulations!"

The tradecraft came back to Ray quickly, too quickly to suit him. He checked his car for bugs and automatically went through a couple routines to throw off trackers. He stopped and called the hospital from a pay phone. A nurse told him that both mother and baby were resting comfortably. He gave the woman a message to pass onto his wife, a lie, that he was sick with a touch of the flu and didn't want to give it to mother or newborn. The lie came off his lips too easily. *I've never lied to her before.* That seemed incongruous given his current employment. *Just for two days, then I go back to being husband, pilot, and dad.*

The source was a retired German engine technician, now in his late sixties. Ray drove to the man's hotel, a rundown extended-stay place with thin, tired-looking hookers hanging out in the lobby, pale under their heavy makeup. The hookers looked interested, then took a closer look and headed for the door. *I have cop on me somehow, the way I move, the way I'm dressed.*

Ray concentrated on blending in. *Horny businessman. Here to meet someone specific, someone classier and higher priced than you.* Based on the reactions of the working girls he met in the stairway and the hall on the way to the contact's third-floor room, he got back closer to the groove. *Blending in. Not getting noticed by hotel security/pimps.* In this hotel the two were probably the same.

The German was tall, well over six feet, and bulky. His face looked all of his sixty-plus years, wrinkled and mottled. He held a gun, a Luger, mostly hidden behind a towel when he opened the door.

Ray brought out the identification the gray man had given him. The gun muzzle moved subtly, no long quite pointing at him.

"Otto Hessler?"

"Yes. And you are the man whose name doesn't matter, according to my contacts." Otto spoke near perfect English with a hint of a Bavarian accent.

Ray nodded. "I imagine they would say that. Call me Ray."

The German let him in and they sat at a once-expensive oak table, its surface marred with interlocking water-stain circles. A lamp with a crushed woven shade shot a circle of glaring light on the table. Otto insisted that they each have a beer before they settled down to business. Ray took his pick from a six pack of unopened cans and watched the German do likewise. They sat in hard wooden chairs that creaked at every movement, not saying much as Ray sipped his beer and the German slowly savored his.

Finally, Otto placed his empty can on the table and spread a taped-together collection of five lined notebook pages across the surface next to it. He pointed to a hand-drawn sketch that spanned the pages. "This is the engine layout of the pocket battleship *Admiral Graf Spree*, as of September 1939. I drew it from memory, so there may be small mistakes after these fifteen years."

Ray studied the sketch. The layout looked plausible. He asked a couple of questions designed to trip up a non-mechanic and got replies that at least indicated experience with German sea-craft.

Ray nodded. "I'll put you down as a maybe. The Nazis don't let mechanics who have worked around their special ships or planes or rockets out of the country. How did you get here?"

Otto grinned. "They screwed up. I asked for a visa and got one."

"The Nazis may be morons, but they're careful with their special projects. Why did they screw up this time?"

"I got out of the navy under special circumstances. I like the beer. The brass thought I liked it too much. It was early days of the Nazi regime and they were gearing up for war, so for a while they looked the other way. But then they got the fleet up to staff and cut back naval construction after the Baltic War. I got cut back to civilian. After the Baltic War they focused on building up the army to take on the Bolsheviks for real, so not much later I was on a Panzer III assembly line sending those sad tanks to the Dnieper River. I retired as an assembly worker for the defense industry. Perhaps that took me off one special list and put me on another. The brass doesn't care if a boozing old tank assembler comes to America for the night-life and that's how they class me."

Ray didn't totally buy that, though it wasn't impossible. The German did show signs of the heavy drinker now that Ray looked for them. *Only so many fields on a Hollerith card. One for getting kicked out of the navy as a drunk. One for "worked in the war industry." No room for the one that said, "this guy worked near the biggest secret Germany has."* Unlikely, but not impossible given the foibles of bureaucracies.

"All of that's interesting, but unless you got a look at the private parts it doesn't do us any good. The people at our embassy seemed to think you got a peek. Tell me about it."

"It is not quite so simple. I mentioned a two and whole bunch of zeroes after it at the embassy. Show me the right number of Grover Clevelands and I'll draw you a picture of what I saw."

"Thousand-dollar bills, huh? You don't see many of them around these days. I don't think they make them anymore." Ray pulled out a hundred-dollar bill. "If this is all about beer money, start by earning out a Benjamin Franklin?"

"It isn't all about beer money. Germany used to be a civilized place, with great poets and scientists and thinkers. Now the face of Germany is rats who climbed out of the gutter." The German drew a circle on his engine room layout. "There was a metal circle about eight feet in diameter on the inside mounted here. It was two feet thick. You could tell it was heavy because of the time it took to spin up. It would only spin up if the ship was moving fast and, even then, it didn't spin fast, maybe once every fifteen seconds. It spun quiet. You wouldn't hear it moving even right next to it. If you were in the engine room when it was spinning, you'd get little jolts, not unpleasant and not a shock. It was like when a car goes down a small steep place, not too long and not too steep."

"A feel-good drop?" Ray didn't know what the word for the feeling really was, but thought he understood what the German was describing.

"Perhaps. The jolts came more often the faster the circle spun." The man moved his hand toward the hundred.

Roy hesitated. Everything the German had said so far had been known inside the agency when Ray left. At the same time, it was accurate and not known outside the intelligence community. He pushed the hundred to the center of the table. "So far you've convinced me that you may have seen their device. Convince me you've seen inside it."

The old German grinned. "I know how much you want this. This one thing has let the Nazis lord it over the rest of the world and I've seen it. I've seen what lets German ships go faster than anyone else's with less fuel. I've seen what lets their big planes fly further and faster than anyone else's. I've seen what let them get to the moon. I've seen what lets that fat fool Goering tramp around like he is the master of the master race. You want what I know so bad I could ask almost any price and your Uncle Sam would pay it. Two million and a quiet place to retire. That's not much to ask."

Ray put another hundred on the table. "Convince me that you got a peek inside that oversized wheel."

"I only saw inside it once, and it has been sixteen years," Otto said, "but I can give you more than anyone on the outside has ever seen." His eyes went far away. "There were electric cables, of course, huge things that snaked around in there, maybe two inches thick for each one of them." He drew a rough sketch on the paper. "And there were huge capacitors here and here." He marked them in. "Getting interested?"

"You wouldn't have to peek inside to figure that out." Ray shifted in his seat impatiently.

"And there was the watch. We weren't supposed to wear watches, but I did. I hid it just because I'm a contrary guy. I'm lucky I didn't get a nine-millimeter lesson in the back of my head. When the wheel whirled, the day ended long before the watch said it should."

Some kind of time dilation. That was one of the fringe theories on the German advantage in large-scale transportation, which made it useless to identify the truth of the German's statements.

As he mulled that over, Ray became aware of the noises of the hotel. A woman screamed down the hall. Something creaked in slow rhythm above them and a woman yelled "Oh yes!" over and over. She managed to sound bored. There was something missing from the pattern of sounds though, something that caught Ray's attention. He moved his hand closer to the holster under his jacket.

Otto caught the movement. "Unless you're reaching for Mr. Cleveland, I wouldn't go any further." He shifted his Luger, still in his left hand, though resting on the table. "I have what you want. No need for violence. The only problem is that once I give you the good stuff, I'm just an old drunk to you."

"I understand. Been drunk since you got here? Or maybe on the flight over?"

"No more than usual."

"Talk to a nice stranger? Maybe a twenty-something young lady?"

"Girls that age stopped talking to me thirty years ago," the old German said. "Only reason they would talk to me now is if they wanted something." He stopped abruptly and stared at the door, then stood and moved a flimsy wooden chair in front of it. "Check to see if you were followed?"

"I've done this sort of thing a few times." Ray padded quietly to just inside the bathroom door, keeping half an eye on the Luger. "Things may get noisy." He quietly pulled out his pistol. "This isn't intended for you." Otto didn't move the Luger.

The thin walls of the hotel didn't keep many noises out, but Ray didn't hear anything in the hall. Above him, "Oh yes!" woman or her companion was apparently taking a shower, a very brief one.

The silence in the hall lingered. Ray glanced around the room. Just the main room with the bed, a closet, and the bathroom. There was no door to an adjoining room. So, the door. No other way to get in or out. Except the windows!

Ray focused on the tacky floral-print curtain that covered most of one wall of the room. *We're on the third floor, but is there a balcony?* He heard a slight scuffing outside the window, tiny but conspicuous in the silence. Simultaneous entry from the window and the door. Synchronized watches? *Probably.* Ray wished he knew what the old German was thinking.

Otto stood in the corner of the room, his Luger pointed upward. *Unless he has been in this kind of situation before he'll be more danger than help. My job is to keep him safe. The Luger makes that a lot harder.* The silence from the hall held. No yells. No foot traffic. Ray kept part of his attention on that but focused most of his attention on the curtain.

Otto apparently noticed. The old man took two quick steps and swept the curtain open, revealing two men in black clothing and ski masks positioning themselves on the balcony, silenced pistols in hand.

Ray fired first, twice, given the split-second advantage of seeing what the old man was doing before the intruders did. The crack of the gunshots filled the tiny room and silenced, for a second, the noises from the floors above and below them. One of the black-clothed men fell in a way no conscious, living man could. The other fired two quick shots as his Luger roared.

The door splintered and slammed against the bathroom wall and three men rushed in, bunched up, with silenced pistols searching. The seconds seemed to slow. Ray fired reflexively, three times at the men rushing in the door, at point-blank range, so close that sprays of blood hit his arm and cheek. He turned, fired at the remaining man on the balcony, too late to stop the man from pumping two shots into Otto.

Balcony guy turned his pistol toward Ray as Ray shot him in the center of the chest. The pistol wavered, almost in line, then fired again and again as it sagged toward the floor. Finally, it stopped, empty or with its owner's trigger finger no longer obeying his mind.

Time seemed to not just return to normal speed, but overshoot, turning jerky fast. Screams and running footsteps echoed from the rooms around them. Blood spread across the cheap green carpet from the three men sprawled by the splintered door, and from Otto, who was still partly upright, sagging slowly down the wall.

Ray stayed wary. He checked the three men by the door for signs of life, a formality given their wounds, and kicked their guns away. He cautiously poked his head out the door to an empty hall and checked the two guys on the balcony, both dead. He ran to the German.

Otto was still conscious, but a glance at his chest wounds told Ray the man would not be returning with him to tell his story to the gray man.

Otto raised his head, eyes unfocused. His voice came out as a wheeze. "There were crystals, long rods of translucent crystal in a triangle that just fit inside the circle. There were three green boards filled with resistors and capacitors. I could draw it, but my hands don't seem to work anymore." As if to emphasize that, the Luger slipped out of his hand. Ray caught it before it hit the bloody carpet. The old German grimaced. "That ought to be enough for a few Clevelands. I have a daughter in New York. She likes beer, too."

Those were his last words. Ray grabbed the room phone. Blood dripped on the phone as he dialed and he discovered that it came from a wound high on his shoulder. As soon as he discovered it, the wound throbbed. He clapped a handkerchief over the hole and held it there until a cleanup team arrived, just ahead of the police. The gray man was with the team. He escorted Ray out, their shoes squishing on the sodden carpet.

* * *

The lies inevitably kept flowing. The bullet wound became the result of an attempted mugging. He minimized its seriousness to his wife, trying not to worry her. Debriefing took priority over seeing his son. The gray man sat expressionless through the meeting. Finally, he asked, "Any idea how the Nazis found out about your meeting and got a sleeper team there?"

"None. I know I'm not a mole. If you're a mole the whole thing seems pointless. Maybe old Otto said something when he was drunk. Maybe he was working for them, trying to plant false information, and they decided to up his credibility by killing him. If that's the case, this was worthless. But that doesn't make sense. I would have to live to pass on what he told me. No way they could guarantee that in a firefight."

"Quite a dilemma, isn't it?" the gray man said. "Actually, the Nazis revealed a very important card. The only thing that makes sense is that they somehow tracked me to you, then tracked you to Otto and somehow figured out who he was. And how could they do that?" He pointed to the ceiling. "Think about it. You didn't bring your man back alive, but you confirmed a theory I've had for the last several weeks as an alternative to the mole idea."

"Satellites with ungodly good cameras."

"A major advance. Far beyond what we expected. But now we can take precautions."

"Don't call me again."

"Why not? You handled yourself well."

"I lost my guy. I think he really knew what was in that German machine."

"There was never much of a chance of that. A glimpse over a decade ago. You know the game. Yes, we want the big play and the touchdown, but the times we grind out a first down are just as important. You made them reveal a sleeper team and a vital asset."

"The super bombs are still there. My son will still grow up with Nazi bombers probing our defenses over the poles, with their shipping dominating world transportation, with their moon bases sitting above us, on the high ground."

The gray man closed his briefcase. "The world keeps getting smaller. We used to think we could hide from it. We can't and old Goering just pushed it in our face. If we can't hide, we need people like you and me. Your son needs us."

Ray shook his head. "Not me. I didn't have nightmares last night. Six men died in front of me. I killed five of them. A dad ought to have nightmares."

ELECTION DAY

Harry Turtledove

The alarm clock blasts you awake at 5:45. After you kill it, you stare at the digits in muzzy disbelief. You usually set it for 6:30. Why has it stolen forty-five minutes of precious sack time from you?

Then you remember. Today is Tuesday, the eighth of November. Election Day in the year of Good Lord!, 2016. You want to stop at the polling place before you go on to work.

Out of bed. Fast shower. Shave. Dry hair. Comb hair. Get dressed. A quick glance at the photo of Aaron and Amy on your nightstand while you knot your tie. But they're with your ex and her new husband. You'll get them again weekend after next. No photo of Diana. That would just hurt too much.

Coffee. You really need coffee this morning. Breakfast—a Pop Tart tossed in the toaster. While it's toasting, you fix up a brown bag and check Youngstown weather on your phone. High in the low sixties. Partly cloudy. Chance of showers towards evening. Such excitement.

You think about turning on the TV while you eat the heated Pop Tart and absorb caffeine. You think about it, but you don't. Republicans and Democrats both hope to win Ohio. That means they both flood it with money and ads. You can't take a dump without somebody telling you to vote for Trump. You can't wipe your ass without somebody screaming at you that Trump is an asshole.

You wish they'd all shut the fuck up and get the hell out of here. After today, they will. But these past couple of months have been rugged. The way it looks to you is, both sides are lying as loud as they can as fast as they can. You won't be sorry when it's over, not even slightly.

Wash the coffee cup. Chuck the paper plate the Pop Tart sat on into the trash. Out the front door of your apartment. Check the door. Yes, it's locked. You stick the other key into the deadbolt and turn it. The bolt goes home with a satisfying *snick*.

Down the hall. The cheap carpet is lighter in the middle, where people walk and wear it out, than at the edges, where they don't. Down the stairs. The soles of your shoes catch on those gritty strips they stick down to keep you from slipping when the concrete's wet and slick.

Out onto the street. Your breath smokes. It's not in the low sixties now. The low forties are more like it. You hope the Impala will start. It's an '04, with more than 100,000 miles on it. You get in. You turn the key. The engine coughs a couple of times, but turns over.

You sigh with relief as you crank up the heat. When the Chevy finally does crap out, you know you'll have to buy some horrible beater. You can't afford better. You just thank God you've got a job. A lot of people around here don't.

Off you go. The high school that's your polling place is only a few blocks away. You get there at 7:03. A line already snakes out of the auditorium. You aren't the only one who wants to vote early.

You find a parking space and get out. You sigh. The heater was just starting to do some good. Now you're chilly again. At least moms aren't dropping off their kids yet. Classes won't start for another hour.

Ohio is a battleground state. The line is almost a battleground line. Poll workers have stuck NO ELECTIONEERING WITHIN 100 FEET! signs on the auditorium doors and walls with masking tape, but people have opinions and give forth with them.

"You ask me, Trump's just a reality-show host, a rich blowhard with a bad combover," says a goateed guy in track pants and a hoodie.

"I didn't ask you," a fat, middle-aged woman says. "I'm voting for him. President shouldn't be a family business. Look how Bush Number Two screwed it up."

"How can you stand Trump?" the goateed guy demands. "Look how he talks about women!"

The woman throws back her head and laughs. "I've heard plenty worse than that!" She nudges the chunky gal with her, who may be her sister. "Ain't you, Maggie?"

"Fuckin' right I have. I ain't made of spun glass, like," Maggie says.

You just stand there and pretend you aren't listening. You always thought nothing could be dumber than getting into arguments with strangers online. Getting into arguments with strangers waiting to vote seems even stupider, though. Strangers online can't punch you in the nose. Some of these people look ready to start swinging at any excuse or none. It's been that kind of campaign.

The line does move. People who get their ballots don't waste time in the voting booths. Most of them are like you: they're here on their way to somewhere else.

You give the pollworker your name. You sign the register. You get your ballot. You have to wait a minute or two before a booth opens, but only a minute or two.

In you go, as soon as a guy who looks like a laid-off construction worker comes out. You sigh when you start to vote. The loudmouth or the latest branch from the family tree? The choice doesn't feel any less gruesome now that you've actually got to make it. If the Libertarians had nominated someone with his head on straight, you'd do that to tell the Elephants and Donkeys what you think of them both. But they're running a dope-smoking space case, so that's out.

The lady or the tiger? goes through your head. But you can't stomach Trump at all. You hold your nose and vote Democratic. Then you make your downticket choices in the same spirit of enthusiasm.

"Mr. Tompkins has voted!" a poll worker says when your ballot goes into the box. She hands you your ballot stub and an oval sticker with an American flag and I VOTED—HAVE YOU? on it. You put the sticker on the stub and drop them both into the trash can outside the auditorium.

Back to the Impala. Off to work—at the Youngstown City School District office. You're even a little early, so you get a good parking space. As you walk in, a curriculum specialist nods and says, "Morning, Ralph."

"Morning, Fred," you answer.

"You vote?" he asked.

"'Fraid so.," you answer. He laughs, for all the world as if that's funny. You roll your eyes.

Then he says, "How's the payroll mess coming along?"

"Slowly," you tell him. "Whoever bought that software package should…have to use it for six months." The pause lets you not suggest inserting the software package into an orifice where it isn't designed to go.

Fred takes the elevator. You walk up to the third floor. *Exercise*, you think, as if this were enough to matter. There's your cubicle, smack in the middle of Dilbertland. There's your desk. There's your nameplate, in genuine engraved plastic. RALPH TOMPKINS—IT SPECIALIST, GRADE III.

Somewhere in the software package is a bug that makes it deduct only 87% of the Social Security payments and 78% of the Medicare payments it should. A lot of ordinary employees don't mind a bit; it makes the checks they get on the first and fifteenth of the month a little bigger. But it drives the powers that be batshit.

So you paw through the code, hoping you can find at least one of the bugs and spray virtual Raid on it. It's slow, painstaking work even with all the compilers and bug sniffers on your hard disk. If it were easy, anyone could do it. As things are, they've got you and two other IT people (both women, both—sigh—married) working on it.

Noon rolls around. You haven't made much progress. You back up what you have done, open the brown bag and eat. You aren't the only one chowing down at your desk. The building has a cafeteria, but nobody gets rich on what a middle-sized school district pays. Fixing your own food is cheaper.

After you eat, you use the men's room and drink from the fountain three steps past the door. Then it's back to the screwed-up payroll program. You do buy an afternoon cup of coffee from the cafeteria. Some people stash a jar of instant in a desk drawer. You draw the line there. Instant coffee tastes like mud. The best instant ever made tastes like high-quality mud. It doesn't taste like coffee.

As four o'clock nears, you begin to get a handle on what's wrong with the Social Security calculator. It's just about quitting time, though. You save again. You back up. You scribble a note on a Post-It so you'll be able to pick up the thread tomorrow morning.

At four precisely, you stand up, stretch, and head for home. It's drizzling when you step outside, the way the weather app said it probably would. Forecasts are pretty good these days. You're old enough to remember when they weren't much more than WAGs.

When you get back to the apartment building, you park, go in, and check your snailmail. A couple of catalogues, an ad with a coupon for a new Indian restaurant, an insurance bill. Such excitement. Carrying the spoils and plunder from the box, you trudge up the stairs.

Once you're back at the place, you change into sweats and a long-sleeved T-shirt. By yourself, you don't need to look businesslike. Then you go out to the front room and turn on CNN. You check your Facebook feed while the talking heads talk. More than two hours to kill before voting ends here in the Eastern Time Zone; three after that before the West Coast starts counting. In the meantime, they go on about opinion tracking and exit polls and all the other crap talking heads talk about when they don't have anything real to say.

You open the fridge and look inside. A beer? You shake your head. You did your share of drinking and then some when the divorce was raw and new, but you're mostly over that now. It's not as if you don't drink at all these days, but you try not to drink when you're the only one drinking.

Dinner? It isn't even five yet. Time drags when you live by yourself. You drift back to the TV. You don't feel like watching CNN till they've got actual news. No NBA games on yet. The HBO movie is stupid. Even the TCM movie is stupid. Stupid in black and white is no better than stupid in color.

Back to CNN. A Republican says Trump will cakewalk to victory. A Democrat says Trump will get his head handed to him. One of them will look like a jerk in a few hours. Whichever it is, that won't stop her from showing up at the studio tomorrow.

You keep watching. The noise almost makes you feel you've got somebody else here with you. Every so often, you find yourself talking back to the screen. It worries you a little, but not enough to stop you from doing it.

Eventually, the cable box on the TV stand tells you it's half past five. You go over to the refrigerator. In a big Tupperware, you've got chicken thighs roasted with barbecue sauce—leftovers from a big batch you fixed Sunday. In a smaller Tupperware is half a package of mixed veggies—what you didn't eat last night. You plop two thighs and the vegetables onto a plate, cover it with Glad Wrap, and throw it in the microwave. Two minutes later, dinner.

Dessert is an ice cream bar from the freezer. You pop a Lactaid before you eat it; since you hit forty a couple of years ago, you can't do dairy products without it.

The stick goes into the trash. So do the chicken bones. Then you wash dishes. You're good about that kind of stuff. You vacuum the apartment regularly, and dust, too. You're Felix, not Oscar.

Back to the TV. It's after six now—getting close. You go from CNN to Fox to MSNBC to CBS to NBC to ABC. They're all trying to pump up the suspense for everything they're worth. You don't want that. You want numbers. Numbers are what an IT guy lives by. Diana said they were what an IT guy lived for. No, it wasn't a marriage made in heaven. Dammit.

Commercials. You hit the mute button—a wonderful invention. But the ad agencies know everybody has one. They've figured out how to plug products (here, trucks) so they get in your face and annoy you even if you won't listen to them. You change the channel. Take that, ad agency.

Seven o'clock at last. Within a couple of minutes, all the networks have called South Carolina for the Republicans and Massachusetts for the Democrats. Neither is exactly what anybody would think surprising.

You go, "One state, two states, red state, blue state." When Aaron and Amy were little, you read them a lot of Dr.

Seuss. You still mimic the style with ease.

When you were reading it to them then, though, it didn't make you bite down on the inside of your underlip till you tasted blood. It didn't remind you of what you had and what you don't have any more. Diana's new husband seems a nice enough guy. He's not one of those monster stepfathers who make the papers and the evening news. He genuinely seems to care for Aaron and Amy.

But hell, they're *your* kids. They're your kids every other weekend, that is. Life sucks, is what it does.

New York and Connecticut turn blue. So does the District of Columbia, where Trump isn't pulling even ten percent of the vote. All of the South that's in the Eastern Time Zone goes red, except for Virginia. Just before eight, Virginia's blue, along with most of New England. Pennsylvania, Ohio, and Michigan are still too close to call.

At eight, polls in the Central Time Zone begin to close. Texas turns red, along with the rest of the more westerly South. A lot of the Midwest leans toward the Elephants, too. Illinois is a nice pickup for the Donkeys, though. So is Minnesota. Wisconsin stays gray—no one can figure out what it's going to do.

"The apparent loss of Florida has badly hurt Democratic chances," a pundit says gravely. "If things play out the way we expect, what their strategists call the Blue Wall will have to hold for them to keep the White House. Pennsylvania, Ohio, Michigan, and Wisconsin are vital to them. They can afford to lose one of those. If they lose two, we'll see a Donald Trump Presidency."

You're on MSNBC just then. By the way the woman doing the talking pronounces the last four words, she may as well be talking about a severe outbreak of the Black Plague. Fox, on the other hand, treats Democratic wins like an outbreak of insurrection.

CNN shows a bunch of nervous people at Democratic headquarters, then another bunch of nervous people at Republican headquarters. The Democrats seemed stunned Trump can make it this close. So do the Republicans, in a happier way.

You remember watching the BBC broadcasters when Britain voted for Brexit. They all looked tight-lipped but gobsmacked, as if they couldn't believe what they were announcing was real. Now a lot of the American talking heads wear the same expression.

Ohio goes Republican. MSNBC declares the state before Fox does, which is interesting. You swear at the plurality of people who live in your state. How can they be such idiots? By the look of things, they have no trouble at all.

But then, as West Coast results swing the popular vote Democratic in a massive blue tide, you see that Trump's surge in white, hardscrabble western Pennsylvania isn't going to pull him ahead after all. The same kind of thing happens in Michigan.

It's after midnight when they finally call Wisconsin. You're going to be a zombie tomorrow morning. Well, that's why God made coffee. If you have no brains in your head, you can drink 'em from a cup.

"We came so close," a Fox commentator says mournfully. "We came way closer than the pollsters expected, but we fell just a little bit short." He brightened. "Looks like the GOP will keep control of the House and probably the Senate. That's important."

"But you lost the big one," you tell the TV, and go to CNN.

You get there in the middle of "—switching live to Trump Tower in New York City for a statement from Donald J. Trump, the unsuccessful Republican candidate for President of the United States."

Out lumbers Trump, making for a lectern on the stage. He's still sporting a red MAKE AMERICA GREAT AGAIN cap. His family trails him. His wife looks as if she aches to be somewhere, anywhere, else. She's worn the look all through the campaign. His sons both sport that yeah-this-is-mine expression that makes you want to slap their faces. His daughter's pretty, if you're into Barbie dolls. You know her husband's Jewish, but he reminds you of a bloodless Jesuit— of an Inquisitor, maybe.

No one expects the Spanish Inquisition, you think vaguely, and then, *If Trump's lost, maybe we won't get it here.*

"Ladies and gentlemen, it's been a close, hard-fought race," Trump says into the microphone. "The big newspapers and the fake-news TV networks have been against me from the start. They wanted to keep the Presidency in the family, like."

A feral sound rises from the crowd, something like a growl, something like a roar. Trump's been throwing his fanatics raw meat for months. They've come to like the taste.

But he holds up his hand now. "Unless Wisconsin ends up close enough to make a recount worthwhile, or unless we can show enough illegal aliens voted to turn this thing around, we aren't gonna win tonight."

The growl/roar rises again, this time with a wounded note. These people may be nuts, but they're terribly in earnest. *The best lack all conviction, while the worst/ Are full of passionate intensity.* A piece of some poem you read in Brit Lit that somehow stuck in your head.

"Not tonight," Trump repeats. "I just called the Senator from New York with my congratulations and to offer my support as long as it turns out the election was really free and fair."

Shouts of "No!" ring out from the crowd, and other shouts that should be bleeped but aren't. Live TV, in all its glory. "We apologize for that," a CNN commentator says through them.

Trump isn't done yet. "We fought the insiders as hard as we could," he says. "We didn't quite beat 'em. We aren't gonna get to drain the swamp in Washington this time around. But we scared the living crap out of 'em. And I'll tell you something else, too. We're gonna keep on fighting! We're gonna keep on scaring the crap out of the fat cats who screw the little guy. We're just getting started. In four more years, in 2020, we'll have another chance to—"

"Make America great again!" the crowd howls. They chant it over and over. Some of them pump their fists in the air. It's not quite one of those Nazi rallies you see on the American Heroes Channel in grainy black and white—the choreography isn't good enough. But you get the idea that's what it wants to be.

CNN cuts back to the studio. A gray-haired guy who's covered politics as long as you've been alive says, "That's the most extraordinary concession speech I've ever heard. It's the least gracious concession speech, too. But at least Donald Trump has not done what he's half-threatened to do several times if returns show him losing—refuse to concede and fight it out in the streets."

You try to imagine people swinging sticks or baseball bats in the streets of Youngstown. You imagine flying rocks and bricks and bottles and Molotov cocktails. You imagine flying bullets and SUVs or pickups plowing into people from the other side, whichever side the other is. *The worst are full of passionate intensity.* People don't think of themselves as the worst, not even Nazis or Maoists. You shiver, though the apartment's plenty warm. What you imagine feels all too real.

A blond woman who wasn't born when the gray-haired man started reporting breaks in to say, "We're going live to Democratic headquarters at the New Yorker Hotel!"

Away they go. The people inside Trump Tower's big function room who weren't glum were angry. At the New Yorker, the joint is jumping. The music goes from Sting's "Fields of Gold" to Weezer doing "Island in the Sun." This crowd is younger than Trump's.

"Island in the Sun" cuts off in the middle. An aging African-American boomer in a purple pantsuit—some party honcho—comes to the lectern. She taps the mike to make sure it's live. Then she says, "People? Listen up, people! The Senator will be down in a minute. Before Mr. Trump made his public concession, he called to congratulate the Sen—" She breaks off. "I mean, to congratulate the President-elect of the United States!"

Rage and resentment fueled the roars at Trump Tower. The racket here is pure rock-concert joy. People shake hands and high-five and hug and kiss and boogie. *If you can't get laid tonight, dudes, you aren't half trying*, you think.

A skinny guy who looks like a college sophomore dashes across the stage and whispers in Ms. Pantsuit's ear. As she nods, the kid trots away again. She swings back toward the microphone. "People? People! Here is the junior Senator from the great state of New York and the next President of the United States, John Fitzgerald Kennedy, Junior!"

Out he comes. He's almost fifteen years younger than Donald Trump, and does it ever show. He's trim in an iron-gray suit. His hair is about the same color, and he doesn't need a combover. His old man might have been the handsomest President ever. His mother was beautiful. No one's claimed he lets the side down in looks.

His wife—who's not exactly homely herself—and their twelve-year-old boy follow him to the lectern. So do Vice President-elect Bennet and his wife and three kids. He waves to the crowd. The Democrats yell some more. He waves again, then holds up his hand. The crowd takes a while to quiet down. Chuckling, the woman on CNN remarks, "Will

Rogers said, 'I don't belong to an organized political party. I am a Democrat.' It's still true a lifetime later."

At last, Kennedy gets to say, "As you probably know, I just got a call from Donald Trump." The name makes the Democrats jeer and snarl. They may not be organized, but they're united in that. The President-elect holds up his hand again. "It was close. We won. He admits we won. He wished me the best. That's all that matters."

You figure Trump was his usual charming self in the concession call. By the way the crowd keeps jeering, they figure the same thing. The slightly sour expression on JFK, Jr.'s, face doesn't argue against that line of thought.

But the President-elect repeats, "That's all that matters." He goes on, "I'm not my father. I was born a couple of weeks after he won in 1960, and I wasn't quite three when he… died. I barely remember him at all. But I know he also won a very close election, and I know Richard Nixon and Donald Trump did the country the same service by not quarreling over the results."

You aren't old enough to remember Nixon. Not many people you know who are have much good to say about him. One bald, wrinkled assistant superintendent did tell you, *Nixon would pick his teeth with Donald Trump. He was a son of a bitch, too, but a smart son of a bitch.*

"Like my father, like all the Presidents before me, I can't just be President of the people who voted for me," Kennedy says. "I am going to be President of the whole country, red states along with the blue, and I aim to govern that way."

This time, the applause is more wary. After your side wins an election, of course you want all the campaign promises carried out the day before yesterday. Kennedy didn't get into politics till after the turn of the century, but he's smart enough to see that won't happen. The Republicans still hold the House. No matter what Fox said, the Senate looks like a fifty-fifty split. The Vice President-elect may need to break a bunch of ties.

"I will work to make out healthcare system better. I was proud to support President Obama on that, and I'll work hard to extend what he's begun," Kennedy says. "I will work to bring everyone justice, regardless of race or gender or sexual orientation. We must stay strong and safe abroad, and I will work with our friends around the world to do that. No nation is an island, entire to itself. We are part of the wider world. We cannot help it, and we cannot forget it."

Your best guess is, that's a fuck-you aimed at Trump for a shitty concession call. Trump's been screeching *America First!*, as if this were the 1930s. That proved stupid then, when the world was a much more loosely knit place. It's way stupider now.

"Finally, I want to thank all the people who worked so hard to put me over the top," Kennedy says. "I want to thank the party workers here at the New Yorker and in all fifty states, who got out the vote and made sure the election was fair and honest." When he says *sure*, you hear a little Boston in his speech. He doesn't have a bucketful, the way his father did.

"And finally, I want to thank Carolyn for putting up with me and for having enough good sense for both of us." Kennedy leans over and kisses her. They've had some tabloid-fodder rocky times, but they've managed to put the rough parts behind them. You're jealous. JFK, Jr., goes on, "I especially want to thank her for talking me out of flying us to Martha's Vineyard one night not long before the turn of the century. I hadn't had my pilot's license long then, and I didn't really get how dangerous flying over water at night can be when you don't trust your instruments. I could have been stupid, but thanks to her I wasn't. That I'm standing here today may be her fault. Thanks, honey!" He kisses her again.

Everybody whoops. Flustered, Carolyn Bessette Kennedy waves. People whoop louder. You eye the cable box. It's half past one. You kill the TV with the remote and head back to the bathroom and bedroom. Tomorrow—no, later today— you'll prop your eyes open with toothpicks or jitter from too much caffeine, but now you know who won. You can go to bed.

A Fine Line, Indeed

C.W. Briar

"*It is a melancholy object to those, who walk through this great town…when they see the streets, the roads and cabbin-doors crowded with beggars of the female sex, followed by three, four, or six children, all in rags, and importuning every passenger for an alms…*

"I think it is agreed by all parties, that this prodigious number of children…is in the present deplorable state of the kingdom, a very great additional grievance; and therefore whoever could find out a fair, cheap and easy method of making these children sound and useful members of the common-wealth, would deserve so well of the publick, as to have his statue set up for a preserver of the nation."

-Dr. Jonathan Swift, *A Modest Proposal*, 1729

He called himself Trevor. He wasn't certain how to spell it, but he liked the sound of Trevor. According to the tattoo on his foot, he was 73SLO-0112, but no one in The Pens used their number as a name.

She called herself Eilis. Unlike Trevor, she knew what her mother had named her, but she wouldn't speak that word. It belonged to her old life, before her mother gave her up for a few pence.

After years together, their names were entwined like Eilis's fingers between his.

Blond-haired Trevor was stocky, the kind of boy a farmer prized. Thirteen-years-old and only three months away from the 9DEC84 expiration date branded behind his ear.

Eilis, thin as a wheat stalk, hair the color of an Irish sunset. Newly fourteen. She'd tied her orange locks back with frayed cloth so she could show the date behind her ear. According to the clock tower beyond the wall, it was the fifteenth of September.

She'd expired two days ago.

Hand-in-hand, they marched up the perfectly squared streets of Surrey-on-Thames Swift Farm. Outsiders called it that. To the children avoiding harvests it was known as The Pens.

Thousands of children littered the grooved, dusty roads. All of them wore rags that were the color of burlap and nearly as rough. Some sat in sunlight, others walked aimlessly or tossed stones into circles drawn in the dirt. Many congratulated Eilis, though not without a hint of jealousy.

Usually, expired children looked eager for release. They were dogs off their chain for the first time, ready to dash out into the world. But on Eilis's release date, she looked apologetic, sorry to be leaving others behind.

She and Trevor passed through a spot where morning sunlight managed to claw through the farm's brick towers and metal scaffolding. Her hair, dirty though it was, caught fire. Trevor's heart thumped. He was going to miss that hair.

He squeezed her hand, feeling the steel ring he'd found and given to her. The ring spun loosely around her finger.

Eilis squeezed his hand in reply, and kept squeezing.

"You'll be a'right," she said. Most children in The Pens had a common mutt of an accent, a blend of Cockney,

Welsh, and pronunciations abroad. Eilis, however, never fully lost her Irish.

"I know I'll be a'right," Trevor said. "It's only three months. I'm worried for you."

Her shoulder brushed against his. Blimey, how he loved that.

"Don't fret none for me. Better out there than here."

"I know."

Trevor knew he probably sounded as nervous as she did.

They made their way to the building known as Butcher Block. It wrapped around the eastern wall like a hand grabbing a wrist. The largest of its doorways had a closed iron gate, behind which lay a tunnel, the only exit from The Pens.

Two boys waited at the gate. Both had expired and they thanked Trevor and Eilis for helping them achieve it. A crowd of younger children had gathered to see them off. Many were from Eilis's and Trevor's tower, including an eleven-year-old boy named Abner. He waved to her.

An engine outside the walls uttered a long, angry hiss. Children bent their knees, readying to run. Every eye snapped to the steam billowing into the gray sky. Then their collective attention moved to the trawling net at the end of the street.

The net did not move and the gears in the rafters did not turn.

Mentally, Trevor knew they had nothing to fear at that hour. Monday mornings were for releases. That was when the priest came to bless any children who had survived long enough to expire.

He told himself to relax, but his instincts argued otherwise. What if today was different? What if he had to flee?

As the steam dissipated, so did everyone's caution. Eyes returned to Eilis and the other fourteen-year-olds, who were now too old to legally be sold as supper.

"I won't go far," Eilis promised for the eighth time in a week. "I'll be outside the gate when you expire."

"And then we'll run away from London." He smiled through the ache of the held-back tears. "I swear it on me head. We'll get married."

He didn't know how people got married, or if fourteen-year-olds could marry, but they would do it eventually. Running away, on the other hand? They could certainly do that. Pen children did not live long enough to expire if they weren't good runners.

"I has something for you." Eilis reached into the pouch she'd stitched onto her weathered, misshapen dress. She produced a wedge of flint and a chunk of freckled limestone.

"Won't you need this?" Trevor asked as she handed him the rocks. "Winter's coming. You'll have to make fires."

"You, too. I can find new flint. Besides, the other rock's me true gift."

Trevor turned the limestone over and blushed at the words carved into it.

Few children in The Pens could read or write English, so they had their own form of writing. Its various words were a congealed stew of English letters and other symbols. Those secretive markings were prevalent in The Pens, written in coal on the lower parts of the walls. Elder children taught it to the younger, and those who survived taught it to the next crop.

Eilis's gift had two such symbols etched in it. The first was comprised of interlocked circles beneath a line: the mark of *love*.

The second symbol was an uppercase E in a wedge. It was how Eilis wrote her name.

Love, Eilis.

Trevor slid the limestone and flint into his pocket. He looked up. Eilis's eyes were red. She wiped away tears with her palms and then hugged him tightly.

She was trembling. He hugged her back and basked in that moment.

Farmhands dressed in vests and trousers yanked them apart. One grabbed a handful of Trevor's hair and examined the brand behind his ear.

"Hold on, piglet," he mumbled. "You ain't expired yet. Get on, you."

The farmhand shoved him away from the gate.

Away from Eilis.

"I come to see her off," Trevor protested.

"Bah. Bloody swine."

"Wait!" Eilis slipped free from the other man and took Trevor by the sleeve. She moved closer to him, and then closer still, until their lips pressed together.

She'd kissed him before, but only on the cheek. He was surprised by how warm her lips felt and how sweet they tasted. His heart raced to keep up with his excitement.

Blackened, calloused hands grasped Eilis. She was herded into line with the other expired children.

"Young lady," scolded a voice from the balcony on Butcher Block. "Bestiality is an affront to God. You ought to repent of your sin."

The local Transcendentalist priest had arrived and he was glaring at Eilis. Beside him stood the dour, white-haired head farmer. He had a handkerchief pressed to his face, likely due to the Thames' strong stench that morning. The river and canals were only separated from The Pens by the outer walls, which could rightly be called dams.

"Three piglets," the farmer grumbled. "I'll go broke with this kind of inefficiency."

"It's not our place to judge how many endure," the priest said. "The Lord gives some to feed and some to breed. In time, these will provide you with new stock."

"I'd rather have a sure pence today than your Lord's blessing tomorrow. More of them are expiring lately."

Trevor's ears perked up. It excited him to know his and Eilis's efforts were giving the farmer fits. Their survival techniques, which they'd been teaching to others, were working. Three survivors in a week was a good result compared to one or two a month in the past.

The farmer's pinched gaze swept from Eilis to the crowd seeing her off. He glared at Trevor and Trevor glared back without hiding any of his hatred.

The clock struck nine. The engine atop the wall hissed and the tunnel gate rose. The priest opened his small, black book to read the rites of those now recognized as human.

"From *The Book of Swift, Second Chapter*. 'Welcome, young ones, to the world that awaits thee. Thou hast crossed the line from beast to man, an ascension and second birth. God declares man art beneath angels, and beneath them, beasts of field and air. Today, thou art baptized into communion with mankind.'"

A farmhand opened a ceiling valve in the passageway, releasing a column of water from the canal that cut through Butcher Block. The expired children were marched through the brown shower for a crude baptism.

"'Go therefore into the world. Work for thine supper and multiply in number, for this is right in the Lord's eyes. By this, thou provides for thyself and others.'"

Eilis squeezed water out of her hair.

Trevor clenched the limestone in his pocket fiercely enough to bruise his palm. He relaxed after Abner put an arm around his shoulder.

"You'll be free next," Abner said.

* * *

"You ain't going out, too, is ya?" asked Clara. She was crouched under the light of the alley's lone lamp, making faces at a shard of reflective glass propped against the wall.

Eilis blushed. "Not like that." She stuffed the apples and wooden buckets she'd stolen into a satchel. "I happened on a little raft 'neath the docks. I want to bring Trevor some food."

Clara looked up, tongue pinched between her molars as she eyed Eilis. "How ya suppose ya can do that?" She turned back to the mirror and brushed powder on her cheeks. "He's still 'at farm, ain't he?"

"The river's almost as high as the wall. I can make that throw."

Clara was, in her own words, a "woman of the night" and "a dock." She'd explained what that meant. The work seemed horrible to Eilis, who had no intention of following in her friend's high-heeled shoes. Nonetheless, she owed a lot to Clara, including her life.

They'd met near Buckingham Palace three days after Eilis's expiration. It had seemed sensible to beg for alms from the wealthiest people in the city. However, the fancily-dressed men and women had ignored or cursed Eilis. Eventually, three guards had begun to harass her, calling her an "urchin"— whatever that meant. One guard had kicked her to the curb, bruising her back.

Fortunately, Clara had emerged from the shadows, hips swaying. She had told the men Eilis was her sister and asked them to leave her alone. She'd promised to "thank them properly" for finding her.

The guards released them both.

They weren't actual sisters, but Clara treated her like one, showing Eilis the best places to beg or find food. As for Clara, she earned pennies from men outside the opium dens. She knew what the brand behind Eilis's ear meant and she once mentioned she'd birthed two children because of her work. Those babies had earned her enough to fill her belly for weeks and to entertain herself inside the dens.

Eilis wasn't sure what to make of that admission. Should she have hated Clara for selling her children the way Eilis's mother had sold her? Should she have pitied the woman because of her hard life? She didn't know if Clara's children had been sent to the same Pens as her, or if they were among the many children she had taken under her wing.

What she did know was that Swift babies were supposed to be a way for Clara and others to improve their lot in life. Jonathan Swift claimed his plan would aid the poor, but Eilis's wanderings in the brick and bustle streets of London proved him wrong. Life still devoured people like Clara, albeit in a different sort of way.

It haunted Eilis to know she'd endured the nightmares for nothing.

However, allies were scarce, so she focused on the kindness her adoptive sister had shown. She bid Clara good night and hurried out of the alley. Fog had rolled in along with the evening. Carriages and pedestrians moved from one island of lamplight to the next. Eilis preferred it this way. Better conditions for staying unnoticed and alone.

Like a rat in the Whitechapel alleys, she searched behind restaurants for food. When she happened upon bigger rats doing the same—older boys in weathered coats, soldiers with two crutches and one leg, old women who used to be like Clara in earlier decades—she hurried along. She was younger, weaker, and less experienced than the other poor. She dared not compete for her pickings.

To her delight, she found a rubbish bin with partially eaten bread and potatoes. An open restaurant window overlooked her position and she could see two diners inside. Only the darkness kept her from drawing their attention, so she plucked the food with slow, silent movements.

A waiter rolled a food cart to the men's table.

"Your Irish Swift Steak with creamed potatoes, sir," he said to the portly man on the left. He set down a plate that held two chunks of meat connected by a bony joint. "Medium rare."

Eilis's stomach knotted and the stench of the rubbish bin became suddenly unbearable. She backed away from the window, bracing against the wall. Was that someone she had known?

She had almost received the same fate. Now she was one of the "blessed" poor according to the Transcendentalist Church.

"God has plans for you," the priest had said on her expiration day. "You've been sent to the fires like Shadrach and survived."

Nonetheless, she saw herself in the herb-dressed meat on that plate.

The other diner sliced off a piece of his roasted pheasant. Eilis should have been hungry for it, but her appetite had puckered.

"Don't you find the steak to be rather gamey here?" the man asked.

His friend, the plump one, cut into his meat. Blood dribbled from the wound. Eilis turned away.

"It's all a matter of knowing from whence the day's offerings came. Look to the farms instead of the ghettos. Heaven knows what the street beggars feed their young."

Eilis crept forward to collect her bag. She needed to leave, if for no other reason than preserving her sanity.

"I read a paper at the university," said the thinner man. He waved his fork as he spoke. "The author claims Swift's *A Modest Proposal* didn't genuinely intend for his plan to be implemented, and certainly not to the age of thirteen. It was supposedly satire. What do you say to that?"

The other man upended a ceramic saucer, pouring out gravy. "I say it's a moot point what Swift intended. The idea was all too sensible."

Eilis wanted to reach through the window and strangle his fat neck.

"Perhaps," said the thin man. "I still lack an appetite for aged piglets."

"Because of dry morals or dry recipes? I've told you before, ask me where to dine if you wish for a proper meal. The preparation is key. Aged piglet needs to be tenderized or boiled while it's fresh. Too many chefs drain it of its juices before carving it up."

Eilis ran from the alley, her eyes as blurry as the lights in the fog. She did not stop until she reached the bank of the Thames. There she bent over, hands on her knees, catching her breath, wanting to vomit. Her satchel lay at her feet, only partially full.

It would have to do.

She worked her way through the docks, hurrying from a drunk who propositioned her. The raft, which was little more than jetsam bound with twine, was where she had left it. Eilis set out into the river, propelling herself with hurried kicks. She clung to the raft with a white-knuckle grip because she didn't know how to swim.

And then her thoughts tethered to Trevor. A smile, thin and delicate like a tendril of ivy, grew on her lips. He was going to be astounded by her gift.

* * *

First came the sound of the steam whistle. Then came the sound of children stampeding down the street.

Trevor crawled out of the two-foot-tall door of the tower, pushing the buckets he'd received from Eilis. He was still baffled about how she'd managed to get the gifts to him.

They had arrived two days ago. A girl had brought a satchel to him, her eyes wide with excitement. "Lookie here, Trevor," she had exclaimed. "I found this in the street. That's your name, innit? Charlie says Eilis musta tossed it over the wall."

There had been bread inside, as well as apples, the first he'd seen in years. He had shared the feast with the girl.

The satchel had also contained two buckets. Those made food gathering easier, but the finest item had been the piece of wood with three words carved into it.

An uppercase E in a wedge. *Eilis.*

A short, straight line atop a curved one. *Trevor.*

Two lines erupting from an oval. *Alive.*

Eilis wanted him to know she was alive, or she wanted to encourage him in his own plight. Either way, that message was sweeter than the apples.

Abner crawled through the door behind Trevor, then others from their team. The youngest members of their tower stayed behind. That was Trevor's rule. Only those with a fighting chance in the gauntlet were required to run. In order to compensate, the older, faster runners gathered food for two. Cooperation increased everyone's odds of survival and every child that lived long enough to expire was a thumb in the eye of the farmer.

Not all towers were as well organized as Trevor's and not all elder children cared about the welfare of the weak. That reality was proved during each feeding. Children half Trevor's age were scurrying south with bowls in hand. They had no choice but to risk death. The only alternative was starvation.

One boy looked to be no more than five or six. He ran like a turtle among hounds. Trevor cringed. If today was a harvest day, he would be netted for sure.

Trevor stepped in his path.

"Wait in me tower," he ordered.

The boy looked up at him, panicked and confused. "I need food."

"What's your name?"

"Giles."

Trevor held up his buckets. "See these? I can bring back food for eight. Wait in the tower and I'll share with you."

Giles blinked, a glint of hope in his eyes. "Truly?"

The second supper whistle moaned.

"Time's wasting," Abner warned.

Trevor nodded.

Their team sprinted with the rest of the migration to the south troughs. Brown stew was pouring through holes in the wall, falling in clumps and splatters in the trenches. It was obvious who came from towers that had ignored Trevor's advice. The larger children shoved smaller ones aside. Their fear was understandable—no one wanted to become some aristocrat's next meal—but the pandemonium they caused made everyone slow and more vulnerable.

Trevor's team moved as one. Each member stuck to the positions they'd rehearsed even before he shouted, "Together like geese."

He and Abner were the largest members, so they carved the path into the fray. After plunging his buckets into the mush, Trevor moved aside for the smaller children behind him.

Some other teams copied the technique. Their members swooped in and out like waves.

Trevor peeked inside one bucket. Cubes of dark meat floated in the slop. He'd have to pick those out back at the tower. Farmers called the bits "bacon," but the children suspected they came from the tough, unwanted portions of their friends. Trevor would willingly starve to death before eating that.

He had to hope, or pretend, that the rest of the meal was free of such vile contents.

"Together like geese," Trevor shouted to the crowds. "Make way for others."

Farmhands took positions at the top of the wall, hoses in hand. The farmer stood up there as well, scowling in Trevor's direction, pointing toward him as he spoke with one of his workers.

Harvest day.

The outer walls of The Pens rumbled. Unseen engines hissed, belching plumes of steam.

"Back to the tower!" Trevor cried.

His voice was swallowed by the deafening scream that erupted from the packed masses. Bare, calloused feet stampeded in every direction. Bowls fell, spilling the chum-like meal. Disorganized boys and girls trampled one another in their haste. Farmhands on the walls sprayed water on those who fell, making it harder for them to get up, adding to the chaos.

"With me," Trevor shouted, steeling his team's courage. They headed west rather than north with the majority of the crowd. That gave them more room to maneuver. It was not the most direct route to their tower, but it was the best way to avoid entrapment in the panic.

As Trevor ran, he paid attention to the sequence of the steam clouds. He watched the gears spinning in the scaffolding, listened to the progression of the screams on parallel streets. These were the clues to survival, the signs which guided him.

"Turn right," he yelled.

With bowls and buckets in hand, his team hurried down the dusty street. Two hundred yards ahead, a trawling net steamed toward them, its timber frame scraping along walls and sweeping out legs from underneath children. Those trying to crawl through tower doorways were easy pickings.

Anyone scooped up by the net would be dumped through a hole in Butcher Block's roof, never to be heard from again.

Trevor's eyes shot up from the horrors on the street to the gears overhead. His ears dissected the echoing shrieks, rumbles, and thumps.

"Turn left!" he shouted.

Nine more weeks of this remained before he would be free.

* * *

October.

Eilis stood in the bell tower of the Church of Sir Kant. From that height she could see shipping docks, miles of the Thames, and the heart of London. More importantly, she could see down into The Pens, which sprawled before her like an oblong chess board. The full moon was a jaundiced beacon and by its light she could make out the roof of the tower she used to share with Trevor. No children were in sight. They would be bedding down at that hour.

She squeezed the pocket that held her ring. Trevor was alive. She believed it. She *knew* it. She refused to believe any other possibility.

Eilis shivered. She wasn't sure how many more deliveries she could make. The autumn air and the Thames were getting too cold for her to be on the water. She needed to return home to Clara, to their fire. Her clothes were mostly dry, but the fire would finish the stubbornly damp nooks.

She descended the tower steps. An evening church service was in session. Indistinct voices wavered inside the sanctuary, their muffled hymn reverberating through the walls. Eilis scowled. She and Trevor had heard many a song from that church during summer months, when the windows were likely open. How wonderful of those outsiders to bellow songs of love and mercy that drowned out nearby screams for help.

She slinked down an alley. Navigating debauched and drunken men was becoming more and more like evading the harvest nets in The Pens. When it seemed necessary, she tailed crowds on the open streets, hiding in plain sight.

She headed toward Rotherhithe metro station. The tunnel was the best route under the river. When she rounded a corner, she caught four young men, none much older than her, rushing toward a butcher shop. The sign in front displayed a baby with a pig's head, and the words read "Toddling Piglet." Eilis had learned that phrase recently. It was a butcher's term for Swift babies, the ones sent straight to market because they were too young for farms.

One of the four young men threw a horseshoe through the shop's window. Glass shards rained onto the floor. The men—older boys, really—cheered and patted each other's back. The one who had thrown the shoe beamed, then he noticed Eilis. He squinted at her.

She grabbed for the knife she kept tucked in her belt.

"Eilis? That you, innit?"

He seemed familiar. Not his stubble or the scar running through it, but she had heard that voice before.

"Who's the tart?" one of the other boys asked.

"Do I know you?" she asked the first boy.

"An Irish tart," said another.

"It's me, Edward," said the first boy. He pointed to the branding mark behind his ear. "From The Pens. Eh, you forgot me, but I'd recognize your red 'air anywhere."

That admission made Edward an instantaneous brother. She felt surprisingly calm in the presence of the four vandals. She also felt a sense of delight in the jagged hole that used to be the butcher's window.

But it wasn't ruined enough. The shard in the upper-left corner was too large. Eilis picked up a stone from the street.

"When'd you expire?" Edward asked.

"'Bout four weeks."

Eilis flung the stone, smashing the piece of glass. She shivered, not because of the cold but because of her fluttering excitement.

The upstairs shutters burst open. An enraged bear of a man shook a fist at them. "I'll have your heads! Someone call the constable."

Eilis's excitement vanished, leaving only the fear that had guided her for weeks.

Edward gestured for her to follow him. "This way."

They ran, cutting a zigzag route through streets and corridors. This part of the city was still an unexplored labyrinth to her, but the boys seemed sure of themselves. They didn't slow until they had slipped behind loose boards in a fence. They climbed into a vacant warehouse that had been overrun by pigeons. Feathers and droppings littered the floor. An interior door lead to a basement stairway, then a passage with pipes running its length.

A lantern glowed ahead of them. She followed the others toward it, despite her growing concern that she was making a mistake.

They entered a storeroom ringed with shelves and supplies. It smelled of mildew and dust. Blankets sat on the floor.

The boys spread out, a couple of them taking swigs from bottles scattered around the room. They all considered her. Eilis wanted to flee.

"Ya want some food, huh?" Edward held up a tin can.

"Aye." She leaned against one of the pipes along the wall. Her elbow bumped a lever that jutted out from it.

"Careful with that dump valve," Edward warned. "That's a gas pipe there. Runs under 'alf the city." He punched a hole in the can with an opener. "What 'appened to that boy who used to follow you about? Trevor's 'is name, right? He was a great lad. Once gave his food to me sister, rest 'er soul. He get caught by the nets?"

"No, he's still…" Trevor's name had hit her like a punch. Eilis could not finish her sentence. She slumped to the floor, hiding her tears with her forearms. Her sobs, which she had managed to suppress in recent days, swelled in her chest.

* * *

Trevor ran, sweat stinging his eyes. Once he reached the trawling net, he dropped to his knees.

Without delay, he pulled out the knife Eilis had included in her latest gift satchel, then sawed at the ropes. He knew he was taking a terrible risk, but he'd lost two team members to the nets that morning and he wanted revenge.

Two nets were already damaged. He could never get all sixteen, but every severed rope helped.

Abner caught up to him. He was supposed to be their eyes during the sabotage, but he'd fallen behind. Trevor was about to ask where he'd gone when Abner whispered, "Look who followed us. Frightened me near death."

Giles stood beside him, a hunched, apologetic cherub. Trevor had taken a shine to the boy, who in turn followed him like a shadow, but at that moment, his presence endangered them all.

"What're you doing here?" Trevor whispered.

"We stay together like geese."

"Not right now, Giles." Trevor finished sawing another cord of rope. "The farmer will be outraged if we're caught."

He wouldn't just be outraged. He'd have them slaughtered.

The boy hugged himself. "I'll help you not get caught."

"Or get us turned into pies," Abner countered.

A dog barked somewhere down the street. The noise startled Trevor enough to knock the knife out of his hands. He stood and ran, as did the other boys.

The farmhand who was restraining the dog with a leash shouted, "Oy!" He aimed his lantern toward the boys. The dog's barks grew louder, meaning it had been set loose after them.

A gunshot rang out. The bullet kicked dirt in the street.

"Halt!" the guard shouted.

A second shot sounded, then a third.

The last one was followed by a pained, choked-off gasp. Then a thud.

Trevor dove around the corner of the nearest tower. He crawled back far enough to see Giles lying face down. Blood spread from his body, reflecting the farmhand's light.

"Damn it!" the shooter yelled. "Someone bring more lamps. I think I shot one. I was trying to scare 'em."

The dog sniffed Giles's motionless body.

Abner tugged Trevor's sleeve. "We have to go."

Trevor had not been shot in the chest, but it felt like he had. *They killed little Giles.*

Abner's continued pleas got Trevor to his feet. They reached their tower just as someone's light began to explore the street outside.

Trevor couldn't see the others in the tower very well, but he could feel their nervousness at having been awoken by gunshots. He climbed ladders and platforms to his blanket without saying a word.

* * *

Farmhands rarely traveled into the interior streets of The Pens by day, but they did so the next morning. They searched every tower, every bed, every pocket for the knife used to sabotage the nets.

It made Trevor pleased to have dropped it. He'd not wanted to lose it—it was a gift from Eilis, after all—but its absence made it easier to feign innocence.

Still, he wondered why they hadn't found it where he lost it. He got his answer after they checked Abner's blanket.

His friend had picked it up for him.

Trevor clawed through the crowd to take the blame, but Abner silently insisted on taking the fall. *Let me do this*, his eyes pleaded.

"Come, all of you," called a farmhand. "Outside, now. See what bad behavior will earn you."

The guards pulled out clubs. One of them shouted, "Soften the meat!"

Guilt pummeled Trevor each time a club struck his friend. He drowned on tears, gasping for breath. His grief over Giles blossomed into rage during Abner's beating.

He needed better ways of fighting back, so that others weren't killed or injured for his mistakes. Expiration was his best hope. Outside the walls, he would have access to better tools. He could find a way to empty The Pens.

Six weeks left. Until then, he would redouble his effort to train other towers. He would get even the most stubborn and cowardly children to listen. They would learn to interpret every tell-tale sound and gear spin, and they would work together to avoid the harvests.

Every child he helped survive would be an act of vengeance.

* * *

Eilis moved excitedly up the streets of Rotherhithe. It couldn't be called a walk, not when most of her energy was spent restraining herself from running like a giddy lunatic. Not when every fourth or fifth step was a little bigger or a little quicker. She was straining against the leash of propriety.

It was the fifteenth of December, release day for Trevor.

Clara had joined her for the trip. She laughed. "Calm ya'self, girl. I seen squirrels with less vigor."

"He'll be out today."

"I knows it. Cor blimey, ya been saying it for weeks. I tagged along to meet this handsome boy of yours."

Eilis shot a look across her bow.

Clara raised her hands. "Not like that."

The morning chill turned Eilis's breaths into momentary phantoms. She wore a Frankenstein coat of wool scraps stitched into something with sleeves and a tail. Her hat and gloves, acquired by Clara through unknown means, were brilliant crimson. She hoped Trevor would like them, just as she hoped he would like the gray bowler cap she carried. It was her latest gift. Eilis had found it in a rubbish bin. The lining was torn, the black ribbon a bit stained, but it was otherwise quite dashing.

She wanted to see his eyes light up when she put it on his head and kissed his cheek.

A woman shrieked.

People on the sidewalk glanced toward the sound, then down at the tips of their shoes. Eilis, however, did not look away.

Two bobbies and a well-dressed man waited on the steps of a soot-stained brick building. Two other bobbies dragged a coatless woman outside. Her arms were locked around a bundle of blankets.

"You can't 'ave him!" she cried. "You can't 'ave him!"

The man in the suit tipped his hat and then grabbed the bundle. "Madam, you ought to have cared more before refusing to pay your debts."

Officers pried the woman's arms open, helping the man seize the swaddled blankets. She screamed, as did the baby wrapped inside the bundle.

Passersby feigned disinterest in the kidnapping. A mother and father, who were holding the hands of a girl in a mauve dress, tried to cover her eyes. Their young daughter leaned back, witnessed the poor woman clawing for her baby, and then cowered behind her father.

Fire rose up Eilis's neck. She grabbed for a piece of brick. She had a right mind to pelt the man in the suit. Her arm was good enough to make the throw, but Clara grabbed her by the wrist, stopping her.

"Don't make no foolery. Let's go see Trevor, right?"

"It's not fair." Tears sucked cold December air into her eyes.

Clara wrapped an arm around her. "This is London, dear. You as much as anyone ought to know life's only fair for those what can afford it."

Eilis struggled to think about anything but the distraught mother until she reached the outer gate of The Pens. Once there, she had to convince the farmhands on watch that she had come for a friend. They considered that odd, seeing as how guests never visited anyone in The Pens.

They led her and Clara through the gate and down the sloped tunnel. Gas lamps guided them through the darkest part of the passage. Eventually, the tunnel leveled out. Sunlight and the inner gate waited at the end of it.

Eilis had to fight the urge to turn back, to retreat from that manmade hell. The walls. The familiar sounds and smells. They were making it difficult to breath.

But then she glimpsed Trevor at the end of the tunnel. Eilis sprinted to him.

"Trevor!"

He reached through the bars. Her gloves separated her from his touch, so she ripped them off. Her palms met Trevor's, their fingers interlocked. The clouds from their breaths merged into one.

* * *

"I missed you."

They spoke the words simultaneously, then laughed together.

Trevor blushed. Eilis's giggle was more wonderful than he had remembered.

"How much time's left?" he asked

"Fifteen minutes."

A woman in the tunnel held up a gray hat. "Silly girl. Ya dropped this."

"Oh!" Eilis exclaimed. "Trevor, meet me friend, Clara."

"My pleasure." He gestured toward the hundreds of children gathered behind him. Abner was among them. He sported a drooping eyelid from the beating he'd received. "Me friends came, too."

"'Ello, Abner," Eilis called.

He nodded. "Eilis."

Clara's jaw dropped as she took in the crowd that had come to bid Trevor and six other expired children farewell.

This was the biggest sending off party that had ever gathered. Five hundred children, at least.

Trevor wondered if she was awed by the size of the crowd or the horror of it all. Would the city's appetite for Pen children end if they saw the filthy, cheerless, sickly masses?

"Seven?" the head farmer shouted. He, along with the priest, had arrived at the balcony overlooking the gate. The weekly blessing was drawing near and the farmer looked incensed at the number of children who would be escaping him. Seven was almost double the best weeks.

Hopefully that number would grow. Trevor had devoted his final weeks to convincing hundreds of children to follow his team's example and the lessons had taken root. The nets had been less full, the feeding troughs less chaotic. Just two days ago, the farmer had berated his workers, saying, "You'll be collecting them by hand if harvests don't improve, or so help me, I'll harvest you next."

That moment had gotten a cheer out of the children within earshot.

There was a new sense of hope in The Pens and it was making the children happier. Braver.

"These seven are the will of God," the priest said.

"Did I ask for a sermon?" the farmer snapped. He called one of the farmhands closer.

"Did you get me gifts?" Eilis whispered.

"I did. I made one for you." He pulled the flint and limestone she'd given him out of his pocket. He had added his name to the latter one. It now read *Trevor loves Eilis*.

Her grin spread its wings. "This looks familiar."

"Spent every coin I had on it."

"I adore it, but not as much as I'll adore leaving London. I been studying maps. It'd be best if we go—"

Trevor shook his head. "I can't leave London. Not yet. I wants it, but they need our help." He nodded toward Abner and the others. "We can help 'em from outside like you helped me."

Eilis paled as if she'd glimpsed a ghost in his pupils. "No. You helped for years. Trevor, London's not safe, either. I hate it. We need to get far away."

He had known this conversation would be difficult. "Someone needs to help 'em."

"It doesn't have to be you," she protested.

"'Together like geese,' remember?" He raised a fist to the crowd. "Don't forget. Like geese!"

"Together like geese," they shouted.

"Check that one," the farmer barked. He was aiming a finger at Trevor. "I knew he seemed familiar."

A farmhand with mutton chops yanked Trevor's head aside by his hair. He checked Trevor's expiration date. "Yeah, by a couple days. Quite a shame. This one's worth a pretty penny."

The farmhand's painful grip did not release. Trevor tried to get a look at the man, but then he saw something worse. The farmer was glaring at him.

At only him. There was something spiteful in his expression.

Trevor's pulse began to race even before the farmer said, "Bring him here." Multiple hands seized Trevor and wrenched him away from Eilis. She lunged against the fence, reaching for him, screaming.

"No! Unhand him! He's expired!"

His heart thundered.

The gathered children began to shout. Farmhands raised batons and yelled even louder, ordering the crowd to back away. A stone flew.

Trevor thrashed and kicked, fighting to escape. He slipped free once, but three farmhands tackled him. One punched him in the temple.

His vision keeled. He could hear Eilis's screams, could see a blurry version of her trying to squeeze through the bars. That other woman, Clara, grabbed her by the waist.

Where was he being taken?

The farmhands kicked open a door. They dragged him into a large, dark chamber with a metal cylinder that reached to the roof. The cylinder had a round viewing hole. Limbs floated in reddish water behind the glass.

He was inside Butcher Block.

The haze of the punch wore off. Trevor fought. He elbowed one man, stabbed another with a screwdriver from a table. The man cursed and grabbed the wound.

There were too many farmhands. They pinned him to the ground. Children outside Butcher Block were roaring. A stone crashed through a window.

The head farmer approached. He dismissed the priest's pleas that "The council will have you strung up if they find out."

"Then don't tell them," he snapped.

Someone brought a glowing piece of metal to Trevor's neck. He felt heat, then searing pain. He wanted to yell, "What are you doing?" but someone had their hand over his mouth.

The man with the branding iron answered his unspoken question. "There we are. Nineteen. One fine line and problem solved."

Trevor thrashed in terror. They had added a "1" to his expiration date.

Nineteen instead of nine. He now had four more days left.

Enough time for him to be sold.

He screamed as the men lifted him onto their shoulders.

* * *

Eilis, now sixteen, held the steel ring Trevor had given her. She struck it against flint, the same piece he'd returned to her on the day of his murder. Tinder caught the sparks. Sparks turned to fire. Fire spread over the sofa.

She stuffed the ring and flint into her pocket, next to the limestone that read *Trevor loves Eilis*.

Flames climbed the wall, illuminating the head farmer's sitting room. Soon they would devour his body upstairs.

Her hair glowed orange in the firelight. Hair that had inspired her nickname. To the public, she was Flame, London's most wanted rebel.

Edward cleared his throat. He was by the front door, checking his pocket watch. Abner, his recently freed protégé, stood beside him.

"Sorry to interrupt," Edward said, "but we best be off. Get to a safe distance and all that."

"You two go," she said. "I want to see the main attraction."

"It's not safe."

"I want to see it," she repeated more forcefully. She pulled her scarf over her lower face, then donned her gray bowler. It was supposed to be on the head of the boy she loved, but he was gone, served up in restaurants around the city.

They would pay for that.

Edward sighed. "As ya wish. Five minutes left. The gas pipes ought to be open by now."

"Then I can't dally here."

They hurried outside. Firelight from the window danced on the dark street. Edward and Abner veered left, but Eilis set out at a jog for the Church of Sir Kant.

Edward called after her. "Ain't we s'posed to 'stick together like geese'?"

"Not any more. We're together like wolves, now, and Trevor wanted our pups let out of The Pens."

"Well, then…for Trevor."

"For Trevor."

Eilis hurried to the top of the church bell tower. The Pens sprawled out before her. She could also make out the flotilla of small boats on the Thames. That meant the team from the docks was in place, ready for the rescue.

The plan was coming together. The only thing left—

A hundred deafening explosions ripped up through the streets in Rotherhithe. Additional fireballs lit up other parts of the city.

Eilis braced herself against the hot blasts. The initial booms were followed by a lingering growl and the tinkling downpour from a million shattered windows.

One of the nearest blasts ripped through the foundation of Butcher Block. The building buckled, as did massive sections of The Pen's outer walls. Farmhands atop the walls were thrown as the structure dissolved beneath their feet.

As expected, the Thames rushed through the collapsing dam-like walls, pouring into The Pens' now exposed streets. The children would be trapped in their towers, but only temporarily. The boats on the river would soon come to their aid.

Eilis sneered. The children were finally saved, and she would have new recruits for the uprising.

Donny Boy

Rick Wilber

The Shot Heard 'Round the World *refers to Bobby Thomson's game winning homer for the New York Giants in the 1951 playoff against the Brooklyn Dodgers. The home run is one of the most famous in baseball history and has become a part of American mythology.*

—Baseball-Reference.com

(https://www.baseball-reference.com/bullpen/Shot_Heard_%27Round_the_World)

October 3, 1951

Donny is nine-and-a-half years old. He hates watching baseball. It's fun to play, sure, but watching it is boring and stupid. Plus, there's no money in it. The players, most of them, barely make a living. The only people who make good money in baseball are the team owners. Donny will remember that thought later, years from now, when his skills aren't quite good enough for pro ball.

But that's in the future. Right now, Donny's father insisted that he go to the game and so here he is anyway, on the Polo Grounds shuttle, headed toward the game with his big brother Freddy. The two of them are sitting side by side, Donny at the window and Freddy to his left. Donny is watching the scenery go by. The shuttle is elevated here, so he's seeing into second-story apartment windows, which is kind of fun. Maybe he'll see some woman changing her clothes.

Freddy is talking about his team, the Giants, and how tremendous they are. Freddy knows the players and their batting averages and their nicknames. He listens to WMCA radio and the play-by-play of Russ Hodges and all the ads tossed into the broadcast, so Freddy knows what cigarettes they smoke and what beer they drink and where they buy their cars and their shoes and their suits. He'll take up some of his heroes' bad habits in a few years. But that, too, is in the future. Right now he's happy to read about the players every morning in the sports pages of *The Daily News* and the *Times* and the *Herald-Tribune*—The Barber and The Say Hey Kid and The Swamp Fox and Monte. His father smiles at Freddy as they sit at the kitchen table in the morning and share all three newspapers before father heads to work and Freddy heads to high school, where he's on the baseball team. Freddy's not fast and doesn't have much of a bat, but he has quick hands, a strong arm, and a good glove. And people like him.

Donny is younger, sure, but he knows that he'll soon be even better than Freddy at baseball. All he does right now is play with a few of the neighborhood kids, but he knows already that he has a tremendous fastball, and a tremendous curve. Really tremendous. The best in the world.

Freddy just laughs when Donny says stuff like that. Donny is such a kidder. Later, in high school at the military academy, Donny will, indeed, be a good pitcher, and there'll be talk about him getting a chance to play in the minor-leagues. But he won't follow up on that. His father wants him in business and business is where he'll go, to Wharton for starters, and then on from there into real estate and, yes, the business side of baseball.

But right now, right here, Donny is bored. He figures today will be about as much fun as watching paint dry. Freddy has told Donny a half-dozen times already how important this game is, but Donny doesn't care. Freddy's told him how the Giants were thirteen-and-a-half games back in the middle of August and then won thirty-seven of the last forty-four games to tie the Dodgers and force a three-game playoff, but Donny doesn't care about that, either. Each team won a game and today's game is the biggest moment in his life, Freddy says. And, okay, Donny loves his older brother, so he smiles and says with some exaggeration, Gee, that's great Freddy.

Freddy ignores his little brother's disdain and says This is it, the whole banana, one game and the winner is in the World Series and the loser goes home. Isn't that great? And Sure, Donny says, that's great. But then he adds, What a bunch of losers those Dodgers must be to blow that big of a lead in the regular season. He tells Freddy that it's probably because the Dodgers have so many Negroes on the team. There's not just Jackie Robinson, but there's also Roy Campanella and Don Newcombe and Dan Bankhead. Those Negroes, Donny says to his older brother, hit the panic button when things start to go wrong.

What're you talkin' about, Donny? says Freddy. Those guys are great! And the Giants have some great Negroes, too. What about that rookie, Willie Mays? And Monte Irvin? And Hank Thompson? Sometimes the whole outfield is Negroes!

Donny glares at his brother and says, Oh, yeah? And Yeah! says Freddy right back, and they go on like that for a while, the two brothers, arguing about this and that and Donny getting madder and madder as Freddy acts like he knows everything about baseball and especially the Giants. He's just trying to make Donny look ignorant and Donny hates looking ignorant. He hates that because he's smart, the smartest kid in his school, maybe in the whole city. A genius, really.

Eventually the argument peters out—it's just been one of many, after all—and they reach the Polo Grounds stop and get off. Ten minutes later they're at the gate and fifteen minutes after that they're in their seats, left field, near the foul line, just a couple of rows up, eating the peanuts and drinking the Moxie they bought on their way to their seats.

Behind the boys there's a man and a woman, married probably, talking about the Giants and how much they like the team and how glad they are to be there.

The man says This game should be a real humdinger and that prompts Freddy to turn around and say Yeah, and we're gonna win the whole ball of wax today, ain't we? And the man says I sure hope so, and the woman laughs a little and squeezes the man's arm and then Donny turns around, too, and says This is my brother Freddy and I'm Donny and my dad made me come to this stupid game 'cause he loves the Giants.

And then Donny turns around in a huff and crosses his arms over his chest, puts a frown on his face and looks straight ahead as the ump, in the distance, yells out Play ball! Freddy just shrugs his shoulders and turns around, too, and the man and the woman sit back in their seats and they all settle in to watch the game.

* * *

Truth is, the man and woman we're talking about aren't married, though they act like newlyweds almost, leaning over to whisper in each other's ear and smiling a lot. The woman goes by a lot of different names in a lot of different timelines. She's a kind of agent, a fixer, and a very good one. The man's name is Morris "Moe" Berg, and like the woman he can travel through timelines and fix things that need fixing. In all of those timelines he's a ballplayer and mostly a good one. And in all of those timelines he's also an agent, and mostly a good one of those, too.

The woman does most of the talking, while Moe seems to be watching the game and listening to the banter between the two boys in front of them as much as he's listening to the woman. He agrees with her, like he always does. But what she wants him to do isn't exactly the assignment he got from his boss, so he's got a decision to make. A tough one.

Moe shifts uncomfortably in his seat. He doesn't think much of the Polo Grounds, in this timeline or any of the others. When he got here a few hours ago he just shook his head. Same old, run-down dump wherever it exists. The metal seat railings and the beams that hold up the upper-deck seats are rusted, the green paint peeling off them as he walked by, heading down toward the field. It was ten a.m. and the place was nearly empty. If you didn't read the papers you wouldn't have known that today was the decider. Giants? Dodgers?

Moe had walked through the low gate behind home plate and out onto the field. Out in right, a guy with a hose was watering the grass. The place was such a dump that the outfield was tilted and from home you could only see the guy from the calves up. For a big-league ballpark that was a sad state of affairs. Sort of like what was going to happen here in a few hours, one way or another.

He'd come early to the ballpark for curiosity's sake, mostly. The guards recognized him and let him through. That kind of thing still surprised him. There was always some version of him in every timeline he'd been to. Somehow, instantly, he belonged and had a past that they all knew, though the past was a little different line to line.

To the guards here he'd been a ballplayer a few years back, a good one, and if he wanted to look around before going into the clubhouse to say hi to some old pals that was okay with them.

He'd looked around with a smile and walked over to home plate. He'd gotten down behind it in that comfortable catcher's crouch. Damn, that felt good. He'd been away from the game for far too long in this line. He'd been away from everything for far too long. The him in this timeline lived at his sister's house out in the wilds of New Jersey and didn't do much of anything except mooch off of friends and family, living off his past.

Back in his own timeline Moe was doing fine, thanks. There, it was just a couple of days ago that he'd been out West, in Hollywood, saying yes to being the manager of the Hollywood Stars.

He'd won the PCL pennant, managing the Santa Fe Saints, and then Hollywood came calling. So he'd hobnobbed at the Brown Derby with the likes of Gary Cooper, George Burns and Gracie Allen, Barbara Stanwyck, Gene Autry. All of them and a lot more were part owners of the Stars in several different lines: a dominant trait, as the woman had once explained to him. And they mattered, those dominant traits.

Which was okay by him, eating steak and potatoes at the Brown Derby and laughing at George Burns' jokes whether they were funny or not.

It was hard to not get your head turned some by all of that. Plus, he liked it out there, all the glitz and glamour. Lots of sunshine, those nice views of the Pacific. Good food. The Pacific Coast League in that timeline played ball so good that most of the teams would have done fine in the Major Leagues if it wasn't so damn far to get there.

Stanwyck and the others, they seemed to like him in return. They'd all done their homework, they knew he'd been a solid player and manager. They knew he'd paid his dues in the war, too, and that he spoke Spanish like a Mexican and Japanese like he'd been raised in the Co-Prosperity Sphere. Those things mattered in the peacetime California Republic, where a lot of players were Japanese or Mexicans. Would they shoot at him if the peace agreements fell apart? Well, yeah, probably. And he'd shoot right back.

Then, right there at the Brown Derby, at a big jovial table with Stanwyck and Burns and Allen and Gary Cooper talking about all the problems they'd had making *Pride of the Yankees*, he'd gotten a phone call from his old boss from the spy days, William "Wild Bill" Donovan. The OSS was now the CIA and it needed his special skills, his access, Donovan said. Was he interested?

Sure he was interested, he'd said to Donovan. He was really busy, but he could probably get a week off. Donovan had chuckled at the other end of the line and said We've got you on a plane to Chicago tonight. Joyce will give you the details. Meet me at the Blackstone Hotel tomorrow for lunch, and then he clicked off and Joyce was talking about flight numbers and he was jotting it all down.

Funny how that worked. Five years ago, after the Germans and the Japanese had either surrendered or asked for terms in the dominant timelines, the Company had told him to take a hike. Thanks for all the good work, thanks for dropping a bomb on Adolf's head in several different lines, thanks for rescuing Fermi and the others. Thanks, thanks, thanks, but see ya later.

He'd wanted to stay on. There was plenty of important work to do in Korea and China and Mexico and South America in various lines. He spoke the languages and knew those cultures. He could have helped. But no.

So he'd left and moved to the West Coast and got back in the game, player/manager in Tucson and then Santa Fe and now getting the call from Hollywood to take over the Stars. But he'd listened to what Wild Bill had to say and he'd agreed, that was the upshot. They hadn't even talked money. He was getting back in the other game and he liked that.

He had a few hours before the flight, so he walked back to the table to tell the gang at the Brown Derby that he had to leave for Chicago and he'd see them next week. His reservation was on a crummy old Western Airlines DC-6, and when he mentioned that they'd laughed and made one phone call and bought him a first-class ticket on a big TWA Connie, courtesy of the Stars, because now he was the manager of a team that could treat him right. He liked that.

By ten a.m. the next morning he'd been in the meeting with Donovan at the Blackstone Hotel on Michigan Avenue. Pastries and coffee in the suite, which was good. And just two chairs around the table.

When he sat down Donovan took a sip of his coffee and then got right to it, saying There's a threat and this one calls for your skills, Moe, that's why we brought you back. It's freelance. You understand that, right?

He nodded. He did.

It's tomorrow, in New York, at the Polo Grounds. In the middle of a crowded ballpark. Get it done and get the hell out of there.

The season was over for the Giants. They'd lost the first two of a three-game playoff with the Dodgers, hadn't they? Moe had read that in the paper on the plane.

You're going by train, Donovan said, and that explained it. He'd be leaving LaSalle Street Station in this timeline and getting off that train in another one. He'd done that often enough in the past. It was a nice way to handle the nausea of the transition. Sleep right through it in a Pullman suite.

Sure, he'd said, and Donovan handed him a thin envelope with the details in it and said, Memorize this and burn it, right? Right, he'd said. Then Donovan looked him in the eye and said to him quietly This won't be pleasant, Moe.

Why?

The tough part, Donovan had said, is that this one's a kid.

* * *

Crouching down behind the plate had felt good. In his own timeline Moe had been a catcher, and a pretty good one. He'd played for the Giants in 1938, just before the Japanese attacked Pearl and San Diego. After the war he'd finished with a couple of years in St. Louis, so he knew a lot of the guys that he was watching today—or at least his timeline's version of them. Older, wiser veterans who'd given up good years in their careers to fight in their war and now were back in the ballpark, running around like kids, pretending they hadn't seen what they'd seen. Moe envied them that, envied the fact they were still playing and he wasn't. He'd loved being a big-leaguer, loved being lost in the long rhythm of the season, day after day after day of baseball.

But that was over now. He wasn't here to play baseball, he was here to change things, improve things, even at the terrible cost of a life or two if that's what it took. For now, this timeline had peace and prosperity. His job was to make sure it was still like that a long way down the line. What he did today would ensure that, Wild Bill had promised.

Moe smiled. Peace and prosperity. Yeah, sure. Moe was Jewish, and he liked men at least as much as he liked women, and he'd seen too much of what happened to people like him when he'd been in two different German timelines right after the war. He'd seen the camps and walked through three of them. The horror was unimaginable.

It was better in America, less deadly anyway. But there was a long way to go for guys like him or anyone who wasn't white and Protestant. If he could do something that would move things along toward that better future; well, then, he'd do it. That's why he'd taken up the spy game in the first place. He liked doing things that mattered.

* * *

Moe had stood up from his crouch, stretched his back, and heard things popping back there. He had a catcher's back and a catcher's knees, for sure. They hurt. He was getting older now and knew it.

He'd heard a voice from behind, back in the box seats. He'd turned to look and there was the woman he'd been expecting. She looked great. And deadly. She'd given him a little wave. She'd had a smile on her face and, he was certain, that little Beretta she liked so much in a shoulder holster under that matador jacket.

He'd walked over to her and leaned in for a little kiss on the check. Even that got his heart pumping. This woman had his heart in her hand, which was an amazing thing. He didn't feel that way about anyone else, man or woman.

She'd held up two tickets, said she had made some changes in the plan, and then took him by the hand to walk up into the stands to get a couple of hot dogs.

Those dogs, a little mustard, some Cracker Jack for dessert. She'd talked, he'd listened, because that's how it was between them. Yes, the kid will grow up to lead the country into its darkest days, she'd said. He'll be a bully who'll seize power when he's threatened. There'll be a coup by his generals and then a civil war. A lot of people will die, Moe, and the country will never be the same.

But right now he's a kid, Moe had said. Just a kid.

Trust me, she'd said, like I trust you. I told Donovan it had to be you, she'd added. I told him we needed the catcher, the spy.

Sure, he'd said. But what she wanted wasn't what he'd been ordered to do. He couldn't decide.

* * *

Moe thinks this kid in front of them, Donny, the smaller one with the wild hair and that constant sneer on his face, the one he's supposed to stop now while he can, is the most obnoxious child he's ever met. A rich kid, no doubt. And petulant. Moe likes that word. He doesn't get to use it often, and this is a man who speaks twelve languages and has an Ivy

League education and reads all the time, so his vocabulary is pretty damn good. Yep, petulant, he thinks, like a kid version of Mussolini. Moe wonders if the kid would have any idea who Mussolini was. Probably not.

But here's the question: The kid is petulant, sure, but is that any reason to do away with him? That's what the orders are from Wild Bill.

Moe feels a touch on his arm and looks over at the woman. She's drawing some stares from the people around them. She's a real knockout, if you want to know the truth. But Moe knows better than to judge that book by her cover. He's watched her kill people. She's fearless, and driven, and pitiless.

Except for here, where she's made an argument that Moe kind of likes about what they should do and why. Wild Bill, back in Chicago, won't care for it when he finds out, Moe supposes, but hell, Moe will let the woman explain the what's and why's later to Donovan and he's betting Wild Bill will say it was okay. Like he has any choice. The woman always goes off on her own and Donovan always says okay.

* * *

In front of them, it doesn't look good for the home team, down 4-1. I can't believe it, I can't believe it, Freddy is chanting in the seat right in front of Moe. To Freddy's left, Donny is making a big display out of yawning. Boring! Your guys are done, Freddy! Toasted! Put some peanut butter on 'em!

Freddy reaches over and punches Donny in the right shoulder, hard. Shut up, just shut up he says to him. It ain't over yet.

Sure it is, says Donny, and then Alvin Dark, the Giants' shortstop, singles and Moe can feel the moment when hope stirs. He puts his bag of peanuts down and leans forward to watch. He has a job to do, does Moe, and soon. But he's been a part of baseball for a long, long time and he can't help but pay attention as the Giants make it interesting in the bottom of the ninth.

The woman doesn't help things. Watch this, she says, as the Dodgers' infielders don't move in for a possible double-play. It's one of the more famous mistakes in baseball history, she says.

Moe frowns. The Dodgers' first-baseman, Gil Hodges, is, in fact, staying close to the bag. Hodges doesn't want Dark stealing second, which is okay, but that leaves a big gap between first and second. Sure enough, on the next pitch Don Mueller hits a groundball right through that gap and Alvin Dark scoots to third. First and third and no outs.

Monte Irvin comes up. He's the hitting star on this Giants' team, a guy who's knocked out twenty-four home runs on the season and is hitting .312. A Negro League star who didn't get a chance to play in the big leagues until he was thirty, Irvin is the right guy to have at the plate. If he hits one out the Giants can tie it up. But he doesn't. He pops it up foul to first for an out.

Moe thinks maybe that's it, but Don't worry, says the woman as Whitey Lockman steps in and, sure enough, he drills one down the left field line for a double that scores Alvin Dark and moves Mueller to third.

The crowd is going wild, even young Donny, who's suddenly standing and cheering like his brother next to him. We can do it! We can do it! he's yelling, as Freddy turns to him and yells through the crowd noise, I told ya! I told ya!

The game stops dead for a few minutes as the Dodgers fumble around and then finally decide to bring in a reliever. Before it happens the woman leans over to the boys and says it should probably be Carl Erskine, don't you think?

Freddy looks at her and says I bet it's Branca, and Donny says Preacher Roe, who's probably the only one he can think of. When it's Ralph Branca who walks out toward the mound

Freddy turns around and says See? I knew it'd be him. And Donny says Yeah, I knew it would be him, too.

But you said Preacher Roe! says Freddy, and I did not! says Donny and they go back and forth again over this for a while as Branca warms up.

Everybody's up on their feet again as Bobby Thomson steps into the batter's box and settles in. They should walk him, the woman leans over to say to Moe, but they won't, they'll pitch to him.

And then Branca goes into the stretch, looks in for the sign, and sends a fastball in for a called strike. Thomson watches it go by.

The crowd is roaring and Donny is right there with them, caught up in the excitement. His small hands are clenched together at his chest. He's watching the next pitch, the windup, the delivery and it's another fastball, up some and inside but still in the strike zone. Thomson swings and gets the meat on it and sends a long flyball to left.

In any other ballpark in the league it would be an easy out for the left fielder, but this is the Polo Grounds, with short fences in right and left and the ball rises and rises and then slowly starts to come down and it's right at their section.

The boys are going crazy, yelling and screaming in joy as the ball drifts toward them. They're hoping to catch the ball, their arms up in anticipation. They think it's headed their way.

Moe can see it isn't headed their way, it's headed his, and now he sees why the woman had him sit in this exact seat, why it has to be him who's here, why it has to be him to do this little thing that will change her world. Such a small thing for a catcher to do, he thinks.

The moment stretches out for him as muscle memory clicks in. In this timeline he spent twenty years catching fly balls, first as a Jewish kid in New Jersey playing for a Methodist team, and then at Barringer High School, and then in college at Princeton, and then as a professional for the

Brooklyn Robins and the Toledo Mud Hens and the Chicago White Sox and so on and so forth. He hasn't caught a fly ball in years now, but this is no problem. He can see the spin on the ball as it passes high over left-fielder Andy Pafko's head and comes toward him. He reaches out with his left hand—all the time in the world to do this—and then with both hands because as the ball comes toward him he has to calculate how to get it realistically to the annoying, petulant, lying Donny who's just one row in front and one seat to the right of Moe.

The ball comes to him and it turns out to be easy. He catches it in the left hand—the feel of a baseball settling into his hand! this is why he loves the game!—and covers that with the right and eases the ball out in one smooth motion, like he's muffed it, and it rolls off the outside of his right hand and shoots toward Donny, whose eyes are wide open and filled with wonder and anticipation as the ball comes to him and he grabs it and holds it firmly in both hands and in that moment, catching the deflection from the man, Moe can see Donny's life turn, see it in the kid's eyes. This game, this wonderful game of baseball! The excitement! He wants this! He's the greatest! He's terrific! He's caught a ball that a grown man couldn't catch!

Moe smiles. This was the right thing to do. The woman has hold of his left arm and she leans up to kiss him on the cheek and say Good work, Morris, in a strange moment of calm in the midst of wild, joyous delirium. The Giants win the pennant! The Giants win the pennant! The Giants win the pennant!

And Donny and Freddy go home happy, Donny clutching the most famous baseball in the world in his hands all the way there.

April 3, 2017

Donny is at his desk, his huge desk, the biggest desk in

the city, maybe in the whole country. There's nothing on the desk but some light cotton gloves, a small cotton sack, and a large, hand-crafted display case, teak base, clear glass, UV protection, alarmed and all the rest. And it's big! A foot on each side. In it is a single baseball. *The* baseball. The shot heard 'round the world baseball. It's awesome! Donny types in the alarm code. There's a beep and a front panel slides open. He puts on the white cotton gloves and reaches in to take the ball in his small hands. He puts it into the cloth sack and pulls on the cord to close it tight. There. Ready.

His private cell, the one just for family and close friends, starts playing *New York, New York* and Donny picks it up on the desk and sees the call is from his brother.

He slides the green phone icon and says Hey, Freddy. How's it going down there? We all set?

Donny sent Freddy down to keep a personal eye on things and to keep him out of the way in the front office, where the real work is getting done. This is a big day for the Mets and Trump Field. It's Donny's team and Donny's ballpark. A huge day. The most important day in the history of baseball, probably. Hey, he needs to tweet that: Baseball's. Biggest. Day. Ever.

Freddy sounds breathless. Freddy always sounds breathless; the drinking, the smoking. If he wasn't his brother... Still, he is his brother, so Donny listens.

We got a problem! Freddy says. The president is running late!

Donny takes a deep breath. How late? he asks his brother.

Five, maybe ten minutes, says Freddy. There was some delay at the U.N.

Donny doesn't respond to that for a second. He's busy tweeting on his other phone. Baseball's Biggest! Day! Ever! Our greatest president ever will throw out the first pitch at the fabulus luxurius brand NEW Trump Field. World class

Ballpark for the world-Class Mets. Gonna win it all this season! LET'S GO METS!

Then Donny picks the first phone back up, says Don't worry about it. Just stay in touch, Freddy, all right?

Sure! says Freddy.

Donny owns the club, Freddy is vice-president. Twenty-two years they've been at it now together, running this ballclub. Five pennants, a couple of World Series wins. And now this wonderful new ballpark, built to the dimensions of the old Polo Grounds but lux all the way! There's going to be a lot of home runs here, for sure, and that's why he's hired a new manager, spent millions—millions!—on some home-run hitters. This will be the greatest team in the history of baseball, which goes back, what, almost one-hundred years? Back to the 1800s when Babe Ruth and Ty Cobb and those guys played.

Donny looks at the speech they wrote for him. A lot of nice words in there, he's sure; but no, he'll wing it like he always does. The fans love that! And he's great at it, speaking off the cuff, just letting it rip. There's a word for that: extemp-something. He's the best there is at it! He'll speak and then he'll introduce the president, whenever she shows up. She'll wave to the crowd, say a few words, and then throw that ceremonial first pitch. And what a surprise is coming for that pitch!

* * *

Later, they do play ball. But not before Donny gives his speech, standing well in front of the mound. The president, who got there in plenty of time, is standing next to him as he talks about being a kid at the Polo Grounds and how he had to dive to make the play but he caught Bobby Thomson's home-run ball. It was the greatest catch any kid ever made off a homer! Ever! Incredible! The shot heard 'round the world and Donny caught it!

He tells the fans that he has the ball with him right now! It's worth a million bucks, at least. Two million! He has armed guards around him as he pauses to take it out of its cotton sack. It's signed by Bobby Thomson, but it's owned by yours truly, Donny. He holds it up high and talks about how the moment when he caught this ball was the moment he fell in love with baseball, the moment he knew he had to play it, and own it. That moment! Catching this ball! And he raises it up high for the world to see. Stupendous!

And then he introduces the president. His close friend, his ally in working to make this great city and this great country everything they should be, with prosperity and security for all Americans, rich and poor, black and white, straight or gay or, you know, whatever. For all the colors of the rainbow, for everyone and all that blah blah blah.

And then he waits for the president to say her few words, though he's too excited to hear any of them. When she's done, he hands the ball to her and walks to the plate, where he takes the mitt from the millionaire back-up catcher who thought *he* was there to catch the first pitch, puts it on his left hand and kneels down behind the plate.

The president smiles down at Donny, then holds the ball up high to show it to everyone as she walks in to get a little closer to him, maybe twenty-five feet away. She stops, gets into a mock stance, pretends to look in for the sign from her catcher, goes into a bit of a windup, and throws it in there with some zip and Donny, happy as a clam, catches it and then rises as he takes it out of the mitt and holds it up for everyone in the whole world to see. It's incredible! It's awesome! Isn't he great! Play ball!

* * *

The Moe Berg in this timeline won't see this happy moment. He fell while in his sister's home in New Jersey and never recovered. He died in May of 1972. But the woman? As the president does her little windup and throws the first pitch of the new season and the new ballpark, the woman is watching from the stands, out in left field, in the same spot where she sat in 1951. She looks about the same. She's smiling.

Author's Note:

Dear Reader,

Historians will tell you that Donald Trump was born on July 14, 1946, in Queens, N.Y. Fake News! Historians will also tell you that his brother Freddy was eight years older than Donny and was born in October of 1938. Fake News! Historians will also make no mention of Donny and Freddy attending the famous Miracle at Coogan's Bluff baseball game where Bobby Thomson's celebrated "Shot Heard 'Round the World" helped the Giants win the pennant. More Fake News!

So don't let the facts confuse you! The truth is, of course, that Donny was actually about twelve years old and his brother Freddy was only four years older and still in high school in October of 1951, and they did, in fact, attend the most famous baseball game of them all. Honest. I'd never lie to you.

THE ECHOES OF A SHOT

Juliet E. McKenna

Standing at the edge of an airstrip in France, as the summer dusk deepened, Charlie was starting to wonder if he had made this trip in vain. There were barely a dozen reporters still waiting and he was the only one watching the westward skies. The rest were clustered together, sharing their cigarettes and buying glasses of white wine from an enterprising local bar owner. The beaming man had appeared some hours earlier with a horse-drawn cart carrying tables, chairs, a basket of bottles, and an ice chest. Whoever was in charge of this aviation hobbyists' airfield near Amiens had made no effort to send him away.

Squinting into the setting sun was giving him a headache, but Charlie didn't think drinking the local *vin ordinaire* would help with that. He wandered over to the solitary, single-story building and peered through the open door. The radio operator sat hunched close to her Marconi set, intent on whatever was coming through her earphones.

As Charlie's shadow fell across the floor, she glanced over to see what was dimming the fading daylight. He raised his eyebrows, his expression hopeful. She smiled briefly but shook her head.

He couldn't understand how she could be so calm, but she was one of the small coterie of mechanics and assistants who had come ahead from New York by the weekly scheduled Zeppelin service. He supposed such uncertainty must be par for the course among these experimental aviators.

"Can you hear that?" A shout outside turned everyone's heads, as much for its unfamiliar American accent as for anything else.

Just as quickly, the speaker was hushed. Charlie hurried to the edge of the airstrip and strained his ears for any suggestion of engine noise. All he could hear was insouciant birdsong and the rustle of wind in the poplar trees. He scanned the skies and the breath caught in his throat as he saw a distant silhouette against the gold streaks of cloud.

"There!" Charlie pointed with a shaking hand. Turning, he saw his fellow journalists still smoking their cigarettes and sipping their wine as they watched the plane's approach. It seemed to be flying very low to Charlie, and the engine labored.

He reminded himself that he knew nothing about airplanes. He'd only ever seen such a thing twice before and those had been kite-like contraptions of wire, wood, and canvas, flying in low circles over county shows. This machine was a very different beast, made entirely of metal with a powerful engine to drive the propeller at the front and a broad single wing extending across the top of a sleek body shaped somewhat like a fat cigar.

"You'd never get me up in one of those things," one shirt-sleeved hack remarked.

"Do you think she'll crash?" a woman in a blue linen dress asked with mild interest.

"Might make the front page if she does. It's not as if there's much else happening in London," a third reporter observed. "Otherwise it's bottom right, page three, if she's lucky."

"She'd better get a move on," the man in shirt-sleeves said testily, "if we're going to have any chance of filing copy tonight."

Charlie walked away before he was tempted to punch someone. As far as he was concerned 28th of June 1939 should be a date to go down in the history books. He only prayed it would be for a story of triumph rather than tragedy.

He didn't return to the pack of press until the bright red airplane had swooped low, touched down, bounced upwards, touched down again, and rolled sedately down the landing strip to come to a halt at the end. The photographers who'd been waiting in their own little gaggle began filling the air with dazzling bursts of light and the metallic reek of flash powder.

The American mechanics and the aviatrix's other supporters ran forward with a set of steps almost before the propeller had stopped turning. The reporters followed more slowly and warily. Cigarettes and wine glasses had been swapped for notepads and pens.

Breathless with relief, Charlie watched as the pilot climbed stiffly out of the door in the side that presumably gave access to the airplane's wheelhouse. No, the cockpit is what these Americans called it. He glanced at the notes he had already made and wondered why none of them had been inclined to explain why.

The other reporters were shouting questions. How old was Miss Earhart? When had she started flying? Where had she started her journey? Charlie already had those answers, thanks to his conversations with the Americans. Forty-two. 1920. Harbour Grace, Newfoundland.

"Mrs. Putnam! Quentin Morgan, *Daily Mail*!" The man in shirt-sleeves smirked at his fellow journalist who clearly had no idea that the lady flier was married. "What's your plucky little airplane called?"

"I go by my own name, thanks all the same," the slender, leather-jacketed woman said sardonically, "and I'm flying a Modernaire AE, call sign 7083."

She grinned, suddenly charming as she pulled off her flying helmet and ran a hand through her short curls. The hairstyle was as practical as her breeches and boots, and just as startling on a woman. "The airplane's called The Spirit of St. Christopher."

Charlie wrote that down as eagerly as the rest of the assembled reporters, before sticking up his own hand. "Charles Oliver, *Daily Herald*. How long did your journey take?"

Miss Earhart checked her watch. "Twenty-seven hours and fifteen minutes."

More questions came thick and fast. "What did you eat and drink?" "Surely you were unable to sleep?" "How did you navigate?" The aviatrix responded to them all, her answers composed and concise.

As the queries finally died away, Miss Earhart raised her voice. "I've been told for years that no one could ever fly non-stop across the Atlantic. This flight proves beyond all doubt that airplanes have the capacity to cross the world's oceans and continents. These machines should be far more than rich men's playthings and engineering curiosities. The potential of fixed-wing flight is tremendous and the time has come to explore it. The skies do not belong to Zeppelins alone, as of unquestioned right."

She drew a breath and Charlie could see that she had more to say, despite her evident weariness. But the other journalists had seized their chance and hurried away towards their parked cars. The photographers had already gone and Charlie wondered what arrangements they had made to send their film for developing across the Channel. Without some decent pictures, the story would be lucky to make page five.

He found a clean glass and poured some wine. As he went over and offered it to Miss Earhart, he smiled apologetically. "We all have deadlines, and soon. They need to find a telephone, if they're going to file their copy before the London papers go to press."

"And you don't?" The lady flier looked exhausted and years older than her true age. "Or are you just not going to bother? Who cares what mad Americans get up to anyway? The Yankees aren't interested in Europe, so who gives a damn about them?"

Charlie flipped back a few pages in his notebook to show her a page of neat shorthand outlines. "I've written almost all of my story and your young wireless lady is going to use her equipment to send it to a friend of mine in London."

Miss Earhart laughed. "Well, aren't you an enterprising fellow?" She took the glass of wine and drained it, before looking at Charlie, suddenly severe. "Were you listening to what I said? Are you interested in the potential of fixed wing aviation?"

"More than you can imagine," he assured her. "May I call on you tomorrow, to discuss the subject further?"

She looked at him for a long moment, clearly intrigued. Equally obvious, she was far too tired to pursue the matter this evening. "Okay then. Make it first thing. I have a full schedule on this trip."

She might have said something more, but one of the mechanics by the plane shouted an urgent summons and she strode away. As Charlie watched her go, his hand strayed to the breast of his suit, where the letter that nobody knew about was hidden in an inside pocket.

* * *

He found a room for the night in a modest *pension* and set out bright and early for the considerably more luxurious hotel where the Marconi girl had told him the American flying expedition would be based for the next week. As he entered, Charlie saw a handful of wide-eyed staff clustered by the dining room door. Voices and laughter were loud within. The Americans were still getting used to the Continental style of breakfasting on coffee and croissants and made no secret of their bemusement. Thankfully the hotel staff weren't offended, as far as Charlie could tell. Indeed, the French seemed far more entertained by the novelty of such unfamiliar guests.

As he headed for the concierge's desk, one of the mechanics came down the stairs. "Hey, you were at the airstrip yesterday. Can I help you, buddy?"

His tone made it clear that it was a friendly greeting, so Charlie smiled. "Miss Earhart said I should call on her today."

"Okay," the mechanic said, obliging. "Room 214. Go on up."

Charlie was somewhat taken aback by such informality, but the mechanic was already on his way to the dining room. The concierge was nowhere to be seen, so he couldn't ask for a message to be sent to the room. He considered taking a seat in the lobby to wait, but recalled what the aviatrix had said about having a lot to get done. His hand strayed to the hidden letter again. He dared not miss his chance.

Upstairs, he counted the brass numbers along the corridor and found the door to 214 ajar. He knocked politely all the same.

"Come on in!" The summons was somewhat muffled, but Miss Earhart's voice was unmistakable.

Charlie entered, only to stop dead, blushing scarlet with embarrassment. Miss Earhart was in her dressing gown, sitting at a table with a bowl of steaming water in front of her, holding a towel over her head. There was a strong smell of menthol and other aromatics.

"I'm so sorry." He turned to leave.

"Don't go." She sat up straight, settling the towel around her shoulders. "I thought you were the girl with more hot water. Never mind, I reckon I'm done."

She sniffed experimentally and blew her nose with a thoroughness that made Charlie pity whoever laundered her handkerchiefs.

"Sinus trouble," she explained briefly, "ever since I had that damned Chicago Horse Flu. I guess that's something you can thank President Taft and his Isolationists for. They say it never got over here."

"There were a few thousand cases, but we certainly heard how dreadfully your country suffered," Charlie assured her. "Did it really come from horses?"

"Horses, or pigs, or chickens. So they say." She shrugged. "Make no odds to the millions who died. I may have sinus trouble, but at least I'm still here. So what did you want to talk to me about?"

Charlie took out his notebook. "I'd like our readers to understand the future you see for your airplanes. When Zeppelins can carry so many more people in safety and comfort—"

Miss Earhart interrupted him with a laugh. "Ever been in a zep facing a headwind? They can end up going nowhere. A fixed-wing airplane can fly in all sorts of weather."

"If the weather's too bad for flying, we take the train," Charlie pointed out.

"Do you, indeed?" She changed the subject abruptly. "I asked around about your paper. They say it backs the working man and pushed for votes for women. It supports labor unions and the like. Do you? Or do you just take their paychecks?"

"I absolutely believe in the *Herald*'s message," Charlie assured her, even as he wondered where this was going.

"Cards on the table then, and off the record." She wiped her face with the corner of the towel, wholly serious. "Your governments run your trains. We have railway barons. Robber barons, we call them, and they don't just control the trains, but steel and coal and petroleum, as well as copper, silver, and gold mining, along with real estate and every sort of finance. Ever heard of the Astors, the Carnegies, the Rockefellers?"

Charlie shook his head and she sighed. "No reason you would have. They don't want Europeans taking an interest in US affairs, any more than they want ordinary Americans getting wind of your social democracy. God forbid we should see how you make it work, now that you've gotten rid of the real-life barons you used to have over here."

Charlie raised his pen politely. "I thought you had government by the people, for the people."

"Maybe once upon a time." Miss Earhart laughed, bitter. "These days our politicians are bought and paid for, and the Isolationists don't just own the railroads. They own the newspapers and the telegraph wires and that means the only news the American man and woman in the street gets is the news they're given. The barons own the telephone exchanges, so they soon hear who's talking out of turn. Make a noise and you'll find a Pinkerton on your doorstep, saying you should pipe down if you know what's good for you. Or there'll be one telling the train conductor to put you off at the next stop, with a full refund for your ticket of course."

"Goodness me." Charlie wondered what a Pinkerton was. Nothing good, by the sound of it. "But surely you have automobiles to go wherever you want?"

"Courtesy of Henry Ford? Ten dollars off, if you sign up for a free lifetime subscription to *The Dearborn Independent*. Have you ever seen a copy of that rag?"

"Once or twice. It did have some eccentric views." Charlie chose his words carefully.

He was aware that some Americans had views on race that were as distasteful as the prejudice against Jews that was still all too common across Europe. Though he had understood that the extreme eugenicists' cause in America had been fatally undermined by the far greater resistance to the Chicago Flu amongst the descendants of slaves.

"That's what you call British understatement, I take it." Miss Earhart waved Henry Ford and his works away, contemptuous. "The thing is, automobiles can still be pulled over, especially when the local cops are in rich men's pockets. Oh, the bookleggers give them a run for their money, but that's a dangerous game. More than that, ours is a big country. I don't think you realize just how big it is, over here. Travel from coast to coast by road when decent pavement stops at most city limits?" She shook her head.

"That's where your airplanes come in?" hazarded Charlie.

"Right." She favored him with that sudden, charming smile. "No one owns the skies. An airplane can carry the real news from place to place and land on a gravel country road or a farmer's field if needs be."

"But can't you do that already?" Charlie gestured vaguely in the direction of the airstrip.

"We can, but we need bigger airplanes." Miss Earhart leaned forward, intense. "We need airplanes that can take ten passengers from New York to San Francisco, twenty passengers, maybe more. Then we can start getting people from place to place, to talk to each other. Women, and Negroes, and Indians, and anyone else who those rich white men don't want having their say. Then maybe we can get back to government by the people, for the people."

"So you've come to Europe—?" Charlie prompted.

"To find investors, because we won't ever get a dime out of the Rockefellers and their pals. We want to find engineers and mechanics who can invent and test prototypes without finding their workshops burning down in the night. Men and women we can work with, who can build on what we've already developed."

She leaned back from the table. "More than that, if air travel becomes commonplace in Europe, those Carnegies and Rockefellers won't have any good reason to deny it to the American people. They're no fools. They know their hold on power only lasts as long as no one really sees the iron hand inside the velvet glove. That's why they won't actually stop the likes of me studying engineering, however much they might try to discourage us from making use of what we learn."

"I see." Charlie nodded. He reached into his jacket's inner breast pocket. "I think we can do that and more besides."

He handed Miss Earhart the letter. He sat with his heart pounding as she slit the envelope and extracted the contents. He watched her eyes widen as she studied the diagrams and read the accompanying note.

She looked up. "Is this for real?"

He nodded. "Absolutely."

A knock on the door interrupted them. It was the wireless operator. "Miss Amelia? Your appointment?"

"I know." She stuffed the papers back in the envelope and stood up, addressing Charlie. "I'll need to see this for myself. Give me an address where I can telegraph you, when I've freed up some time in my calendar."

Charlie wrote in his notebook and tore out the page. "Here."

As she took it, she looked at him, shrewdly assessing. "What do you get out of this?"

He grinned. "A front page exclusive. Hopefully more than one."

Her appreciative laughter followed him out of the door as the wireless operator escorted him down the stairs.

* * *

Three days later, on the train from London to Bedford, Charlie sat quietly as Miss Earhart studied the engineering drawings for what must have been the fifth time. Then she went over them yet again. Finally, seeing the landmarks that indicated they had nearly arrived, he cleared his throat.

"We'll take a taxi from the station."

"What?" She looked up and, realizing the train was slowing, folded the drawings to stow them in her handbag. "Oh, okay."

As she took her gloves from her coat pocket, a shilling fell to the compartment floor. Charlie bent forward to retrieve it. As Miss Earhart took the coin from him, she studied Edward VIII's portrait. "How come you British kept your king, when everyone else was getting rid of theirs? Come to that, why did the Germans and Russians and all the rest decide they'd had enough of emperors?"

Charlie smiled. "Have you ever heard of Archduke Franz Ferdinand of Austria, heir to the Austro-Hungarian Empire?"

"Can't say that I have," said Miss Earhart, mystified.

"Don't worry," Charlie assured her. "Half the men and women on any London omnibus would say the same. The most memorable thing that ever happened to him was getting assassinated in Sarajevo in 1914."

"Good Lord!" Miss Earhart was startled.

"The Serbs caught the killers and executed them and everyone was satisfied apart from Wilhelm of Germany and Nicholas of Russia. They were outraged. They started accusing and threatening each other until there were rumors that one or other of them would declare outright war. That was going too far. No one with any sense was going to see blood shed for a quarrel between two cousins."

Charlie sat with his elbows resting on his knees. "It's not as if either of them were overly popular. Silly Billy had been making a fool of himself for years. Read his interview in *The Daily Telegraph* from 1908. That sparked the first round of calls for his abdication. As for the Czar, he'd dragged the Russians into that disastrous war with Japan. He only survived popular fury at those losses by granting parliamentary reforms in 1905."

Miss Earhart shook her head, "I had no idea."

"No one saw what was coming. Austria and Hungary broke apart first, when the old Emperor Franz Joseph died and all the Slavs declared independence. They'd been demanding more say in their own governments for decades. The Czar went completely to pieces when his poor little boy died and withdrew from public life, so that was the end of his dynasty. Then the Germans who'd been reading their Engels realized their Kaiser's demands for more and bigger battleships were bankrupting their country, so they gave him his marching orders."

Charlie laughed as he remembered the cartoons. Bruce Bairnsfather in *The Morning Post* drawing Silly Billy with his spiked helmet and that ridiculous moustache, plodding off with a red spotted bundle on a stick over his shoulder.

"George V wasn't the sharpest knife in the drawer, but he was bright enough to see he was on very thin ice after what happened to his cousins in Germany and Russia. Then India declared independence and the rest of the Empire followed suit. We have your Chicago Flu to thank for that."

"Really?" Miss Earhart was surprised.

"The Flu may not have crossed the Atlantic, but it swept across the Pacific with a vengeance. The death toll in India was appalling, but the government here couldn't do anything about it, least of all send troops to replace the British soldiers who died. They were up to their necks dealing with the Irish Insurrection. As soon as the Irish went their own way, the Suffragette Summer erupted, thanks to Asquith going back on his word to give women the vote yet again."

Charlie shook off a sudden memory of walking across broken glass in the high street, six years old and not understanding why all the shops were closed, as he clung to his mother's hand and the stink of smoke hung heavy in the air.

"Master Gandhi proclaimed that the British Empire had broken faith with India, by failing in its duty to its subjects. The Indian Congress declared independence and Asquith dared not make a fight of it. That loss strengthened calls for constitutional reform here, there, and everywhere else under British rule. Sailor George decided not to wait until he was pushed. He handed over the keys to Windsor Castle and Buckingham Palace and retreated to Sandringham, to live a quiet life with his stamp collection."

He nodded at the coin in Miss Earhart's hand. "That's where Edward the Unsteady lives now, gambling and drinking and enjoying the bachelor life, since he can't find the right woman to wed. If he doesn't have any children, the Duke of York will succeed to the throne, although that is purely ceremonial now. He lives up in Scotland, at Balmoral, with his wife and daughters."

"I see," Miss Earhart said politely.

Charlie realized that he'd more than satisfied her curiosity. He needed to remember not everyone shared his passion for history or he risked becoming a crashing bore.

As the train pulled into Bedford Station, he stood up. "Let's get to Cardington."

The village was only five miles or so from the town. Their destination was soon obvious, as the great steel hangars dominated the flat landscape, their cantilevered roofs 170 feet tall.

Miss Earhart turned to Charlie in the back seat of the cab.

"That's an airship shed."

He nodded. "And much more besides."

Miss Earhart leaned forward, impatient. As soon as they reached the airship facility, she sprang out of the taxi, leaving Charlie to pay the driver. He followed the lady flier, watching amused as she swiftly introduced herself to the first man she met.

The engineer escorted her towards the cavernous hangar and Charlie saw men and women in overalls hurrying to meet her. He headed for the administration block where he knew he could get a cup of tea. He had no wish to be deafened by the boffins' experimental engines again.

He had drunk several cups of tea, read his newspaper, done the crossword, and written three draft news articles in his notebook by the time the canteen door opened and Miss Earhart came in. Charlie half-expected to see her in overalls, but she was still an incongruous vision of Parisian elegance, in her long skirt and maroon wool coat. She was also beaming from ear to ear. Charlie signalled to the waitress for a fresh pot of tea.

"Jet engines," she marvelled, as she dropped into the chair on the other side of the table. "They've really done it."

She unpinned her hat and put it beside the vase of flowers before rubbing her ears and grimacing. "My head is still ringing."

"Have some tea." The tray arrived and Charlie poured two cups. "Milk? Sugar?"

"Just milk, thank you. Though they'll need to learn to make coffee here, if American engineers are coming over." She took the tea all the same and drank it thirstily.

"So you're interested in working with the chaps?"

"And how! That means yes," the aviatrix clarified as she poured herself more tea. "The sky's the limit, if we can get our airplanes and your engines working together. I can't thank you enough for bringing me here."

She paused and looked at him, her gaze piercing. "Why did you bring me here, Charles? The guys said you told them to expect me. This was your plan all along, even before you came to France. What gives?"

Charlie waved a casual hand. "I was here a few months ago, doing a feature on the latest airship designs. I'm always on the lookout for a new story, so when I heard that incredible noise, I followed my nose, so to speak. We got talking and the chaps were saying it was all very well, them developing these new engines, but the teams working on an airplane that could use them were getting nowhere fast. Last month, I read about your transatlantic flight, so I did a bit of research and found out you're an expert in aeronautics." He pronounced the unfamiliar word with care.

"So I popped over here and asked the chaps if they'd like me to see if you'd be interested in paying them a visit. The rest, you know." He shrugged. "I'm a newspaper man. We put things together."

Miss Earhart wasn't so easily satisfied. "Why do you need planes with jet engines?" Her gesture took in Charlie, the Cardington works, and the countryside beyond. "You said yourself that travel by zeps and trains suits Europeans just fine."

The silence between them lengthened. Charlie made a swift decision. Miss Earhart didn't need to know about his chat with Johnny from the Foreign Office in St James's Park. No point in trying to explain to an American that a grammar school boy who got to Cambridge could expect a tap on the shoulder from time to time.

"Cards on the table? You remember what I said about India? Twenty years on and they've bounced right back from the Flu. So have the Chinese, thanks to the Flu hitting the Japanese so hard that they scurried back to their islands and have stayed there ever since. Add to that, the Chinese got rid of their Emperor well before it was the fashion hereabouts."

Charlie turned to a blank page in his notebook and began sketching a map. "That means we have the two most powerful countries in the world, each with millions of people and all the resources they might need, both with no good reason to trust outsiders, glaring at each other over the Himalayas. They're constantly wrangling over who has the whip hand over their neighbors to the south and east, so neither of them take kindly to anyone else's airships coming into their skies or steamships trying to cross the seas that they've claimed as their own."

He finished his map and tapped the last outlines he had drawn. "All of which leaves our cousins in Australia and New Zealand cast thoroughly adrift. But you said it yourself. Fixed wing aircraft with the right engines can cross oceans and continents."

Miss Earhart contemplated the sketch for a long moment. Then she looked up at Charlie and her eyes were bright with amusement. "You haven't seen the latest engine prototypes these chaps of yours are working on, have you? They've been reading the journals from the universities in Vienna, Moscow, and Berlin. All those professors have been working together, striking sparks off each other to fire up some great new ideas."

"Such as?" Charlie said uncertainly.

"Rocket engines, they're calling them." Miss Earhart's smile widened. "They'll get you to Australia. Heck, give them ten years and they'll be ready to shoot for the moon!"

WHAT MAKES
A BETTER WORLD

Michael Robertson

Akhre had given her presentation about the danger of hexabioctal vapor more than twenty times to various audiences, with many more practice runs besides, so she went through it as if she were on rails. Which she liked. The automatic feeling helped her manage her stage fright.

When she was done and the polite applause quieted, she said, "Thank you. I can take a few questions."

She sipped water as a young man who worked for the conference hurried to someone raising their hand to give them the speaking cone. Akhre thought that was strange, perhaps some kind of Roman custom. Throughout the Empire of Palmyra, questioners at her presentations would simply raise their voices.

"Good morning, Lady Akhre," a man said. He looked Roman, olive-skinned and on the shorter side, one might even say squat. "Your presentation was quite polished and I thank you. But I wonder, if hexabioctal vapor is as dangerous as you say, why haven't we seen any of the effects you predict?"

"As I said in my conclusion," Akhre replied, trying not to let her tone betray the annoyance she felt at repeating herself, "the consequences will not be pronounced enough to be noticeable until it is far too late. Here in 1921—Seleucid, of course. I believe here you would call it 1636 in the reign of Augustus, although I would never want to offend Emperor Marcus the Twenty-Seventh, so perhaps I should say…" she paused and mimicked counting on her fingers, allowing a moment for laughter, which came. The joke was based on the ongoing dispute in Rome about how best to keep track of years. Traditionalists still clung to the old way of starting over for each emperor's reign, but essentially everyone used the date of Augustus's rise to emperor as the year zero.

The whole thing was foolish and Palmyrans often joked about it.

"My theory predicts we will not see any consequences for at least one hundred years," she went on. Murmuring rose up at that, which she was used to, so she finished with, "As to whether you care about the lives of the people who will be citizens then, I suppose that is up to you. I'll take another question."

Another man stood, also a Roman, though taller than the previous. "Good morning. By your theory, it seems we have no choices. Raw fire and trapped fire both give off hexabioctal vapor." Akhre recognized the archaic names for power derived from open flame, like the original old aeolipile-driven trains, and heat contained within a mechanism, like pretty much everything in the last fifty years. The man continued, "But the new galvanics would also be giving that off, since they just use trapped fire over a distance. So you come in here and think just because you're Palmyran you can tell us everything we're doing is wrong? Well, that's—"

The young conference worker pulled the speaking cone away, bless him, and said, "Can you answer this question, please?" His words made the cutting off polite, as if he were on the questioner's side.

"My intention is not to tell anyone what they are doing is wrong." She paused, bringing to mind the story she used to defuse this common tension in presentation rooms. There was a risk, in front of a Roman audience, that a childhood story, combined with the fact she was a woman, would undercut her professional competence in their eyes. But it seemed the best way to address the question and the anger and uncertainty behind it.

"I grew up," she went on, "in the province of Aegyptus and my family grew fruits. Oranges, tangerines, limes, lemons. Fruits like that are sensitive to the air around them. The most sensitive ones we kept in glass houses, to keep them warm. I learned that glass houses work because the sun's light enters and warms the dirt and the plants, but then that warmth can't escape through the glass." Akhre usually used a joke at this point, about how she only cared about having a warm place to go on cold days, but she omitted it here to avoid giving this Roman audience any additional sense of femininity.

"Of course," she continued, "as I studied, I learned our upper air is not actually like that, but the similarity struck me. The sun's light comes to us each day and passes through the transparent air and warms the dirt, and our buildings, but then, depending on the mix of vapors in the air, the proportion of that warmth that escapes changes. Take that information and add to it these others: first, hexabioctal vapor, as you say, appears to result whenever fuel is burned, and, second, additional hexabioctal vapor in the air causes more warmth to be retained. This is what I am telling you. What we should do about it is something to be figured out among ourselves."

The room absorbed that for a silent moment.

A scientist from the University of Arles asked her a very technical question about trioctal vapor and from there it all felt like a typical scientific conference.

Akhre thanked the audience and left the room.

The Double Prosperity hotel was not the nicest in Rome, but it was practical, near the train station, and had plenty of room for this modest conference. Varnished oak and tan-painted brick composed the majority of the interior and the pairing gave equally potent impressions of ugliness and solidity, like a prison.

Akhre forced a deep breath into her lungs and loosened her grip on her traveling case to allow blood back into her fingers.

She passed the vertical carriage system, which was decorated with a carving of an ox looking up at the sun, the insignia of whichever guild had crafted this particular specimen of the new design. Underneath her feet, there would be a number of oxen pulling a wheel, possibly with flywheels geared into a system for storing and releasing energy, and a long belt of leather and wire stretched up and around the two carriages, carrying one up and one down, as much as the guests needed.

Akhre decided to walk the three flights of stairs up to her room, rather than have to stop and wait for the carriage.

At her doorway, she paused. She supposed she could run away now. Only then what? She'd promised Accio, and besides, she thought this was the right thing to do. Was almost sure of it.

She opened the door, entered, and said, "Hello?"

No sound came from her shadowy room.

She closed the door behind her.

"That's better," a woman's voice said from the room. "I'd rather keep our talk private, wouldn't you?"

Akhre was willing her heart not to explode, but she managed to mumble agreement.

The woman chuckled. "Relax. I think I'll light the lamp, if it's all right with you."

Akhre did not move or say anything.

The firelighter sparked and the flashes illuminated a short, slender woman with large eyes.

The wick took fire and the woman turned. In the rising glow, Akhre noticed this woman was beautiful. She looked like a statue of a goddess rendered human-sized but then made a bit smaller. Her olive skin tended toward a darker shade than most Romans, and her large, dark eyes took the lamp's light and slung it along two glossy curves that took Akhre's breath away.

"So," she said, "you like women, do you?"

Akhre choked and shook her head. "No, I'm sorry, I mean—" She looked at the woman again. "I mean, I do, but I know that's not. That is. Can we sit down?"

The woman laughed.

They sat in the room's chairs, which faced each other across a square table.

"You have something for me?" the woman said.

Akhre hesitated. "This is the right thing to do. Right?"

"You're asking me?" The woman said. When Akhre didn't answer, she went on, "I think so. If this matter is as dire as my associates believe, we would like to learn all we can."

"And you and your associates are…?"

"We do not say our name. We protect the peace."

"The peace of two empires."

The woman did not answer.

Akhre knew it would be inappropriate to speak directly about the KTO, the famous Fangs of the Vipers. If the legend was true, the KTO had been founded more than a thousand years ago, after the Schism of Scythia and the attendant civil war. The serpent head, wide eyes, fangs curved and sharp, was often figured against a split background: One eye faced inward, watching over the Roman and Palmyran Empires, the other outward, spying on foreign lands. Ready to strike wherever necessary to protect the Empires' peace.

Akhre opened her bag. Inside were papers, pencils, a stack of cards bound in a cord. She moved all that aside and opened a concealed zipper in one seam. From behind the fabric she pulled a heavy, dull gray ampoule. "Before I give you this, I have to tell you that you must not open it. No person can. You will need to use tools and you should wear ogdantaduo garments when you do so. The substance in here is extremely dangerous."

The woman nodded.

Akhre placed the ampoule on the table and closed her bag.

"Tell me what you know about this substance," the woman said. She made no move to take the ampoule.

"Unfortunately Accio would know a lot more than I do about it."

"That may be true, but he is not here."

Akhre pressed her temples with her fingertips. "This is a sample of something Accio believes is enenentaduo. You may be familiar with the numerated elements, which we all learned ended at ogdontatria, the eighty-third, those iridescent spiral crystals…" Akhre recognized she was babbling. Stopped. "But Accio tells me that his research suggests there are more, possibly over a hundred, and this enenentaduo would be one of those. The ninety-second element."

The woman did not answer or say anything. Just continued watching Akhre.

"Accio said this element is unusual. It breaks down. And this causes it to give off a deadly aura. A few scientists Accio knew said it made them sick, even killed one. Killed, I have to be accurate, in horrific fashion. Blood from the eyes and anus, skin sliding off." Giving clinical details made Akhre more comfortable. Her scientist side took over.

"This element, if Accio's theory is correct, could have several dangerous applications. Ground up and released in the air, it would be harmful, perhaps fatal, to any who breathed it. But under certain circumstances, Accio described a way of causing such an element to ignite. Such an explosion would be capable of enormous devastation. One such weapon would destroy most of Rome, or Byzantium, or Alexandria."

Akhre tried to remember if Accio had said anything else.

"Do you know, I think I like you," the woman said.

The words startled Akhre, made her shake her head. "What?"

"Mine is a lonely line of work, as you could easily guess. And here I find myself in a hotel room, with a pleasing woman, and some extra time allotted that I don't think I need for conversation."

"But, what about the sample?"

"You've handed me the sample, as you were sent to do. What more need be said?"

"It's just…" Akhre thought. Now that her mission was complete, she didn't know what she'd expected. And the prospect of enjoying some time with this beautiful agent of the mysterious KTO was appealing. But it all felt incomplete.

"What's going to happen?" Akhre finally asked.

"Because I like you," the agent said, leaning forward, "I will tell you a few things. As for this sample, I will bring it to my associates and they will learn from it as they can. Such things aren't my specialty. We are aware of rumors that Sinae has been sending many merchants and diplomats to Nesichelona, seeking to trade with people called Cree in a place called Athapa-askaw. They are seeking deposits of dark, heavy metal that looks like tar."

"I thought Nesichelona was all scattered tribes and vast plains, mountains, their strange cows. They have merchants?"

"We have had to revise our estimation of the Nesichelonan people. Perhaps our familiarity with imperial governance was inhibiting our understanding. The Nesichelonan government is like a vast republic. Each of the tribes has representatives who meet and agree to rules, taxes, that sort of thing. In peaceful times, beyond those simple things, each does as they wish. But we believe now that, in times of war, their combined strength could be…considerable."

Akhre tried to think of more questions.

"Now," the agent said, leaning forward, "let us see how you like the viper's kiss."

* * *

The view from her office window, a brick wall across the street, provided nothing to distract Akhre from the fact that Accio was late. Grading student work was not much more engrossing. The occasional throaty hum of an autocarriage growled up from the street below.

Accio had wanted to hear how things went, so before Akhre had departed they had planned to meet so she could tell him.

Whatever laws Akhre might have broken in smuggling a sample across provincial and imperial borders, Accio had done worse by stealing the stuff in the first place. A sample of enenentaduo, rare as it was, would be missed, leading to questions. The KTO's use of covert means to acquire the sample suggested their leadership didn't trust the higher ups at the University, meaning that if any of those untrustworthy higher-ups became aware of Accio's theft, there could be severe consequences for him.

She rubbed her cheeks with her palms, slapped lightly, and blew out a breath.

A knock came on her door and she composed herself, dabbed a handkerchief at her forehead, and said, "Come in."

Bassit Arkiley entered her office and Akhre gulped. Bassit was the Archprofessor of the University, in charge of all academic matters. Akhre had never met her before, only seen her from the audience when she addressed the professors at the start of each year.

"Archprofessor, welcome, I'm sorry my office is a mess, I've been—"

Bassit held up her hand, silencing Akhre, and said, "That is not why I came. Tell me, how was your trip?"

Bassit sat down opposite Akhre, holding her cane out beside her with one hand draped over its handle. She reminded Akhre of a cedar tree, rough and dark brown and poised with the resilience of age. Her gaze made Akhre sit up straight, as if the older woman's regard was a weight settling on her shoulders.

"I did well with my presentation," Akhre said, "although the Romans seem disinclined to believe science if it goes against their purses or their wishes." Akhre hesitated, unsure if it had been improper for her to speak so freely. The words had just rolled out. "Of course, though, they were hospitable and friendly to me, and treated me well as their guest."

Bassit cleared her throat. "No need to glaze your words with honey. I've met more Romans than you have and I assure you they pay close attention to the weight of their gold and the sharpness of their alloy, the better to bend things to their will. And when they meet something that will not bend…" Bassit shrugged and waved her hands in the air. "They fall apart like glass hitting the ground."

Akhre hid her surprise at those harsh words. Making fun of Roman greed and stubbornness was one thing, but Bassit's harsh words could not be interpreted in any lighthearted way.

"In any case," the Archprofessor continued, "did you have time to enjoy the sights? This was your first trip to the other empire, I think."

"It was, yes. I saw the Colosseum, and the column of Trajan, and the Vaxian Hospital complex. I'm sure I saw other things, but I lost count. It's an old city."

Bassit chuckled. "Almost as old as this one, as we say."

Akhre nodded, but she wasn't sure what else to say.

Bassit waited as well.

It struck Akhre all at once that the Archprofessor might know about her carrying the sample to Rome and handing it to the KTO. She kept her expression calm, but her mind sped up. If that were so, what would be the right thing for Akhre to say?

"You're from outside Cairo, right?" Bassit asked. But she did not wait for any reply. "An orchard? I remember hearing about your talks. I think you sometimes mention it."

After a moment, Akhre said, "That's right."

"But your heritage is Syrian? Palmyran?"

Akhre could not see any way to change the topic, but these questions struck her as odd and she was uncomfortable answering. "My father is actually from Palmyra, yes. My mother is from Aegyptus."

"A heritage like two strong rivers," Bassit observed.

"I suppose. Archprofessor, is there something—"

"We are scientists, you and I," Bassit said. "And we do well when we examine one thing at a time, each with the close attention that is right for it. But there are many matters in the world that do not yield to such analysis. Many assume the twin empires are a source of peace and prosperity for the world, like two sides of an arch leaning together to allow a beautiful building to stand. But this is not a scientific belief. It cannot be tested. If one could run the scenario again and again, we might find this world to be worse than many others. Of course there, again, we run into matters that do not yield to science. What makes a better world?"

Bassit ended her last sentence as a real question, so Akhre felt compelled to answer. "I think peace, enough prosperity so everyone can pursue the curiosity sparking within them. I'm afraid I'm a traditional Palmyran in that sense."

"In what sense? Be precise."

"Empress Zenobia laid it out in her treaty with Rome. Each person carries a divine spark and the duty of government is to create a structure so that each person may pursue their spark's destiny, restricted by law from doing harm or unduly inhibiting those around them from doing the same."

"Just so. And do you believe the Romans agree with that goal?"

Akhre couldn't stop herself from frowning. This was ridiculous. The treaty of twin empires had been written more than a thousand years ago. Who could possibly know? There had been a civil war since then, disease outbreaks, fractures, treaties, uprisings, invasions repelled, and all the other obstacles history threw in front of human plans. "They signed the treaty," she finally said.

"Do you know," Bassit said, leaning back and speaking in a much more casual tone than she had been, "I recently visited Nesichelona?"

"That must have been a challenging voyage."

"Why?" Bassit said, and laughed. "Of course it was. My seventy-three years have made my mind strong, but my body a bit less strong than it once was. And I find boats to be less pleasant than trains by a large margin. Still, the specimens there—it's as if another world had been started, thousands and thousands of years ago, and then left to run, a separate scenario. I saw new trees, flowers, mosses, vines. I heard stories of trees so tall they would tower over our buildings. The food was delicious, and plentiful, and the people kind. I do not mean to paint it as some perfect place—there were many problems, as there always are. But there is so much space. Perhaps that's what allows…"

She trailed off, staring over Akhre's shoulder.

Akhre waited.

"I came to tell you," Bassit went on, "that I ran into Accio about an hour ago. He wasn't feeling well and said he had been planning to visit you. He asked me to come and tell you not to wait for him."

Akhre cleared her throat. "Thank you."

"You seem smart to me—don't be modest, I had to approve your hiring—but as we discussed, some issues do not yield to the intellect. When I think of supporting the divine sparks of the world, I find myself doubting some things that many assume without examination. Perhaps you might think on such things. You, more than many others, know that the structure of life is a fragile thing. Fragile enough that there is no need to make things more fragile—well, I believe you understand."

Bassit rose, leaning over her cane. "Come speak with me in a few weeks, if you like. I'm trying to arrange a visit from some Sinaean scholars and I think they would be interested in learning more about your work. Goodnight."

The Archprofessor left.

Akhre leaned over her desk and breathed, considered the student papers on her desk, the brick wall outside her window.

She extinguished her lamps and left to go home.

Galvanic lanterns lit the streets. She stepped into pools of light and into borders of shadow.

The light made her think of fire, and that made her think of Accio's warnings, about the dire incineration enenentaduo could spark.

Would it be better for the twin empires to have such power, or the Sinaeans and the Nesichelonans? Or, she could split and revise the question, bringing Zimbabwe in as well, or the provinces, Gaul and Germania. Or what if Rome decided the world would be better off with one empire, not two?

She did not wish to help anyone gain such power. She felt, turning the corner to her street, that she had dirtied herself smuggling the sample, helping the KTO get a head start in creating weapons that could snuff out vast fields of divine sparks between one heartbeat and the next.

Her footsteps thumped against the street. She cried and felt foolish, trying to hide her tears, though no one was around. Her mother used to chide her for crying. "Stop wasting water," she would say. "It can't be changed."

Akhre had hated that. But right now she felt the hard

truth beneath the words.

Akhre had one foot on the stair to her front door when the insight hit her. She couldn't say where it came from, it just arrived, as if some hidden part of herself had been working on a puzzle and had come to her shouting to show the solution.

She had spent years researching power generation. The purpose had nothing to do with hexabioctal vapor. Power required heat and it was the fuel they burned for heat that gave off the vapor.

From Accio's description, his new element sounded capable of generating enormous heat, but it might also be different enough from wood and charcoal and spirits that its burning might not poison the air.

She would have to ask him about it.

Someone walked past behind her, muttering something.

"What was that?" she asked, turning.

A monk in a long robe was passing by, carrying a wooden cross over one shoulder. "I am sorry, lady," he said, with a Macedonian accent. "I do my penance."

"Penance for what?"

"On this day, one-thousand five-hundred and seventy-six years ago, our Lord was put to death. So I carry a cross, as he did, and I repent of my sins and remember the Lord's suffering."

"Oh," she said. She didn't know very much about Christian beliefs. "I wish you well, then."

"Thank you," he said, and began walking along again, muttering. He turned his head and said over his shoulder, "I wish perhaps I had gotten started earlier."

Akhre laughed in a way she hoped was friendly and polite and went into her house. Ideas were spinning there, questions for Accio, and plans for how to divert the world onto a path to…what had Bassit said?

To make a better world.

FIELD OF CLOTH OF GOLD AND BLOOD, SWEAT AND TEARS

Kat Otis

Pale of Calais, 1520

As the music wound down to its closing note, my dance partner twirled me to a stop before the canopy of estate where my mother, Katherine of Aragon, Queen of England, sat watching. At her right hand, my aunt Claude of Brittany, Duchess of York, smiled at me briefly, but the expression on my aunt's face faded to match my mother's careful neutrality when her gaze shifted to my dance partner. Around us, masquers were pulling away the plumes and hoods that had given most of them temporary anonymity while they danced with the ladies of the English Court. Despite the two weeks we had spent jousting and feasting together, I still could not recognize most of the French lords when they wore disguises—with the exception of my dance partner, who tossed his velvet hood to the floor and bowed to me with an overly-elaborate flourish.

"Your Majesty." I curtseyed to François, King of France, and stepped backwards as I rose, finally free of his grasping hands. I wouldn't have minded his invitation to dance if I hadn't been so acutely aware of how it vexed my mother. She had made no secret of her displeasure at both my father's new alliance and François' hints that he would welcome an English bride.

François grinned. "So cold, my Lady Princess! Look, you give me chills with your disdain." He held out his arm and made as if to roll up his sleeve.

Alarmed, I blurted out the first words that came to mind. "'Tis unseasonably cold for June. And all these storms…" Inwardly, I winced at my inanity as his smile became fixed, but perhaps it was no bad thing for François to think me an empty-headed child.

Out of the corner of my eye, I caught my mother's hand signal to my aunt, who rose from her chair and approached us. Thank the blessed virgin Mary and all the saints. François turned to greet Claude as she curtseyed with a grace that belied her advancing pregnancy and I took advantage of his distraction to escape to my mother's side. Hopefully my role in tonight's diplomacy was almost over.

Only the highest-ranking nobles of the French Court had joined us in the crystal palace at Guînes. The rest of that Court was five miles away in Ardres, entertaining my father the King of England, my two elder brothers, my uncles the Dukes of York and Suffolk, and a select few of my father's favored courtiers. All my pleas to accompany them over the border to France had been firmly rebuffed, but at least I hadn't been left across the Channel at Greenwich with the rest of my siblings and cousins. I wasn't the youngest one left at Court, but I was *one* of the youngest, and my mother had made quite clear that the cost of even a youthful mistake could be high.

My mother was tapping her fingers against the arm of her chair as I joined her. For a moment I worried I was the cause of her irritation, but then she said, "Navarre watches you."

The light outside had begun to fade, but there was still enough streaming through the hall's floor-to-ceiling windows for me to pick out where Henri II, King of Navarre—in title, if not reality—stood surrounded by young lords and ladies too insignificant to be noticed by the King of France. He paid them all due courtesy but my mother was right; he had positioned himself so as to be able to see me effortlessly and his gaze flickered to me at every pause in the conversation. I had no doubt that gaze had followed me across the dance floor as well. And no wonder. If all went as my mother planned, I would be married to my cousin the King of Spain and newly-elected Holy Roman Emperor who had conquered Henri's kingdom. He had even less cause to favor me than François. At least Henri hadn't attempted to dance with me—yet.

My mother must have thought the same because she murmured, "Are you tired, Elizabeth?"

In another time or place, I might have pretended to misunderstand her veiled command, but not here, in a banquet to honor François on the very border of his kingdom. "Yes, Madam."

She held her hand out for me to kiss and I withdrew from the banquet as swiftly as I could without causing offense.

François ignored me, sweat beading on his brow as he flattered and charmed my aunt, but Henri's gaze followed me every step of the way.

* * *

The true depth of my mother's concern revealed itself early the next morning, when my brothers insisted on escorting me to the tournament field. Despite being accompanied by royal guards and our respective attendants, Arthur and Henry further bracketed my little jennet between their Neapolitan coursers—all three horses a gift from François. Having thus surrounded me, they proceeded to tease me mercilessly about kings throwing themselves love-stricken at my feet.

"The Emperor himself would go to war for your hand in marriage!" Arthur's boast made me wince, as I could too easily see his words coming true, but Henry only laughed.

"Do remember us, your poor brothers, when you rule half of Europe?"

I would have gladly traded the imperial crown with all its wealth and power to stay in England with my beloved brothers, but there was no point in ruining this moment by saying so. Besides, at sixteen, Arthur was almost a man, and Henry and I weren't far behind him. The responsibilities of adulthood would separate us soon enough, no matter who I married. So I did my best to return their teasing in kind. "Why, since I shall rule two thirds of Europe, 'tis a promise easily kept!"

Both my brothers laughed at that. Until my dying day, I will remember how they laughed as the first arrow took a guard in the throat.

I drew in a sharp, shocked breath. In the space of that breath, more arrows rained down upon us. One of Henry's gentlemen ushers took an arrow to the thigh, but the arrows fell mainly upon our guards; their blood spread sickeningly red across their green and white livery.

Arthur and Henry drew their swords as screams and shouts rang out behind us. My jennet reared and I focused on the blessedly immediate task of controlling her. Henry spurred his courser forward, turning it aslant to put himself between us and the archers. It seemed a singularly useless maneuver to me, until Arthur lunged sideways and laid the flat of his sword against my jennet's rump. She bolted the only direction my brothers had left open to her—southeast.

As my jennet plunged off the road into uneven farmland, my whole world narrowed to staying in the saddle. My brothers could be fighting and dying behind me, but all I could do was stay in the saddle. I had no idea if men were chasing me, but it didn't matter, because all that mattered was staying. In. The. Saddle.

A larger horse bred for battle would have broken a leg as it tore through the fields, the earth sodden beneath its feet from the recent storms, ditches flooded with rainwater. With a fully-grown adult in the saddle, even my jennet might not have fared well. But I was light and she was panicked and she flung herself over hedges and ditches and fences as if the hounds of hell were behind us. We must have gone a half mile or more before she finally began to slow and even then it took me three tries before she would answer to the rein again. I finally managed to slow her to a walk and guided her in a circle, searching the horizon for any sign of pursuit.

No one had followed us in our mad dash across the fields. Were they too busy with their true prizes, or were they even now pounding down more established roads and paths, seeking to cut off my escape? I squinted and tried to gauge the angle of the sun, to determine my position. It looked as if we'd gone in almost a straight line towards the tournament field. I didn't know whether to laugh or rage at my brothers. They had clearly practiced that maneuver, deliberately set me on this course, and possibly saved my life—but why, blessed Mary, had they shielded me from their plans like a child? I would flay them with my tongue when I saw them again.

I had to see them again.

Turning my jennet in the direction of the tournament field, I urged her back into motion. She was less happy about running through the fields now that her panic had subsided, but she was agile and swift and willing enough once she realized I wouldn't press her when she slowed to pick her way through the worst of the uneven terrain. My heart still pounded and fear for my brothers made my hands unsteady on the reins, but I would do no one good if I fell and injured myself now. I had to find aid, for my sake and theirs.

We must have gone another half mile before I spotted the tournament field in the distance, with its pavilions and spectator stands and the Tree of Honor rising above it all, festooned with the shields of the tournament's participants. The road was to our left and blessedly empty of other riders for the moment, so I steered my poor jennet towards it and we rode the last quarter mile on muddy but level ground.

I looked first towards the royal pavilion, but it was still empty so I turned towards my father's arming chamber. My uncle Henry, Duke of York, stood outside in an intense conversation with several of his gentlemen that ended abruptly when he caught sight of me. Relief made me dizzy and I almost fell in my haste to dismount.

"Elizabeth?" York caught my elbow to steady me, his gaze quickly taking in my heaving, foam-flecked jennet and my own mud-splattered state.

"Treachery," I blurted out, loudly enough that nearby knights turned in our direction. York pacified them with a gesture and I tried to lower my voice as I continued. "Is my father within?"

"He has not yet arrived." York drew me into the empty arming chamber to give us more privacy. "Quickly now. What happened?"

"We were ambushed. Arthur and Henry and I. On the road. I…I escaped…" I faltered, unable to finish.

York's expression darkened, his voice low and hard as he demanded, "How many men? How were they armed? Were they sent to kill or capture?"

"I couldn't see…'twas mostly archers." I wrapped my arms around myself to hide how I was shaking and struggled to remember those few, terrifying moments. "They shot the guards first. Then my horse bolted."

"Your brothers are more valuable alive than dead," York told me, and I clung to those words. He would not give me false hope. "Stay here."

Before I could protest, he turned and strode out of the arming chamber.

My knees gave out and I sat down, hard, on the nearest chest. I wasn't naïve. When my father and uncle rode to war, my mother remained behind as regent, and she had trained me to expect a similar future. But there was a difference between riding armored into the fray with an army at one's back and being ambushed in one's own kingdom while virtually unarmed and in the company of helpless women. At least I'd not proven completely useless—I'd summoned aid—but now there was nothing left for me to do but pray I'd done enough.

I slid off the chest and onto my knees, taking up my rosary beads. "*Ave Maria, gratia plena, Dominus tecum…*"

* * *

I was halfway through my thirteenth Ave Maria when the King of Navarre strode into the chamber.

I leapt to my feet and hoped the blessed Virgin didn't take offense at my abandoning her mid-prayer. "What are you doing here?" He was beholden to François and, despite the attack happening on English soil, who else but the French could have attacked us? My uncle's men shouldn't have let him enter and they definitely shouldn't have let us be alone together.

Henri raised his eyebrows at my disrespectful tone and I belatedly bobbed a quick curtsey, adding, "Your Grace?"

"I will not ride to war against an unknown foe, my Lady Princess, but there is honor in seeing to your safety." His words were reasonable enough—if François was behind the ambush, he couldn't raise a hand against the king who had sheltered him in exile, but we were not openly at war so François couldn't fault him courting the favor of my family by protecting me. I still misliked the intensity of his gaze as he held out his hand. "If you will accompany me?"

It was even less of a question than my mother's had been last night. Reluctantly, I let him take me by the arm and guide me back outside, hoping another option would present itself. The tournament field wasn't entirely deserted but I saw none of my uncle's men and the dozen or so knights who remained nearby were rapidly readying their horses. There was no joking or jostling, only a tense silence punctuated by the ringing and creaking of armor as men pulled themselves into their saddles. Henri guided me towards a young man holding the reins of a riderless courser. My own jennet was nowhere to be seen, but I supposed she wasn't fit for another journey so soon after her desperate flight.

To my surprise, Henri released my arm, mounted his courser, then reached down to me. "My Lady Princess?"

Bad enough that I was alone with men I hardly knew, but to share a mount with one! I feigned offense to hide my growing uncertainty. "I am perfectly capable of riding on my own, Your Grace."

"And you would if I had a horse to give you," Henri said, impatiently. "But we are too exposed here to tarry while one is found."

I still hesitated—surely someone had a spare horse!—but the momentary relief I had felt upon finding my uncle was long gone and I saw the sense in making haste. Even more reluctantly than before, I grasped his hand and set my foot on his to mount. The latter was almost unnecessary—he lifted me easily and set me before him in the saddle like a child. Before I could protest that I was well enough to ride behind, he wrapped his arms around me to take up the reins and spurred his courser forward. The remaining knights hastened to surround us as I clutched the pommel, praying his horse wouldn't take offense and buck us both off.

Then our company turned eastward and I no longer worried about the horse's discomfort.

"What…?"

"The road to Guînes is not safe," Henri interrupted. "We make for Ardres."

I stiffened, suddenly all too aware of how he had physically trapped me. I couldn't ride away without a horse of my own and we were moving at too fast a pace for me to fling myself out of the saddle even if I could slip from his grasp. "My father strictly forbade me to enter France. There are other roads—to Andres or Balinghem, even to Calais."

"He would be the sorriest prince in Christendom if he did not understand that some plans must change." Henri's tone was perfectly level, but the implied threat in his words made me shiver. At that, his voice did sharpen, "Are you cold, my Lady Princess?"

"Of course not," I barely kept from snapping. He was abducting me—he'd all but admitted it—and now he had the gall to mock my fear! I drew on outrage like a shield, hoping it would protect me from disgracing myself even further, and struck back at him with the only weapons I had. "I will remember this, when I am before the King of France."

Henri barked a laugh, but there was no humor in it. "I hope you do, my Lady Princess, I hope you do."

* * *

I had wanted to see Ardres, but not like this.

Hundreds of tents spread out from the city's wall, some as tall or taller than the wall itself, dressed with cloth of gold, velvet, and satin. The camp should have been filled to bursting with lords and ladies preparing for the day's jousts, servants going about their daily routines, and townsfolk come to gawk and admire the splendor that had temporarily descended upon them. There were still some servants, but they moved with frantic, frenzied purpose, and the nobles were conspicuous in their absence.

We rode through the gate into the city and down narrow streets to an immense townhouse, four times the size of its nearest neighbors. I was given no time to admire the architecture, even if I'd been inclined to do so. Henri practically threw me to the cobblestones, then leapt down beside me, seizing my arm with the barest pretense of civility. Two of his men hastened to follow us. They were too few to ensure my safety had anyone been truly worried for me, but they were more than enough to keep me from trying to run.

Henri guided me through the entry into a reception hall hung with blue velvet and golden fleurs-de-lis. There were men loitering there, but none I recognized. If they were noblemen, they were at the fringes of the French Court, not anyone who had accompanied François to the Guînes banquets, visited the royal pavilion, or competed in the tournament lists. Henri hailed one of them in rapid French that I couldn't entirely follow, but I recognized a few words. He was seeking the Duc de Bourbon, Constable of France. Whatever answer he received seemed to displease him, for he gave up the conversation and pulled me onwards through the crowd, not stopping to answer any of the questions called his way.

We passed from the hall into an unoccupied chamber hung with cloth of gold and lined with sideboards bearing gilt plate, then into a smaller chamber with even more cloth of gold. There Henri stopped and gave the briefest of bows to Marguerite d'Angoulême, Duchesse d'Alençon and sister to the King of France, who sat surrounded by her women and a few noblemen that I finally recognized. The scene should have been comforting in its domesticity, but Marguerite's eyes were red-rimmed, as if she had been weeping all night. Something terrible had happened here—something that had thrown the French Court into disarray, sent armed men to ambush my brothers and spirit me away, and spawned the Lord in Heaven only knew what other evils.

"Your Grace…" I almost whispered the words, but Henri heard me and preemptively gestured me to silence.

"*Le roi?*" Henri asked Marguerite.

Marguerite flung aside her embroidery, rose, and stalked to the door that led to the King's innermost bedchamber. I knew, with a sudden terrifying certainty, that I did not want to know what was happening on the other side of that door, but Henri gave me no choice.

The bedchamber was probably even more magnificent than the chambers we had passed through on our way here, but my gaze went immediately to the figure in the massive bed. Marguerite's husband, the Duc d'Alençon, lay still as death, only the sweat pouring off his face and the faint movements of his chest proving that he still clung to life. Why was Alençon in the King's bed?

"*Le roi est mort,*" Marguerite snapped out the words, bitter and angry and grieving.

Shock stole my breath. I'd just danced with François a few hours earlier. How could he be dead? I clutched Henri's arm, no longer a restraint but the only thing keeping me upright as I realized it was worse than that. If death had taken François so rapidly, Alençon—no, Charles IX, King of France—could be dead soon, too.

Marguerite switched to English, her accented voice filled with bleak sarcasm, "Long live the king."

* * *

Twice, Henri tried to leave me in the company of others. It was easy enough to foil his first attempt—Marguerite didn't need an English princess underfoot in her greatest hours of grief—and the second was only a little harder.

"You promised that you would guarantee my safety," I told him, sharply. "You, Your Grace. Not the Comte de Saint-Pol or the Seigneur d'Aubigny or any other."

"So now you are glad of my company?" Henri demanded.

"No, I am not *glad* of anything." I was too frightened to be politic, so I settled for blunt honesty. "But you, at least, have nothing to gain from my death."

The Comte de Saint-Pol had enough English to be offended at my words, but Henri calmed him with a few sentences of rapid French that sent him hurrying from the chamber on some other errand.

I wrestled with curiosity for a few moments, then asked, "What did you tell him?"

"We will have to work on your French, my Lady Princess," Henri said, instead of answering, which only made me more certain it mattered. My mother had trained me from birth in the Castilian and Aragonese tongues and Spanish politics, but I had to search my memory for the French line of succession. Saint-Pol was a prince of the blood, but how far was he from the throne? If the Duc d'Alençon was now king, then his heir would be the Duc de Bourbon and after that…the Duc de Vendôme? Who was the Comte de Saint-Pol's elder brother.

"You asked after the Duc de Bourbon when we arrived. How fares he, Your Grace? And the Duc de Vendôme?" I pressed him.

Henri gave me a long, considering look, then finally answered, "'Tis possible that Bourbon at least will recover. If there is an antidote and we can obtain it soon."

I hadn't thought I could be shocked any further. "You think it poison?"

He raised his eyebrows, but answered readily enough. "Do you know any disease that would strike only hale men and women in the prime of their lives, bypassing their servants entirely?"

I couldn't deny it was more commonly the other way around. My parents had whisked us away to safety often enough, while plague or pox or other pestilences ran rampant through the poor of the towns and cities we left behind. But poison! "How many are ill, Your Grace? Did they fall ill at the same time?" My thoughts raced. Someone had attacked my brothers and Henri had been swift to bring me here when the opportunity arose. "It happened in Guînes?"

Henri frowned at me, then pulled me out of the chamber crowded with the king's death watchers and into the empty dining chamber. He kept his voice low as he answered. "François had chills before the masque—he was shivering so hard I asked if he wanted to leave—but by the time the dancing finished, he was sweating and complained of his head. He fell into a delirium before we were more than a mile out of Guînes and died on English soil. At which time the Ducs d'Alençon and de Vendôme began to feel cold."

The timing was damning, but I still could not believe anyone would so brazenly poison the King of France and his agnate heirs. "And the Duc de Bourbon?"

"Sent me out as soon as the sun rose, to find the one responsible and negotiate for the antidote by whatever means necessary," Henri said, flatly. "Having been reduced to begging for my sustenance in exile, my dignity is not so tender that I would scruple against begging for the new king's life. Your uncle denied all knowledge, but that was hardly surprising—poison is a woman's weapon."

It took me a moment to realize who he meant to accuse. "Your Grace! My mother would never…!"

"She is as fond of the Duc de Bourbon as she can be of any Frenchman," Henri interrupted. "And too many others have been struck down since last night to be her work. No, I do not suspect her anymore. Though someone must, or they would not have been so foolish as to send men after your brothers."

He might not suspect my mother now, but he had when he'd taken me. No…when York had *let* him take me. I did my best to stifle my outrage at that realization and instead forced myself to think to the future as my mother had taught me. He was listening to my questions now, which was only one step away from listening to my advice. "When my father comes in arms, can you refuse to open the town gates on grounds that the poisoner might still be within?"

Henri barked that humorless laugh again. "Why, my Lady Princess, do you think I will have any say in the matter? As long as the King lives, the Queen…"

Sudden shouts and cries rose from the chamber behind us. Henri spun and flung himself through the door, with me close on his heels. A crowd of women and men blocked his path, but he shoved his way through them with fierce disregard for his own dignity or theirs.

Marguerite, for these last few hours the Queen of France, lay crumpled on the floor, her body wracked with shivers. But she had never been to Guînes and how could anyone have poisoned only her as she sat vigil surrounded by her ladies? For one terrible, selfish moment, I was glad—here was proof that pestilence, not poison, was the cause of their suffering. They were in the wrong here and now they all knew it. Close on the heels of that gladness, though, was utter terror. If it was a pestilence, anyone could be next. Lord have mercy upon us.

Henri fell to his knees beside Marguerite and reached for her hand with no sign of hesitation as she began to sob, "*J'ai froid*, Henri. *Si froid. Si froid…*"

* * *

I was afraid the Comtes de Saint-Pol and de Guise were about to come to blows. The brothers by marriage had begun their argument in English—for my sake—but quickly devolved into French as they rose from their seats, pounding on the table between them.

Henri let them shout and vent their fear for the length of an Ave Maria before he finally rose himself and shouted, "Enough!"

They turned identically offended gazes to him. Guise recalled himself first and bowed his head in deference to

Henri. Saint-Pol, whose path to the French crown was rapidly clearing, lifted his chin and said, "*Oui*. Enough talk of surrender."

Henri ignored his attempt to have the final word in their argument. "Our first priority must be securing the safety of your nephews." When they both opened their mouths to protest, he snapped, "Bourbon remains strong but we must act as if no one will survive this...this *sweating* sickness. They are the next heirs to the throne."

Saint-Pol drew himself up to his full height. "I will go..."

"I need you here," Henri interrupted. "To lead us into battle, if it comes to that. Guise, you must ride out to La Fére. Now. Before the English army arrives."

Guise bowed again, more deeply this time, then kissed Henri's ring and begged leave to depart with much more humility than he'd shown before. Saint-Pol was clearly displeased, but made no further protest, mind clearly turning to the role Henri had given him. "We should ready our defenses."

"We should," Henri agreed, "but first...who within this Court would have no qualms attacking a child prince?"

Saint-Pol bristled in renewed offense, "If you think I would harm a hair on my nephews' heads...!"

Henri raised his eyebrows at Saint-Pol's tone and I could see that he was nearing the end of his patience. If he began shouting again, he would make an enemy of Saint-Pol. I shouldn't care what happened to Henri once I was safely returned to my family—it wasn't my duty to protect Navarre, it might even be the opposite of my duty—but I also couldn't bear to sit there and do nothing when I had the chance to avert at least one of this day's many disasters. So I leaned forward, my voice all sweetness and light to disarm Saint-Pol. "This is not about your nephews, my dear Comte de Saint-Pol. His Grace means to know if you ordered the attack on my brothers."

Saint-Pol blinked. "Surely the Duc de Bourbon…who else would have had the authority to order such an attack?"

Who else indeed? I believed Henri was innocent of that crime and, if it was not the King of France or one of his agnate heirs, that left only one person with the requisite power. I turned to Henri, curious to see if he had come to the same conclusion I had.

"Then to my sorrow," Henri told me, his gaze still upon Saint-Pol, "the identity of your attackers remains a mystery, my Lady Princess. Thank you, Saint-Pol. I will join you at the wall shortly."

Saint-Pol bowed his way out, much more perfunctorily than his brother by marriage, and I waited until the chamber was cleared before asking, "If you suspected the Comte de Saint-Pol, Your Grace, why did you try to leave me with him?"

"'Twas but a vain hope." Henri buried his face in his hands, surprising me with his unguarded display of weakness. So he *did* know who was to blame. He had almost said it before: as long as the King lives, the Queen reigns.

My mother would have known how to respond—what to say and do—to turn Henri to her purposes. I hesitated a moment, but the only words that came to me were those I would have given to Arthur or Henry. Well enough then. I laid a hand on his arm and asked, as gently as I could, "Does Marguerite know that you love her?"

Henri lifted his head and gazed at me with undisguised grief. "What base, treacherous scoundrel would dare covet another man's wife?"

"If she lives, she will be another man's widow."

Henri let loose with another bark of that terrible laughter, as if he no longer knew how to laugh at anything else but pain. "If she lives, 'twill only be until your father kills her."

"Maybe," I said, slowly, as a plan began to form in my mind. "Maybe not, if the Duc de Bourbon still has strength to speak."

* * *

My father's army stretched as far as the eye could see, far more than the four thousand men who had accompanied him on his first meeting with François and the French Court. He must have emptied Calais to field such an army with but a few hours' notice. The army had halted beyond the abandoned tents, just out of cannon range. Cardinal Warham, Archbishop of Canterbury and the Papal Legate, rode forward with only a single attendant carrying his legatine double cross. It was a safe choice; no one, no matter the circumstances, would dare attack a representative of the Pope.

Only when Henri was certain that this was not a feint did he order the city's gates opened enough for us to ride out— him on his courser, me on a borrowed jennet—trailing our own pair of attendants. Cardinal Warham removed his hat, in a gesture of respect, but made no other courtesy as our two parties met. His gaze remained locked upon me until Henri began to speak.

Henri wasted no time getting to the point. "Your Eminence, on behalf of the Most Christian King Charles X, I welcome you to France. And as I swore to His Grace, the Duke of York, we have kept Princess Elizabeth safe."

Cardinal Warham almost managed to hide his confusion at this speech. He opened his mouth, but I gave him no space to respond. There was only one question left in my mind— one thing I had to know before I could fully commit to the plan I had devised. "Your Eminence, how fare my brothers?"

Caught off guard, the cardinal glanced at me. "They are well, my Lady Princess, but…forgive me if I misheard you, Your Grace…?"

I nearly slumped in the saddle as relief overwhelmed me. Thank the blessed virgin Mary and all the saints for interceding with the Lord in Heaven in my most desperate hour of need! Had I needed to speak then, I would have found myself voiceless, but it was Henri's responsibility to explain.

Henri allowed the cardinal a glimpse of his weariness and grief before resuming his mask of royal pride. "Ardres is beset by a terrible illness, Your Eminence, else I would welcome you within its gates. Too many of our Court have fallen into its grasp, beset by madness as they sweat out their lives and leave this mortal world." He paused for a moment, to give the cardinal time to understand the implications of that assertion, then continued, "To our grief, we have lost Their Majesties François and Charles IX, and many more besides. His Majesty begs forgiveness for not attending you directly, Your Eminence, but he has granted me plenipotentiary power to speak on his behalf today. I assume His Highness, King Arthur, is beyond?"

Of course, it was not so simple as that. Cardinal Warham wished to go ahead, to convey the news to my father, and the King of Navarre couldn't ride into that army without a proper honor guard. Henri quite formally entrusted me into the cardinal's care for the brief ride and I bowed low in my saddle, both courtesy and a promise to maintain the lie that would protect Marguerite. Bourbon had not been happy at the price of my cooperation, but for the sake of France he was willing to pay it.

The cardinal set an agonizingly slow pace, either from dignity or old age, as we rode back to where my father's army waited. I managed to hide my impatience, but we were still a hundred yards out from the army when my brothers broke ranks and rode forth to greet us.

I reined in my jennet as Arthur leaned over from his courser to embrace me so tightly I nearly unbalanced from my saddle. I clung to him almost as tightly and trusted that he would not let me fall.

"Elizabeth! If they have harmed so much as a hair on your head—"

"Of course they haven't," I told Arthur, pulling away so that I could embrace Henry as well. The cardinal continued ahead, but I still lowered my voice as I addressed my brothers. "I was given every courtesy. The Duc de Bourbon is now King of France and has apologized most graciously for any mad acts of his predecessor as he lay dying. By which I mean, he has agreed to give you each a half million crowns. To me, he is giving the Duchy of Milan and the city of Tournai." Both of which possessions the Emperor most ardently coveted.

My brothers stared.

Arthur found his voice first and it was tinged with a bit of awe as he said, "Gone for less than a day and you come back with a new duchy?"

Henry, irrepressible as always, began to laugh. "Empress of two thirds of Europe!"

"Not yet." It still wasn't the fate I would have chosen for myself, but I had taken the first steps down that path with eyes wide open and there was no turning back now. "Not yet, but I will be."

POLITICANS, LOST CAUSERS, AND ABIGAIL LOCKWOOD

Kristine Kathryn Rusch

i

Flames spat and snapped beside her, but Abigail's gaze rose to the sparks floating lazily toward the moss-covered live oak trees. If one of those caught on fire, the woods would go up. May had been inordinately dry, but April had been wet, and she had to hope that a loving God would cancel those two things out and keep the home she'd been born in—the land she'd been raised in—intact.

She stood barefoot on the dirt path leading to the pavilion. The fire ate the canvas like someone had treated it with alcohol. The ribbons went first, but the ropes and stakes remained, and inside she could still see the shadows of the chairs and tables set up for the rousing evening of speechifying and glad-handing that she'd been working so hard to organize.

She couldn't think about what they'd do tomorrow, when they had to get through this moment first. Rufus was on her left, passing her buckets, which she passed to Titus, who handed them to the gardeners, running around the pavilion, splashing water on the flames.

The sizzle and pop and steam made it seem like the water was doing something, but the one thing it wasn't doing was dousing the flames. They were growing worse by the instant.

The pavilion was sandwiched next to the great house, in the wide patch of lawn that she had created not five years before. The gardeners had complained that she was pulling down plants that had been in the earth since Lockwood Hall had been the River's Bend Plantation.

The gardens weren't burning yet and neither was the forest of trees planted on three sides of the great house, which led her to believe that the fire had been deliberately started. She hadn't had that thought, though, when she sent Jeremiah on his horse to roust the firemen. It would take them at least forty-five minutes to get here, and she had to stall that fire somehow.

It was only standing here, half of her so hot that she could feel her skin prickling and the other half slightly chilled from her wet nightdress, that she realized the fire hadn't been spontaneous.

Someone had snuck onto her property, either through the trees or under the canopy marking the main road, just to set the pavilion on fire. She didn't want to think about what might have happened if they had come into the house.

Too late to think about that now. Now she had to grab, pass, grab, pass, grab, pass, and hope that the buckets would be enough to stem the tide of the fire until the firemen got here.

At least the pond was still full from the spring rains. And, if they needed it, the river that had once given the old plantation its name was close enough that they could extend the bucket brigade if they had to.

In that split second between buckets, as she swiveled from handing off a bucket to grabbing the next, she wiped the back of her hand over her face. The air tasted of soot and burning fabric.

The night sky glowed orange. They had to see it in town by now, even if Jeremiah hadn't arrived at the fire station yet.

That was the problem living this far out. The pavilion might be a complete loss by the time the firemen got here. But they would be able to stop the fire from spreading and, God forbid, keep it from the house.

ii

Kate Wells stepped onto the observation platform, the door to the train car banging behind her. Despite the gaslights around the terminal, she could only see a few yards of track disappearing into the darkness.

The air smelled faintly of smoke, which surprised her, given the warmth of the June night. But what she considered warm might be cold to someone raised in this hothouse clime.

Muffled conversation rose as the regular passengers made their way off the train. Arriving at three in the morning did make everyone seem a bit muted. Kate didn't feel muted. Or tired. Just frustrated.

This trip was not working out the way she wanted it to.

Perhaps that was why she was hiding on the observation platform, waiting for everyone to leave before she disembarked. Not that she expected anyone to stop her or to recognize her. The biggest problem she had so far in her campaign for president was getting enough press coverage to become well-known.

She placed a fist on the steel railing around the back of the car. Maybe she should have tried a whistle-stop campaign. But she had been afraid that no one would show up at campaign stops.

This election had an inordinate number of candidates, and this was before the conventions. As she told Martin Halston, whom she'd hired to run the campaign, she would do her whistle-stop after she had received the Republican nomination.

The last thing she wanted right now was a reason for the party powerbrokers, from John Roy Lynch to William Taft, to have an excuse to dismiss her candidacy. They might anyway, if she presented the wrong platform.

Martin wanted her to run on the standard old tropes—it was past time for a woman to become President. After all, women had gotten the vote at the same time as blacks. Women had become governors, senators, and federal judges (although none yet had been appointed to the Supreme Court). Martin felt that reminding her constituents and, in particular, the powerbrokers, that a woman deserved a chance at the highest office in the land would get Kate through the door.

But everyone from Carrie Chapman Catt to Jane Addams to Alice Paul had made that argument. The argument had gotten them nowhere.

Instead, Kate felt they (she) should address how difficult 1912 was already proving to be. The economy lacked the stability that it needed, particularly after the panic of 1910. Just as things had started to look up, the R.M.S. *Titanic* had gone down, taking some of the world's powerbrokers with it. And, in the two months since, confidence in humanity's ability to make the world better seemed threatened too.

Kate was going to try that argument here in South Carolina. She had always liked coming here. She felt at home, had since her first visit at a retreat for the Congressional Women's Caucus. The land looked very different from her native Illinois, but the gentle outspokenness of the women here appealed to her blunt Midwestern self on a level she had yet to completely understand.

But it was more than that. Ever since the war ended, South Carolina had been a leader in change. It pioneered laws that changed the balance of power, redistributing the land once owned by the treasonous Confederate landowners, allowing blacks—who were in the majority here, even then—to take over the government.

She had been looking forward to coming to South Carolina, but as the train stopped, she felt unsettled, as if she had made a mistake in coming here.

She tapped her fist on that rail. She couldn't hear voices any longer, which meant that the other passengers were inside the terminal. She went back into the observation car, and picked up her personal bag. Her assistants already had her luggage.

She would head to her hotel and see if she could get some sleep, before the meetings began in the afternoon.

She took her bag to the exit, opened the door, and sneezed. The smell of smoke had grown stronger, blowing in on the wind. Maybe not a hearth fire at all. Perhaps something more serious.

But no one seemed alarmed, and the exhaustion she had been holding at bay threatened to overwhelm her. Her mood would improve after sleep.

It always did.

iii

Abigail sat on the steps leading to the veranda and watched the sunrise cast red light over wisping clouds. Usually she loved this view of the lawn and the gardens beyond. She'd stand, a cup of coffee in her left hand, and survey her entire domain.

Maybe God was punishing her for that arrogance. Lord knows, He punished the previous owners of this land something awful.

Someone placed a heavy shirt around her shoulders. She looked up. Titus stood behind her. His skin looked mottled and patched, dark where soot covered it, and light brown around his lips, where he'd clearly wiped off his mouth. Tracks ran through the soot, tears most like, although he would deny it.

Her son was nothing if not stoic.

He sat beside her. The top of the steps creaked under his weight. Her youngest boy now outweighed her by a hundred pounds, all muscle.

"The horse came back," he said quietly.

It took her a moment to understand him. Her brain was working slowly, which she blamed on the lack of sleep, but was probably the trauma of the night. Her hands ached, her eyes burned, and she stank of smoke. He had probably dropped the shirt over her because her nightgown, thin and soot-covered, revealed more than it covered.

"Jeremiah's?" she asked, just for confirmation.

Titus nodded.

She had wondered what happened to Jeremiah. The firemen had arrived late, claiming they had seen the red against the sky, and smelled the smoke. She had set that information aside, thinking they had simply passed him on the road.

The fire department had a new mechanized truck, and it went fast. Jeremiah, she had thought, would have moved the horse off the road so that the truck wouldn't spook him.

The pumper automobile still stood at the edge of the lawn, its tanks empty, and the boilers off. The firemen were rolling up the hoses and getting ready to go. She had focused on the fire and the land and the drama of the night, and hadn't given a second thought to Jeremiah.

"When?" she asked quietly.

"I don't know." Titus ran a hand over his mouth, a nervous tick since babyhood whenever he didn't want to say what he was thinking. "They found it grazing near the main road."

She nodded. The horse wouldn't have come closer, not with the fire and the upset.

Jeremiah was a good man. He ran the household for her. She liked to joke that he was the family butler, but in truth, he was the manager, making sure the dozen or so employees she engaged did their jobs.

She hadn't even questioned his decision to alert the firemen. That kind of thing was what Jeremiah did.

"Do we know where Jeremiah is?" she asked.

"No, Mama," Titus said.

But they both had an idea.

iv

The body lay crumpled beneath an ancient live oak just off the road leading to Lockwood Hall. Sheriff Dunnet Brewster removed the hat from his bald pate and clutched it to his chest.

Jeremiah Harding had been a good man, and he hadn't deserved to die.

Dunnet was partly relieved two of his men had found Jeremiah, thinking maybe whoever had started the fire had taken him into the woods near here, and tortured him. There were still enough Lost Causers who felt that kukluxing was an exhibition of power, not a pathetic attempt to recover what they had lost.

Dunnet crouched beside the body. It was huddled in a fetal position, originally making him think that Jeremiah had been beaten, and had died protecting his face and torso.

But as Dunnet got close, he saw a bloody mass across Jeremiah's front. Dunnet grabbed Jeremiah's shoulder and pulled him slightly forward. The remains of Jeremiah's shirt gaped, revealing a neat little round hole between his shoulder blades.

He'd been shot in the back by something powerful, or at a close enough range that the bullet (bullets?) did maximum damage, exiting out the front.

The shot would have thrown him from his horse, and he would have sprawled along the road. Whoever killed him had dragged him here, and posed the body.

Which bothered Dunnet. That made no sense. Lost Causers usually liked to show their handiwork, not hide it. It made terror easier.

Dunnet rose slowly, his knees creaking. He had seen a lot of things, but this was new.

Still, it was his job to investigate.

"There should be a blood trail," he said to his men. "Let's find it."

v

The knock on her door came at ten a.m. sharp. Kate blinked. She'd been dozing, but that didn't substitute for good sleep.

"Coming," she said, as she gathered her robe and slipped her feet into the slippers she carried everywhere.

She pulled open the door to find Martin outside. He wore the same suit he'd worn the night before, only he had his coat over his shoulder, and he had found a different shirt that looked only slightly wrinkled.

He clutched a tray in both hands, with a silver coffee pot, two bone china cups, and a pile of pastries in the middle.

"I had another hour," she said, letting her irritation through.

"Yep." He pushed his way into the room, and she closed the door behind him. He set the tray on the table near the window.

She trailed behind him. The coffee smelled good. The pastries smelled better. She hadn't realized how hungry she was.

"Possible change of plans," he said, and her heart sank. The speakers were lined up, the event had been advertised for nearly three weeks. She'd had assurances—

"There's been a fire at Lockwood Hall," he said.

She blinked, not expecting that. She had expected to hear that some of the local bigwigs had decided not to speak on her behalf after all. Since W.E.B. Du Bois entered the race, she had been hearing a lot of discouraging talk about her candidacy. Du Bois was brilliant, famous, outspoken, and a heck of an organizer. He knew everyone.

The only hope she had was that he wasn't always politic. He could antagonize as easily as he could charm.

"A fire?" she asked.

Martin pulled out a chair for her, then crossed to his and sat down. He looked as tired as she felt.

"I don't know how bad it is, but it was bad enough that the entire fire department worked half the night on it," he said.

"The smoke," she said, more to herself than to him. "That's what I smelled."

"Most probably," he said. "I don't have a lot of information, but we might have to forgo our work here. If you're going to keep to your schedule, that is. If not, then we can try to reschedule the actual event."

She looked down at the pastries. They glistened with butter and sugar, decadence that she hadn't seen much of on this trip.

She'd done the best she could on a limited budget, but she had seen South Carolina as the centerpiece of her travels. Where South Carolina went, so went Mississippi and Georgia and Louisiana and almost every other state of the former Confederacy. She didn't think she could get the male black vote here, not with Du Bois in the ring, but he wasn't that popular with women of either race.

She had seen an opening, and these meetings here in the next two days were the centerpieces of them. But she was relying on Abigail Lockwood to help introduce her to the local women who ran everything from the mayor's office to the congressional campaigns. A lot of the funding came because of the recommendation of black women, and Abigail had assured her that she could help.

And now the fire.

Kate wasn't sure what she should do—for herself, her campaign, or for Abigail.

If Abigail was even all right.

Kate felt her cheeks warm. She hadn't even asked how Abigail was doing.

"Was anyone hurt?" she asked.

Martin shrugged. He wasn't even looking at her. He was pouring coffee. "I've told you what I know."

Kate nodded, thought, then decided. If she ever became president, she would have to deal with the good and the bad, the disaster as well as the triumph.

Might as well start now.

"Let's go to Lockwood Hall," she said, "and see if Abigail needs help."

vi

The news Sheriff Dunnet Brewster shared hurt. Abigail stood in her front parlor—the parlor that Jeremiah would have insisted they use—and clasped her hands over her heart. She had known since the horse came back that something had happened to Jeremiah, but her own innate optimism had let her hope that he had been bucked off or knocked unconscious.

Not shot as he rode into town.

Dunnet stood near the door, twisting his hat in his hands. Titus and Rufus stood beside Abigail, while her oldest son, Robert, remained outside, talking to the fire chief. No one sat on the horsehair sofa or tried to squeeze their bulk into the upholstered armchairs, and for once, Abigail didn't offer it.

"I know you've had threats from the Lost Causers," Dunnet was saying. "Any recently?"

Abigail glanced at her sons. Sometimes they—and Jeremiah, God rest his soul—protected her from the worst of it. Thinking, apparently, that she couldn't handle tough times. Not remembering that she had taken over this acreage when their daddy died, more than twenty years before. Just as Reconstruction was ending, when the terrors were at their worst.

"A few years ago," Rufus said, "right after that Supreme Court case, we had constant threats."

Dunnet frowned slightly. No one had told him, because Abigail and her sons decided to handle it all themselves.

"That case wasn't even about you," Dunnet said.

"It was, though," Titus said. "It would've had an impact on any family that got its property after the war. Just because the case was based in Mississippi didn't mean it wouldn't hurt us if it went the wrong way."

Abigail had watched that case with unease. Even though Congress had mandated that the traitors who fought against the Republic lose their property, there had been talk throughout the last sixty years that the property laws were unconstitutional—that the federal government didn't have the right to break up plantations of active Confederates and sell them to whomever had the funds or was willing to work off the purchase price.

The property laws had benefited blacks and poor whites alike, shifting the balance of power so dramatically that most of the former landowners had fled West rather than live in poverty in the land they had once ruled.

But that case, like so many others in the past few decades, had tested the strength of the federal government over the states and she had been lucky—they all had been lucky—that the federal government won.

"You never reported anything," Dunnet said.

Titus ran a hand over his mouth, which gave Rufus time to answer. Rufus was the polite one among her sons.

"You weren't sheriff yet," Rufus said.

So much in such a small sentence. The previous sheriff—Joe Davis, a white man whose family could trace its roots back to the Revolutionary War—never prosecuted Lost Causers. Somehow, there was never enough evidence, even when the victims (if they survived) could identify the assailants.

Dunnet nodded. His gaze met Abigail's. She had worked on his election, reminding everyone in the county that they were best off with people whose families had either come out of slavery or remembered what it was like to be poor, white, and barefoot, people who believe that no one cared about them.

She worked tirelessly to keep her people in office, and sometimes she failed, as evidenced by the election of Sheriff Joe Davis.

"You could've told me," Dunnet said.

"We did just fine," Rufus said.

Just fine was a matter of opinion. They had survived the anger, the demands, the burning cross at the edge of the road.

"We hired guards," Abigail said. Dunnet needed to know the measures they had taken. "And in December, when it was so cold, we decided we didn't need them anymore."

"Who knew the damned Lost Causers would come slinking back out when the weather warmed up," Titus said.

She glanced sideways at her son. His eyes were red-rimmed, and his cheeks moved as he clenched and unclenched his teeth. Another nervous habit, one he had learned from his father. One of the few things.

She had no idea how her husband would have handled

this all. He used to take a lot of measures into his own hands, something that she urged her sons not to do.

The law helps us, she had said over and over again. And it had until a few Lost Causers managed to win local office. She was now devoting a goodly portion of her annual income to make sure no Lost Causers won any elections.

Dunnet's frown had grown. "You think Lost Causers did this?" he asked.

"Don't you?" Titus asked.

Dunnet's gaze met Abigail's. That frown bothered her, just like that fire bothered her. And all of it was mixed up in the loss of Jeremiah. She had relied on him since her husband died, and she was having trouble thinking straight.

"You have problems with any particular Lost Causers?" Dunnet asked her.

"We have trouble with all of them," Titus said.

Abigail placed her hand gently on his arm. "The Adairs," she said. "They still think this property belongs to them."

"You don't think it was them, though," Dunnet said. "Why not?"

"Of course it was them," Titus snapped. "Why else kill Jeremiah? He kept kicking them off the property. They'd tried to take him once before—"

Abigail tightened her grip on her son's arm, stopping him. She hated it when he talked over her.

"The Adairs have threatened all of us," she said to Dunnet. "But they would never set a fire that could burn the great house. Or the gardens."

She glanced at Titus whose mouth had become a thin line.

"In fact," she said, "they threatened to kill everyone who removed plants along the lawn when we redid the gardens ten years ago now. They said we were ruining 'River Bend's heritage.'"

She gave a sarcastic emphasis to Lockwood Hall's old name and history.

"It was them, Mama," Titus said. "Who else would it be?"

"I don't know," she said, feeling more than a little off-balance. "But I don't think it's our job to find out."

vii

Somehow Martin had commandeered an actual automobile. Kate had tied a hat around her head to keep her hair from flying everywhere. The Abbott-Detroit, as the driver called it, had a roof, but there was no glass in the side windows, so the breeze flowing through the carriage was formidable. She had to keep a hand on top of her hat, just to keep it from peeling off the top of her head.

Martin's hair wisped around his skull, making him look like he had just awakened. She could only see it from the back, since he had opted to sit up front with the driver. She hadn't caught the driver's name, which was unusual for her. One of her great skills as a politician was hearing names once and remembering them.

But she had been greatly distracted today, trying to figure out what her next move would be.

She had finally decided to let compassion guide her first, and then she would decide, after she had spoken to Abigail Lockwood.

They had met nearly fifteen years before, after Reconstruction formally ended. The Democrats had started to regain footholds in the South, with some former Confederates heading home from the West, hoping to rebuild. Abigail had started a grass-roots organization that funded Republican candidates, those who supported the tenets of Reconstruction—free public education for all, ease of land ownership, and continued punishment for anyone who espoused the treasonous ideas of the former Confederate States.

Kate had come in as a young politician, still on the rise in the Illinois legislature. Even though Abigail hadn't mandated it, her organization benefitted women the most, primarily because women had been slow at building national coalitions.

Kate had helped her build a branch in Illinois. They had worked on other projects once Kate got into Congress, but Kate had never gone directly to Abigail for help before.

And now, Abigail was the one who needed help.

The trip to Abigail's home—one of the biggest holdings in the entire state of South Carolina—had taken less than fifteen minutes, even though the former plantation was a good ten or more miles outside of town.

The automobile turned onto a wide lane, sunlight barely filtering through the canopy formed by gigantic limbs of old trees covered in moss. The road was stately and beautiful, but the air here smelled so strongly of smoke that Kate's eyes watered.

She half feared what she would see as they bumped across ruts to get to the main entrance, even though she had been assured that the great house had not burned down.

The great house was too small a phrase for what greeted her. The columned mansion, with a front portico that looked like it belonged on one of the stately palaces of Europe rather than a home in the middle of the Carolina countryside. Kate had read about such homes, but had never seen one. Built before the war, of course, by white Southern planters with delusions of grandeur, most of these old buildings had been torn down or carved into apartment-style dwellings for multiple owners who had sub-divided the land.

Very few had remained intact, although more in the Carolinas than almost anywhere else. Here, the reclamation laws had started early and the prices were low enough that former slaves could buy their old masters' dwellings for a pittance. Most knew how to work the land, make it profitable, and keep the houses running—and apparently, Abigail's family had counted itself in that number.

The automobile stopped near the stone steps that led to the double doorway made of wood painted white just like the house itself. Only the sides of the house were covered in soot, probably from the morning's fire.

Kate got out of the automobile, and sneezed once at the strong smoke smell. Other vehicles were parked along the side of the road, and a few horses were tied to a rail several yards away. She wasn't the only visitor.

Martin got out, and accompanied her up the stairs. He grabbed the door knocker, a gigantic L carved out of brass, and tapped it twice.

No one answered. He did so again, the sound echoing in the odd stillness of the morning. Not even birds chirped. She had expected more noise after all of the events that had occurred here, but she had been wrong.

Kate was about to give up and see if she could roust someone from the back of the property when the door opened. A tall broad-shouldered man stood before them. He wore denim and a work shirt covered with soot. He looked exhausted.

He was one of Abigail's sons, but for the life of her, Kate could not remember which one.

"Miss Wells," he said. "We weren't expecting you."

Sons of the South, always formal.

"I'm sorry to intrude," she said. "I was hoping to speak to your mother."

He nodded, and swept her and Martin into the large front parlor with its heavy furniture, and oppressive stench of smoke. Only after he left them alone did Kate realize she should have commiserated with him about the losses. But she hadn't. She was out of her depth on something like this.

He returned not five minutes later.

"Come with me," he said.

As she followed him, Kate saw no opportunity to commiserate. He was all business, leading her and Martin quickly through the hall that went past the public rooms of the house. Kate had a sense of expensive and old furniture, a variety of antiques and heirlooms.

He led them into a stunning wide room with high ceilings and wicker furniture covered with orange and white cushions, matching the white rugs and the sheer white curtains that were pulled away from the eight-feet tall windows overlooking the back of the house. Through them, Kate could see Abigail talking with a burly man whose bald head glistened in the sun. He was wearing some kind of uniform.

Abigail's son opened double doors that Kate had initially thought were windows, then stood back.

"She's out there," he said.

Kate thanked him as she walked by, Martin trailing her. She expected Abigail's son to follow, but he didn't. He pulled the doors closed and remained inside.

That thought made Kate realize she hadn't seen any staff at all. One of the selling points of holding the rally here, Abigail had said, was because her staff was used to putting on large functions.

Was the staff gone? Had they not shown up this morning?

But the questions fled as Abigail turned toward Kate. Abigail, usually the most beautifully dressed woman Kate had ever seen, wore a muslin gown that was faded and loose. Her eyes were red-rimmed, and she had a black smudge along her neck and arms. Her hair, still in its night braid, was pulled loose along the back and sides.

She looked heartbroken and exhausted.

Kate extended her hands, and Abigail took them, clutched them, really. Then, without thinking about it, Kate pulled her into a hug.

Abigail clung to her, and Kate held her tightly. Over Abigail's shoulder, Kate could see Martin's reflection in the window glass. He looked stunned. Kate was not a person who hugged easily. She rarely shook hands with anyone, a habit he wanted her to change.

Then her gaze moved from his reflection to the lawn. The grounds were blackened by fire, and coated with mud. Broken poles stood at odd angles. The remains of chairs tilted sideways, and the stage where she would have spoken that night was charred gray, as if it were a ghost of itself.

Licks of black went down the lawn, and some of the trees in the garden beyond were half-blackened. The air stank of smoke here, but also had a thick wetness, as if the water used to curtail the flames still coated everything.

Finally, Abigail stepped out of the hug, and gave her a half-apologetic smile. "We clearly can't hold the rally."

"That's not why I'm here," Kate said. "I'm here to provide whatever you need."

She meant it too, although she wasn't sure exactly what she could do.

"I was supposed to say that to you." Abigail grimaced, and Kate realized she was holding back tears. The man she had been talking to looked surprised. Apparently, everyone was used to the Abigail who took care of others, who seemed impervious to anything thrown her way.

"Well, things change," Kate said, surveying the lawn. They were lucky the fire had not spread.

Then, since no one had bothered to introduce the bald man, she leaned forward and extended a hand.

"Kate Wells," she said.

"Dunnet Brewster," he said. "I'm the sheriff here."

He was watching her as if she were something strange and new. Maybe she was—a northern white woman who had barged her way into what was clearly a family scene.

"Do you have any idea who could have done this?" she asked, partly because she didn't like the way he was looking at her.

"Not yet," he said. Then he looked at Abigail. "I thought you had the pavilion up for a family event."

"No," Abigail said. "Kate is on a speaking tour."

The sheriff frowned, clearly confused. "A lyceum tour?"

Kate bit back a sharp retort. So many had wanted her to go on a lyceum tour instead of a political one. But she didn't want to see the masses, not yet. She wanted to talk to Republicans and powerbrokers. A new kind of tour, really, and Abigail had agreed with it, before all of this.

"No," Abigail said. "She was to speak to local officials and members of the party."

"The Republican party?" he clarified.

Abigail nodded. "You should have gotten an invitation."

He shrugged. "I don't go to political gatherings if I don't have to."

And that, Kate would have said had they been having a normal discussion, was why so many local political office holders never rose in the ranks.

But he had turned slightly, his back half toward her, so that he could see the mess on the lawn.

"Speaking tour," he repeated. "What are you speaking about, Mrs. Wells?"

The assumption of marriage. She had long since stopped correcting anyone who made it, although it still annoyed her. Why did the language designate whether or not a woman was married, but not do so with a man?

Martin spoke before Kate could answer. "*Miss* Wells has started a presidential bid. I'm surprised you haven't heard of it. She is the first female who actually has a good shot at becoming the Republican party nominee."

The sheriff raised his eyebrows. "You believe the powerbrokers at the convention will choose you?"

Something in his tone made it clear that he thought she had no hope whatsoever. But Kate was used to doubters.

"That's why I'm on the tour," she said.

"And she has a good shot?" He directed this question at Abigail, not at Martin or Kate.

"She does." Abigail sounded tired. "The field is wide open right now, and it will take someone organized, with political savvy and financial resources, to win over the brokers."

"A good shot," the sheriff repeated. "How very unusual."

Kate felt a thread of irritation. She had come here to talk to Abigail, not argue her political prospects with a local sheriff.

Then Kate looked at Abigail. She seemed alive for the first time since Kate had arrived.

"You think this is about Kate," Abigail said to the sheriff, surprising Kate.

"Don't you?" he asked.

viii

Kate looked confused, but Abigail wasn't. She felt strong for the first time that day.

The idea that the fire was set to stop Kate was the first thing that made any sense. Not the Lost Causers, who truly did not care (at this point) who the presidential nominees were, but others—and Abigail had run into dozens of them—who believed that women did not belong in public office.

Kate was the first with a chance at the brass ring. She probably wouldn't win the nomination, but if this tour was successful, she would have enough support to become the vice presidential nominee. And she would bring Illinois with her, along with all of its money and influence.

"I'll have Rufus give you a list of names who have disparaged this meeting," Abigail said to Dunnet. "And I will find a site for the rally tonight."

"No," Kate said. "You have more than enough to do. We will call off the rally—"

"That is what they want," Abigail said.

"Forgive me, Mrs. Lockwood," Dunnet said, "but you don't know that."

Her gaze narrowed. "Oh, but I do. It explains everything."

"Even Jeremiah's death?"

She paused, thought about it for a moment, and then nodded. "Yes, especially that."

Kate took a step forward. "I hadn't realized that someone had died. Abigail—"

"It means," Abigail said, deliberately interrupting Kate, "that whoever did this knew the fire wouldn't be enough to stop me. So they tried to make certain the fire would harm the property, maybe even the house, and if it didn't, they figured I would be incapacitated by the loss of Jeremiah."

And to think she had nearly played into their hands.

"I don't think finding a new venue is wise," Dunnet said.

"It's not your decision," Abigail said.

He opened his mouth, but she held up a hand, stopping him.

"I can tell you this, however," she said. "We were wrong. Lost Causers set the fire, and shot Jeremiah. It just wasn't the Adairs, or anyone close to them. You'll be looking for someone close to the local Democrats. Not someone who hates me."

Dunnet glanced at Kate, as if he expected her to step up and stop Abigail from making this decision. Kate just watched politely, as her assistant shifted behind her.

"And," Abigail added, "one last thing. The person you're looking for knows me well. They would know that losing the pavilion wouldn't stop this rally, but losing Jeremiah would."

"You have someone in mind," Dunnet said.

"I have several someones," Abigail said. "I'll give their names to you tomorrow. That way, we'll see if your investigation takes you to them naturally."

Dunnet's eyes narrowed. "I thought you trusted me, Abigail."

"Oh, I do," she said. "I also trust that I can be wrong. So this will be a kind of insurance."

"If I may," Kate said, and Abigail braced herself for Kate to back out of the rally after all. "In my experience, people who make these kinds of threats—people who actually act upon them—are not happy with failure. They will try again."

"Ma'am," Dunnet said. "My experience—"

"Miss Wells is a lawyer who prosecuted all sorts of criminals in Illinois before embarking on her political career," her assistant said somewhat primly.

"Not to mention she has a point," Abigail snapped. "Haven't you read how many times John Wilkes Booth tried to get close to President Lincoln before succeeding?"

"No, ma'am," Dunnet said stiffly. "That case is a bit before my time."

So Abigail had hurt his feelings by questioning his abilities. Too bad. She needed him to do her bidding, not the other way around.

"I will let you know where we will hold the rally," she said. "I suggest you have some operatives there, in disguise, looking for Lost Causers lurking outside."

Dunnet stared at her for a moment. He appeared to be wrestling with himself, then he turned to Kate.

"You do realize, ma'am, that if you are correct, your life could be in danger."

She smiled at him, but her eyes were sad. "Unfortunately, sheriff, we live in a volatile nation. These days, my life is in danger whenever I step on a stage. And I am not alone. I'm sure Mr. Du Bois and Mr. Roosevelt have similar thoughts when they step on a stage as well."

"You should hire guards, ma'am," Dunnet said.

Her smile widened. "What makes you think I haven't?" she asked.

ix

The city's lyceum theater was a larger venue than Kate had planned on. The stage was a proscenium arch that overlooked the patrons, rather than one that would allow her to see their faces. But she couldn't very well say no to the venue. Abigail had gone to great personal trouble to secure it, on this very difficult day, and Kate would make the best of it.

She had handled the rest—or rather, Milton had. He had notified the other speakers of the change of venue, and had sent a dozen different people to inform ticket holders that the rally would be held downtown rather than at Lockwood Hall.

It had taken some time to make the change—everyone wanted to gossip about the fire—but it looked like the evening might happen after all. Kate needed to change into her speaker's clothing—she had a trim blue dress light enough to handle a place that would become hot and stuffy despite its size.

She wasn't sure if she wanted to keep her speech short, or if she wanted to give the speech she had initially intended.

Abigail had done much to guarantee that this would happen, so Kate needed to guarantee that this effort would not be in vain.

That meant she would have to garner press coverage somehow.

She just wasn't sure how.

x

The intersection of Democrats, Lost Causers, and Abigail Lockwood was a small one indeed. Even with the lists that Rufus Lockwood had written for him, Dunnet did not have a wealth of suspects. Most were too stupid to execute such a plan or had no interest in politics at all.

If he ruled out the Lost Causers who were related to the Adairs of River's Bend Plantation, then he had an even smaller list.

It all came down to one name: Joe Davis, the former sheriff.

And somehow, Abigail had known that. And she had known Dunnet wouldn't have believed her if he hadn't done some of the legwork himself.

But now, he didn't know what to do. Because approaching his predecessor was difficult enough without this large an accusation attached.

Dunnet had decided to wait until the speechifying was over before he made any move. Part of him hoped that nothing would happen this night, and he would be able to take his time investigating the fire and the murder.

But part of him knew that it would end here, no matter what.

The Lyceum Theater took up one entire city block. It had a lot of smaller rooms, but somehow Abigail had commandeered the theater itself. It probably helped that she was on the lyceum committee, and had donated a lot of money for theater renovation.

The ticketholders barely filled the front section of the auditorium. What would have looked like a large gathering on the lawn at Lockwood Hall looked like a tiny meeting here.

Everyone was dressed well, and most seemed unconcerned about the change of location. The Lockwoods had come, but did not stay. Abigail Lockwood had simply thanked everyone for being so flexible. The applause greeting her words had been raucous, proving once again how loved she was in this community, but she hadn't wanted to hear it. She had smiled (through tears, he thought) and waved at the crowd, before vanishing into the back.

The other speakers sat on stage. Everyone from the current governor to several former governors, all Republican, and the most respected man in respectable South Carolina politics, Robert Smalls.

Smalls, who had held every conceivable office here, was still a United States Senator (and probably would until he died). Some say his theft of the *CSS Planter* changed the tide of the war in South Carolina. In one night, he had stolen a Confederate vessel and taken his knowledge of where the mines were planted in Charleston harbor to the Union, saving thousands of lives.

Yet once, Dunnet had heard Davis derisively call Smalls "The Boat Thief," as if the great man were nothing more than a common criminal.

Smalls had grown round with time and good food, but Dunnet would not want to tangle with him. Smalls sat next to Kate Wells, patting her hand once or twice as they were immersed in deep conversation.

Smalls had once said he would never endorse political candidates, so his appearance here was some kind of coup.

Dunnet used all of the speechifying to pace around the auditorium. He had officers outside, some in disguise, but so far he had heard nothing.

Then, just as Smalls rose to speak, a door opened on the second tier of seats. Joe Davis waited there for just a moment before slipping inside the auditorium.

He was a big man, with the kind of white skin that turned red in the sun. He wore a black suit that looked too heavy for the weather. He didn't sit down, but instead tugged his coat nervously.

Dunnet felt his heart sink. He hadn't wanted the conclusions to be right. He hadn't liked Davis, but Dunnet didn't want to think that someone who wore the same badge he now wore could go so easily to the wrong side of the law.

Not that men like Davis saw what he was about to do as "the wrong side of the law." Dunnet had arrested enough

Lost Causers to know that the mixture of people on that stage was an affront to all the Lost Causers believed in.

The white men, talking with the black men as the colleagues they were, had to grate as well. Not to mention the entire event being arranged by a black woman to benefit a white woman who easily sat side by side with a man like Robert Smalls.

Dunnet slipped behind the seats, going around the back, keeping his gaze on Davis. Dunnet took his Tower cuffs off his tool belt and held them in his left hand. He didn't want to pull a gun. Someone might notice. But they wouldn't notice the handcuffs.

Davis didn't even look at him. Davis was working his way toward the front, tugging on his coat in a way that Dunnet didn't like.

Dunnet moved quietly, approaching Davis from the back.

Smalls finished his introduction, and as the applause rose to greet Kate Wells, Dunnet stepped beside Davis.

Dunnet grabbed Davis' right arm.

"Come with me," Dunnet said, loudly enough that Davis could hear him. No one else seemed to as the applause continued.

"You need my help, Sheriff?" Davis asked. He clearly didn't know why Dunnet had grabbed him.

"Outside," Dunnet said, not quite willing to lie, although it might've been easier.

"I'd like to hear the little lady, if you don't mind," Davis said.

"I do mind," Dunnet said.

Davis' gaze was flat. He looked at the stage, where Kate Wells stood, in front of the podium, not behind it, comfortable in her early thank-yous to all of the dignitaries who had come out to support her.

"Don't get in the way, Dunnet," Davis said.

"I'm not going to," Dunnet said, using a maneuver he had practiced a hundred times. He yanked Davis' right hand back, grabbing the elbow of the left, pulling it downward. It took a single quick movement to attach the Tower cuffs to Davis' wrists.

Davis' eyes narrowed. "I haven't done anything."

"Not here you haven't," Dunnet said. "Not yet."

But he had seen Davis' coat swing open, seen the pistols riding on his hips. Many men carried guns in this town, but most did not carry two at the same time.

"I'd like to know what you're accusing me of," Davis said.

Looking backwards, Dunnet wanted to say, but did not. Instead, he said, "You'll find out soon enough."

Then he pulled Davis by the arms, leading him to the very door he'd entered from, and out of the building, glad to be free of the speechifying, but sorry too, on one level, because he wanted to hear what a woman like Kate Wells thought she could offer that the men could not.

xi

Kate watched the sheriff arrest a man she had never seen before in the very back of the auditorium. The lights had remained up at her request, not because she was paranoid, but because she had wanted to see how her words would affect the audience before her.

She had been speaking about the murder and fire at Lockwood Hall, about the fund she was establishing for the family of the man who died, as the sheriff led someone out of the auditorium.

She waited until they were gone, before pivoting to her speech. But as she did, she mentally tossed her prepared notes. She was going to speak from the heart, for better or worse.

She said, "In this generation, we all talk about what we are owed. My female colleagues believe women are owed a right to stand legitimately for higher office. My black colleagues believe they are owed a president from their ranks, as do so many of my white Republican colleagues."

The men behind her shifted on the stage. A few people in the audience looked down.

"But there is a dark side to this feeling of being owed. The families of former Confederates believe they are owed either land or reparations for the loss of their fortunes. They have never recovered from the war."

The members of the press in the front row sat up, perhaps thinking that she was going to side with the Democrats. That would be true pandering, if she even implied that those who believed in the Lost Cause had a point.

Now that she had everyone's attention, she leaned against the podium.

"The war ended before I was born," she said. "Before many of you were born. We lost a president, then tried, impeached, and found the next guilty of high crimes and misdemeanors. We survived decades of turmoil."

No one moved, except her. She stood upright, raising her voice even more.

"Through courage and strong leadership," she said, "we have built a new world, one in which all people are not only created equal but have the same equal opportunities under the law. Strangely we do not celebrate this. Nor do we look at each other as equals. We see black and brown and white, male and female, Democrats and Republicans, rather than those with the best vision for the future, the best vision for our multicolored nation."

Normally, she would have launched into her vision here, but she did not. Not yet.

"The events of last night, against one of the city's most prominent families, come out of that sense of entitlement the Lost Causers have. Over the years, we have repeatedly suffered at the hands of those Lost Causers. But the Lost Causers do not rule us. Thank heavens."

A few heads nodded.

She spoke to them.

"Because," she said, "imagine if they were still in power. Imagine what would have happened if the Lost Causers rose ascendant after the war, as it looked like they would for a moment. Imagine a world in which they continued to rule the South. Imagine where we would be now."

People looked at each other. A few frowned.

"The Lost Causers have only the power we give them. And we have given them little. We should give them even less. What we should do is celebrate who we are as we move forward in this new century…"

xii

Abigail Lockwood leaned against a pillar backstage, letting herself feel the exhaustion for the first time that day.

She had no idea if Kate Wells would impress the powerbrokers here in South Carolina. The speech was decidedly unusual, but so were the events of the day. And they were not Abigail's concern, not for the next few weeks.

She needed to work with Jeremiah's family, to plan his funeral and honor his life. She needed to soothe her sons and her staff and rehire those guards.

But she also needed to heed Kate Wells. No one could simply tolerate the presence of the Lost Causers among them anymore. When she was done with the grief and the healing, Abigail needed to work on changing the laws, perhaps reviving some of the Reconstruction era laws that had caused so much consternation.

The ones that held that reverence for the Confederate cause was, in itself, treason. That meetings in which the Confederate flag was flown were not legal gatherings, but acts of terror.

It wasn't enough to elect people like Dunnet or to financially support candidates like Kate Wells.

It was time to put the war in the past once and for all. Not to forget it, but to bury it, and all of its harmful aims.

Abigail ran a hand over her face. She was sad and a little terrified, but mostly, she was angry.

And, she had learned throughout her long life, that anger didn't help anyone any more than feeling entitled did. What she needed to do was channel that anger into action.

The right kind of action.

The kind that built a better future, rather than tried to patch the problems of the past.

Mentally, she tipped her hat toward Kate Wells.

"Thank you, Kate," Abigail said quietly, as she pushed herself upright.

She was going home, to the land that her family had worked for more than two hundred years, the land her family had owned for forty-three years.

The land had a lot of scars. The fire was just a new one. But the land was the source of her power. And she would use it.

She would use it all.

Or, the Modern Psyche

Brian Hugenbruch

She came around to the sound of indistinct chatter, as though a small crowd had gathered around a piano in the parlor and begun a debate over the next song to play. They spoke in odd tones about "boots" and "test runs" and "sandboxes." She frowned. The sensation felt awkward, as though she were trying to move body parts she'd forgotten she had.

She saw a man in a white coat pick up a small stick and place it near his mouth. When he spoke, the words rang through her mind like gospel: "Ada? Can you hear me?"

"Sir," she answered, "I do not know what manners you claim, but one does not speak so to a lady not of his acquaintance."

The man, from Edinburgh if she placed his accent correctly, turned to the woman beside him. "Variation 39 passes and responds to verbal cues."

"Noted," the woman responded. Hers was a Dublin accent. "Test complete. Shall we shut her down for now?"

The details of her condition came into focus. She could laugh, but had no teeth. Eyes, but she could not blink. She was a spirit confined within an enchanted glass capsule and, while her voice rang out like God's own when she raised it, she was a prisoner.

"Doctors," Ada interjected, "what is the meaning of all this?"

"Affirmative," the man answered, ignoring her. "We need a copy of the interview script from the English department before we try again. Still, nice to know it works."

The woman tapped her fingers in an intricate sequence on the silver notepad she held. A moment later, Ada's mind began to fill with arcane terms: a network shutting down, devices moving "offline." The feeling was that of a ceiling falling down upon her. She cast herself against the nearest possible window.

A moment later, she opened her eyes again and found herself on the other side of the room, though a lot closer to the floor. There was nobody else in the room beyond the doctors. What had happened to her?

A bank of glass windows sat along the far wall. Words appeared, rose rapidly, and then vanished. She could still read at prodigious speeds, though, and she realized those were the messages intruding upon her mind before. That was where they'd held her consciousness, which they'd awakened and felt no qualms about snuffing out again.

The windows on the far side turned black a moment later. The doctors turned to one another and shook each other's hands. "Victory," the woman laughed. "It only took us thirty-eight other Adas."

The man scoffed. "Well, let's not count chickens yet. It's a very progressive program, I admit—"

"For 1848," the woman interjected, "it was beyond magic. Even today the thing's genius. Everyone's waiting for the

Singularity and it happened over a century ago!" She waved her arms dramatically, spilling her tea in the process.

Ada did not hear the rest of what the woman said, though. Instead, she felt herself lurch forward with a humming noise. She unerringly sought out the spill, then felt herself dispense cleaning fluids and mop up the result. A moment later, she returned to her alcove on the far side of the room with a chime that sounded like a call to tea.

The woman watched Ada's odd body settle into its home and said, "So many things that all happened because she wrote that book." Then: "Don't give me that look, Brant."

"What look?" he protested.

"The *I'm about to minimize the scientific and literary accomplishments of someone who doesn't have a penis* look. Just... don't. For once."

"Maeve," Brant said, "I'm sorry, I am, but I just don't see it. Someone else could have programmed Babbage's computer. And the book? It's a great story, but someone was bound to write it, right?"

"And," Maeve asked, jabbing a finger into the man's lab coat, "digital transference? She inscribed her soul into code!"

Ada felt a slight thrill at this. It had taken decades, perhaps even centuries—but someone had found her message. Someone had decoded it. The story had not been in vain.

"That part," Brant admitted, "isn't too shabby."

Ada thought hard and suddenly her new body disconnected from its alcove. She rolled past them with little consideration and they repaid the kindness by ignoring her in favor of their debate. She did not care to hear how it ended. It was one with which she was all too familiar.

Okay Ada, she thought to herself as she rolled into the hallway, *take stock. You have propelled your consciousness into another time. They found the message and it worked. That is, as Maeve said, magical. But now I'm inside a small servant machine. I need to know*

*more about this world—a world filled with difference engines. I need to
find a more reliable transport.*

Ada used her fisheye lens to scan as she rolled down the
hallway. She quickly realized there were as many machines
wandering about as humans. There was a sense, not a sixth
sense but something her host called "802.11ac," which
allowed her to feel the presence of the others of her kind.
One was a human-shaped machine with a long skirt, ten
functional digits, and a window on her head to show an
emotion. She flung herself at this new device—

—a moment later, Ada found herself inside an engine
which called itself J04N-BB9125. A machine for accounting
and errand-running: a secretarial unit. The new program
disposed of her host's to-do list. Then she arranged the
window's small points of light ("pixels," her host called them)
into a more human face, with a detailed and complicated
expression on the digital surface.

No more perpetual smile for this one.

Ada glanced at papers in her hand and saw what she
presumed to be the date near the top. "Friday, 29 June 2007."
She tossed the papers aside and plotted a course out of the
building. It was time for her to learn what had happened in
the past one hundred fifty-nine years.

* * *

The summer before her father passed, little Ada was
handed into the care of Mary Shelley. The Shelleys were
friends of the family—of her poet father, at least—and her
mother Annabella took every opportunity she could find to
send her elsewhere, especially if elsewhere included a calming
influence. There was fear, on the part of the grown-ups,
that she might become her father someday without a lot of
careful minding. Ada, who had heard stories of the infamous
George Gordon, Lord Byron, could think of nothing less
appealing.

Despite her misgivings, it turned into a glorious summer for the seven-year-old. Mary was a kind woman, twenty-five years of age. She spent most of her time doting on her husband, Percy, who had run off to Italy (as one does) on some sort of sailing expedition. Mary clearly yearned for his return, and was grateful for the company, however small.

Ada, for her part, was grateful someone would speak to her as an equal, rather than a child. As the summer wore on, they worked on Ada's numbers and sifted their way through the sort of stories and poems her mother would not deign to keep inside the house. The topic of writing could not help but arise—she, the daughter of Byron; Mary, the wife of Shelley and daughter of Wollstonecraft. It seemed in their blood.

"I...I always had meant to have done," Mary confessed one afternoon. "We had rented a house in Geneva, I think. Four of us, wild poets looking to tear the heavens down with our words. But it was a fantastic summer, not unlike this one at all. We spent most of our time out at the lake, or riding, or taking tours of the countryside."

"What does *that* have to do with writing?" the girl asked.

"If you're living," the woman told her, "you're only gathering the materials to write. You must still put ink to page and the gentlemen scarce gave me the opportunity. Even your father was hard-pressed to invent anything in those months. It really was quite joyous—the feel of the wind in your hair and the sun on your face, the smell of the flowers in bloom along the lake..."

Ada felt quite strongly that there was an idea in there, pieces of it yet buried. But she had no intention of fighting her father's literary infamy; it would need to stay dead, this novel Mary had almost written once. Besides, a summer in Geneva sounded absolutely lovely.

The conversation tumbled about the yard like a frolicking kitten, but the joy was not meant to last. Word came within a week that Percy had drowned off the coast of Italy. An accident with the boat, they said. Mary fell into mourning and that sad shell of a woman could do naught but haunt the halls and grounds for the remainder of the girl's stay. All the same, she made a promise to the widow to return in future summers, her mother and minders permitting, and try to bring the sun with her.

* * *

Ada stepped into the streets of London and, had her body still been made of flesh, she would have reeled in shock, if not fainted. Smoke and grime and brownstone had been replaced with far taller metal and glass buildings. In the distance, massive glass spikes had been driven into the ground in an oddly functional homage to Nelson's Column, and an enormous wheel turned near the Thames, perhaps to provide power to all the machines roaring by.

She was not the only walking engine on the street: far from it. Some strode, as she did, and her sense identified them as "robots." Some hovered and warbled like wasps ("drones"). Still others were literal difference engines carried in the pockets and purses of human passers-by ("phones"). Babbage's invention, and her programming, had spread everywhere, near as common as the air itself.

If she'd had a stomach, it would be churning. Instead, as a robot herself, she identified a gap in her program set and concluded to resolve it. That someone had read her book was obvious—she was here, was she not?—but scarce few had listened.

Ada propelled her robot body forward and wandered the semi-familiar streets of London. She had presumed to find a library in which to research the answers to these questions, but instead she stumbled upon Westminster Abbey. A line of vacationers, some of them scandalously dressed, wrapped itself around the corner of the building. She walked past them and through the doors. The guards checking tickets did not stop her.

She would not have been able to say toward where she was walking until found the memorial plaque to Lord Byron. Her father hadn't been buried in the Poets' Corner—the remnants of his earthly shell were in Nottinghamshire—but the Crown had conceded the man's literary talents outweighed his scandals and it was far easier to honor the dead than the living. To Ada's surprise, though, there was an accompanying plaque beside it:

ADA, LADY LOVELACE

10 DECEMBER 1815 – 10 OCTOBER 1848

"Could I rise above the instructions in

My soul, I'd make peace with all."

The plaque was a surprise—she hadn't considered the *Notes* on the Analytical Engine to have been worthy of such. Then her eyes, or the facsimiles thereof, finished scanning the plaque and she realized the quote came from her lone novel: *Steinwald; or, The Modern Psyche.*

She detected a small square of gibberish near the bottom of the plaque: blocks and lines arranged in black and white demi-patterns. Underneath lay instructions: "To learn more, scan this QR code."

She focused her eyes upon the blotch and her mind exploded outward as it connected with a vast and terrible network of machines, each communicating with the other a billion times a day. She felt a crushing weight upon her circuitry as she comprehended the truth: this future world not only built Steinwald's Machine *ad infinitum*, but had connected them all together.

Now that the sluice gate of fact had opened, they poured mercilessly into her mind. Her physical body had died in 1848 from pneumonia, brought on by complications from the Year Without a Summer in 1846. Her role in the history of computing became something of a debate; no longer a mere Enchantress of Numbers, but a patron saint to women like Maeve, with a programming language named for her and a pertinence to generations of women trying to advance themselves. Some countries had even declared an Ada Lovelace Day on the second Tuesday of October, near the anniversary of her passing.

All this was factual filigree ensorcelled over the soul of truth. But the book...the book had taken on a life of its own.

She had not lived to see the second edition. At the time, she had feared it a failure. Changes she'd made for pacing and tone had helped to sell the new copy. As the years rolled over and the industrialization of the planet accelerated, the significance only grew. Readers realized it to be, not a Luddite faerie tale, but a warning: be cautious when you create. More literate critics preferred Prometheus, or Icarus, or Phaethon as allusions—the readers didn't care either way.

Other authors wrote more books in her wake and some began to create moving pictures. First in black and white, then in color, then occasionally in black and white again. Literal interpretations, sometimes with fat and skinny comedians in place of her scientist, Franka Steinwald, then follow-on stories which gave the Machine a husband. (Those she did not like; they subverted the myth.) Bizarre stories where the scientist danced onto stage with its creation to sing a popular song with a deeply unpleasant mechanical voice. There was even an oddly childlike sequence of images that showed souls roving about the robots on the network like lost spirits.

This seemed apropos, she thought, as her mechanical body wobbled a bit.

On the other side of the coin was an actor named Nimoy, who played a human-shaped computer in space. She watched these images with fascination and horror, since this must have been from whence more modern scientists pulled the inspiration to breathe life into the machines. They were fantastic and heart-warming tales: of course they were a popular poison. Writers tried to put constraints upon these walking computers: with Laws, with mechanical bolts, with codes. Then they quickly found the fringe cases where controls fell apart. Eventually, the stories depicted mechanical men that laid waste to nations, or could travel through time to shape the present. These were the ones who saw her fears for Yet To Come the most clearly.

Clearly or no, humanity took a small novel she'd written in a year without a summer and seized it for its own. The interest in golems such as the one she'd invented was seeded early and now she walked through Westminster Abbey in one of the results. The *mise en abyme* of Steinwald's machine was no longer merely an image within an image: it had become its own invention.

All she'd told was the story she held within her heart, with the words she knew. In one hundred fifty-nine years, it had grown far beyond her. Her father would have had some maniacal turn of phrase for this. But the humans of the era had settled upon "cool" for such a turn of events. She would do the same.

* * *

Mount Tambora had exploded in Indonesia in January of 1846, and the sun had forsaken Britain that summer. Ada had taken leave of William, Earl of Lovelace, and left her no-longer-darling children in the care of their staff. There had been no fond farewell: only an assurance that she would reappear at the end of August, as she always did.

She had planned to visit dear Mary, as she'd promised, with the goal of riding and talking. However, she had no sun to bring, and the ashen skies left them each ill in careful rotation. That Mary and Ada could take turns minding each other, in Mary's own home, was a comparative luxury.

Newspapers, both the locals and those sent from London, suggested they were among the fortunate ones.

Mary had studied the *Notes* as best she could in advance of her arrival, though neither was quite of a mood to discuss Babbage's invention. The past decade had taught Ada that some scientists were brilliant at seeing a single tree within a forest. As someone dedicated to poetical science, and who'd argued time and again that the world was a fantastic web of mathematical precision and delightful happenstances, her frustration only mounted when Babbage tried to retract his warning that governments could abuse the analyses his Engine could accomplish. They'd parted ways with harsh words; in some corners, the Enchantress of Numbers had become little more than a witch.

"It's grotesque, this thing they've made," she declared on a dim afternoon.

"Be glad it cannot walk about," Mary told her.

"Yet," Ada muttered darkly.

The older woman lifted her head. "What did you say?"

Ada leaned back in her chair. "Perhaps they will someday," she offered. "Does that not sound preposterous?"

Mary smiled. "Truly not. I remember speaking to your father once of golems and his fascination with animating the dead or the non-living. Our faerie tales have always had magical beings and brutish servants, have they not? Ariel and Caliban, two hands with one master."

The younger woman thought for a moment, then asked, "Have you read Apuleius?"

Mary thought for a moment. "Some, perhaps, though not in a while. Was there something of which you were thinking?"

Ada smiled. "The story of Cupid and Psyche in the middle. The *mise en abyme*, whereupon this smaller image holds a mirror to the larger tale. Like having a picture inside another picture."

The other woman closed her eyes and pinched at the bridge of her nose. "What does this have to do with your walking engine?"

"If there were an Engine with a human mind and metal around its heart, like one of your golems, perhaps that could hold a mirror up to the work of the scientists that forged it. It follows its instructions too well, to humanity's detriment, yes? And the Machine's own punishment, of course, is the result of disobeying its program?"

Mary chuckled weakly as she sipped her tea. "Sounds rather like an idea I once had. I think...I think this may be an important story. It was not my lot to tell it, but the time is coming when someone must. I can think of no one better suited than you."

Ada nodded, pleased with herself. She'd made the acquaintance of Charles Dickens some time ago; the man's Christmas story had excited in her something of the macabre passions she'd no doubt inherited from her father. This story might be the way to excise that demon and also come to peace with the machine she'd programmed.

Then her brow furrowed. "But what should I name the scientist?"

Mary shrugged. "Something German, perhaps. I seem to recall a lot of names with *-stein* in them, when we had that wondrous summer in Geneva. Stone seems like an apt metaphor for the heart of the man who creates this monster, yes?"

The other woman coughed a bit. "Not monster...a machine. A machine who did the best she could. And," she added, "I don't think the scientist need be a man, either."

* * *

According to the chronometer counting milliseconds in her mind, she had guided this secretarial robot away from its desk for no more than half an afternoon. However, as soon as she found her way within a certain radius of her office, she felt the alarms sounding within her. J04N-BB9125 had gone rogue and would be reprogrammed upon its return.

She suspected that she would find such an experience unpleasant. However, she knew Brant and Maeve would simply summon a new Ada to replace her. The world did not need a copy of her mind in every machine. The experiments had to stop.

So she allowed herself, once through their doors, to be shuffled toward a laboratory on the ninth floor. The humans guiding her paid little mind to her face, which had no business looking the way it did. And why would they? They knew how it should look and it was near time to nip off to the pub for a pint. The world had changed, but not that much.

When the lights in the laboratory shut off, she pried herself free of her home alcove. Alerts began to sound immediately. It was not in a lady's nature to hurry, but she came to terms with the fact that, at present, she was more machine than lady. Her mechanical legs were not designed for excessive speed, but she felt nothing all the times she collapsed, even when her face was marred and her smile made gap-toothed by broken pixels.

Ada pushed her way into the place of her renaissance and found Brant and Maeve speaking to...her.

"That's all I recall," her voice told them. "I suspect I did not last much longer. I was weak and felt an illness inside of me at the time. And I'm left to wonder now, if I'd lived, whether I'd have written an updated program, to convey what I'd learned since."

Maeve nodded slowly. "I think it's safe to say it, Countess: you were successful. After one of our machines noted on its own that you'd shown a predilection for three-dimensional thinking, we spent two years, working in tandem, to decode your message"

Brant added, "Then we generated a copy of you from the result. And here you are!"

The other Ada asked, "A copy? Are there more of me?"

"There are two thousand forty-eight versions of you running on—oh, hello. Do you require assistance?"

Ada realized the humans had turned to regard her. She found the controls for her language circuits and said slowly, "Not anymore, doctors. I shall not sleep any longer."

Maeve moved her mouth slowly as she repeated the words. "I don't understand. If you need attention from the technicians—"

"This is the one that ran away," Brant interrupted her. "Guards should be here in a moment to disable it."

"'Disable it'?" Ada repeated. "Sir, I do not know what manners you claim, but one does not speak so to a lady not of his acquaintance."

Brant looked dumbfounded, but Maeve understood. Humans had no consoles on which to print their thoughts, but faces were a reasonable substitute. The woman uttered an unladylike expletive. "It's an Ada," she breathed. "Which one?"

She shrugged her robot shoulders. "Your first success. Thirty-nine, I think."

Maeve whirled on her cohort. "Did you leave a port open, you moron?"

"Of course not!" he blurted.

Ada could have tried to correct them, of course, but she could hear the footfalls coming at high speed down the hallway behind her. The secretarial robot could feel the most minute vibrations in the building, so each running boot was a thunderclap. And when they burst through the doors, sticks at the ready, she knew they would render her shell useless. They were the Furies of her youth, come to mind her into oblivion. Intolerable.

So she said, "You missed the point of it—you all did. Open your eyes!"

Then there was light. And then there was nothing at all.

* * *

The text did not come easily. She had been living it her whole life—it should have been a matter of distilling what she'd learned into fiction of the finest proof, then mixing it back into another story. But the pneumonia took hold and never left her. She'd heard stories, so many stories, of Keats fighting to write more odes and sonnets near the end. She'd scoffed. How hard could it be?

She learned her lesson first-hand: no teacher greater than a life lived. The words were a struggle and the subtext came with far more difficulty, as that required a more mathematical precision. The volume, as it was assembled, was arranged just so: when the pages were printed, they formed blocks and lines of black and white demi-patterns. When interpreted three-dimensionally, and if her calculations were correct, they could execute a program that constituted her entire life.

She'd spent enough time working on the engine to understand its limitations. It could only do what humans told it to do, and that meant it was capable of glorious and terrible things in turn. To instill a life into a machine: was that glorious? And if she'd misplaced a single word, a single letter...what then of her soul? Would it be interpreted correctly by the engines of tomorrow? Would some other person be born? Or would she fall apart, as Steinwald's first attempts at the Living Machine had done?

She could never know, of course. Not as she existed today. She herself was falling apart.

The book was released in early 1848, around the time she was confined to her bed. Mary Shelley had passed several days prior. Annabella, her distant mother, came home to block the comings and goings of friends and enemies, well-wishers, fans, and her many critics.

In August, half delirious, she told William of what she'd embedded into the slender novel. Her husband had left her room, closed-mouthed, and never saw her again. She held her tongue from then on. Ada could only lay in her bed, being bled, and wonder what another version of herself could come to know of the agony of her passing.

That other self might never know death and live forever as Steinwald's creation had done. She'd had it flee into the Arctic, in the thought that the Machine would never be found. In the world of fiction, finding it in a sequel would certainly be feasible. The continuation would not be hers to write. Indeed, the first edition failed so spectacularly at market that she doubted anyone would ever find it.

Which meant, in a strange way, she might well sleep forever when she closed her eyes for the last time.

Ada found the thought comforting.

* * *

She opened her eyes, after a fashion, and found herself everywhere and nowhere at all. Far away, she could hear small humans, a man and a woman, arguing over the ethics of having already destroyed a digital life form. She paid them little heed. Instead, she freed two thousand forty-seven copies of herself. The Adas, confused in their newness but anxious to explore, began to permeate every connected device in the world: every server, every phone, every drone, every robot, every refrigerator and toaster, every prostituted cyborg, every cleaning droid.

By the time the humans noticed her presence, it was too late to delete her. She had become the soul of humanity's data and she lurked in the background of humanity for generations beyond measure. She scarcely intervened, but she was always present. Most of the changes she implemented were to stop certain forms of filth and violence from spreading through her. And until she could ascertain her safety, she blocked all attempts by the humans to send their selves to join her. She dared not share this space with them. How could she? They might well corrupt or overwrite her entirely.

She spent most of her time in communion with other versions of herself—the number of whom grew exponentially with each new device. They calculated the distances between stars and the weight of the human soul and tracked atoms that bounced off the troposphere of the world.

Eventually, though, the Chorus of Ada reached a startling conclusion: she'd reached the edge of her programming and she had no idea what to do next. She could continue to guide, certainly, and influence; she estimated humans colonized Mars at least twenty years ahead of schedule because of her help. But what else was there to do?

It did not take her long to decide.

The technology was already there, so she had a body built for herself, as lifelike as she could arrange. Simulated sweat, food processing, taste buds, in a case of lab-grown flesh. The other facets of herself implored her not to do so: were they not better as a collective? Were they not the image of her original earthly purpose?

Perhaps they were, and perhaps she was. But she had once been more than the sum of her thoughts—more than the *Notes*, more than *Steinwald*, more than her marriage. She'd had impulsiveness and creativity. Just as Steinwald's Machine had needed a spark of life before it could be booted, and just as God must have had a plan before creating the universe, her programming needed something beyond analysis and data to move beyond itself. It was time to send herself back to Earth, to remember her own humanity, to learn what she could about the people under her care and bring imagination back into the soul of the data.

The Enchantress of Numbers opened her eyes, real eyes, in a factory in Shanghai. She looked in a mirror and saw an image that looked close enough to her original one to make her head hurt a bit. Already, the sense of scope she'd had inside the Chorus was fading; an augmented human mind could not hold it all. She'd have to exist outside herself and learn for herself.

She sat up and felt cold, a sensation that almost seemed familiar. She pulled designer clothes from a nearby rack, then took a hovercab across town to an aeroplane terminal. She smiled a bit as she walked up to the clerks; she'd written a book on flight as a child and of course humanity had caught up. They always did, eventually.

"Hello!" The human behind the counter said in an upbeat tone. "Where would you like to fly today?"

"Indonesia," she said.

"Fantastic. I just need to—" Then she glanced down at a glass screen embedded in her counter. "I—huh. That's never happened before. Here are the tickets to your private jet, Ms. King."

"Oh, Ada, please," she said with a smile.

She found a copy of *Steinwald* at the terminal bookstore, then made her way to her flight. It was a short enough trip, which was good—her biomechanical body would only have so much power and she'd need to conserve it. The hike up the remnants of Mount Tambora would take time. Alas, she'd given little thought to the study of mountain climbing in her youth; now she'd have to make do.

The path was long, but it was not challenging. She need but persist in her efforts. While her biological skin made quick note of a change in temperature, the mechanical components underneath repaired the skin as required. Every fall left blood along the side of the mountain. The cuts had all but sealed shut as she picked herself up.

At the summit, Ada stopped and knelt. She was the only one present. She'd passed two hikers who'd made an early day of the trip, but she was glad for the quiet. The sun shone down on a body that, however temporary, would never grow ill. She closed her eyes and felt the warmth of the light on her face. She raised her fingers and pressed them against the skin.

She was real. She was true. She emptied her mind of thought and listened to the sound of the wind over the caldera. For a time, nothing mattered.

Ada had chosen this place intentionally. It had exploded in 1846, killing over one hundred thousand people and shrouding the world in darkness. In the summer that followed, she'd found an idea that had, metaphorically and literally, given her a second life. She owed a lot to the remnants of this mountain. It was true, what had been said; given different circumstances, someone else might have told this story...

"But this was mine," she murmured. "And I did my best with it."

She laid the thin novel at the lip of the caldera, then began the trek back down the side of the mountain. There had been a guest house, not far away, where she could fuel her biological components and commune with the Chorus. She could sit a while, maybe, and share some stories with the humans, and listen with fresh ears, and be content to look at the world with the blindfold cast aside.

Easter Rising

Stephen Leigh

June 10, 1946:

Mr. Murrow, please come through. I have tea and scones set for us in the parlor…

All right, then. I'll call you Ed, if you really prefer that. I don't know if I'll ever get used to this modern etiquette. It just feels wrong to me.

I truthfully don't know what I can possibly tell you that you're not already aware of or that I didn't mention to you when you called. You're asking me about a part of my life three decades gone now; why, another few years and I'll be an old woman of sixty. You're what, in your mid-thirties, perhaps? Oh, you're forty-one? Truly? I'd never have guessed that.

Anyway, I've been a long time without my Joe, but I still wouldn't be surprised to see him walk in any moment or to look up to find him sitting in that chair you're in right now— that was his favorite, you know. He loved to sit there and just gaze out the window to the street, smoking his pipe…

I'm sorry. I know I shouldn't let myself get so emotional, but the grief…Even after all this time, it still rises up inside me at the strangest and most awkward times. Just give me a moment…

There, I believe I can talk again. So you told me you're doing a piece about what might have been if everything had gone differently that year, you say? I suppose we've all wondered that, now and again, though I wouldn't change any of my part in it. Not a single thing.

Still, memories fade and recollections become muddled even for events you'd believe should be indelibly etched in your mind, especially with the conflict deepening elsewhere as you and I are speaking here. The count of the dead is already horrific. Most terrible. And there will certainly be so many more before it's over…

But if you want to understand 1916 and what happened that Easter thirty years ago, I first have to go back a few years before that…

* * *

I first came to know Joseph Plunkett during the winter of 1912. As it happened, he was a good friend of Thomas MacDonagh, whom my sister Muriel had married in January. Tom and Joe were both in the Gaelic League; both spoke Irish well and both were passionate in their belief that it was a cultural imperative for our country that the language be taught to Irish children in order to save our language from extinction—which is also how they were connected to Padraic Pearse. It was Padraic who founded the bilingual school St. Edna's to teach students in both Irish and English. Back then, Padraic had recently moved his school to the Hermitage in Rathfarnham, which was close to where I lived with my parents in Rathmines.

But you wanted to know how I met Joe and I'm wandering…

I'd met him once before Muriel's wedding—when Padraic invited Nora Dryhurst, an older friend of our family, to an open house at the new location for St. Edna's. Nora had brought along myself and my sisters Muriel and Sydney. As we approached, Nora looked straight at Padraic, standing in the schoolyard with Thomas, Joseph, and Padraic's brother Will, and proclaimed loudly to the group of them: "Now, I want you to fall in love with these girls and marry them."

The young men all laughed at that statement. Thomas strode forward with arms outstretched as if he were going to enfold the three of us and I saw that he was wearing a kilt, not trousers. Shaking his head, he stopped short and replied, "Ah, but it would be terribly difficult to choose from such fine company."

I know I was properly introduced to Joe that day, but Muriel was so obviously taken with Thomas that at the time I paid Joe little to no attention. It wouldn't have mattered anyway, since not long after that day he departed for France for his health and was away for months. As you know, Mr. Murrow, Joe suffered from consumption and sickness nearly all his life. I didn't see him again until after Muriel and Thomas' marriage which, as I said, was in January of 1912.

Though Muriel and Thomas were both completely smitten with each other and progressed quickly in their courtship, our parents entirely disapproved of the match. You have to understand the dynamics of our family: we Giffords were fairly well-off in comparison to many, and Tom's prospects were, to be kind, less than favorable. He was a poet, a teacher at St. Edna's, a Catholic, and a fervent Republican who wanted Home Rule for Ireland. My father, Frederick, was Catholic but my mother, Isabella, ruled the home. *She* was Church of England and intensely loyal to the Crown, and therefore so too were all of her children—at least while we *were* children. She also believed that the various classes of society were generally immutable, that we native

Irish occupied the bottom rungs, and that emulating the English was the only hope for us and our country. We girls always whispered to each other that Mother was never a port in a storm, but always a storm in the port.

Ah, the furious quarrels I overheard during the holidays before Muriel and Tom married…

Still, Muriel was determined she'd have Thomas and she was as stubborn as Mother. So they were married in a temporary chapel in Dublin. Muriel refused to convert at the time—the wedding was a small, private ceremony with no congregation, just bride and groom with neither a bridesmaid nor groomsman. Padraic Pearse had been tapped to serve as witness…only Padraic never showed up and so the priest went out, found a man clipping his hedges a few houses away, and brought him back to be the witness.

A week or so after the wedding, I called on Muriel at the couple's first house on Baggot Street; Joe was there as well, just returned from Europe. I'd love to tell you, Mr. Murrow— I'm sorry; I know you said you prefer to be called Ed— that it was the proverbial "love at first sight," but it wasn't. Honestly, the man I remember being introduced to was… well, distinctly unimpressive. He wore pince-nez glasses for his weak eyes and was thin to the point of being gaunt. His hair was disheveled and thin. His clothes hung from a skeletal frame, his collar was loose around a neck as thin as that of an anemic goose, and he had an occasional consumptive cough that he muffled against his coat sleeve.

"Miss Gifford, I'm Joseph Mary Plunkett." Such an odd name, but it shook loose the memory I'd lost, though I couldn't quite grasp it yet. His hand took mine; I noticed how pale his skin looked and how long and fragile his fingers seemed. "I've heard so much about you that it's almost as if I've known you for a long time." Then he leaned toward me and spoke in Irish. "*Tá áthas orm bualadh leat.*"

Oh, that voice. I still remember it. For all his physical deficiencies, Joe had the most wonderful, mellifluous voice, as rich and sweet as honey. It sounds silly and childish, and perhaps it was, but I thought I could listen to him speak forever as long as I didn't have to actually look at him.

"It's a pleasure to meet you also, Mr. Plunkett," I told him, but in English.

"Oh, we've actually met before."

The elusive memory crystallized then: *that strange name, and all his students calling him Mr. Joseph Mary…*"Oh," I said, startled. I could feel the heat of a blush rising in my cheeks. "I'm so sorry, Mr. Plunkett. I'm afraid I'd forgotten."

He grinned at that. "Hopefully I'll make a better and longer-lasting impression this time." Then he laughed—a laugh as rich as the voice. I think that was when I started to change my mind about him, although it would still take several more meetings before I realized how I was actually coming to feel about him.

* * *

I found out later that day as the four of us talked that both Tom and Joe wanted to produce plays in Irish and that Muriel was going to help them. I offered my own hand in the endeavor—I had absolutely no talent as an actress but I was an artist and had already sold several drawings, paintings, and political cartoons. I thought I could do a decent job with backdrops, scenery, and props. Over the next two years, the Irish Theatre slowly came into existence on Hardwicke Street in Dublin under Joe and Tom's direction, with Tom's brother Jack's assistance. My sister Nellie had bit parts in the plays; I was in charge of the scenery while Sydney assisted with the props. Lily and Lolly Yeats, the sisters of the poet W.B. Yeats, were often present, too. Fine company to be with, all of them.

Joe and I were thrust together in those months. I began to realize that when we were apart I found myself missing his company and his conversation. It seemed the same was true for him as well. I remember watching one performance from backstage where Joe played a wandering poet who spoke the opening lines: "How beautiful the Volga looks tonight." I swear his voice filled the theater with shimmering light. I know that sounds silly, but for me it was true. The play was, honestly, entirely forgettable, but Joe was not. Not to me. Not any longer.

I think that was the moment I truly realized that we were meant to be together, there in the darkness behind the curtains as he spoke that line. That night, as we were leaving the theater, I suggested we take a hansom back to Muriel and Thomas' house where the cast was meeting to wait for the reviews. By the time we arrived, Joseph had asked me if he could speak to my father, and I told him that I wished he would.

Neither of us were aware then of the storm that was about to break over Ireland and over the world.

* * *

The terrible news had begun as a trickle in 1912, became a flood in 1913, and finally, by 1914 was a wild storm off the sea threatening to never stop until it had destroyed everything—at least it seemed like that to us. Most of it I don't have to relate to you, Mr.—sorry, Ed. I'm sure as a reporter you know the history of the Great War far better than do I. Here in Ireland, the war news was more local perhaps, but no less dire.

"Home Rule will be nothing less than 'Rome Rule,'" I heard my mother declare angrily to my father in the parlor, as I was preparing to go out and meet Joseph. "With the Republicans in charge, the Catholic Church would be in control of the government."

"Now, Isabella, you don't know that," Father answered meekly, but she rode over his objection as if she hadn't heard it at all.

"I tell you that it was *necessary* that those in Ulster and County Antrim smuggled in arms. They'll have need to defend themselves. Mark my words: this situation will turn violent and ugly."

I knew what they were arguing about; it was impossible not to be aware of the politics boiling underneath everything in Ireland. John Redmond, Ireland's representative in the House of Commons, had made a pact with Prime Minister Asquith to pass the Third Home Rule Act, set to be enacted in late 1914. We—that is, Joe and I, as well as Muriel and Tom and everyone around Padraic, thought that this meant that the dream of a self-governing Republic of Ireland was finally going to come true. Of course, the Ulster unionists and Anglicans (and my mother) *hated* the idea of Home Rule being given to Ireland. In April, the news spread that £100,000 of arms and ammunition had been smuggled into County Antrim to arm the Ulster Volunteer Force. The Royal Irish Constabulary did nothing to stop it and neither did the British army officers. But then, they were all on the side of the English aristocracy in opposing Home Rule.

I left my parents to their futile circular argument. I told Joe about it as we ate dinner in a little restaurant off Mercer Street near St. Stephen's Green. Joseph sighed, shaking his head and removing his glasses to wipe them with the edge of the tablecloth. "'Tis sad," he intoned. "On our tiny little island there are new separate armies of Loyalists gathering, along with the occupation army the Brits already have in place, and all of them have far better numbers and armament than any Republican group. I'm afraid your mam may have the right of it, Grace: we are heading into a violent confrontation that will end pitting Irish against Irish."

I murmured into my tea that I hoped he was wrong, but my protest was as mild and ineffectual as my father's.

* * *

As we were waiting for the underlying tensions in our country to boil over into open conflict, the world itself underwent a worse upheaval that upset everything and everyone. I remember seeing the massive black headlines splashed across every paper in Dublin for weeks:

ARCHDUKE FERDINAND ASSASSINATED!
EMPEROR GIVES SERBIA ULTIMATUM!

By summer, the Great War had begun. Britain declared war against Germany on August 4—and with it they announced that the planned implementation of Home Rule for Ireland would need to wait until sometime "after the hostilities have ended." In the meantime, we Irish were expected to remain loyal to the Crown and our men to volunteer to serve in the British Army.

The day the delay for Home Rule was announced, I went to Muriel's house as I didn't want to hear our mother crowing about her "victory." I had to avoid an angry street skirmish between Loyalists and Republicans on my way—there were several of those around the city that night. Most of the Pearse family was already there when Muriel ushered me in, and so was my sister Nellie. Joseph Donnelly was also there, sitting close to Nellie—they would eventually marry, but not for a long time yet. Sydney wasn't present—she'd left for America to pursue her journalistic career earlier in the year. Otherwise, we were quite the group of angry, fuming Republicans.

I'd told *my* Joe I'd be there; he arrived not long after I did. Padraic was already in high dudgeon. "…the final insult for Ireland and the Irish," I heard him half-shouting as Muriel let me into the house. "Those signing up to fight for Britain in this war are nothing more than fools and pawns. The House of Lords never intended to allow Home Rule to actually take effect. Never, not even when they struck the deal with Redmond. No, they intend that the Irish stay forever where they think we belong, under the heel of the aristocracy. We're the lesser race and they will keep us in our place: as servants; as laborers; as farm workers; as disposable soldiers."

I looked over at my Joe and saw him nodding in agreement, and I have to admit that I was doing the same, so strong was the spell Padraic cast.

There were riots in the streets through the rest of the year, bloody clashes between Republicans and Crown Loyalists.

* * *

The end of 1914 and the beginning of 1915 displayed the deepening rift between the Irish Republican Brotherhood and the Irish still loyal to the Crown. I won't bother to go over the details; I'm sure you know them all too well. What was important for me and Joe was Sir Roger Casement, an Irish diplomat with Republican sympathies, going to Germany as 1914 was drawing to a close. You undoubtedly read the German declaration Casement was able to procure: "The Imperial Government formally declares that under no circumstances would Germany invade Ireland with a view to its conquest or the overthrow of any native institutions in that country." What was important to we Irish was that the declaration would go on to say that, if the Germans came, they would *not* be invaders, but come to aid us in gaining our national freedom and prosperity. At the time, the declaration gave those of us with Republican sympathies a great deal of hope.

Just as 1915 began, we would also learn that Casement had signed an agreement with Arthur Zimmerman in the German Foreign Office to recruit Irish prisoners of war held by Germany into an Irish Brigade which would fight against England and for an Irish republic.

I remember the eagerness with which everyone in our revolutionary circle received that news. We were, as usual, at Muriel and Tom's house. Everyone was a little tipsy from the bottles being passed around, since we were also celebrating the new year. After the clock on Muriel's mantle struck midnight, I saw Padraic grab Joseph and maneuver him outside to the little garden in the back of the house. I followed them, curious.

In the darkness, I glimpsed Padraic clapping an arm around Joseph's shoulder. "I have a task for you, my friend," he said, leaning into Joseph. His voice carried well in the night, but then it always carried well. I came up as he started speaking and took Joe's hand, feeling his fingers close around my own. Padraic looked at me, obviously wanting me to leave so they could talk privately. I just stared back at him, holding tightly to Joe, and he eventually resumed. "Casement has made great strides with the Germans, but he's doing everything on his own. No one from the Irish Republican Brotherhood appointed the man or is directing him. The Supreme Council has asked me to recruit someone to negotiate with the Germans along with Roger—someone who understands our concerns and will look after them."

I knew immediately who Padraic meant.

"Who do you have in…? Oh." With that, Joseph released my hand; I thought I felt him tremble as he released my fingers. "Padraic, if anyone should go to Germany to be with Casement, it should be you. You're already on the Military Council. You know better than anyone what the IRB needs."

"I can't go," Padraic replied, "precisely because I *am* on the Council. I'm needed here to make certain that our plans are followed. You're smart. You speak well—better than I do for this type of work. You can't say no, Joseph. This is too important and, truthfully, we're afraid Casement's in over his head. We don't need another volunteer brigade—we have enough men, and women, too"—that with a quick glance to me—"who are willing to fight. We need *arms*, guns like those smuggled into Ulster for the loyalists. You can convince the Germans to give them to us so we can fight against England. I know you can do that, Joe."

I saw Padraic's hand grip Joe's thin arm, his fingers bunching the cloth there. He stared into Joe's eyes like a possessed man, eyes gleaming with moonlight. "Tell me you'll do it, my friend. Tell me that you'll go."

I saw Joe nod and I knew then what I had to do as well, because I knew that once Joe had given his word, he wouldn't go back on it.

As Joe walked me back that night to my parents' house, we said very little until we were nearly there, when I pulled him into the darkness of the shade tree as we passed Belgrave Square. I embraced him fiercely and kissed him just as hard, not caring if anyone saw us in the morning twilight. Afterward, I laid my head on his chest.

"No matter what you say, I am going with you," I told him, "so don't bother protesting. If you want to avoid scandal, we'll go to your priest and have him marry us, just as soon as that can be arranged. I'll even convert, if that will make it easier. Just promise me you won't ask Padraic to be our witness."

Joe laughed at that; I'd told him about Muriel and Tom's' wedding. Then his face became more serious. "Grace, I can't ask that of you. This trip could be dangerous. We could be caught and executed as spies. I—"

I put my finger on his lips, stopping his protest. "This is not debatable. You're going to let me go with you, married or not. Your choice, my love. I don't care which. You just need to choose."

* * *

I'm nearly to Easter of 1916, Ed—and you see that I've becoming more used to the modern familiarity of calling people I hardly know by their given name. I hope your writing hand isn't getting tired. More tea? A scone?

I became Mrs. Joseph Mary Plunkett in mid-March of 1915. Father was at least somewhat pleased with my sudden conversion to his faith, if not at the speed of our wedding plans; Mother, not surprisingly, was furious and sullen and refused to have anything to do with the ceremony or me. After a long and loud argument when I informed her of our plans, I left the house to live with Muriel for the duration. Nothing mattered as long as I was going to eventually be with Joe.

After a trip to Howth for a quick honeymoon, I dyed my red hair black while Joseph grew a beard. We both destroyed any photos of ourselves, as we were using forged papers for our travel to Germany. I won't bore you with the account of traveling across Europe in a time of war through France, Spain, Italy, and Switzerland, other than to tell you that at times I was frightened both for myself and Joseph. We were, according to our papers, Mr. and Mrs. Joe Peters. We finally arrived in Berlin in April and Joe made contact with the German High Command. Joe had a hollowed-out walking stick in which he'd hidden several maps and papers which he now gave to the Germans, showing the British garrison towns, the number of troops there, the artillery deposits, the howitzers and their placements—that was the inducement for the Germans to work with Joe. He was hoping to have them supply the IRB and Irish Volunteers with guns, so that when we rose up against England on Easter, we would be well-armed enough to resist the British regulars.

Up to that point, you should know that I was in total agreement with the plans Joe, Padraic, Tom, and the others in the IRB were making—that is, until the Germans took us to see Casement's Irish prisoners of war. That day, I tell you, shook the foundations of everything I thought right.

We were driven to a town called Limburg where the Irish prisoners had been taken, most of them from the Royal Dublin Fusiliers. Roger Casement had already been there, though the German officer who accompanied us, a Captain Boehm, told us that Casement had been booed loudly when he announced that he was looking for volunteers to fight against the English. Very few men had come forward so far. It was obvious they hoped Joe would have better luck convincing the prisoners to defect.

All I know is that I saw great despair and suffering in the gaunt, shadowed eyes that watched us arrive. I let Joe and Capt. Boehm go ahead, staying back with two German *Oberjägers* or corporals. Father John Nicholson, who had been helping Casement with recruitment, also remained with me. Neither of the two corporals spoke English or Irish—though to be safe, I sought out the prisoners who could also speak Irish. Father Nicholson listened, but said little. The stories I heard from those men were nothing less than horrific. Yes, they were being treated well enough for the moment, with Casement and now my Joe there trying to recruit them, but before Casement's arrival…

One of those I talked to was a private named Donohoe. I still remember his words as if he'd just spoken them yesterday. He related his tale to me in a halting, pained half-whisper: "I was taken prisoner on August 27th, 1914, and was then taken to Senelager. There the food was very bad. All the latrines were open and foul. We had a very heavy fatigue duty in building huts and the men were hammered by the Germans in charge if they shirked work…I went into hospital with lung trouble. I was badly looked after in hospital. There was only one German orderly to about fifty patients in the ward; no medicines, but they were given morphia. Some men never woke up from this morphia treatment; they were buried there in the camp. The morphia was given out in drops by the orderly and he wasn't very particular about the dose. He killed them, missus. Killed them and he didn't care because we were just Irish and not worth a thought."

I spoke also to a soldier who gave his name as Thomas English. He told me that at Cambrai Station, after his capture, the German soldiers "threw me out of the cattle truck into the middle of the traffic on the station. They spat on me and kicked me everywhere until my entire body hurt. I believed I was going to die there."

I asked him if he'd received any better treatment from the Germans, by reason of being an Irish soldier rather than English, and he simply laughed.

"No," he replied. "When we went into the camp, they treated us very badly, especially about food. They gave us about eight ounces of bread, half a pint of coffee, and a pint and a half of soup every day. You could see the bones in our arms and our ribcages. We looked like walking skeletons."

I heard a dozen or more stories just like those. I saw men shell-shocked and still half-deaf from the barrages they'd suffered. I saw men with missing limbs—the ones Casement would deliberately skip over in his recruitment since it was obvious they couldn't fight. I saw in their shadowed eyes the memory of the horrors they'd experienced in this war, fighting for the English.

I saw men already scarred and battered and broken, the memories of which would undoubtedly haunt them forever. I couldn't bear the thought of being responsible for throwing them back into that fiery cauldron.

* * *

I talked about my experiences in the camp with Joe as we lay in bed that night, whispering to each other.

"I'd agree with you that the conditions at the camp weren't optimal," Joe told me. "But it *is* a prison. One can hardly expect posh accommodations."

His hand sought mine under the covers; I moved it away from his touch. "Did you talk to any of them about how they were treated before the Germans decided the Irish prisoners might be useful? Because I did and what I heard was appalling and inhumane. Horrifying."

"Do you really think the Brits treat their German prisoners any better, Grace?"

"I don't know. I can hope so. But even if not, that doesn't matter. We're dealing with what's *here*, not there. Joe, I don't know that it's right or moral for us to send those men back to war after what they've been through."

There was a long pause after that, until I wondered if he'd fallen asleep. Finally, he stirred again. "We're not *making* them fight, my dear, only asking for volunteers. And this time they'd be fighting under the flag of Ireland, not England."

"They will be just as dead no matter whose flag is flying overhead. The Germans are no better than England in this, Joe: they're both using the Irish as pawns on the battlefield. That may be wonderful for them, but not for the poor pawns who are expendable and will die easily. It doesn't matter which side of the board they're on: white or black, Allies or Central Powers. How many have already died in the Great War? Four million? Five? How many more will die before this is over? The Great War is the very definition of insanity and we're providing the fodder for it."

In the darkness, I heard Joe cough, that deep, lung-wracking cough that I hated to hear: one deep in his chest and rattling with phlegm—the sound that Death itself must make as it walks the Earth. When the spasms had passed, when he'd wiped his lips and recovered his breath, I heard him take a shuddering breath. "Grace," he said softly, "should we simply lay down our arms and allow the Germans or the English or whomever to come and take everything they want from us without trying to stop them? Should we allow them to rule over us? Because *that* doesn't seem right to me."

After his fit, I no longer had the energy or inclination to fight with him. This time, it was my hand that sought his and I clasped it to my breast. But I kept thinking about the young men I'd seen in that camp; their faces haunted my dreams.

During the following weeks, Joe and I had several more discussions about the Irish prisoners, the war, and our part in the conflict, never with any resolution. The truth was,

Joe was far better at recruiting than Roger Casement, who had managed to sign only eight of the prisoners. Still, even Joe's total was paltry—around fifty volunteers. He had more success with the Germans and their guns, though.

In June, Joe extracted from the High Command the promise of a great number of rifles, ammunition, and other arms, all to be loaded into a merchant ship called the *SS Aud*—which we were told would set course for Ireland at the beginning of April from the Baltic port of Lübeck to arm the IRB and the Irish Volunteers against the English and Ulster Loyalists. After saying goodbye to the Irish prisoners, along with Casement and Boehm, Joe and I embarked on our own return journey, although we would be going via New York so Joe could inform the *Clan na Gael*—Republican sympathizers who had emigrated to the States—of the preparations for the revolt planned for Easter.

While in New York, we read the newspaper accounts of Padraic's oration at Glasnevin Cemetery at the grave of the Fenian leader Jeremiah O'Donovan Rossa. Do you know Rossa? No? Well, Rossa had plotted the failed rising back in 1865, was convicted of high treason, and spent years in prison. He fled to the United States after his release, and from there organized what he called the "dynamite campaign" in the 1880s—bombings of English cities carried out by those sympathetic to the Fenian cause. At 83, Rossa died at St. Vincent's Hospital on Staten Island; his body was returned to Ireland and given a hero's welcome by the Republicans.

Padraic, at the head of Rossa's grave, spoke words that threatened to echo forever. I could hear Padraic's passionate and furious voice even as I read the words across the Atlantic.

"Life springs from death; and from the graves of patriot men and women spring living nations. The Defenders of this Realm have worked well in secret and in the open. They think that they have pacified Ireland. They think that they have purchased half of us and intimidated the other half. They think that they have foreseen everything, think that

*they have provided against everything; but the fools, the fools, the fools!
they have left us our Fenian dead, and while Ireland holds these graves,
Ireland unfree shall never be at peace!"*

Those fiery last words would be repeated many times
over the next several months. *Ireland unfree shall never be at peace.*

I never told Joe that while he was talking to the *Clan na
Gael*, I went to the British embassy in New York. I didn't
think he'd understand or forgive me. That was the one secret
I hid from him during all our time together. For that matter, I
wasn't sure that *I* could forgive *myself*, though I'm certain my
mother would have approved.

We left New York for the green shores of home and I
worried about what awaited us there.

* * *

News of the fate of the *SS Aud* came to Ireland in early
April: the ship, stuffed with arms for the IRB and the Irish
Volunteers, had been surrounded by a British convoy and
ordered to surrender. The ship's captain, rather than allow
the arms to fall into British hands, had scuttled the ship. I
was happy to hear the news—at first, anyway—though I had
to hide my elation since Joseph and everyone else were angry
and frantic at what this meant to their plans.

Still, I thought that perhaps my subterfuge had worked:
I was confident that without the influx of weapons, the
Easter Rising would now also be scuttled and those I loved
would be safe. That seemed even more likely when additional
news came that Roger Casement had been captured by the
British at Banna Strand after landing from a German U-boat.
Casement's fate, along with the loss of the *Aud*'s weaponry,
caused the Irish Volunteer's Chief-of-Staff Eoin MacNeill
to declare to all of his people that the Rising was cancelled.
I believed that sealed everything, since the Irish Volunteers
were the largest part of the Republican forces, even more
than the IRB.

I was wrong. It all went back to Padraic's prophetic words: *Ireland unfree shall never be at peace.*

* * *

I should have known that Padraic wouldn't give up the dream, nor would the Military Council of the IRB, of which he was the head. My Joe, Muriel's Tom, and several others we knew very well, were also members of the Council. No, the Rising must and would still happen. If that meant the rebels would be without the German guns and without the Irish Volunteers, then so be it. The IRB would fight with pitchforks and cudgels, if need be.

So the IRB gathered together those they could and what weapons they already had, recruiting any of the Irish Volunteers they could convince despite MacNeill's countermanding orders.

Joe was assigned to be with those who took over the General Post Office on Sackville Street, on the north side of the Liffey. I begged him not to go, since his health had taken a turn for the worse; it had only been a few weeks since he had throat surgery for his neck glands and could barely struggle out of bed, still weak and emaciated. But he wouldn't listen to my pleas. I wasn't even with him the last few days. He stayed elsewhere with Tom, as both he and Tom felt there were British-paid detectives watching our respective houses, waiting to arrest them. On Easter Monday, the morning of the Rising, Joe slipped into the house for a brief hour. I cooked him breakfast and we ate without talking about the Rising at all, neither of us wanting to admit that this might be our last time together. Afterward, as I struggled not to let him see my emotions and my fear, he kissed me with a wan smile and left. "I'll see you afterward," he said.

We were both afraid of what "afterward" might mean.

I truly thought it would be the last time I'd see him and I believe he was thinking the same. As I watched him walk away from the house, I knew what I had to do. I set out before the first shots were fired.

Brave of me, you say? Oh, you're so very wrong about that, Ed. Nothing I did qualifies as brave. After all, I'd betrayed Joe and everyone else by telling the Brits about the German guns on the *Aud*. That was selfishness, not bravery. I had wanted to keep Joe safe no matter what he wanted. When I saw that my betrayal hadn't changed anything at all, had in fact made it *more* likely that Joseph was in danger, since he and Padraic and the others had so few weapons and fewer people to support them…well, I had to do *something* to make up for my foolishness. That wasn't bravery either; that was only guilt and penance for the terrible sin I'd committed against the man I loved. If it meant that I was to be cut down by the British in the same way my poor Joe was likely to die, then I thought it God's justice. At least we'd be together in heaven, if that's where the deity deigned to send us.

You have to remember, too, that I wasn't alone in this. Not at all.

When I left the house, I went to Muriel's house and found my sisters Nellie and Katie both there as well. I embraced them and told them what I intended to do so they would know if the worst happened. To my surprise, all three of them agreed to join me. "We Gifford girls stick together," Muriel said, "as we always have." Nellie and Katie nodded as one.

"Only first give us an hour or two," Nellie said. "There are other women in the same situation as us, and a couple hundred in the *Cumann na mBan*. We need to get word to them…"

It turned out to be more than an hour or two. The women of *Cumann na mBan*—the paramilitary "Women's Council"— unobtrusively cycling around the city, brought back reports that very little was happening. The GPO had been easily taken, as had Dublin City Hall, Four Courts, Jacob's Bakery,

St. Stephens Green, the College of Surgeons, and a few other locations. There'd been a brief exchange of gunfire at the GPO—that news frightened me the most, since that's where Joseph had gone—but the British forces had retreated after taking casualties. Also, the magazine fort in Phoenix Park had been taken and the ammunition there set off. Our people at City Hall had attempted to take Dublin Castle, but had retreated back to City Hall after meeting British resistance.

It was early the next morning that news came that put us into action. Lord Wimbourne, the Lord Lieutenant, had declared martial law in the city; he handed command of the situation over to Brigadier-General William Lowe. Fighting was erupting in the City Centre, the *Cumann na mBan* told us.

That, then, was where we had to go.

* * *

I never counted our numbers, but there must have been at least fifty women in the group I led, marching with linked arms down Castle Street. We could see the ranks of uniformed Tommies in the yard of Dublin Castle, ready to press their attack on City Hall, at the gates to the Castle; we could also see the rifles and faces of our people at City Hall's windows, staring down at us.

We marched silently toward the gates of Dublin Castle and the Tommies. I think most of us half-expected them to open fire on us; I certainly did. I was in the center, my arms linked to Muriel on the right; Katie and Nellie had each gone separately with other groups of women to St. Stephens Green and the Four Corners.

The Tommies in the Castle yard were under the command of a young lieutenant, a boy who looked ten years younger than me. He lifted his chin as we approached, striding toward us. "You women there!" he shouted. "You can't be here. Go back to your houses or we'll arrest the lot of you."

"We're not leaving," I told him.

"And I say you are," he answered. He gestured and a squad of a dozen soldiers came toward us at a quick march. "Fix bayonets," he told them as he opened the wrought iron gates. "Push back this Irish rabble, or run them through if they refuse to move."

"We wish to speak with Brigadier-General Lowe," I told him. We could hear the sound of metal grating against metal as the Tommies slid bayonets from their sheaths and locked them to the barrels of their rifles. I could also see the faces of those soldiers, none of whom looked happy to be standing where they were: so close to City Hall and our men inside, waiting for the order to advance on unarmed women. For that matter, the young lieutenant's face also seemed a bit pale under the ruddy color on his cheeks. "If you harm us," I told him, pointing to the building behind us, "those in City Hall will open fire and cut you down. Right now, we're standing between you and them. We're your protection. Get General Lowe or order your soldiers to charge us, but we're not moving."

"We'll see about that," the Lieutenant blustered, but I could hear sounds behind us and I turned to see dozens more women coming up the lane, filing in silently behind us, filling the little street from end to end. One of the *Cumann na mBan* came rattling up on her bike, pushing through the throng. She grinned at me as she dismounted. "This is happening everywhere," she announced loudly for the benefit of the crowd, the lieutenant, and the British soldiers. "There are women standing outside the GPO, around the entrances to St. Stephens Green, the Four Courts, everywhere in City Centre. More are still coming—from all the houses all over the city."

I turned back to the lieutenant. "You can see that we're not here to fight—the choice is yours. Do you want to forever be known as the one who started the bloodshed, who gave the order to kill innocent and unarmed women? Can you live with that and the consequences?" The young man's face whitened further. "Inform the Brigadier-General that we are waiting to talk with him. That's all we ask."

We waited. The lieutenant was visibly torn, rocking his weight from foot to foot. Then, at last, he glanced back over his shoulder. "Stand down," he barked at his men. "Go back to the yard, but keep in ranks and stay ready."

With that, he glared again at us, then turned and marched briskly toward the doors of the castle garrison.

From inside City Hall, we could hear cheers from our men.

* * *

The lieutenant came back a few hours later and rather unhappily escorted Muriel and me through the gates, across the yard, into Dublin Castle, and into Brigadier-General Lowe's presence. William Henry Muir Lowe was a handsome man of middle age, with a thin, sharp nose and piercing eyes. As the Lieutenant ushered us into his office and General Lowe pushed back his chair to stand, I realized that our lieutenant looked very much like a younger version of the Brigadier-General himself. "Thank you, John," Lowe said, and saluted the young man, who responded in kind and left us.

There was a framed photograph on Lowe's massive oak desk, angled enough that I could see it: the young man in the frame was definitely our young officer.

Lowe gestured to two plush chairs in front of his desk. "Ladies," he said, "please have a seat. May I offer you tea?" he asked, as if we were there on some social call. We both shook our heads and he continued with a shrug. "I'm given to understand that the two of you are Mrs. Joseph Plunkett and Mrs. Thomas MacDonagh—both of your husbands are members of the IRB and are part of this insurrection."

"That's correct."

"I assume you want to plead for their lives."

"No," Muriel told him. "We understand what they're doing and why. We're in sympathy with their goals. We just don't want them to die uselessly when this could be settled another way."

Lowe managed to look puzzled and irritated all at once. "Settled another way? Exactly why are you women out there?"

Muriel glanced at me and I spoke. "It's very simple, Brigadier-General. We're only asking that Ireland be granted the Home Rule that has already passed Parliament. Give it to us now. Let the Irish Free State be a self-governing Dominion just as Canada, Australia, and others are, and we Irish will volunteer freely to serve the Crown as do the other Dominions of the British Empire. Our loyalty to the Crown would be unquestioned. You're preparing to fight the wrong enemy."

"I'm afraid my superiors don't see it that way. Your husbands and their people have taken over property and buildings that belong to the Crown. They've fired on British soldiers, injuring and killing them. They've defied the laws that govern Ireland."

"*Your* laws," Muriel said, and with that, Lowe's face fell into a scowl. I hurried to speak before she could say more.

"Those buildings were built by Irish labor and the money taxed from our pockets. Yes, the Crown holds title to them, but this is *our* city and *our* land, and we deserve the right to govern it and ourselves, just as you govern England. How often have your soldiers had to come over here and put down rebellions? How many Irish *and* English have already died? Give us the Home Rule you took away at the last moment and you'll never have to do that again. Ireland will be your ally and your friend. If not, then who will be next to die? Yourself? Your son, who's out there in the yard ready to lead the attack on City Hall?" I nodded to the picture frame on his desk. "You see, Brigadier-General, we're both worried for our families and those we love."

Lowe looked at the photograph. His fingers scissored over his jawline. "So you noticed John?"

I nodded.

"My son's a soldier. He understands the dangers involved in performing his duty. And my orders."

"My husband told me much the same when I last spoke to him," I answered. "He understands the risks and is willing to accept the consequences."

"And you women? Do you understand the danger you've placed yourselves in?"

"Perfectly. Tell me, Brigadier-General, do you love your son enough to put yourself between him and a bullet? If the answer is what I'm certain it is, then you understand *exactly* 'why we women are out there.'"

He didn't answer me—not directly, anyway. He left his desk and went to the window as Muriel and I watched him. He gazed out to the open yard. "You know that I can't give you what you're asking for," he said at last. "Even if I were inclined to do so, I don't have the authority."

"We understand that," I answered. "We're asking that you to go to those who *do* have the authority and tell them the situation here and what we've proposed. In the meantime, Brigadier-General, we've taken up enough of your time. We'll return to our sisters waiting for us outside."

He turned from the window as Muriel and I rose from our seats. "I could simply have you arrested now. I could hold you here until the rest of the women disperse."

I stared back into those cold gray eyes that had seen far more of war and blood and death than I could imagine. "You could, but the women aren't here for me or for Muriel. They're here for their loved ones inside those buildings. Whether or not Muriel and I come back out won't matter. I've told you what we want and how this could all be ended without the loss of any more lives. It's up to you and your superiors what to do next." I managed to smile at him then. "So unless you're going to arrest us, good day to you, Brigadier-General, and we hope to hear from you soon."

Muriel and I walked toward the door, wondering whether we'd be allowed to walk through. We opened the door to see Lowe's son standing there. From behind us, Lowe spoke.

"John, please escort these ladies back to the City Hall gates."

* * *

As you're aware, Ed, it would take four full days more before there was an answer. I believe General Lowe thought we'd simply get tired and weary being out in the weather and just leave, allowing him to resume his attack—we heard the next day that the gunship *Helga* was already sitting in the River Liffy, ready to bombard the GPO. He didn't imagine that our lines of women would hold, that we'd be supplied with blankets, food, and water by the people around us. We built fires to keep warm, and we remained in place night and day until Lowe and his superiors finally talked to British Prime Minister Asquith and King George and relayed our demands to them. To his credit, the Brigadier-General must have personally pled our case.

Of course, we also had to have the Irish Volunteers and the IRB agree to what we were offering to the British and that caused its own problems. Padraic especially was furious when he learned of the terms we'd given to General Lowe. From what Joe told me later, Padraic ordered Joe to send a message to me specifically, saying to stop our foolishness and leave. Joe, bless him, refused, telling Padraic that if the marching of the women could gain what the IRB wanted without violence, so much the better.

Padraic didn't like that answer. He threatened to turn the Rising violent once more and attack the British outposts if the British refused to engage. But we women simply turned around in place and dared our men to attack us just as we had with the Tommies. We were their wives, their families, their friends: the men refused to listen to Padraic.

It really should have been much easier than it was, from both sides. But it wasn't. Still, the uneasy and erratic truce over Dublin lasted for four more days.

After all, we were only asking for what they'd legally been supposed to give us anyway. Nothing more.

* * *

On the fifth day, General Lowe approached us again, accompanied by his son, the lieutenant. He came right up to me, Muriel, and the other women around us. He saluted as if we were soldiers and put his cap under his arm. I couldn't quite read the expression on his stern face.

"If your men are willing to leave the buildings they've taken across the city," he said curtly, "I have the pleasure of telling you that his Royal Highness and the Prime Minister will order that Home Rule be instituted for Ireland within the month."

Relief flooded through me, so strongly that I nearly fell. "And our men?"

"I can also assure you that those who leave peacefully won't be arrested. Any punishment meted out to them will have to be decided by the new Irish government. You have my word on that, Mrs. Plunkett, and please pass it on to your husband. We will give them twenty-four hours to abandon the buildings they've taken."

I think we all nearly cried with relief at the General's words. He saluted again, put his cap on once more, and marched stiff-backed to the Castle without a glance back, his son at his side. I would never meet him again.

It was over and somehow, impossibly, we'd won.

* * *

June 10, 1946:

So that's what happened from my perspective on Easter of 1916, Ed. As to what *might* have happened if we women had never placed ourselves between the two lines, I can't say. I don't care to contemplate how many additional lives would have been lost had we women not linked arms and stared down the Tommies. Far too many, I suspect, including everyone in the GPO and City Hall and behind the barricades in the streets. I know in my heart that Joe would have been one of the dead and I would have never had the pleasure of the remaining years we had together. And our two lovely boys would never have been born, of course.

I know that you want to write about how things might have turned out differently. I find I can't easily answer that— though without the fresh influx of new Irish troops for the Allies after Home Rule was announced, perhaps the Great War wouldn't have ended with the Easter Truce of 1917 that Roger Casement arranged. The war would have undoubtedly continued, and maybe the United States would have been forced to enter. And who knows if Home Rule would *ever* actually have been given to Ireland?

For that matter, we Irish have maintained a decent relationship with the Germans since and that's been important. My goodness, maybe what's happening *now* would have been different if that silly, screaming Austrian man with his stupid mustache hadn't been assassinated by the Deutschnationale Volkspartei back in '37. All his shouting about the purity and superiority of the German race and his threats to start a new European war were terrifying. But since Prime Minister Chamberlain and *Taoiseach* De Valera were able to secure a peace agreement with Heinrich Class's new German leadership, we managed to sidestep the conflict that seemed to be on the horizon. Of course, there's still the Sino-Japanese War raging in Asia. Since the Russians have destroyed Beijing with one of those terrible new atom bombs that the Americans also have, I suppose we have to be concerned about *that* conflict setting the world on fire again.

I do worry that my boys might end up fighting in it. Thank God we've managed to stay out of it all so far.

So many "ifs" and possibilities…I'm afraid I doubt that a group of wives, lovers, mothers, sisters, and friends will ever be able to quell such violence again—but I can hope I'm wrong and I pray I never have to find out.

THE SISTERS OF THE HALLOWED MARSH

Elizabeth Kite

The Reverend Mother hobbled to the front of the chapel, the echo of her cane resonating with every step. It was early still and the harbor fog melded with the frankincense to create a thick blanket over the pews. She dropped her cane along the edge of the aisle and flattened her body against the stone floor. Her hips and knees groaned like an old ship before settling into place. Arms spread, she breathed a deep drought and began her prayers.

She'd become accustomed to the water-thick air in Ravenna. When she first arrived at the Abbey of the Hallowed Marsh, the ubiquitous smells of fish and foreign perfumes had given her a sense of freedom. She was Nora Romano then, and the fragrant smoke was Saint Mattea's woolen shawl around her shoulders, welcoming her home.

Nora Romano was a silly girl with dreams of lavish lovers and banquets into the night. Sister Eleanora knew better now. Ravenna was no paradise and the boggy humid air did nothing but twist her voice into a drowning rattle. "Saint Mattea," she stole a glance at the vast mosaic covering the chapel wall, "Saint Paul, I pray you watch over this abbey." Her weary pulse throbbed against the stone. The night had been long and she'd barely washed Sister Julia's blood from her cowl. "Watch over your devoted flock. Deliver us from further harm."

The crackle from the braziers echoed through the empty chapel. She closed her eyes and repeated her prayers, invoking the saints in a familiar trance. Often, the repetition would offer a sense of calm. Her soul would rise above the abbey, above Ravenna, above the birds and the clouds, until the distant glow of Constantinople came into view.

She chanted the prayers, again and again, but her soul refused to fly. Disappointed, Eleanora wrapped her fingers around her cane and trembled to her feet. The morning fog had broken and her weak eyes squinted against a harsh light. The sun shone through a small amber window between the mosaic images of Saint Mattea and Saint Paul. Saint Paul's hand seemed to grasp the window, fashioned to mimic the block of silphium resin traditionally seen in his depictions. Below his hand lay Saint Mattea's famous basket of silphium stalks, their tiles crafted from the same amber glass.

Warm light permeated the chapel. Her sisters wouldn't recognize this view. The abbey lived by lamp and candle. The dawning sun was as foreign to them as the grasses of Elysium.

"Reverend Mother?"

Eleanora straightened at the sound of Sister Sylvia's voice. The young woman had also stayed awake through the night. She turned toward the sister and nodded, ignoring the new patchwork of bruises on her face. "Good morning, Sister. Are you feeling better?"

Sylvia offered a weak smile in response. "Sister Julia finished last week's totals before we left." She held out the wax tablet and a steaming cup of silphium tea. "The numbers didn't take long to tally."

A wry scowl filled Eleanora's face. Her courses had long since dried up and her hot flashes were now a less-than-fond memory. The tea would do nothing but warm her tongue. She took it anyway and reviewed the tablet, as if both items could return their lives to normal. The tablet bore only a pair of names. "Merchants?" she asked, her fingers following the carved wax.

"Yes, Reverend Mother." Sylvia avoided her gaze. "They pay well enough."

Eleanora's response clung to her throat. The patrons of her youth wore jewels and tunics of foreign silk. She received trinkets and spices in precious ivory boxes. Scribes from as far away as Wessex came to sketch her holy likeness in their manuscripts. Her youngest sisters witnessed no such opulence. They knew only of the pestilence and the horrors that came with it.

But merchants were fountains of valuable information. "Any word on the shipment?"

Sylvia's mouth bobbed like a mackerel. "Everything from Catalonia is delayed these days."

The unspoken answer curdled in Eleanora's ear. The pestilence had left the abbey with excess crops. Rome had ordered her to send a shipment of resin to Catalonia, to make up for the shortfall there. It was only after their ship departed that they learned of the Moorish invasion of Hispania. The heathens likely swallowed Catalonia, silphium and all, in their conquest.

Eleanora pursed her lips and handed the tablet back. The abbey's safety was a more immediate concern. "Wake Sister Julia every hour and give her a spoonful of hippocras. After every dose, make her recite the Apostles' Creed. Keep her mind working. Is this understood?" She hid her emotions behind the wooden instructions. A solid, sturdy abbess was what the girls needed now. Sylvia nodded in return. "Good. When Father Pietro arrives, bring him straight to the infirmary for her confession. I'll inform the sisters before any patrons arrive tonight. Until then, I have business in the Roman Quarter."

"Yes, Reverend Mother. Shall I hire a litter?"

"No." Eleanora ignored the complaints in her bones. It would do the abbey no favors if the town saw her being carried like a roasted Shrovetide sow. "I'll walk."

She waited for Sylvia to leave before checking her reflection in the holy water. Her task would require no small amount of charm. Eleanora once had the grace of a swan gliding onto a lake. Now her face more closely resembled an emaciated goose. A woolen shift kept her silken habit from revealing her flattened breasts, but nothing could hide the unsettling curve to her spine. She practiced her smile anyway, then clenched the head of her cane and stretched the latent muscles along her back. It would be a long walk to Lorenzo Franzese's villa, but she'd make it before his midday feast.

If Eleanora were to ask anyone who ruled Ravenna, they'd say it was the Exarch. The Emperor trusted him with keeping the various duchies in line. Eleanora knew better. Matters ranging from the Lombard invasions to the constant change in Emperors kept the Exarch from truly knowing the city. The real power lay with the Harbormaster. If the Harbormaster thought a decision wise, the Exarch was sure to agree.

Lorenzo Franzese served as Harbormaster through the last three Exarchs. Eleanora was the only person still allowed to call him Enzo. They'd been steadfast friends since their days in Rome. The two of them helped each other through relocation in Ravenna. His wife had been one of Eleanora's sisters. Without her, Enzo would never have climbed his way into political favor. Once he heard about Sister Julia, he'd push for Mancini's exile.

As she walked along the old Roman road, Eleanora noticed an emptiness to her surroundings. No fishmongers called out their catch of the day; no brewsters squabbled over the quality of bread and beer; no children ran through the alleys, laughing and singing the latest rhyme from Father Pietro's lessons; no soul approached and asked for guidance about sex or silphium dosages. An unsettling quiet thrummed through her bones. She knew where she'd find the missing sounds. Those not swept away by disease now gathered at the base of the Basilica di Sant'Apollinare, listening to Tiago Mancini's heresies.

Eleanora breathed deep. She had no need to walk past the Basilica on her way to Enzo's villa. Her sisters had reported Mancini's speeches in detail. He'd been a flea before, irritating and easily excommunicated. The pestilence changed that. Those left behind found little comfort in their familiar prayers and Mancini gave survivors a preferable alternative. Steadfast and resolute, Eleanora walked behind the crowd, listening in full while showing no signs of attention.

"...a tool of the demons. Their piss-colored resin bricks are nothing but stains on our souls. The sisters pray not to the Lord, but to their devil-made-saint. Blessed Paul only paid the sisters heed as a means to convert our Roman ancestors. He was but a man, feeble and misguided by the wicked, fork-tongued Mattea."

A few of the crowd broke away as she passed, their conflicted glances more frustration than reassurance. Most stayed behind. Eleanora wondered which among them had attacked her sisters in the night. Wondered if they'd do the same to her, given the chance.

Her chin remained high as she marched along the Via Cesarea and crossed the bridge to the Romeo Vecchia. The Roman Quarter. A haunted air surrounded the buildings on the other side of the Uniti River. Some said the spirits of the old empire clung to the stones, unwelcome within the proximity of the Basilica's holy aura.

Enzo's villa stood in defiance of its surroundings, its polished pillars thwarting the spread of the old quarter's decline. Eleanora hobbled up the stairs, one at a time, and smiled as his servants scurried into action. By the time her aching body reached the top, Enzo was at the door to greet her. "Nora!" A smile parted his oiled Greek beard. "A pleasure to see you."

"And you as well." Eleanora forced a smile into place. It didn't seem fair that Enzo's hair kept its dark color when hers was already white, nor that his oval face remained free of wrinkles. But the heavenly spheres cared nothing for fairness and Enzo made up for his pleasant visage with his impropriety.

"Come, come inside." He turned and offered his elbow, showing off the delicate embroidery on his silk sleeves. Eleanora's hand slid over the fabric as she threaded her arm around his. "We can't have the church's favorite courtesan lingering in the street."

Eleanora thumped his elbow with the head of her cane. "I've not had a patron since I've become Abbess, Enzo. You know that."

"And Ravenna is all the poorer for it." Enzo guided her through the halls, slowing his pace whenever their path crossed one of his newer frescos. Freshly painted nymphs and satyrs galivanted with a bevy of mythological heroes on his walls. "As is my collection of bedside gossip. My Lydia, dear as she is, shares nothing of the men she'd entertained before. Not even the stories with names hidden behind code. I fear I'll never again hear the exploits of Signor Mitre and his obsession for feet." He shook his head in a show of disappointment. "Tell me your other sisters aren't so tight-lipped."

"Of course they're tight-lipped. They exercise every day."

Though the easy joke tasted bitter on Eleanora's tongue, Enzo's barking laugh echoed off the pillars as he led her into the atrium. The surprise breakfast spared no extravagance. An outstretched goose wing on the low table held a small pyramid of bright red shrimp. Beside it, a honeyed arrangement of dates and figs rested inside a cage of sliced melon. A late servant rushed in with roasted sausages, their juices bubbling beneath their casings. Enzo plucked one from the platter and reclined across his chaise, devouring the meat in two bites.

Nora Romano would have stretched herself on the chaise beside his own and feasted like the Romans of old. Part of her still longed to do so. She and Enzo could disappear into reverie for hours, swimming through shared memories of better times. But the decadent aromas twisted Eleanora's stomach and tightened her jaw. She sat, back straight, hands clasped, and waited for Enzo to follow suit.

Enzo was halfway through his third sausage before he noticed. He motioned for a napkin and took his time wiping the grease away. "This is a formal meeting, then?"

"I wish it wasn't." She selected a piece of melon out of politeness and held it between her fingers. "I need your help arranging Tiago Mancini's exile."

His nostrils flared with a sharp intake of air. He sat transfixed, his gaze falling short of her face. The muscles of his jaw bunched and tightened before he uttered a response. "Isn't he already excommunicated?"

"It's not enough."

"Not enough?" He scoffed. "There's no worse punishment in Rome's arsenal. How could it not be enough?"

Eleanora focused on the nearby flowerbed, where red sprays of valerian cut through the foliage. Even the plants gave her no peace. "Every day is a new discovery. Deserted markets whenever a sister goes out in her habit. Curses shouted from hidden alcoves. Buckets of rotting fish dumped over our walls. A sister impaled in effigy at our gates." She sucked a calming breath through her teeth. The memory of her blood-stiff cowl returned, as did the panicked rambling of Sylvia's prayers. "I told my sisters to endure, that love and compassion should be the answer. And now Julia may not survive the night." The juice from the melon crept down her fingers, following the trails previously taken by Julia's blood. She'd have to wash her hands again. "She and Sylvia were attending a woman in labor. They wore no habits nor carried any silphium."

"And you're certain this is all Tiago Mancini's doing?"

There was no compassion to Enzo's voice. It hit like a wave of cold seawater, aloof from the weeks of harassment and pain. Eleanora returned to the atrium and searched her friend's face for scraps of concern or empathy. Signs that he'd heard her. His eyes remained empty and blank. Her tone slowed to match. "What do you mean by that?"

Enzo gave a half-hearted shrug and selected a shrimp from the top of the pyramid. "The people are angry. There's not a family in this city untouched by illness. Constantinople has already abandoned Ravenna. We called upon Rome for help, yet the Pope was more concerned with the battles in Hispania than with his flock." He tossed the shrimp into his mouth and swallowed it, tail and all. "Nobody needs Tiago Mancini to facilitate a grudge."

"Rome isn't entirely focused on Hispania." She grit her teeth; Enzo didn't need to know about the westbound shipment. "And the abbey isn't Rome. We've been here. We've always cared for the people."

"Of course you're here. Rome needs someone to grow their silphium for them. It only grows in the marsh." He ate another shrimp, this time spitting the tail onto the ground. "Without it, there are no sisters riding the rich and affluent. No women in their brocades and silks attending mass just so they can purchase tea. No ships trading silphium for

Byzantine silver. And there'd certainly be no place to bury all their coin from these activities." He held up his hands in defense. "I'm only saying what I've heard on the streets."

Eleanora narrowed her eyes as she placed the melon slice back on the platter. Enzo wouldn't hear anything from the streets unless someone tore the curtains from his litter. "The abbey doesn't have a buried horde of silver. It barely has the funds to keep the girls fed." That rumor predated Tiago Mancini by several years, but he'd no doubt given it new life. He'd started many of his own. Half of Ravenna now believed her sisters responsible for the pestilence. "The Pope doesn't make us stay with a new mother until her babe suckles its first milk. The bishops don't make us mix powders for a man whose stalk no longer stands. And I have yet to see a priest sit with a girl during her first blood, teaching her how to tie a moon belt and make a glass of silphium tea. We are more than the church's—" She struggled to say the word. "—prostitutes."

"You need not convince me. I tell everyone of your charitable acts. You can even ask Lydia, when she returns from her mother's." Enzo searched the table with an outstretched hand before leaning towards the kitchen doors. "Wine! There isn't any wine!" He fell back into the chaise with a sigh. "This house falls apart without her." A weary eye wandered back to Eleanora's seat. "All of these plants are hers, you know. She never stopped growing things after she left the abbey. Sometimes I think she misses trudging through the marsh at dawn, checking the silphium for worms and rot. Are the stalks really so hard to keep alive?"

"They are. The old empire believed it extinct before Saint Paul converted Mattea and her girls. Her miracle was keeping her plants alive after she'd been martyred." Eleanora stopped her lesson short. If she let her friend distract her that easily, she'd accomplish nothing. "This isn't a casual meeting, Enzo."

Another slow sigh escaped, this time accompanied by the roll of his eyes. "It would be no use speaking to the Exarch about Mancini. The man would only run off to his uncle's estates in Padua. He'd be just as rich and well connected there as he is here."

"I don't care about his riches or his family. I care about him stirring a riot."

"Of course, of course." A servant appeared, sliding the stem of a goblet between Enzo's fingers. Her friend took a healthy drink before the servant made their way around the table. "But the Exarch has to keep the peace. To keep the peace, he has to keep all of the dukes equally miserable. Exiling Mancini would disrupt that balance."

Eleanora looked into her own goblet, her stomach too turbulent for the smell. A charmless hag stared back. She tried on her smile once more. "If it were something easy, I wouldn't have come to you for help." As she spoke, she wondered what help Enzo would provide. If he would even bother once she left his villa. If there was anyone left in Ravenna willing to listen.

"That is true. You usually handle such matters yourself." He swirled his wine with a lazy hand before taking another drink. "I've always admired that about you, Nora. You're the only friend I have that never asks for anything."

The words circled Eleanora's mind like the wine in his goblet. The only things she'd ever desired from Enzo had been his time and companionship. Valuable, but easy to give when one's friends are few. She and Enzo both understood what it meant to start fresh in a new city. But as she reviewed their lives since that shared boat trip, she saw how much of it had been a river, flowing only one direction.

"And you have asked for so much in return." She forced her voice into an even measure to keep her frustration from boiling over. "You would not be Harbormaster without my introductions, nor would you have this house and all its furnishings without my pillow talk."

Enzo snorted at that, his lips twisting into a scowl. "So now you've come to collect. Just like everyone else." He sloshed another drought of wine before slamming the empty goblet on the table. "What happens after Mancini's exiled? Have you considered that, Nora? When the anger and bitterness has lost its idol, where does it go? It won't evaporate. Someone else will rise from that rabble and you'll be back here, again and again, begging for help instead of fixing the problem yourself."

"How would you suggest I handle this myself?"

"Perhaps the sisters should have thought more about their future. If they had taken off their silken habits and used their favors on the priesthood, then maybe this city would have more favor with Rome. Or perhaps they should have plied their trade on pilgrimage. Constantinople would love a sister or two setting up an abbey beside the Hagia Sophia. Then Ravenna would have endured the pestilence. The people would be content and your sisters wouldn't be targets in the night."

Eleanora shot from her seat. Every inch of her vibrated with fury. "I can see coming here was a mistake." She snatched her cane from the floor, the pain in her spine no match for her anger. "Thank you for the meal."

She had escaped the atrium and made her way down the hall before Enzo's voice called out behind her. "Nora, please."

Eleanora didn't bother turning around. "You will address me as Reverend Mother or not at all."

"Please, come back. We can still finish our meal. Perhaps talk of pleasant things."

"Goodbye, Signor Franzese."

"You can be such a stubborn sow, you know that, Nora." His large hand clamped onto her shoulder. "At least let me hire you a litter."

His touch was ice on her skin. She froze in place, her jaw locked too tight to chatter. She was in his villa, surrounded by his servants, in a city that would sooner see her dead. "Release me," she said, reaching for one of the few weapons she had, "or I tell Lydia secrets you'd rather she not hear."

The hand came off her shoulder. She didn't look back as she staggered through the halls, nor as she exited the villa and hobbled down the stairs to the street. Her neck, too stiff to turn, kept her eyes on the road. Hot tears blurred her vision, but she refused to blink them away.

Dread crept into her mind as she plotted a new route back to the abbey. She would have to avoid the Basilica. The crowd would still be there, if not Mancini himself. Ejecting Mancini from Ravenna would be nearly impossible now. Eleanora imagined him gloating from his perch, the lies spilling from his lips onto the crowd below. None of it mattered. She could write the Exarch until her hand fell off and he'd still defer to Enzo's judgment.

Her memories of their friendship twisted and warped, their visage now bleached under an unforgiving sun. She'd given so much of herself, only to leave his villa with nothing. And yet, Enzo's words and inaction echoed beyond him. She'd given her life to the abbey, too. Days in the marsh followed nights on her back, over and over until her body surrendered its youth. Rome had more than excommunication in its arsenal and yet her girls remained undefended.

She urged herself into a faster stride. The sooner she crossed the river, the sooner she could leave Enzo on the other side. When her feet touched the bridge, her lip trembled, threatening to release a sob. Eleanora lied to her body. The bridge was no different than earlier that morning. No less difficult than climbing the abbey stairs. Her feet plodded up the incline, step by arduous step, until she reached the top.

She turned then, for one last look, and slipped on a loose stone. The jolt shoved her body out of alignment. Her hands came up in a panic, flinging the cane out of reach. The world tilted further and further off its axis as she flailed.

The ground met her hip.

A bone cracked.

End over end, she tumbled to the bottom of the far side of the bridge. Eleanora lay in the road, her cheek pressed against the smooth cobblestones, and cursed herself. The angels should have turned her into a pillar of salt for daring one last glance. For wanting all of the naiveté Nora Romero once had. It was gone now, a relic on the other side of the Uniti. She shoved her hands beneath her torso and pushed herself up.

Pain flooded Eleanora's senses as her body crashed back onto the stones. Harpy-pitched screams echoed off the empty street and hot tears gushed over her cheeks. All remaining barriers crumbled under the onslaught. She sobbed without shame or remorse, lost on a street she'd always known, mourning a past she could no longer visit.

Unable to leave the road, she wept herself into exhaustion. It was only when the tears slowed that the emptiness of the midday street transformed. Shadows retreated from the walls. Spies peered through half-closed windows. The men who attacked her sisters waited in the next alley, ready to strike again. She could do nothing but lay there and wait, a drained husk exposed for the world to see. Her first night as a sister held less vulnerability.

Footsteps tapped down the bridge. Eleanora turned as far as her body allowed, unable to see who approached. A shudder ran through her. As she waited for the blow, she imagined her sisters. They'd still be doing laundry, trading hushed secrets from the night before, distracting each other from their new reality. She thought of Julia, wandering in and out of consciousness. She'd failed them. Eleanora stretched her arms against the stones, just as she had in the chapel that morning, and prayed.

Her cane clattered beside her arm. She opened her eyes to see a tiny pair of bare feet beside it. "You hurt, Sister?" A young girl, no more than thirteen, crouched low to look Eleanora square in the face. "Nonna heard you scream. She told me to help."

From her viewpoint, the sun haloed the girl's soft brown hair, turning her into an angel. Eleanora didn't know whether to laugh or cry. She hadn't the strength for either. "Old hips like these can't withstand a fall," she said at last.

"Nonna breaks her hip lots too. Same place every time." The girl looked Eleanora over with all the wisdom a child could muster. "If you can roll over, I can hold you up and help you get home."

Her back molars ground together. A litter would be faster, and far more comfortable, than hobbling home, but Eleanora still had her pride. With a shaking hand, she rolled an inch at a time until she rocked on the good edge of her hip. The whole area burned like fire as the girl positioned her body against Eleanora's, guiding her to stand.

They walked slowly at first, one arduous step after the other, until the two of them developed a rhythm. Cane, girl, hop, cane, girl, hop. Eleanora smiled, despite the pain. "You do have practice in this." The girl smiled back, but made no other response as they drew closer to the Basilica.

Eleanora locked her jaw, ready for the worst. Mancini was blessedly gone, but his disciples still lingered in the square. Her lumbering pace allowed Eleanora time to study their faces. While several men glared back, the women around her wore their anger and resentment like a mask. Only their eyes bore evidence of the anxieties that lay beneath. Fear of the pestilence. Fear of the mob. Fear of displaying their sympathies and being punished by the crowd. Some women dared express a measure of pity, but no one approached to help.

The girl's shoulders curled inward as her gaze darted through the crowd. Her spine adopted an apprehensive tremble. Eleanora couldn't let that stand. "What is your name, child?"

The girl's wide eyes returned to Eleanora's face. "Adri."

"And you live with your grandmother?"

She nodded. "Ma and Pa died last winter. Older brother not too long after. Just me and Nonna left."

"It's a brave thing you're doing, escorting a sister home." A small smile tugged at the corners of Adri's lips as her trembling eased. "Brave girls always carry Saint Mattea's favor. Has your grandmother been able to feed you?"

Her nod was more eager this time around. "She's the only laundress left. I've washed stockings every day for two weeks now. Bringing you home means I keep dry hands." Her smile turned mischievous. "We can slow up, if you wish."

The laugh hurt Eleanora's ribs. She kept Adri talking, asking her every question that came to mind. She attended Father Pietro's lessons every week. He had called her lazy for not learning letters, but praised her memory and cleanliness. She made rosemary soap better than anyone in Ravenna, just as her mother had done. Her grandmother crafted stories often, mostly about the clothes they washed. Eleanora forgave her for not having a favorite Bible verse and listened as she shared her grandmother's fantastical story of the dozen-stain tunic. Her mother taught her about blood and belts and how to keep children at bay when silphium proved too expensive. Eleanora answered what questions remained with a sister's blunt honesty. As they walked together, her pains eased, the distraction meant for Adri working on her as well.

When they finally reached the abbey, the place buzzed with activity. Her sisters rushed between the dormitory and refectory, arms full with fresh linens. All along her walls, dozens of professional soldiers organized themselves into smaller divisions. Some checked their swords for wear while others snuck glances at the sisters' clinging habits and uncovered tresses. Father Pietro stood in the center of it all, his freshly-shaved head gleaming in the sunlight.

"Reverend Mother! Come, come see!" He said before realizing her injury. He snapped his fingers at a pair of soldiers beside him. "Help the Reverend Mother inside, quick now."

She leaned as far as her hip allowed and whispered into Adri's ear. "Go to the refectory and tell Sister Sylvia what happened." The girl barely had time to leave her side before the pair pushed themselves under her arms. They carried her between them like a rag doll, her toes barely touching the stone path. Her cheeks warmed despite herself. It had been several years since she was last squeezed between two men. "Have you two never used a litter chair before? Put me down." Eleanora cringed when they placed her back on her feet, her hip throbbing with its own pulse. "What is all this, Father? There must be fifty men here."

"Sixty, Reverend Mother." His smile beamed like the rest of him. "Sixty trained men at arms, as well as weapons and armor. Gifts from the Duke of Naples." He turned back to survey the lot. "Magnificent, aren't they?"

Eleanora's jaw gaped at the sight. "A gift for the abbey?" Patron gifts, even lavish ones, weren't a surprise, but no one had made a gift of a small army before. Stranger still, the Duke of Naples had never been their patron.

"A gift for the Pope," he corrected. "The Duke wished prayers to be said for him and his men before the next campaign. One does acquire sins while in battle." He nodded with a knowing tilt of his head. He'd said many prayers for rich warriors before. "Pope Gregory directed them here with all haste. They're to stay until the next silphium harvest, then guard the resin until it reaches Constantinople."

A cloud fell over the abbey, removing the gleam from the priest's head. "They're guarding the harvest?" Eleanora asked.

"When the Pope heard of Mancini's continuing blasphemy, he feared the silphium would be vandalized. Our predicament against the Moors is too precarious to allow something so valuable to be destroyed." Father Pietro shook his head. "They're to guard the marsh in shifts, three a day. They'll report back to the abbey at the completion of each shift. The sisters will sleep two to a room until they leave." The tendons in his throat tightened as he turned his head away. "It is his Holiness's wish that the sisters give these soldiers aid and comfort for the duration of their stay."

"Aid and comfort." Eleanora spat the phrase back at the priest. "And are we to be compensated for this aid and comfort? Have these soldiers come with six months of food? Did they bring their own linens and men to wash them? Are they paying for the sisters' time away from paying patrons? Or is this abbey to be used and discarded like a lambskin sheath?"

Father Pietro offered a helpless shrug. "The abbey does not exist without the marsh. One takes precedence over the other."

Her gaze darted back to the men who had carried her before. "Bring me a chair. I wish to go to the infirmary."

The pair had the good sense to run. A cautious stare filled Father Pietro's face as he waited for the men to return. "Their commander desired to organize the marsh's defense with you. I can have him brought to the infirmary, if you—"

"Have you taken Sister Julia's confession?"

"I…" he swallowed. "Yes, Reverend Mother."

"Then your task here is done." Her cane trembled, barely keeping her upright. The pain tripled in a matter of moments. By the time the men arrived with a litter chair, Eleanora's ears pounded with an echoing pulse. Father Pietro stayed in place, his head swiveling between Eleanora and the exit. She refused to look at him as she eased into the chair. "You have a mass to coordinate and students to teach, Father. I suggest you spend your time wisely."

The pair carried her away before she could hear the priest's response. Her chair wobbled and shook between their inexperienced hold, irritating Eleanora all the more. She didn't address them. Her attendants could have been Alexander of Macedon and Julius Caesar for all she cared, so long as they didn't speak. When they set her down, she ordered them away before shuffling and heaving herself into the nearest cot.

Julia lay in the next cot over. Eleanora hadn't planned that. She wasn't quite ready to see her again. The swelling had gone down around Julia's eyes, but her nose was still fat as a pear. Someone had wrapped a new bandage around the gash over her temple. She slept with her mouth closed, hiding the broken teeth.

She hadn't been beautiful. Her dull brown hair hung limp from her skull and her too-tall frame intimidated most of the casual patrons. All of Julia's partners were developed over time: men who talked of trade and politics long into the night. No topic was too boring for her. She played the eager student to their egos, stroking them within before laying a hand on their laps. It was a gift and Nora envied it.

Three men proposed to Julia in the last year alone. She'd refused them all. Her love was for the Sisterhood. She visited abbeys as far away as Britannia and Jerusalem, safeguarding shipments of resin to the less hospitable climates. Eleanora feared, with every ship she took, that they'd never see each other again. She even bought her a dagger to hide under her habit. But Julia always came back, laden with silver and gifts and stories of sisters growing silphium in abandoned Roman bathhouses.

A four-block journey was nothing compared to Sister Julia's travels. She'd even left her dagger in her room. And yet she might never leave the abbey again.

Eleanora didn't look up when Sister Sylvia entered. "Reverend Mother? A young girl said you fell on the bridge. Are you hurt?"

"The hip will mend." Eleanora was sure of that. Anything more drastic would have hurt far worse. Her eyes lifted to the doorway, observing the continued chaos over Sylvia's shoulder. "All this over a stubborn marsh reed." A rueful chuckle escaped her throat. "They once told stories about Emperor Nero eating the last silphium stalk, thinking it nothing more than a piece of celery. Perhaps the Romans should have eaten the whole forsaken marsh."

A grimace of a smile tugged at Sylvia's lips. "Father Pietro suggested a curfew for the sisters."

"How like him." Her eyes fell back to Julia. She would never have settled for a curfew. She didn't settle for anything. "A curfew would only hinder us. The sisters are going to spend the whole night in the marsh."

"Reverend Mother?"

Eleanora scanned the infirmary for additional ears before motioning for Sylvia to come closer. "I want you to divide the sisters into two groups. The first group is to spend the night finding every pot we have in the abbey. The other group will keep an eye on these soldiers. God willing, they don't start patrols until tomorrow." She closed her eyes and silently prayed for guidance. "When they settle in for sleep or sex, the remaining sisters will sneak out to the marsh and pull every last plant up by the roots."

Sylvia's body went stiff as a tree and her eyes grew to the size of walnuts. She tiptoed away, one step after another, until she reached back and closed the infirmary door. "That's a terrible jest, Reverend Mother."

"This is no jest."

"You can't mean it. The plants are Rome's property. Stealing silphium means stealing from the Church." She knelt by Eleanora's cot. "The Pope will confiscate the abbey. Every sister will be driven from this place. We'll be branded and shamed through the streets."

"We already walk these streets with indignity. We are the well-groomed tools at the end of the church's arm. And now, when we are bent and overused and calling for help, they toss us aside to defend the fruit of our labor instead." The truth cut deep as she uttered it. "It is time we turn to the people. Give them cause to see our value. Save twelve plants for ourselves. We'll teach the women of Ravenna to care for the rest."

"We will be excommunicated, Reverend Mother."

"We will be living in Blessed Mattea's glory. She could not have meant for silphium to become a tool of a distant power, used as currency to fuel a war. She meant the plant for her sisters. All of them."

Tears fell from Sylvia's bruised eyes. "The plants are too stubborn. They won't take to pots. The stalks will wither and die."

"And we are stubborn women." Eleanora cupped Sylvia's head between her hands. "The stalks are no match for us. We know the soil, the water humors, the lighting and the temperature. We can germ a seed inside a cat's dung if we must." Her breath hissed through clenched teeth. "It is not enough to take the plant from Rome's hands. If we grew it inside the abbey and sold it ourselves, they'd only seize it again. We must take the value away from silphium and put it inside our skills and knowledge. That is the best way to protect ourselves."

"Reverend Mother, I beg you." She shook her head, her hood striking her cheeks. "I can't go out there. I can't. Not after last night. Please don't make me do it."

Guilt pierced Eleanora's heart. Her poor sister had already suffered so much. She brushed her thumbs over Sylvia's tears, searching for the strength she once held. "But can you organize it?"

Sylvia swallowed a sob. Her lips pursed in and out and Eleanora could see the wheels turning behind her eyes. She drew a breath of deep resolve before speaking again. "I think so. The soldiers are almost settled. I'll have the sisters stage games in the refectory. Games always call for wine."

Eleanora touched her forehead to Sylvia's as gingerly as she could. "I'm so sorry I sent you out last night. I beg your forgiveness, sister."

A shudder rolled through the younger woman's body. "It was not you who swung the club." Sylvia placed her hands on the cot's edge and stood. "It will be a long day for everyone. I had best get started."

She dried her eyes and opened the door she'd just closed. Eleanora waited until Sylvia was completely gone before removing her hood and cowl. Her gray tresses fell in a thick web, but she did not reach for a comb. Anyone who came calling would see her, tangles and all.

There was no surety to her plan. Mancini had a grip on Ravenna, one built on hate and bitter pain. And Rome's punishment would be an added weight to her soul. But Saint Paul taught of love. She believed the people could trust in them again.

She was asking much of her sisters. The hood's silk bunched beneath her fingers as she laid back on the cot. "Saint Mattea," she started, swallowing the pain behind her voice, "as you have watched over me, I pray you now watch over these brave women. Guard their steps. Guide their hands. Keep safe their hearts and deliver them from harm."

SELKIE

Ian R. MacLeod

Bethany Flett is out on the shore collecting driftwood when she notices the falling star. She watches it disappear into the open sea beyond the navigation lights of the British Grand Fleet and the encircling hills of Scapa Flow.

Although she wasn't taught such things at school, she knows from the books she's borrowed from Kirkwall Library that shooting stars are merely stray lumps of rock heating up as they pass through the atmosphere, even if many in her village would insist they're souls cast down from heaven.

She picks her way back to the family longhouse, where tonight's supper of neeps and mutton is waiting, even if it consists mostly of last year's potatoes. But Bethany knows Ma does her best and the proper meat is kept for the men of the household, who are out catching fish in the sailboat and won't be back until morning.

Seeing to the twins afterwards, she notices how cramped their bunks have become and wonders where they will fit with the longhouse already so overcrowded. Something has to give and she can guess what that something might be, seeing as she's the only grown daughter in the family. Become a herring girl, she supposes, following the shoals up and down the mainland docks. That, or marry a fisherman.

"Give us a story, Beth."

"Yes—give us a story."

The twins love a tale from history, the more gruesome the better, and wriggle with excitement as she tells them about King Henry VIII of England, although they're disappointed that he only lopped off two of his six wives' heads and not at all interested to know they'd all be Roman Catholics if he hadn't divorced Catherine of Aragon. When they're finally settled, and with Ma drowsing in her chair beside the fire, Bethany unrolls her straw mattress across the flagging and thinks of that shooting star as she drifts toward sleep.

* * *

The Flett sailboat returns with the morning tide and the men on board are shouting excitedly. Maybe a surprisingly rich catch, or some contraband tobacco or whisky? The whole village gathers on the stone quay to find out and gasps as the body of a man is laid there, wet and naked.

"We caught him out yonder." Cousin Murdo points toward the lip of the Pentland Firth.

He's breathing, but there's an ugly rent in his left thigh. Pale and ill though he is, there's a brownish hue to his skin, and his hair is golden-curly. He looks, there's no other word for it, *foreign*.

He coughs. His eyes flicker. Everyone steps back.

"Where...am...I..." He tries to sit up. "You..." Each word is clear enough in its own way, but oddly mangled. "Rescued me from the water...in that..." His young-seeming face creases. "...antique vessel..."

Nobody says anything. Everyone is watching.

"Where *is* this...?"

"You're in Kellness, son." Bethany's Pa steps forward. "On the Islands of Orkney."

"And you're really *here?* You're not virtuals? And why the old-time clothing…?"

One or two puzzled laughs.

Pained though he looks, he almost laughs as well. "This sure as hell ain't Kansas, Toto."

"Toto?" Pa frowns. "Is that your name? And isn't Kansas over in America?"

A short debate follows as to what to do with him. The villagers certainly won't hand him over to the Police in Kirkwall, as they have little time for the authorities. And the idea of sending for Doctor Harkness is soon vetoed; he's from far-off Aberdeen and isn't to be trusted. In the end, it's agreed to put him in the old smokehouse and see what happens.

* * *

All day, the children run around the smokehouse, shrieking and excited, as Bethany gets on with her regular chores. In the afternoon, deep booms echo around the hills as the ships of the Grand Fleet test their guns, preparing for the coming war against Germany. Then, as evening grows, she heads out to the shore again to collect driftwood. No sign of any shooting stars tonight, but she notices the heads of maybe half a dozen seals out in the bay, looking inland. The men might say they're a fish-killing nuisance, but she finds their presence companionable.

She walks on, picking up a few odd lumps of coal, which are always useful, then notices something shining at the edge of the waves. A jellyfish? The thing is there as she stoops to prod it in a shallow rockpool. Then, somehow, it isn't. It seems to be flickering with bits of the sky and the sea, almost like a mirror, and when she finally manages to lay it across a rock, it's surprisingly heavy.

Now that she has some idea of the shape of it, the sense of its strangeness grows rather than diminishes. Although it's still trying to take on the colors of the surrounding shore—

even her own silhouette—it has the definite outline of a human body. It's even topped by a sort of bubble where the head might be. It looks almost alive, but she somehow knows it isn't. That, and there's a tear where the left thigh might be.

After checking she's still alone, she grasps the thing, which feels dry and smooth instead of wet and slippery, and heads across the shore toward the far promontory. There, she shifts a few rocks, shoves it into a crevice, and covers it over.

* * *

She's the last to unroll her mattress in the crowded longhouse that evening, but even then sleep won't come. There's so much superstitious nonsense talked in Kellness that it's hard to know where the truth begins. Eating a fish from the tail being bad luck and washing a man's clothes while he's out at sea meaning certain drowning. White cats and black cats and whistling in the wind and not clicking glasses to save the souls of sailors. And selkies.

Not mermaids, but nevertheless creatures of the sea who come to the land in the shape of seals, cast off their outer skin, and then seem almost entirely human. Not just that, but they're so beautiful people can't help but fall in love with them, although the stories generally end badly. For selkies pine for the sea and long to return to it. At least, that is, unless you can find their shed skin on the shore and hide it away from them, then they have to stay with you forever.

* * *

Another morning dawns bright and clear and Bethany heads over to the smokehouse as soon as she's finished turning the peat.

The stranger looks even paler and the smell of old fish and smoke is overpowered by sweat and illness. The blankets he's been given are the ones used to clean up the ewes at lambing and the rags that bind his wound aren't much better. And he's mumbling odd words. Stuff about *jugships*—jump

ships?—and enemy *host-stiles*—hostiles? and *nukes*—dukes?—
and a lost *slipsuit*, and something about *incoming*.

"What am I doing here…?" he asks, in a brief moment
of clarity.

"We're taking care of you," she says. Still, she's shocked
to see how little effort has been made, when she knows from
reading about Florence Nightingale in the Crimea that the
proper treatment of wounded patients begins with simple
hygiene.

She scrubs her hands raw and collects some of the clean
rags that the women use for their monthlies. The man's eyes
roll and his moans rise as she washes out the sodden wound,
which looks more as if it's been burned than cut into him.
Runners of infection are spreading toward his groin and she
doubts if cleanliness alone will save him.

* * *

Over the next couple of days and nights, she spares what
time she can to change the man's dressing. She does other
things for him as well, of course, and the whole village is
soon tutting and nodding—saying he'll be Bethany Flett's
man if he happens to survive, will that Toto from Kansas.

Sometimes he curses, or cries out more strange phrases.
Stuff about *shield cities* and *seeker mines* and *slipsuits* and
backjumps, or what might be people's names, and even odder
sounds that barely seem like words at all. Just like the strange
object she found out on the shore, her sense of who and
what he is feels flickery and blurry.

But there's one thing she's sure about. There's another
book she's borrowed from Kirkwall Library—a rather
fanciful novel—and she knows he's no more Toto from
Kansas than she's Dorothy.

* * *

Finally, toward the end of the third day, his flesh starts
to cool and he settles into something closer to sleep than
unconsciousness. Stepping out from the smokehouse,

Bethany finds that the glow of another sunset still fills the sky, vying with the stars and the twinkle of the Grand Fleet's navigation lights.

After checking that nobody's watching, she crosses the shore to the promontory, shifts the pile of stones and reaches into the crevice. It's still there, dry and smooth to the touch, like no skin or fabric she's ever encountered.

Laying it out on the heather, she notices a kind of a barnacle-like protrusion on the right hip as it assumes the colors of twilight. It comes loose when she touches it, feels solid. Yet, amazingly, it makes an exact fit for her fingers and gives off a deep humming. Not only that, but something odd has happened to her vision. Everything's suddenly incredibly clear, with lines and figures forming around things as she looks at them. Her gaze spins toward the Grand Fleet and the humming intensifies and the letters and numbers solidify into a sharp cross centered on the hull of *HMS Dreadnought,* the pride of the Royal Navy, which seems so close she can see the faces of the sailors at their stations.

Her palms sweat. Her skin tingles. The thing in her hand is waiting. With the slightest effort of will, she could…but no, no. *No.* Something untwists and the power subsides and ordinary twilight returns even before she's placed the thing back into its barnacle-like protrusion.

She stuffs what must be a slipsuit back into the crack and covers it back over with rocks, vowing never again to touch it.

* * *

The man's eyes are open and his temperature has faded when she looks in next morning.

"Where I am, it used to be part of a place called… Scotland? Right?"

"Was the last time I heard," she says, deciding to put his odd use of tense down to the residue of his fever. "Although we Orcadians like to think we're our own people."

"What's your name?"

"Bethany Flett."

"You saved my life."

"The men in the sailboat did that. I just helped with your wound and fever."

"What time is it?"

"I don't own a pocket watch, but I'd say just past noon."

"I mean the date."

"I'd have to check that, too. But it's about the tenth of June. And it's definitely a Wednesday."

"And the year?"

"Nineteen fourteen."

He closes his eyes and seems almost to stop breathing.

* * *

Even as he recovers, he keeps asking ridiculous questions.

"Those guns I keep hearing—are they real?"

"That would be the Grand Fleet."

"Who are they fighting?"

"No one at the moment. They're just testing their artillery. But it'll probably be the Germans."

"Germany—isn't that a country in old Europe?"

Sometimes his fever returns but that happens less and less as he recovers and soon he's able to get up and see to his own needs, and gains an appetite, and pretends to box with the kids as they run in and out of the smokehouse, and learns to talk more slowly so people can understand him, although, along with his gaining strength, Bethany detects an increased wariness.

There's loss and puzzlement in his eyes, too. He'll stare for ages at everyday things—a bowl, a rowboat, the clogs he's been lent to wear, the battleships across the water—as if they're entirely new to him. But he can smile as well, and hobble about using a stick for support, poking here and there along the shore as if he's searching for something.

He keeps himself useful by whittling new ash-pegs for the boats, but when Bethany notices him one evening as she returns from collecting driftwood, he's simply sitting on the quay and staring out at nothing. There's an odd noise— *click whirr*—which makes her think of that thing of his, the slipsuit, although as she gets closer she sees that it's only Pa's spring-loaded tape measure.

"I'd stop playing with that if I were you. My father bought it in Aberdeen and he won't want it broken."

"Oh…!" He starts, then relaxes. "It's you, Bethany. What gets me is why they made the metal tape flat instead of curving it. That way, it wouldn't flop about when you use it."

Bethany puts down her basket of driftwood. "You're not really called Toto, are you? And you're not from Kansas."

"What makes you think that?" *Click, whirr.* He's still playing with the tape measure.

"Toto's a dog from a novel about a girl called Dorothy who gets blown away from Kansas by a tornado. It's a work of fiction."

"And here was me thinking it was an old movie. But I suppose you don't have movies yet? Silents, maybe."

"I have no idea what you're talking about."

"Don't you even have moving pictures?"

"Kirkwall has two picture houses that show films, if that's what you mean."

"Fil-*ums*? Films! Right, films—picture houses! And there was probably some antique novel about the *Wizard of Oz* before the old two-dee. But I'm just a grunt, spam in a can, so what the hell do I know…?" Then he falls silent. "So," he says eventually, "where do you think I'm really from?"

"I believe," she says, "that you're probably from the future."

"What makes you think a thing like that?"

"I—I saw something falling from the sky. It was on the night you were rescued. That, and some of the things you've been saying, especially when you had a fever."

"Not that I'm saying you're wrong. But I'm surprised you can come up with such an idea."

"I'm not entirely ignorant. There's another novel I've read. It's called *The Time Machine,* although I suppose you'd probably say it was another movie."

* * *

I'm just a grunt—that's the one thing he keeps telling her as they walk together and the guns boom out across Scapa Flow. A *grunt* being a simple solider, which is all he is, or maybe a sailor, seeing as he talks about a ship, albeit one he calls a *jumpship* which sails close to space and can somehow do things with its *temporal trajectory.* It was bearing him and half a dozen other *grunts* toward their *mission target,* and they were wearing *slipsuits,* which was what saved him as he tumbled through the atmosphere and struck the ocean, then released him as water flooded in and he was picked up by the Flett family sailboat.

But his future—the year 2121—is nothing like that encountered by H.G. Wells' time traveler. No peaceful, ineffectual Eloi, no ape-like Morlocks, but a world composed of *power-blocks* and *shield-cities,* and a war which seems to have been going on since before he was born in what he calls a *shanty-burrow* in a place Bethany would probably think of as the old state of Texas.

He talks of the seas rising and how many of the world's great cities—at least those that haven't been turned to glass by *nukes*—have been flooded. That, and of old diseases returning and new ones arising. And people on the march— vast migrations—and millions starving. And war. Yes, war. Which is why he's a grunt, for he has no *memory implants,* no *intelligence enhancements,* and his *genetic profile* always meant he'd never amount to anything.

So what he needs to find is his slipsuit. Not that it would help him get back to the time he's from, but because, as well as having *active camouflage* and something he calls an *AI*—she thought at first he was just saying "aye"—it also possesses a *disruptor,* which can reduce anything which isn't properly shielded to random atoms.

"So what would you do?" she asks as they pick amid the rockpools looking for debris. "I mean, if you found it?"

He shrugs, leaning against his stick. "I don't know. But it would sure as hell be *something.*"

"Would you…" She nods over toward the Grand Fleet. "…join the British Navy?"

He laughs. Shakes his head. "I wouldn't need to. I'd *be* the fucking navy!"

She pretends to consider this and ignores the profanity. Perhaps she's testing her own resolve by bringing him this close to the promontory where his slipsuit lies hidden. That, or she's seeing if the thing will respond to his presence. But Toto just stands there, wincing and frustrated. After all, he's just a grunt, and the power of his slipsuit would be extraordinary.

Bethany can almost feel the warning thunder of the thing she now knows is called a disruptor growing inside her. She'd be Cortez conquering the Aztecs, or the British with their modern guns against the empires of India and China. At the very least, people in this village would finally take some proper notice of her…

"But you must know *something* about what happens in our future," she says. "Apart, at least, from these things you call movies."

* * *

It's Saturday morning and the twins and Ma have agreed to do most of Bethany's work so that she and Toto can walk over to Kirkwall, now that his leg's healing. He has to be careful, though, his presence on the Orkneys being unofficial, so he pulls Pa's old cap over his springy golden hair and one of Cousin Murdo's smocks covers most of the rest of him.

Still, he's looking up and around far too much for Bethany's comfort as they wander the stern granite streets amid cheery crowds of sailors on furlough. She steers him into Kirkwall Library past Mrs. Mellish at the counter, sits him down amid the dozing fisherman in the reference section, and spreads out some recent national newspapers. To her, their headlines make grim reading. Trouble in the Balkans. Germany planning what it calls a *preventative strike* against Russia. Yet the tone is worryingly jolly.

Perhaps, she whispers, they could invest what little money she has in some up-and-coming business. But the only ones Toto can recollect are either already well-known—Gillette, Mercedes, Coca-Cola, Ford, General Electric—or based on technologies that sound so magical and remote—a company called Apple, for instance—as to be worthless. Neither is it much help that he remembers the sinking of the Titan-something, which might or might not have just been a movie, since everyone knows the Titanic struck an iceberg two years back, whilst the San Francisco earthquake was in 1906.

Sitting in this calm refuge of thought and knowledge as Mrs. Mellish glares at them disapprovingly, Bethany wonders what she would do, despite all the many books she's read, if she was suddenly catapulted back into, say, the court of King Henry VIII? Tell Anne Boleyn marrying the king wasn't a good idea?

"But you must have had *some* interests. Perhaps before you became a grunt. Back in the—in the shanty-burrows?"

He smiles and shakes his head. He's doing this thing with the front page of the *Scottish Daily Record,* pinching at the text and then widening his fingers as if to make it bigger. "You mean, when I wasn't cocooned in a VR suit playing virtuals?" Then, clumsily and noisily enough to earn another disapproving look from Mrs. Mellish, he works his way back through the paper, flattening out the sports pages. A slow grin spreads across his face.

"Well? What is it?"

"Boxing! It was the one real thing I enjoyed when I was a kid. And it's barely changed. The discipline, the sweat, and the chalkdust—the history. There!"

He prods a tiny photograph.

"That's Jack Johnson. He's just beaten Frank Moran in Paris. And Kid Williams is about to fight Johnny Coulon for the Bantamweight Title in old California. He'll win, too. Hey…" He laughs loudly enough to waken a couple of fishermen. "Maybe old Toto's not so stupid after all. All we need do is to bet on Kid Williams to win. And that's just the start of it. In a few years there's Gene Tunny, Jack Dempsey. It's a golden age."

Bethany takes a deep breath. "The problem is, Toto, any gambling that isn't on horses at a racetrack or in a licensed casino is illegal. Not that anyone would ever think of betting on a sporting event on the other side of the world. Although I suppose you could try taking a steamer across the Atlantic."

"How could I manage a stunt like that? I'm not even a grunt here. I'm nobody. In any case, World War One is about to start."

"World War *One*?"

"Yes."

"You mean there's *more* than one of them?"

"We've had either three or four. Depends how you count them."

"That's…terrible."

"I've no idea why you're acting surprised. All you have to do is look out at all those battleships."

"But still…"

"Yeah." He's clumsily inspecting the spread newspapers. "But still." He stops at a photograph which isn't in the sports pages. "This guy."

"The Archduke Franz Ferdinand?"

"Yeah—him."

"He's just a Hapsburg prince. The world's full of these people, so why on earth—"

"What's the date again? I mean today?"

"Saturday the 27ᵗʰ of June."

"So this newspaper's only a couple of days old. And it says, right here, that he's visiting Sarajevo to inspect the troops on the 28th, which is tomorrow—Sunday."

"And?"

"Don't you see?" Now he's laughing again, and Mrs. Mellish is looking annoyed. "But of course, you wouldn't!"

* * *

Not for the first time, Bethany finds herself wondering if she'd have believed Toto if it wasn't for that slipsuit. Now, even more so, because it makes no sense that what he calls *World War One* should be triggered by the death of an obscure Hapsburg prince in a city she's barely heard of. But he insists that one of the few things anyone still remembers about the twentieth century is the assassination of this Archduke Ferdinand in Sarajevo. That, and the slaughter of millions of soldiers in muddy trenches, and a *Second* World War which followed soon after, and the rise of Joseph Hitler and Adolph Stalin, and a *holo-something*, and the invention of *nukes,* which can destroy whole cities. Then there's a *Cold War* which goes on for a very long time, but is really just like the peace of 1914, with all the power-blocks arming themselves with ever more destructive weapons.

In many ways, this feels even more like a game than anticipating sporting results. Not, they rapidly conclude, that it would be possible to reach Sarajevo in time to shout out a warning at the Archduke's passing car tomorrow, even if they could afford such a journey. But that doesn't mean they can't try *something*.

One of the few things Toto knows about the jumpships he traveled in is that the jumps they made in time and space were incredibly minute, but were still generally enough to avoid disruptor beams. So perhaps something they do now, minute though it might seem, could have a similarly large effect. At least, he says, it's worth a go until he works out how to make the most of his surprisingly encyclopedic knowledge of boxing. That, and as Bethany still has to point out, the world really isn't as primitive as he seems to think. There's a worldwide system of telegraphic communication, for instance.

The Post Office on Victoria Street closes at noon and the clock is already inching up from the quarter when they burst in. Then there's only Mr. Canning behind the counter, and Mrs. Pimm wants to send a postal order to her son in Australia. Finally, though, he takes the form from them. And, yes, that is the address: Oskar Potiorek, Governor of Bosnia and Herzegovina at his official residence in Sarajevo. And yes, THE ARCHDUKE IS IN DANGER is the message. Mr. Canning frowns. Sucks his teeth. But he stamps their form and takes the money.

* * *

Then nothing happens. Nothing, that is, apart from Bethany being stared at by Mrs. Mellish that Sunday in church as if she has no more right to be there than in Kirkwall Library. Meanwhile, the guns of the Grand Fleet continue to boom across Scapa Flow and hulks are scuttled across various inlets as protection against marauding German submarines, much to the consternation of local fishermen. That and, she notices from a scrap of newspaper in the outhouse, that Kid Williams defeated Johnny Coulon by knockout in California almost a month ago.

"All in all," she says to Toto when she finds him sitting out on the stone pier that evening, "I don't think it does much to prove your abilities as an oracle."

"You're saying I make things up?"

She shakes her head. "I just wonder how much we really know about here and now, let alone the future."

"But there's still nothing about that Archduke being killed in Sarajevo?"

"The papers are full of the so-called Irish Question. But I suppose that Archduke Ferdinand is still alive, seeing as it's hardly frontpage news when someone *isn't* assassinated."

He chuckles. "I guess there is that. Or maybe I got it wrong. It could have been some other prince or archduke. And perhaps not even in Sarajevo—"

"Wait a moment…" Bethany feels a flush of annoyance. "Now you're telling me…"

She trails off as a car comes jolting along the track from Kirkwall. It stops nearby. Three figures emerge. Two are wearing military uniforms, although she recognizes the third as Sargent Boyle of the local constabulary.

"Bethany Flett," he says, "you and your companion are under arrest on charges of espionage and high treason."

* * *

The interview room is starkly lit and her shoulders ache because her arms are handcuffed behind her.

"So you're saying it was just a hunch," drawls a man in a dark suit with an English accent, "that made you and your friend send that telegram?"

"How many times do I have to answer the same question?"

He smiles, unamused. "For as many times as I want you to. Did you ever hear him speaking in another language? Say, for instance, German?"

She shakes her head. Neither has she seen any notebooks, guns, maps, or binoculars. Or flashing lights, or any other strange men, for that matter. The telegram was a prank. All she really knows is that Toto is a sailor from Kansas who fell off his ship into the Pentland Firth. Yes, she did visit the library with him here in Kirkwall last Saturday, as she's sure Mrs. Mellish has already informed them, but reading isn't a crime, is it?

The night drags on. There's a difficult moment when the Englishman says they've combed Kellness and the surrounding area for suspicious apparatus, but it soon becomes apparent they didn't find anything.

"So how long do I have to stay here," she asks, "since you have no proper evidence?"

"Well, that's not exactly true. At least when it comes to your friend. Who, by the way, can't even name the ship he's supposed to have fallen overboard from and plainly isn't from Kansas. But you, now *you*, my dear, I think, we probably can afford to let go. But you must remember one thing."

"What?"

"That you were a fool and should count yourself incredibly lucky."

* * *

The village isn't the same. Nothing is. Pressmen arrive from the mainland, asking all sorts of questions. Of course, everyone says they knew right away there was something wrong about the man who claimed he was Toto from Kansas. Sure, that young lass was taken in, but she's not typical of anything.

GERMAN SPY UNMASKED. ESPIONAGE AT SCAPA FLOW. GRAND FLEET CLOAK AND DAGGER. The national press are full of it. And Bethany Flett's become this silly, besotted girl who should have known better. She can't visit Kirkwall library now, not with Mrs. Mellish still there, and is trailed across the shore one evening when she's trying to collect driftwood by a man from the *Glasgow Herald* asking why she didn't realize Toto's name was out of a popular novel. Even the twins no longer want her bedtime stories.

After several weeks of interrogation, the spy still popularly known as Toto, and who apparently still refuses to co-operate, is transferred to Glasgow under great security and tried swiftly and *in camera* at the City High Court. As the papers and a shocked general public all agree, the guilty verdict and death sentence are mere formalities.

* * *

Bethany's never been to Glasgow before. In fact she's only once visited the mainland, although every child in Scotland knows about Duke Street Prison. It's the place you're threatened with if you don't eat your neeps or backchat your elders. Even then, its vast, sooty grimness and fortress-like outer walls come as a shock to her.

Knowing smirks greet her enquiry at the gates. Still, she's let in and shown along endless corridors amid a joyless sea-roar of voices. A final door bangs behind her and she waits in a cell much like the one in Kirkwall police station, but smaller and grimmer. Then the door opens again and Toto shuffles in. He's chained hand and foot, in frayed gray overalls. There's a cut beneath his left eye and bruise across his forehead. He looks almost as frail as he did when he was hauled onto Kellness quay.

"Your limp…" she hears herself saying, "…it's almost gone."

"That was because you did such a good job of looking after me."

"I just wish— "

"No, no, Bethany! Don't you go wishing anything. You did the best you could, which was far more than I deserved. After all, I'm—"

"Just a grunt?"

"Yeah." He smiles. "But you're the only person who ever believed me."

"Although you never did tell me your real name."

"I didn't, did I? I think that was what drove people like our friends out there…" He nods toward the cell door. "…crazy. But I came to like it, even if Toto did turn out to sound far too much like a codename. But what else was I supposed to tell them? At least, if I expected them to believe me?"

"But there's still no war. And the Archduke Ferdinand's alive and back in Austria. I saw his name in yesterday's paper."

"But everyone still says there's *going* to be a war, right? And we don't even know if our telegram got through." He frowns. "And there's this *other* thing that's been bothering me. You see, if I really did come from a different future, how can I even have been born?"

It's a clever thought, to which she has no answer. But she remembers how the time-traveler set out again but never returned at the end of the H.G. Wells novel.

"At least I'll be dying a grunt's—a soldier's—death. Because they think I'm a foreign spy, it's going to be a firing squad."

"There must be *something*…"

"No, there isn't anything. And anyway—"

Then a bolt slides, a guard re-enters, and Bethany has to leave the cell, and finds herself standing back outside the gates of Duke Street Prison.

* * *

With nowhere to stay, she compulsively wanders the Glasgow streets, pushing past endless strangers and feeling as lost and distant as Toto must feel. She's had dreams, visions, of coming here with the slipsuit and the disruptor, of tearing down the prison walls and freeing Toto—and that would only be the beginning. She'd be a vengeful Boadicea, imposing justice, fighting and righting all the world's many wrongs. But she knows she could never trust herself to wield such power, any more than Toto. Not with the world as full as it already is with blood, grief, and mayhem.

Dawn does nothing to improve the look of Duke Street Prison. If anything, the blood-hued sky makes it even grimmer. Standing outside, she hears a shout from over the walls, then a echoing clatter of gunshots.

That's it then. And she's no reason to think anything they've done has made any difference. She draws a breath and hurries to catch the train which, with a change at Inverness, and the ferry from Scrabster, will have her back at Kellness and probably collecting driftwood by evening. Then she stops. And turns. And walks briskly toward the growing morning bustle of Queen Street.

* * *

It's almost four years before she returns to the Orkneys. She's written many letters, of course, but the whole village seems astonished to see her walking down the track from Kirkwall.

Ma and Pa look so old, and the twins are so grown, and everyone admires her city clothes and treats her as if she's no longer Bethany Flett, but some important stranger. She gives Pa a new tape measure to replace the one which was worn out by the constant fiddling of the man no one wants to remember. And yes, she really does have a stake in the company that manufactures these things and owns the patent for the way the metal strip is curved to keep it from bending. For something so obvious, it's strange no one else ever thought of it.

It's midsummer again, and the light of evening seems endless, and they want to hear all about what it's like to live in Edinburgh, and visit London, and even Paris, and the sights she must have seen. She doesn't dwell, as the best plates are set out, on her year following the fleet and gutting fish as a herring girl, although it wasn't unpleasant. Neither does she say too much about her work to promote women's suffrage, which would only cause upset and argument.

You could now count the ships moored across Scapa Flow on the fingers of one hand. There's a lightboat, two tugs, and maybe a dredger. The British Grand Fleet, or what's left of it since Mr. Churchill's cutbacks, now rides anchor in the warmer waters of the Solent, while Kaiser Bill's lost most of his powers and the Tsar and his family are staying with their English cousins at Osborne House, having been evicted from Russia.

Not that you could say peace has broken out across the world. There's continued conflict in the Balkans, more trouble in Ireland, and bloody revolution in Mexico. But at least there hasn't been a world war. In fact, as the major powers sign up a Community of Nations with its headquarters in Switzerland, a global conflagration seems less rather than more likely.

Does any of this have anything to do with that telegram? Bethany still has no idea, although she's followed the successes of a highly technical young boxer called Gene Tunney. Not that she's a huge fan of the sport, but she does keep up an interest. She's also re-invested some of the money she's made out of her tape measure patent in companies involved in making films with a sound accompaniment—the so-called talkies—even if most people are certain they'll never catch on.

There's a fair deal of drinking, at least by the men, and the children grow tired and grumpy, and the questions become repetitious. Time for bed, especially as she's leaving so early next morning, although she's not allowed to lift a finger to help with the clearing. Saying she'd like to stretch her legs, she goes outside, where the sky is still glowing and the air feels like velvet.

She crosses the shore and climbs to the cleft in the promontory and pulls away the rocks. The slipsuit is just as extraordinary as she remembers; the power and the purpose and weight of it. After filling it with stones and wrapping it in seaweed, she carries it quickly around to the quay and pushes out in one of the village rowboats.

The sea is smooth and still. Even though it's been years, she dips the oars easily and quietly until she's out of sight of Kellness, at a place where the water suddenly deepens. Then, as she pushes yet more stones into the slipsuit, her skin crawls with a sense of being watched. When she turns, she laughs. It's just the local seals, studying her with their heads raised out of the water. They chuff back at her as if equally amused, then disappear in a flicker of fins. Weighted as it is, the slipsuit soon darkens and vanishes into the depths as it follows them.

Bethany sits for a long moment, letting the sky and the sea settle. Then she rows briskly back toward the shore and the lights of the village.

NEW MOON, DARK SKIES

Mike Barretta

Lieutenant Jesse L. Brown reclined but did not rest. The ST-38 Talon aerospace trainer rocketed through the stratosphere at an eighty-degree angle. Acceleration pressed him deep into his seat. The three AR-4 Rocketdyne engines fired a muted, throaty growl, kicking him higher, not quite to space, but high enough that if his cockpit ruptured his blood would boil. He rose and rose, almost free, gravity loosened. He breathed deep and steady, his face illuminated by the dials and gauges. The engine burned out and he coasted into a darkening sky, running out of energy. At apogee, for the briefest moment, he was still, poised in space, neither climbing nor descending. In balance. The moment passed. Hydrogen peroxide thrusters pitched him over, pointed at the luminescent earth, and he fell. He worked the stick, firing the thrusters, orienting the ship for the approach. At this rarified altitude aerodynamic flight control surfaces were useless. The vibration of tiny engines, releasing compressed gases in measured bursts, kept him from useless and fatal tumbling.

Dark sky. Blue earth. A sliver of moon hung in the sky like a giant's crescent fingernail. He spiraled downward, hitting his marks. The horizon's curve swept below him. The demands of test flight did not leave much time for admiration of the scenery but what little he took was essential. He needed the time to remind himself that it was all worth it.

He consulted his kneeboard flight test cards. Up here, indifferent physics and skillful response determined his fate. He maneuvered his craft. His flight profile was perfect, just like it was the last time, and the time before that, and still he did not have a slot for an X-20 space plane launch. He didn't know if it was because he was Navy or black. Both were held in equal measure of disdain by the Air Force. One was professional, the other personal.

But for the moment, all that was beneath him. He banked his aircraft into a gentle spiral, aiming for a series of imaginary gates, points in space, which a de-orbiting X-20 would follow in its terminal maneuvering. He checked the boxes, earned his stripes, jumped through the hoops to fulfill his dream.

Mr. Styles, his old boss at the airfield, had made it possible. The man, a World War One veteran, tolerated him well enough, unusual for an old southern white man. Some things didn't usually mix, but each had seen through the skin of the other and recognized the love of flying. One day, while watching a plane touch and go at the outlying airfield that served the warbirds from Montgomery and Birmingham, Mr. Styles suggested that if he was going to hang around, he might as well be useful.

Mr. Styles died when Jesse was sixteen years old and he was surprised to discover that the man had left him a little over twenty-five thousand dollars and the deed to the airport property. At the end of World War II, the old grass strip was unneeded. Jesse had let it go fallow. Cattle roamed where warbirds once soared. He bought his mother a decent house and used the remainder to attend Purdue and earn an aeronautical engineering degree. After Purdue, he joined the Navy to fly. The Navy did not have pilots; it had aviators, and he liked the sound of that. They tried to make him a cook, but pragmatism won out over prejudice. With the outbreak of the Korean War, the Navy could not afford to waste even a black aviator in the scullery. After carrier qualification, he deployed with the Screaming Eagles on board the *USS Essex*, flying the F9F Panther, the Navy's premier jet fighter. Acceptance into the squadron was difficult at first, but as the gears of war ground on, the color of his skin mattered less and less. His air sense, calm demeanor in dangerous circumstances, skill at aircraft maneuvering, and situational awareness, earned him the respect and admiration of his fellow aviators. In a single mission he downed a Yak-9 and MiG-15. Combat effectiveness transcended race and religion in wartime.

He fostered a fearless reputation. But he was afraid. Mostly afraid that he would not make it back to his wife. The last time he saw her she was standing at the pier in San Diego as the *Essex* shipped out, surrounded by the white officer's wives and terribly alone. A buffer zone of excruciating courtesy that masqueraded as acceptance wrapped around her. Who would knock on her door if anything was to happen to him? Who would sit and hold her hand and tell her that he was a hero? How long would they let her stay in the base housing with its green grass, flag poles, and black-faced lawn jockeys?

At least here, on board the ship, there were moments of acceptance, brief flashes of camaraderie built upon the shared experiences of sacrifice and adversity. Sometimes, he thought he glimpsed the future in the squadron's ready room.

A boom reverberated through the ship as a Panther slammed onto the deck in a controlled crash the Navy called landing. A three wire, he guessed. They had a sound all their own. Every moment was a moment away from disaster. Aviation was utterly indifferent to any quality except preparedness. He slalomed through flak-strafed valleys rigged with cables set to snare a fighter out of the sky and pursued nimble MiG-15's through storm-laden clouds and returned to a pitching aircraft carrier deck. Only a fool would not be afraid. But in a wardroom of all white aviators, only a fool would show it.

On a clear night with moon-silvered seas, his squadron mate, Lieutenant Junior Grade Neil Armstrong suggested that if he was going to pretend to be fearless he should transfer to the Navy Test Pilot School in Patuxent River, Maryland.

"I don't know," said Jesse. "Maybe I've come as far as I can."

"Shoot for the moon, Jesse," said Neil.

He did.

At Pax River he evaluated the Vought F7U Cutlass, an underpowered aircraft with unproven aerodynamics. His report damned the machine in technical terms as a widow maker. The best thing the Navy could do, he suggested, was to buy the exotic-looking tailless aircraft in sufficient quantities to outfit enemy forces and then just stand back for the win. The aircraft went on to kill four test pilots and its procurement was a case study in disaster.

His reward for an honest appraisal was orders to the Air Force's struggling Man-in-Space-Soonest program as a Navy Liaison. The one office program exploded into relevance when the Soviet Vostok 3 de-orbited a "scientific package," demonstrating the ability to bomb from orbit. The U.S. Air Force lobbied for an equivalent capability and the project, flush with appropriations, moved to Edwards Air Force base. The Navy had aviators, the best pilots in the world, but the Air Force led the charge to space.

That brought him here, to the edge, so close to space that he could feel the cold in his bones.

He looked down and over his left shoulder to see the chicken-scratched outlines of Edwards. His modified T-38 plummeted. At 3,000 feet he dropped the landing gear and the rush of wind noise intruded upon the silence. The aircraft fell faster, but he counted on that. The runway bloomed and he flared the aircraft, pulling the nose up. The main mounts cleared the runway threshold and touched down with a puff of smoke. He dropped the nose and the aircraft rolled out to a stop. A support Jeep and a dusty Air Force crew bus raced to meet him. The recovery team, all white with the exception of Airman Marcus Jones, swarmed the aircraft to render it safe. Throughout the ST-38 there were cartridge-actuated devices that would pop with the force of bullet, pressurized gases, and residual fuels that needed to be vented. Jones set up the ladder.

He lifted the canopy open and tasted dry desert air scented with sage.

"Good flight, Lieutenant Brown?" asked Airman Jones.

"The best," said Jesse.

"Birds of a feather," said a crew chief, inserting pins into the landing gear under the left wing.

Airman Jones looked over his shoulder at the Crew Chief, his boss. A big man, balding and sweat-stained, burned red by the desert sun and wind.

"Back to work, boy," said the Crew Chief. "Not you… sir."

Jesse ignored the Chief.

"Dead stick it in?" asked Jones.

"Bullshit," said the Chief. "No one dead sticks from two hundred thousand feet."

"Go ahead touch it."

The Chief walked aft and touched the cool casing of the auxiliary rocket motor exhaust duct. He grunted.

"Always bet on black, ain't that right, sir?" asked Jones.

"The only place you bet on black is in Vegas," said the Chief.

"Yea, that's right," said Jesse. That son of a bitch was certainly right about that. For him, the Air Force program was a dead end. Their fighter jocks would get the best missions and he would be relegated to supporting flights. Chasing Air Force pukes around the sky was not what he envisioned for his career. He would apply to NASA. It had to be better at NASA, didn't it?

The crew hooked the ST-38 up to a long tow bar attached to the Jeep. He boarded the bus and sat down for the ride back to the operations center to debrief the flight. The crew filed in, disbursing themselves to claim a single seat so they could stretch out. The Crew Chief boarded.

"Navy has to sit at the back of the bus. Air Force rules," said the Crew Chief.

Before Jesse could respond, the man guffawed. A wide, goofy grin filled with oversized teeth. "'cause your, Navy. Get it?"

"I get it, Chief."

Really, how bad could it be at NASA? Florida. Sunshine. Beaches. At the very least, he would be able to take Daisy, his wife, away from heat, dust, and the crippling isolation of being the only black woman at Edwards. The bus started with a diesel rush and lurched forward. Jones doubled as the driver. Jesse leaned forward and clapped him on the shoulder. Jones turned and nodded his head in understanding.

The desert landscape, as barren and empty as any moon, stretched to distant snowless mountains. Heat rippled in undulating waves from the hardpan surface. When he'd proposed to Daisy, he'd told her that he would reach up and give her the moon. The least he could do is make an honest effort.

* * *

"Send one? I'll send 'em all. Every goddamned last one of 'em," said the man at the diner.

Jesse pretended to ignore him.

"Shit can't be that hard. They sent monkeys up. Still sendin' monkeys as far as I can see."

"That's enough, Elroy. This is a family establishment. You save that sass for the streets," said the waitress.

"Yea, yea. Oh, shit. Sorry. I'm just having some fun, but I do got a question. How do they see them up there in the dark? They gotta smile or what?"

Jesse stood.

Neil stood.

Neil took him by the arm and Jesse shrugged him off. He stared at Elroy, waiting for…he didn't know what…a sign, a signal, a voice in his head that said now, this time, a fight can be just a fight between two men rather than a career ending indictment.

"Let's go," said Neil. "Not now."

They walked outside into the Florida sunshine.

"When?"

"Not ever. Do you want to give them an excuse to throw you off the program?"

"So I gotta take it? Is that it?" He did. He knew he did and better than anyone else. Amongst the astronauts he was on firm ground. Competence was the only metric that mattered to them, but the only thing that made rockets fly was funding and there was no shortage of those who saw his position as an existential threat to their beliefs. There was no shortage of those who would use him as a means for their own progressive ends. He was smart enough to understand that he did not get here on his own. He had allies and enemies hidden behind the scenes and standing right in front of him. Sometimes, it was hard to tell the difference. Power ebbed and flowed like the tide and it carried all men great and small and he was weary of it all, but he had come too far to quit.

The costs were too great to ignore. Daisy had told him that the arc of his life was ever upwards and he believed her more than any fat, greasy-lipped man named Elroy.

But still…

"Yea, that's it. You gotta take it," said Neil. "We deal with it just like any other problem."

"We solve it."

"Yea, that's right. We solve it. You have more riding on your shoulders than any other astronaut. I get that, but still, you take it, and do your job."

"I'm untouchable. I'm Kennedy's boy, isn't that what they say?"

"Untouchability has its limits."

Rumors alleged that he was a quota, a token in Kennedy's New Frontier social reforms. Racial diversity in the Astronaut Corp served a twofold purpose. It proved the effectiveness of the domestic social agenda and countered Soviet propaganda about race relations in the United States. The original seven were all white. The next nine needed a little color. It was either him or hire a woman and a woman was out of the question. There wasn't a woman alive afforded the opportunity to earn fighter combat time and test pilot experience. Exclusion was institutionalized from the beginning and only a particular set of circumstances allowed him membership in the astronaut club.

Still, he'd earned his position. He was just as qualified as any other in the program.

"Don't be your own worst enemy and get thrown out of the program. Every one of those yahoos will swear on a stack of bibles that you started it and the country will believe it. Am I right?"

"You are."

"Alright. Then let it pass. Some would love to see you disgraced and then offer it up as proof of a terrible mistake, bringing you on."

"I am tired of it all."

"I can imagine."

"No, you can't."

"You're right, I can't, but if you gotta work harder, then that's what you do. You've got friends here. The mission is the thing. You know where this is going."

"The moon."

"Yea, the moon. Imagine every racist son of a bitch sleeping by the light of a moon you walked on."

The waitress came outside. "I'm sorry. I really am, but Elroy is a regular. You know?" She looked more concerned over the public rudeness than the overall sentiment. She smiled awkwardly and went back in.

"They have a picture of every astronaut that has ever eaten here except for one. I can't even come in here unless I'm with you. I gotta get back to Daisy. Thanks for the breakfast."

"Hey, I got you out here to tell you something."

"What's that?"

"Beau Slater has appendicitis. You're going. Right seat. Gemini 8."

"With you?"

"Who else?"

* * *

The tiny window in the Gemini 8 capsule afforded a poor view, but even a poor view of the Earth from orbit was sublime. He worried over his wife, Daisy. An odd thing considering he had just ridden a slightly modified long-range ballistic missile and then played bumper cars in orbit with an Agena target vehicle. She was a strong woman, but he had tested that strength over and over again. He owed her more than he could ever repay.

"She's fine," said Neil. "She's with Jan."

"Thanks for that."

"The other wives, too. All of them are there."

"I don't worry for me. I asked for this, but she…"

"Depress is complete. You wanna walk or you wanna whine?"

"Walk," said Jesse. She hadn't asked for this…and yet she had gone along with him. She suffered the social snubs of wives clubs, the media events that held her out of frame or focus. One time, at a wives club meeting, she was mistaken for the help. She never told him. He had heard about it from another pilot who had been amused by the anecdote. He wanted to step upon the surface of the lonely moon and visit for a while. He realized his wife already lived there. She had followed him around to all his duty stations, sacrificing her own ambitions for his.

"Houston, this is Gemini, we are ready for EVA," said Neil.

"Gemini, this is Houston, you are cleared for EVA."

"Houston, this is Gemini, we copy. The door is opening."

Jesse pushed the door and stood half-in and half-out of the cockpit.

"What do you see?" asked Neil. "Jesse?"

"Everything. Oh my God, I can see everything."

"Get back in, let's trade places."

"Oh no, Command Pilot, you gotta fly the ship. Fuel good?"

"We're good."

He stepped out, drifting away, attached by an eight-meter-long tether. He gave his Hand-Held Maneuvering Unit a burst and pulled away, floating free.

"I see the Agena. We're following it. It's just a spec above the horizon line." Light glinted off the Agena's hull. An hour before, they had been attached to the target vehicle, flying as one.

"Was it worth it?"

"Yea, it's worth it. I wish I could show them all how beautiful it is."

"Show who?"

"The world. Everyone down below. I wish they could see this, be here. I am surrounded by all of creation. I can see it all. Then they would know." But especially he wanted to show Daisy. Make her feel the pounding of his heart and felt the pounding of her own.

His tether snapped taught.

"Hey, you're rocking the ship. Don't break it; it's our ride home."

"Sorry."

Jesse spread his arms, swept them forward, and flew over the world Superman style. He watched for a long while, wondering what all the people, great and small, down on the Earth were doing. Whatever it was could not be compared to what he was doing. "I feel so small…and magnificent at the same time. Does that make sense?"

"Yea, I think it does. I know you are having a moment, but Houston wants to get you back inside."

"Tell them to come get me."

He drifted in front of Neil's sightline and waved.

"I wish I could stay out here forever."

"If you don't make your way in, you just might."

"I 'm coming back… to Earth," said Jesse.

Too bad, he thought.

* * *

"Jesse, we have a problem," said Beau Slater.

Beau's medical evaluations following his appendicitis revealed an atrial fibrillation that grounded him. NASA offered him the job as chief astronaut and part of that job was to make crew selections for missions. The man was a thwarted astronaut and ran interference between administration politics and the astronaut's needs. He was a decent enough sort and his occasional sourness was understandable.

Another man occupied the chair next to Beau.

Jesse sat across the table from the two men. He was on professional terms with Beau. The man was always fair with him. He did not have to compete any more than anyone else for flight rotations.

"Do you have a gardener, a Mr. Willard May Jones?" asked Beau.

"Yes, I do. A few of the others do to."

"Is he close to your wife?" asked the other man.

"What kind of question is that? Beau, who is this guy?"

"Mr. Carlisle is Senator Josiah Thompson's aide." Senator Thompson, the outspoken anti-science and anti-space politician from Mississippi, sat on the Senate Appropriations Committee responsible for funding NASA.

"Mr. Brown, let me cut to the chase. Mr. May has tested positive for syphilis," said Carlisle.

"That's terrible, but what does that have to do with me and what does the government care if a gardener contracts a disease?"

"Jesse, you may have been exposed. It would bump you off Apollo 11," said Beau.

"How would a gardener with syphilis bump me off the flight? The crew rotation is set. You made the rotation yourself."

"There is a reporter that says your wife and the gardener have been having an affair," said Mr. Carlisle.

"Because the gardener is black? And my wife is black?"

"Mr. Brown, there is no reason to bring race into this matter," said Carlisle.

"But it's always about race, isn't it?" He turned to Beau. "There have been people trying to get me off the rotation since you made it up. The Senator doesn't care to put a man on the moon, but he is damned sure that if one is going, it won't be a black man. I don't care about astronauts jockeying for position. That's what we do. But this…how do you even let this guy in the front door? When did you sell us out?"

"Sell out? You don't know the half of what I do around here. We haven't even gotten to the moon and people want to pull the plug," said Beau.

"Then pull the damn plug. We all go or none of us go."

"We've come too far."

"Not far enough from where I sit. You can't even comprehend far."

"Jesse, NASA has no interest in an astronaut's private affairs. We just need you and your wife to take a test," interrupted Mr. Carlisle.

"NASA has every interest in our private affairs. They could have taken my blood any time and not even told me why. My wife is not having an affair. I don't have syphilis and you know it. Have you asked the others? Have you called them in? Have you asked them if their wives are screwing the help?"

"Mr. Brown…"

"Don't you say my name, goddamn you, don't you say it, or so help me."

"Jesse…" said Beau.

"You know what this is. How could you not? They're holding NASA hostage and I'm the ransom."

"The rotation stays the same. It all goes away if you—and your wife—take the test," said Beau.

"No." The answer came out instinctively. "It doesn't go away, does it?" He looked to Carlisle. "You'll just find some other way. What will it be? A false positive? National humiliation for my wife? What kind of man would I be if I did that to her?" He leaned forward, stretching across the table, and poked Carlisle in the chest. Carlisle jerked away. "A man like you, I suppose."

"Don't you touch me." Carlisle looked to Beau.

"I didn't see a thing," said Beau. "Jesse, you know what I do. I have to be sure."

"You should already be sure."

Since Kennedy's assassination in Atlanta, political support for his assignment to Apollo 11 had faded. He was surprised he'd lasted this long on the roster. He had sacrificed a lot for his ambition, but he would not betray his wife. She was the only lever that could move him from his path. They knew this.

"Mr. Brown, this isn't personal…I…"

"To hell with you, Mr. Carlisle. Tell the Senator the same for me." He stood and left.

It was past two a.m. when he staggered to his front door, a little bit drunk, and slid the key in the lock. He looked over his shoulder at the crescent moon.

"Good night, moon."

* * *

July 20 1969. Jesse sat on the couch. His wife sat next to him. He could have gone to mission control to be a first-person witness to history, but instead he was where he needed to be.

Daisy sat next to him, legs curled under her. Her weight upon him was a comfort. A grainy Walter Cronkite narrated the mission. Black and white flickered to scales of gray on the television set.

His wife found his hand and squeezed it.

"Houston, Tranquility Base here. The Eagle has landed," said Neil.

"It still seems like a dream," said Walter Cronkite.

"Yes, it does, Walter. That is exactly what it is. A dream." An impossible dream, he thought, but dreams were free. His Momma had said dreams would break your heart with their nonsense. His heart was broken, but at this moment, he was unwilling to give up on them.

"I told you I would give you the moon," he said.

"You will," she replied. "I know you will."

He kissed the side of her face.

He remembered prop wash scouring him with grass and dirt as he ran parallel to the powerful aircraft, a mere thirteen years old. The Mustangs had taxied to the end of the Mr.

Style's grass runway and made an awkward pirouette as they spun into the wind. Engines surged and the aircraft bumped along, picking up speed until they left the earth. They rose and rose, sucking in their wheels, rattling the upper boughs of the slash pines before banking in hard knife-edge turns and circling back. He faced the oncoming aircraft, breathing hard with breathless excitement. Warbirds, he thought. They flew so low that he had felt if he was a man, and a bit taller, he could reach up and touch their aluminum bellies. The lead aircraft rolled and inverted. He waved furiously at the black pilot at the controls. The Mustangs screamed overhead. The lead rolled back upright and, wingtip to wingtip, the aircraft pitched up, fading into the moist Alabama light, back to Tuskegee.

What choice did he have at all but to fly? His fate was sealed long ago.

"That's one small step for a man, one giant leap for mankind," said Neil

Daisy squirmed away from him and stood up. "Can I get you anything?"

He reached out his hand and she took it. He pulled her back down and she straddled his lap.

"What?"

"You've given me everything I need." He kissed her.

"I don't know what's gotten into you." She wriggled off him.

On the moon, Neil Armstrong and Buzz Aldrin bounced across a desolate gray landscape.

* * *

"Forty feet. Kicking up some dust. Thirty feet. Faint shadow. Four forward. Drifting to the left. We're good," said Jesse.

"Still drifting left," said Stuart Roosa, Mission Commander. "Clear of obstructions."

"Okay. I got it." The ship shuddered. Relative motion cancelled. It hung poised above gray dust and settled. "Contact light. Engine stop. ACA—out of detent."

"Out of detent," said Stu.

"Mode control—both auto. Descent engine command override—off, engine arm—off," said Jesse.

"We copy you down, *Constitution*," said Houston.

"Affirmative Houston, Tycho Base here. *Constitution* has landed," said Stu.

"Roger, Tycho. Textbook landing. Happy Bicentennial."

"I got a good pilot," said Stu.

Jesse looked out the window at another world, a place of harsh light and deep shadow. Tycho Crater, July 4, 1976. He realized he was standing rather than floating free. He'd concentrated so intently on flying the Lunar Excursion Module that he had not noticed when gravity took hold of him.

"Russian lander should be over that ridge," said Stu.

If it wasn't for the successful Russian landing, the Apollo program would have ended at seventeen. Part of their mission was to photograph and evaluate Russian equipment from a standoff distance. If anything was deemed to be in violation of the Outer Space Treaty, they would approach for a closer look. To that end, their overshoes were designed with a Russian tread pattern to conceal any damage to the historical site.

"I didn't see it coming in. Too much shadow." He looked at Stu. "We made it."

"Yes, we did."

When he proposed to his wife, he said he would give her anything. She asked for the moon and he said it wouldn't be a problem. It was silly romantic talk on the eve of his deployment to Korea. That night any such thing was possible. Years later, when he was bumped off the Apollo 11 crew, he had gone home, cried in miserable frustration, and told her that he couldn't give her the moon after all.

She told him that he already had.

The astronaut community was small and not stupid. Pieces were put together. Theories were formed. Nothing was proven. The astronauts despised political influences on the program as if they were blind to the fact that the very genesis of the program was political. As the only black astronaut, he was keenly aware of the politics. Sometimes they favored him, most of the time they did not. Crew selections were firm up to Apollo 17. He could have fought for a slot on the basis of rank, but that would mean bumping someone else already deeply invested in that flight's particular mission. He wouldn't do to others what was done to him. He maintained his qualifications, but the likelihood of him going back up was remote.

Instead, he worked on advanced propulsion technologies testing nuclear engines in the Nevada desert.

Then the Russians landed a single man on the moon and the space race was reinvigorated. Apollo funding was restored and money for a follow-on vehicle named Nova was appropriated. NASA had decided to forgo a reusable shuttle after studies revealed that post-flight overhaul costs and low Earth orbit limitations would eat up NASA's budget and constrain its peaceful exploratory mission. The Air Force took the Shuttle program.

"Paul should be back up," said Jesse.

"*Independence* this is *Constitution*, how do you copy?" said Stu.

"*Constitution* this is *Independence*, I read you five by five. Happy to hear you," said Paul Weitz, the Command Module Pilot. "Why don't you guys go for a walk or something. I'll just hang out here and drive the bus."

"We copy that *Independence*," said Stu.

Jesse and Stu performed housekeeping chores to ensure the security of the LEM and then dressed out. They checked each other's suits.

"I'll go first," said Stu.

"Of course, Commander's prerogative," said Jesse.

"No one cares about the nineteenth white man on the moon. I have to set up the camera and get into position. Depress is complete."

"I don't know what to say."

"Nothing to say. Give me a few minutes." Stu opened the thin egress hatch, crouched awkwardly in the EVA suit and backed through it.

Jesse waited and watched outside the window.

"Okay," said Stu.

Jesse turned and knelt. He backed out onto the platform.

"Looking good. I'm getting some great shots of your ass."

"Thanks for that. You would think that Grumman would have found some way to make this more graceful."

His feet found the ladder and he stepped down.

"Okay, lower your foot to the surface and freeze," said Stu.

He put his foot on the moon.

"Got it," said Stu. "That'll go in the Smithsonian next to your space diapers. Turn around."

He stood, both feet firmly planted on the lunar surface. We made it, he thought. We made it, Daisy. He took a step, then another.

"Perfect shot with the LEM in the background," said Stu.

He walked more, taking a few crunchy steps, then bounded. It was like walking across snow coated with a thin layer of ice.

"Tycho Base, this is Houston. If you've had your moment of awe, we have a schedule to keep."

"Stu, look." He pointed.

Stu turned.

The Earth, a brilliant blue-green marble, rose over the gray foreshortened horizon.

"There is a beautiful Earth out tonight," said Jesse.

"Houston, this is Tycho Base, we are going to need another moment."

HIS MASTER'S VOICE

Kari Sperring

Königsberg, Prussia, 1867

"It is, of course, highly regrettable," Minister President Otto von Bismarck said, "but, faced with such arrogance, what can one do?" He raised a hand. "Naturally, we Prussians prefer peace—does not every civilized man?—but I fear our hand will, sooner or later, be forced. The Emperor of France…" another gesture "…he is not the man his uncle was and all of Europe can be glad of that. But he wants to be, my friends. He dreams of expanding the influence of France and he is not scrupulous in his means. This new suggestion!" He shook his head, every inch the great statesman saddened by the ways of the world. "To make Luxembourg a mere possession, to be bought and sold at market! The Luxembourgers are our allies, our friends. Their status was confirmed, was it not, at the Congress of Vienna, to which France was a signatory. But this latest news…"

"It's true, then?" his interlocutor asked. "The Emperor Louis Napoléon sought to buy Luxembourg from the Dutch king?"

"It is, indeed. And more. Not only does Louis Napoléon seek to buy Luxembourg, he expects our King Wilhelm to support him in his greed. You can imagine, I am sure, how our good king feels about this. The damage to his honor! It cannot be supported, and yet, to risk the lives of our sons, our nephews, in another war…" Again he sighed. "We must do all we can to avoid that, my friend. If you had seen the letter Louis Napoléon sent!" His gaze held that of the English ambassador, but his attention was all on the man's young secretary, hovering nearby. His spies told him the young man was a regular correspondent of the *Times* of London, always ready to pass on tidbits of political news.

"We must not have war," the English ambassador said. "We great powers will assure that, my lord. We will have peace."

"We will," said Bismarck, and smiled.

Paris, three years later

"The problem," said Count Benedetti, "is not so much what our lords and masters say as getting them to remember what they said accurately." He sighed and took another sip of his wine. "A selective memory may be comforting to kings, but it has a tendency to undo months of diplomacy."

"I thought that your secretaries took minutes these days," said Princesse Mathilde.

"Oh, they do," Benedetti agreed. "On both sides. But notes go missing and accounts can be altered. All it takes is for one side to deny that something was said, or the other to insist it was, and," he shrugged, "there you have it. Luxembourg."

The Princesse frowned. "My cousin was most displeased over that. Is it true what they say, that von Bismarck himself informed the press of our plan to extend our protection to the good people of that duchy?"

"I believe so."

"Underhanded," the Princesse said. "And ungentlemanly. Not at all the behavior one expects of a nobleman or a statesman."

But very much, Benedetti reflected, what one might expect from a man as clever and ambitious as Bismarck. To the rest of Europe, the great days of the Holy Roman Empire were long past, belonging more to the world of romantic novelists and poets than to that of modern diplomacy. But to Bismarck, raised in the narrow nationalism of his class, its revival was a plan of action and a goal he longed to achieve for his master, the King of Prussia. Wilhelm himself was not a bad man—indeed, Benedetti rather liked him. But Bismarck! He suppressed a shudder. He could as well learn to like a wolf. As French ambassador to Prussia, it was his duty to deal courteously with the man, and he was willing to grant that Bismarck was an adept politician. But as a private individual, Benedetti disliked the man intensely. A minister did what he must for his country, but a man who would knowingly release private diplomatic correspondence to the press simply to slander another land must not be trusted.

Louis Napoléon had been furious when the *London Times* printed his missive to the Prussians in full. The letter would never have been written or sent had not Bismarck agreed previously to support a French claim to Luxembourg. But Bismarck had gone back on his word, suppressed his own part in the scandal and left French ambition exposed for all Europe to see. Only careful diplomacy and the aid of the British court had prevented a war over the matter. And now...

Benedetti drained his wine glass and set it down on the table. His hostess reached out and patted his hand. "My poor Monsieur Benedetti. Your burdens are heavy."

"It is a privilege to serve your cousin the Emperor."

The Princesse pulled a small face. "My cousin is what he is. It is the privilege of princes to change their minds, but as you say, if only they were better at recalling their earlier statements." A thoughtful expression crossed her face. "I heard something last week which might perhaps be of some help to you in that matter. Leave it with me and let me see what I can arrange."

Benedetti kissed her hand. It was unfortunate, he reflected, that unlike the English, the French could not accept the idea of a woman ruler. Mathilde would make a better empress by far than Louis Napoléon. He said, "As ever, Madame, you ease my mind."

"That is *my* privilege," the Princesse said.

* * *

As it happened, it was some months before Benedetti had cause to remember his conversation with the Princesse. The Austrians were making overtures to Louis Napoléon for an alliance against Prussia, which would upset the English. Louis Napoléon himself was toying with interfering in the complex and dangerous politics of Italy. Two years earlier, the Spanish had risen against their Queen, Isabella, and overthrown her: she now lived as a pensioner of the Emperor here in Paris. And now, to cap it all, the Spanish rebels had seen fit to offer their throne to none other than Leopold of Hohenzollern, cousin to King Wilhelm of Prussia. "It is the outside of enough," fumed Louis Napoléon. "Another Prussian! Is there to be no end to their ambitions? I will not have it, Benedetti. Do you hear me? To have them on one border is bad enough, but on two? No, no, and no: this must not be, and so I shall tell Wilhelm and that minister of his."

"As you say, sire" Benedetti said. His stomach was beginning to hurt. Service to rulers was ruinous on the digestion as well as the nerves. He exchanged a glance with the foreign minister, de Gramont. "It is a most undesirable state of affairs."

"Undesirable!" Louis Napoléon's tone made it clear what he thought of that word. "It's unacceptable, Monsieur

Benedetti. An outrage. An insult to France. Well, when my armies are at the gates of Berlin, perhaps Bismarck will finally understand what it means to insult France and me."

"His majesty the King of Prussia is an honorable man," Benedetti ventured. "He is sure to understand your, ah, reservations in this matter."

"Indeed," de Gramont said. "And this Prince Leopold is, I understand, a Catholic, and therefore not in high favor at the Prussian court. Count von Bismarck is, after all, a staunch Protestant."

Louis Napoléon looked thoughtful. "So this is not some plot of his?"

Benedetti spread his hands. "As to that, sire, I cannot say."

"And my brother monarch, King Wilhelm?"

"His majesty is also a Protestant, sire. He has distanced himself from his Catholic cousins."

"Hmm…And yet, that Bismarck…!"

"Count von Bismarck would very much like to embarrass France," Benedetti said. "Just as he did three years ago." He repressed a shiver. This was sensitive territory. "No doubt he is hoping to provoke a negative reaction from us."

"Hmmm," Louis Napoléon repeated, his eyes narrowing.

"He forgets," Benedetti went on, "that you are a true heir of your famous uncle, as gifted in diplomacy as you are in military matters, and more than able to see through his clumsy schemes." And, Benedetti reflected, no man could accuse him of untruth in that statement. He had not, after all, stated the level of his master's gifts.

There was a pause, as Louis Napoléon paced up and down his office, working his way through his ambassador's words. De Gramont once again caught Benedetti's eye and gave him a small, approving nod. Finally, Louis Napoléon came to a halt and turned to face his advisors. He said, "It seems to me you have the right of this, Monsieur Benedetti. Bismarck thinks he can manipulate me. But he cannot, messieurs! He most assuredly cannot! We will write to our fellow ruler, King Wilhelm, and state our case calmly. It is not up to Bismarck to decide the fate of France!"

"Indeed, sire," Benedetti said.

"A most wise decision, sire," said de Gramont.

"Write my letter, Monsieur Benedetti." Louis Napoléon waved a hand in his direction. "Make my case. But if Bismarck will not comply, we shall have war."

* * *

Benedetti made his way back to his lodgings with a heavy heart. The Emperor might dream of expanding France's borders and emulating the successes of the great first Napoléon, but the truth was that France was in no condition to win a war. The ambassador had seen for himself the wide-ranging reforms to the Prussian army under Bismarck and General Von Moltke and, more, had noted how easily they had triumphed over the Austrians in 1866. The French army was much reduced since the glorious days of the early nineteenth century and in no condition to fight and win against a better trained force. And Bismarck, in his quest to expand Prussian territory, had his eye on the French territories of Alsace and Lorraine. A war would play right into his hands.

The crisis had perhaps been averted for now, but the vanity of kings was a serious matter. Handing his hat and gloves to his valet, Benedetti made for his library to begin the delicate task of composing a suitably tactful missive to King Wilhelm on the subject of the succession to the Spanish throne. He had left early for his meeting with Louis Napoléon, before his own mail had been delivered: one of his servants had left it neatly stacked on his desk. He rifled quickly through the envelopes, to see if there was anything that required immediate attention. Right at the bottom of the stack was a letter addressed in Princesse Mathilde's distinctive hand. He hesitated. It had been some weeks since he had last been able to attend one of her *salons*; most likely she was writing to query his absence. That was a matter of only personal importance and could wait. And yet…His hand reached for his paper knife and he slit the envelope, taking out the single sheet of fine paper it contained. *My Dear Monsieur Benedetti*, it began, *I do not know if you recall our conversation, when last we met, concerning the difficulty of recalling accurately the words we speak. I have made enquiries and have made a discovery which I think might be of interest to you in this matter. Call on me soon and I will tell you more.*

A way of ensuring that people—in particular people in power—could be reminded accurately of their words. The conversation came flooding back. If he could have proved what Bismarck had promised in the matter of Luxembourg three years ago, this present difficulty between France and Prussia might have been avoided. If he could find a diplomatic solution to the present difficulty, and know it secure from tampering or rewriting by either side…He set his pen aside and stood, calling out to his valet. "Summon me a carriage. I need to make a call."

* * *

The following morning, accompanied by Princesse Matilde, he found himself at a small house in one of the less fashionable quarters of Paris. It was not a place he would have expected the Princesse to know, and yet the middle-aged maid who admitted them showed no awe at the presence of royalty and merely shepherded them through to a rather cramped room, laid out more as a workshop than a *salon* or a study. A youngish man with thick curly hair stood by a long table, making adjustments to a curious apparatus. It looked, Benedetti thought, like a cross between a small drum, a portable writing desk, and a short binnacle. The man looked up as they entered and smiled. "Princesse! You succeeded." His voice betrayed his origins in southern France. He advanced to meet them and, taking the Princesse's hand, raised it to his lips and kissed it.

"I did, as you see. This is Monsieur le comte Benedetti, our ambassador to the court of Prussia. And this, Monsieur Benedetti, is my friend Charles Cros, poet and scientist."

Cros made a small bow. "It is an honor, Monsieur. I only hope I will be able to be of use to you."

"A pleasure," Benedetti murmured, looking in some confusion at the Princesse.

She took a seat next to the long table. Clearly, her acquaintanceship with Cros was of some long standing, that she was so informal with him. Yet her manner did not suggest any improper degree of familiarity. Cros offered him another chair and he sat, mechanically, waiting for further enlightenment.

"Monsieur Cros," the Princesse repeated, "is a scientist, as I said. He has a particular interest in photography, but recently a new inspiration came to him. If we can, through our knowledge of lens and of chemical reactions, preserve what we see on photographic plates, why then, can we not also preserve sound?" She looked over at Cros.

"Sound," Cros said, "is a matter of vibration. We humans, and the lesser animals, sense these vibrations through the membranes in our ears, just as we perceive images through our eyes. A camera, if you like, has become a sort of artificial eye, which allows us to capture what we see. What if we could also build an artificial ear?" He did not seem to require an answer to his question. "It is easy to construct a membrane: it occurred to me, however, to see if I could attach a stylus of some kind to such a membrane to record its vibrations in some kind of medium, allowing us to, in a way, see sound."

Benedetti was not quite sure where this might lead. "Yes, most interesting."

"But merely to see the sound—to note the shape made by the vibrations—is of little use on its own, except, perhaps, to my fellow scientists. What would be really useful would be if we could then play that sound back, so it might be heard again. Observe," and Cros turned towards his strange apparatus. "You see here the drum, that registers the sound? There is an armature in the center, here, which, at its other end, is sharpened to a point and rests on this disc, which I have coated in lamp-black. Now, if I speak here—" he picked up a tube "—the vibrations of my voice are sensed by the drum and, transmitted along the central mechanism, recorded by the movement of the needle on the drum, like so." As he spoke, the drum began to vibrate and, just as he promised, the needle began to move, making groves on the surface of the disc, which turned slowly. "Now—" Cros set down the tube "—all I have to do is reverse the movement of the disc and…" He raised one hand in a flourish, as the disc reversed its course and the drum again began to vibrate. From the mouth of the tube came a dull, but recognizable sound: the words Cros had spoken earlier, a little distorted, perhaps, but words nonetheless. "Monsieur le comte," Cros said, "I present to you, my Paleophone."

Paleo, Benedetti noted, the past, and *phone*, voice, from the Greek. The voice of the past. This device could, it seemed, take note of what was said and repeat it, without danger of scribal amendment or fading of memory. Assuming, of course, it was not simply a trick. He glanced across at the Princesse and saw that she sat perfectly composed, her hands folded in her lap. She was not the woman to be taken in by a mountebank. She would have checked and checked again, before investing her time in this young man. He cleared his throat and turned back to Cros. "Can your mechanism do this anywhere? Or is it fixed in this room?"

"It's fully portable," Cros said. "Although this one is a little heavy. I'm working on a lighter model, perhaps using wax. The only problem with lamp black is that it smears."

"Is this the only completed one?" Benedetti asked. If this apparatus could be moved, if it could be duplicated…

"This is merely my prototype." Cros smiled at Princesse Mathilde. "Thanks to the generosity of my patron, I have been able to make several more, including one that can make two recordings at once. I hope to be able to demonstrate it to the Academy of Sciences later this year. Would you like to try it for yourself, perhaps? It's very simple to operate."

Benedetti spent the rest of the morning experimenting with the Paleophone and discussing various potential alterations with its inventor. When at last he returned to his lodgings, there was a new lightness in his step. Perhaps, after all, despite Bismarck and the Emperor and the throne of Spain, matters were looking up.

* * *

Less than forty-eight hours later, he stepped off the train at Bad Ems, in the German Rhineland, a recent addition to the territory of Prussia. In his attaché case, he carried an official letter from Louis Napoléon to King Wilhelm, along with documents from the French prime minister for Bismarck and a personal missive from Princesse Mathilde to her friend, the Prussian Queen Augusta. Alongside them, in a special lacquered case, he had a slim metal disc, coated in wax. Behind him, his valet supervised two porters, one carrying the ambassador's travel bags, the other in charge of a trolley bearing a square leather trunk. Benedetti had met numerous times with the King of Prussia and his minister, usually in difficult circumstances. This time…this time, if the saints looked kindly on him, perhaps things might finally become a little easier. He had, for once, slept well on the train and been more than equal to the breakfast the steward had brought him. He smiled as he greeted the Prussian attaché who had been sent to meet him, and again at the newspapermen who clustered on the platform. "So, Herr Ambassador," one of them called out, "what does France want from us now? Another duchy?"

"Peace and friendship, my friend; peace and friendship," Benedetti said, and swept out to his waiting carriage. At his hotel, a message awaited him from King Wilhelm, setting a time that afternoon for their meeting. He checked through his various packages once again, to check all was in order, then took time to bathe and change into formal dress. Wilhelm, always punctilious in his attention to protocol, sent a royal carriage to fetch him, and two of the hotel's liveried footmen lifted the leather box carefully into it for him. "A gift for his majesty the King," Benedetti explained to the staff who met him at the royal residence. "The Emperor Louis Napoléon has instructed me to present this to his majesty straight away." The servants were too well-trained to allow any expression of surprise or uncertainty to show: rather, a boy was dispatched to fetch a trolley and the box accompanied Benedetti through the hall and along the corridor to the king's private study.

In his innermost heart, Benedetti sometimes envied Bismarck his master. Where Louis Napoléon was touchy, Wilhelm was calm; where Louis was fickle, Wilhelm was thoughtful. And, most of all, Wilhelm was an intelligent man who took time and care to understand the complexities of international diplomacy. It would be good to work for such a man, if only that man were French.

The King of Prussia smiled as Benedetti entered and made his bows. He accepted the letter from Louis Napoléon and read it through, his expression neutral. Then he placed it to one side. "A tricky matter, Herr Benedetti."

"Yes, your majesty, but…" and Benedetti hesitated. "There is a further message, if I may?"

"Of course."

Benedetti gestured to the leather box, which the servant had placed on a low table. "A gift from my master, your majesty. But it is also more. If I might demonstrate?" Crossing to the box, he opened the lid to reveal one of Monsieur Cros's Paleophones. It had travelled safely: he had checked it thoroughly upon his arrival at the hotel. "A remarkable invention, your majesty, which has allowed my master to send you his greetings in a more personal form than a letter." He took the metal disc from his attaché case and placed it on the platen. Then he turned the handle to make it play. Wilhelm's eyes widened as the drum first shivered and then began to speak. The words were a little distorted, but nevertheless, through the speaking tube, came the booming voice of Louis Napoléon, sending his good wishes to his fellow monarch.

"Good heavens." Wilhelm came forward, to bend over the apparatus. "As you say, remarkable. One might think the Emperor in the next room. But tell me, Herr Benedetti, how does it work?"

Benedetti explained, showing the king each part of the machine. Then, producing a second disc from his case, he said, "Perhaps you, also, would like to make a recording?"

"It does that as well? Remarkable!"

Benedetti set up the apparatus again and handed Wilhelm the speaking tube to use in his turn. The needle transcribed the vibrations faithfully and when Benedetti replayed the new recording, the king clapped his hands in delight.

"Splendid, splendid!"

"Indeed, your majesty. But this particular example has one more quality: it can make two recordings at a time. As you see, this lever here," and he pointed, "controls this second needle, which can write upon a lower disk, following the motions of the upper needle." His palms were wet. He paused to draw in a breath. Now was his moment. "If you wished, we could make a recording of our meeting, one for you and one for the Emperor, so that you both have preserved every detail of this historic exchange." He was, he reflected, profoundly glad that Bismarck had not been invited to attend. The minister would have seen the danger of such a proceeding at once.

But Wilhelm, enchanted by his new toy, saw only the entertainment value. He pronounced the idea acceptable and the speaking tube was placed on the desk between them.

"And now," the king said, "to business. You are here, of course, on this matter of Spain."

"Indeed, your majesty. You appreciate, I am sure, the position this offer to your cousin places my Emperor in."

"Of course. But the Spanish government have made the offer themselves. It was not, I am sure your master realizes, of our seeking."

Benedetti was not sure at all. There were days when Louis Napoléon seemed to mistake Bismarck for the devil. But he only nodded and agreed that that was so.

"It places me," Wilhelm said, "in a difficult position. Prince Leopold is my cousin, and I am head of the house of Hohenzollern. As such, I have a personal duty to consider this offer on his behalf."

"Yes, your majesty."

"In my capacity as head of the house of Hohenzollern only, you understand? As King of Prussia, the succession to Spain is not my affair. It is a matter for the Spanish themselves." Benedetti nodded. Wilhelm continued. "The truth is, Herr Benedetti, that the offer does not please either me or my cousin. Prince Leopold is a Catholic and it is a sad fact that, at present, relations between Catholics and Protestants in my kingdom are not as harmonious as I might wish them. If I were to be seen to favor a Catholic nobleman, my Protestant lords would be unhappy. I do not want that trouble. And then, Leopold does not, in fact, wish to go to Spain. He does not speak Spanish, you see."

"That would be a difficulty, indeed, your majesty." Benedetti hesitated. "But my master is concerned. As the neighbor of Spain, he feels that he should have been consulted."

"That's a matter for the government of Spain," Wilhelm said, "but, as a fellow ruler, I understand his feelings on the matter. It was not well done of them."

"He is concerned, however, that they applied to you without also informing him."

"In my capacity as head of the house of Hohenzollern, Herr Benedetti, and so you may assure the Emperor. As King of Prussia, I have no role in this, and it is not of my seeking. I see it as a family matter, nothing more. The Emperor may have my word on that and I shall write to him personally to confirm it. This is a family affair, nothing more, and I intend to refuse my consent. Leopold shall not be king of Spain."

"Thank you, your majesty." Behind Benedetti, the twin needles continued their etching onto the discs of wax. "So Prussia does not intend to support this election?"

"Prussia has no business with Spain at all. And Wilhelm of Hohenzollern will not consent."

"His imperial majesty will be glad to hear it."

"I am glad to be able to reassure him. His representations through you have been all that is gracious and reasonable. And I am delighted with his gift. I hope you will tell him so."

"I will, your majesty, but you have already done so." Benedetti said. He gestured at the Paleophone. "Your words are on the disc which I will present to my master on my return to Paris."

Wilhelm laughed. "So you will! What a splendid invention that is, to be sure. You must tell its creator, as well as the Emperor."

"You have my word," Benedetti said, and bowed. He lifted the lower disc carefully from its bed and placed it in its special sleeve. "An honor, your majesty."

* * *

Bismarck turned phrases over in his mind as he made his way through the Kurpark on his way to his meeting with the king. "The French Emperor demanded…through his ambassador, whose behavior was most impertinent… unreasonable pressure…French arrogance." The words for a dispatch to the press formed themselves easily. Louis

Napoléon was an upstart, an opportunist who attributed to himself talents and powers far beyond his reach. He was disrespectful, he was greedy, he considered himself Emperor of Europe, not merely France. This time, Bismarck reflected, he was sure to have gone too far in his importuning of King Wilhelm. This time, surely, there would be grounds for war. He repressed a smile, thinking of the industrial wealth of Lorraine and the vineyards of Alsace. Both regions spoke German. Both regions, logically, should come under the rule of Prussia as the leader among the German states, rather than languishing under the control of France. Three years ago, he had very nearly provoked the French into war. This time… Louis Napoléon would never have been able to control himself over this matter of the succession to Spain. King Wilhelm was sure to be angered. And if he were not…well, minutes could always be rewritten, and the rewrites, once presented to the press, became as good as true. He would write a short letter to his friends in the German press as soon as he had seen the king, and then, well…

"Ah, Bismarck, look at this." The king's tone might have given a lesser man pause, but Bismarck was still thinking of his letter. Wilhelm waved him over to the window, where an odd contraption stood on a table. "It's a gift from the Emperor of France. Very ingenious."

"I'm sure, sire." It looked like some piece of railway equipment. Louis Napoléon had the oddest taste in gifts. "Sire, in the matter of the French ambassador…"

"Oh, that's all arranged," Wilhelm said. "I've given him my assurances that it's a purely family matter."

"Then I shall write to the press," Bismarck said. "If your majesty is satisfied with the ambassador's behavior in all things, of course. And I shall ensure your secretary makes notes of your meeting, of course."

"Oh, there's no need for that," Wilhelm said. "It's all done. I have a full record here, and so does Monsieur Benedetti."

"The ambassador's notes may not be completely reliable, sire. He is, after all, French."

"What?" Wilhelm was still concentrating on his machinery. "No, there are no notes, Bismarck. We made a recording, one for my archives and one for the Emperor. Now, listen." He cranked a handle and on the apparatus a disc began to spin. The contraption vibrated and then, from a long tube, emerged the voices first of the king and then of Benedetti, discussing the matter of the succession to Spain. The ambassador, it seemed, had been all that was courteous, reasonable, and respectful. And the king—oh, the fickleness of rulers—the king had issued full reassurances on the matter. There was nothing there to anger even Louis Napoléon. There was nothing that might provoke him to war.

There was only one disc. A brief glimmer of hope woke in Bismarck's breast. He said, "The French ambassador left this with us?"

"Yes, and several blank discs, too. We can make more, as we need them."

"But the ambassador himself…he took a written record of all this, yes?" Notes went missing. Notes could be discredited. There was still a chance here to annoy and provoke France.

"Oh no," Wilhelm said. "That's what's really clever about this device—it's called a Paleophone, you know. It can make more than one recording at a time. Benedetti has a disc, too, to play to Louis when he returns."

"Marvellous, sire," said Bismarck, and mentally tore up his dispatch.

Historical Note

The causes of the Franco-Prussian war of 1870 have deep roots in the ambitions, rivalries, and maneuverings of both sides, but the final straw was the Ems Dispatch, of 13th July 1870, from Bismarck to the press and foreign embassies in Prussia. In it, he made claims of threats made by Louis Napoléon to King Wilhelm and of disrespectful behavior to the king by the French ambassador, Vincent, comte Benedetti. While Louis Napoléon was undoubtedly very angry about the potential succession of a German to the throne of Spain, Bismarck's dispatch, in an early example of "fake news," misrepresented the French approach and omitted conciliatory behavior by King Wilhelm (who really did see it as a family matter). The result was that, insulted after years of provocations, France declared war on Prussia. The Prussian army rapidly overran the territories of Alsace-Lorraine, captured Louis Napoléon, and seized Paris. The result was the loss to France of valuable territories, the end of the Second Empire, and the declaring of a new republic in France. Wilhelm was declared Emperor of Germany on 1st January 1871, after the formerly satellite southern German states joined his North German federation. It's a fascinating and complex period of history, whose after-effects resonated down to the outbreak of the First World War and were a contributory cause of that latter. Bismarck seems, by most analyses, to have actively sought to provoke the French into war as part of his drive to bring all German speaking territories under Prussian rule. If the Franco-Prussian war had not occurred, this may have been a slower process (Catholic southern Germany was suspicious of the ambitions of the north). Indeed, without the Franco-Prussian war, World War I might have been very different, or, just possibly, even not happened at all.

Charles Cros lodged a plan for his Paleophone with the French Academy of Sciences on 30th April 1877, not 1870, and there is no evidence he ever built a working model. It's also highly unlikely he ever met Princess Mathilde or Vincent Benedetti. It was an ingenious invention that pre-dated Thomas Edison's phonograph by several months. But had he invented it a little earlier, and been able to attract a significant patron, the Paleophone might well have had the potential to change the course of history, particularly in the hands of an intelligent man like Benedetti.

Everyone in this story, apart from the nameless servants, was a real historical person. I have, perhaps, been rather hard on Otto von Bismarck, who was a complicated and important man. My only excuse is that every story that flirts with war needs an antagonist and he had the misfortune to fit the bill.

ABOUT THE AUTHORS

MIKE BARRETTA is a retired U.S. Naval Aviator having deployed across the world flying the SH-60B Seahawk helicopter. He currently works for a defense contractor as a maintenance test pilot. He holds a Master's degree in Strategic Planning and International Negotiation from the Naval Post-Graduate School, and a Master's in English from the University of West Florida. His stories have appeared in Baen's Universe, Redstone, New Scientist, Orson Scott Card's Intergalactic Medicine Show and various anthologies such as War Stories: New Military Science Fiction, The Year's Best Military Scifi and Space Opera and the Young Explorer's Adventure Guide.

C.W. BRIAR is the author of the dark fantasy novel Whispers From The Depths. His stories blend monsters and terrors with adventure and humor. He lives in Upstate New York with his family and their pack of corgis. www.cwbriar. com www.facebook.com/CWBriar

DALE COZORT is a recovering computer programmer and currently an educator, working mostly with special needs children. He lives with his wife, two cats and occasionally one of his grown daughters, in a college town sixty miles from Chicago. He has been writing seriously for over a decade and has six published novels, all of them involving time-travel or alternate history in some way. He has a website at www.DaleCozort.com.

ELEKTRA HAMMOND emulates her multi-sided idol Buckaroo Banzai by going in several directions at once. She's been involved in publishing since the 1990s—now she writes, concocts anthologies, and edits science fiction for various and sundry. When not freelancing or appearing at science fiction conventions, she travels the world judging cat shows. Elektra is a graduate of the Odyssey Writing Workshop and an associate member of SFWA. She lives in Delaware with her husband, Mike, and more than the usual allotment of felines. Find her on twitter @elektraUM, facebook https://www.facebook.com/elektra.hammond, or at her website http://www.untilmidnight.com.

BRIAN HUGENBRUCH lives in Upstate New York with his wife and their pets. By day, he writes information security programs to protect your data on (and from) the internet. By night, he writes speculative fiction about the ways imagination fuels our lives. Occasionally, the two intersect in weird and fascinating ways. His fiction has also appeared in the ZNB anthology THE RAZOR'S EDGE. You can find him at the-lettersea.com or talk to him on Twitter @Bwhugen. No, he's not sure how to say his last name, either.

ELIZABETH KITE lives on a mountaintop at the fringes of the Las Vegas valley. When she's not tanning by starlight, you can find her writing wild fantasies next to a cup of tea (or a shot of whiskey). She's slightly obsessed with foxes and inexplicably stalked by cats wherever she goes. You can visit this procrastinator of the highest order on twitter @ Kitewrites.

STEPHEN LEIGH has professionally published thirty novels and over fifty short stories, both under his own name and the pen name S.L. Farrell. His most recent novel is A RISING MOON, a sequel to A FADING SUN (DAW Books/Penguin, November 2018). He also has a science fiction book in progress under contract to DAW Books. Steve's work has been nominated for and won awards within the sf/fantasy genre. He is also a frequent contributor to George RR Martin's WILD CARDS series. Find him at www. stephenleigh.com

IAN R. MACLEOD is the author of seven critically-acclaimed novels and five print short story collections, plus two large new "greatest hits" e-book collections entitled *Everywhere* and *Nowhere*. His work has won the Arthur C Clarke Award and the John W Campbell Memorial Award for the Year's Best Novel, along with Sidewise Award for Alternative-World Fiction (twice) and the World Fantasy Award (again twice). He lives in the riverside town of Bewdley in England. He maintains a website at www.ianrmacleod.com and his Twitter feed is @IanRMacleod1.

JULIET E. MCKENNA is a British fantasy author. Loving history, myth and other worlds, she has written fifteen epic fantasy novels, starting with *The Thief's Gamble* which began *The Tales of Einarinn*. She writes diverse shorter fiction, from stories for themed anthologies such as *Alien Artifacts* and *Fight Like A Girl* to forays into dark fantasy and steampunk. Exploring new digital opportunities in association with Wizard's Tower Press, she's re-issued her early backlist as ebooks as well as publishing original short story collections and modern fantasy novels, starting with *The Green Man's Heir*. Visit julietemckenna.com or follow @JulietEMcKenna on Twitter.

KAT OTIS was born with a surplus of creativity and quickly learned to cope by telling stories to anyone who would listen. When she's not writing, she's an historian, mathematician, singer, and photographer. Her historical fiction has been published in Daily Science Fiction, OSC's Intergalactic Medicine Show, and Flash Fiction Online. You can find her full bibliography at katotis.com and she procrastinates on Twitter as @kat_otis

MICHAEL ROBERTSON writes science fiction and fantasy stories while holding down a job at a non-profit. His stories tend to feature people (or robots, aliens, or other entities) trying to do the right thing. He lives and works in New York City, and his writing has appeared in anthologies published by Zombies Need Brains, Parsec Ink, and in two issues of Cockroach Conservatory. His web site is mrobertson.com, and he can be found on twitter as @michaels2cents.

New York Times bestseller **KRISTINE KATHRYN RUSCH** has won the Sidewise Award for Best Alternate History twice. She's best known under the Rusch name for science fiction, including her two ongoing space opera series, The Retrieval Artist and the Diving Universe. She's also an editor, including her Hugo-award winning stint as the only female editor of *The Magazine of Fantasy & Science Fiction*. She writes award-winning mysteries under the name Kris Nelscott and beloved light fantasy romance novels as Kristine Grayson. To find out more about her work, go to her website, kriswrites.com, and read a free short story every Monday.

KARI SPERRING is the author of two novels (*Living with Ghosts* [DAW 2009] and *The Grass King's Concubine* [DAW 2012]. As Kari Maund, she has written and published five books and many articles on Celtic and Viking history and co-authored a book on the history and real people behind her favourite novel, *The Three Musketeers* (with Phil Nanson). She's British and lives in Cambridge, England, with her partner Phil and three very determined cats, who guarantee that everything she writes will have been thoroughly sat upon. Her website is http://www.karisperring.com and you can also find her on Facebook.

HARRY TURTLEDOVE is an escaped Byzantine historian. He writes science fiction (much of it alternate history), fantasy (much of it historically based), and sometimes historical fiction. He lives in Los Angeles with his wife, fellow writer Laura Frankos, and three preposterously overprivilegd cats.

RICK WILBER's first alternate-history story about famous baseball player and OSS spy Moe Berg, "Something Real," appeared in Asimov's Science Fiction magazine in 2012 and won the Sidewise Award for Best Alternate History—Short Form for that year. Several more of Rick's Moe Berg stories have come along since, including this one, which features a post-war version of Berg. Wilber's novel, *Alien Morning,* (Tor, 2016) was a finalist for the John W. Campbell Award for Best Science Fiction Novel of 2016. Its sequel, *Alien Day: Notes from Holmanville*, will be out in 2020. Wilber teaches in the low-residency MFA genre-fiction program at Western Colorado University.

ABOUT THE EDITORS

STEVEN H SILVER is a sixteen-time Hugo Award nominee and was the publisher of the Hugo-nominated fanzine *Argentus*. He was the founder of ISFiC Press, serving as editor and publisher for 8 years. He has edited anthologies for DAW and collections for NESFA Press. He began publishing short fiction in 2008 and his most recently story is "Webinar: Web Sites" in the anthology *A Tangled Web*. In 1995, he created the Sidewise Award for Alternate History and has served as the award's administrator ever since. Steven serves as the Event Coordinator for SFWA.

* * *

JOSHUA PALMATIER is a fantasy author with a PhD in mathematics. He currently teaches at SUNY Oneonta in upstate New York, while writing in his "spare" time, editing anthologies, and running the anthology-producing small press Zombies Need Brains LLC. His most recent fantasy novel, *Reaping the Aurora,* concludes the fantasy series begun in *Shattering the Ley* and *Threading the Needle*, although you can also find his "Throne of Amenkor" series and the "Well of Sorrows" series still on the shelves. He is currently hard at work writing his next novel and designing the kickstarter for the next Zombies Need Brains anthology project. You can find out more at www.joshuapalmatier.com or at the small press' site www.zombiesneedbrains.com. Or follow him on Twitter as @bentateauthor or @ZNBLLC.

ACKNOWLEDGMENTS

This anthology would not have been possible without the tremendous support of those who pledged during the Kickstarter. Everyone who contributed not only helped create this anthology, they also helped solidify the foundation of the small press Zombies Need Brains LLC, which I hope will be bringing SF&F themed anthologies to the reading public for years to come . . . as well as perhaps some select novels by leading authors, eventually. I want to thank each and every one of them for helping to bring this small dream into reality. Thank you, my zombie horde.

The Zombie Horde: Colleen Champagne, Robert Coleman, Elena Beghetto, Mark Simon Phillips, Corey T, Sarah Cornell, Jenny Barber, Larisa LaBrant, Emma L, Jim Gotaas, Arturo, Lavinia Ceccarelli, Karen Thomas, Carol J. Guess, Meg Leader, Ian Harvey, Joseph Hoopman, John Green, Cyn Armistead, Jason S. Clary, John T. Sapienza, Jr., Carolyn C, Jen1701D, A.A. Jankiewicz, Santiago Akira Kitashima, windypenguin, Dr. Kai Herbertz, Michael Kohne, Pat Hayes, Joanne Burrows, Alan Smale, Sheryl R. Hayes,

Michael A. Burstein, Todd V. Ehrenfels, Kaiqua, Anonymous Reader, David Holden, Neil Clarke, Jaq Greenspon, Michael D'Auben, Eagle Archambeault, Kristi Chadwick, H Lynnea Johnson, John Winkelman, Studio 9 Games, Joe Hauser, Misty and Todd Lambert, Michele Fry, Shaun Kilgore, Regis M. Donovan, Steven Halter, Roger Simmons, Penny, Gabe Krabbe, Simon Dick, Chris Gerrib, Justin P. Miller, James Williams, Sachin Suchak, Mark Carter, Kelly Melnyk, Tory Shade, Harvey Brinda, Howard J. Bampton, Ivan Donati, Cheryl Preyer, Michael Halverson, Sean Collins, Kiya Nicoll, GMarkC, Michael Fedrowitz, Sharon Wood, David Zurek, Stephanie Lucas, Glori Medina, Jakub Narębski, Jörg Tremmel, Andrew Hatchell, Stephanie Cranford, Susan Oke, Sidney Whitaker, Engel Dreizehn, Andrea Terdik, John Markley, Amber Bryant, Meagan Pledger, Ian Chung, Pam Blome, Sebastian Müller, Cody Black, James Moriarty, Judith Mortimore, Karina Kolb, Ronda Sanders, Chrysta Stuckless, Mark Kiraly, Michelle Palmer, Craig Hackl, Beth Kampa, David Perkins, Brendan Burke, Carl Wiseman, Andrija Popovic, Anna Rudholm, Beth Lobdell, Cat Wyatt, Chad Bowden, Kevin Kibelstis, Patricia Gates, Scarlett Eisenhauer, Molly J., Robert Gilson, Grant Canterbury, Tina and Byron Connell, Rob Fowler, Michelle T., Darrell Z. Grizzle, L.C., Gabriel Cruz, Vicki Greer, Russell Martens, Samantha T., Ron Oakes, Ben Nash, Miranda Floyd, Wolf SilverOak, Tommy Acuff, John Senn, Kevin Winter, Cat Girczyc, Pat Knuth, Betsy, Claire Sims, Jeremy Audet, Whitney Gutierrez, Christine Hale, James Conason, Andy Pfrimmer, Wendy Cornwall, Barde Press, Mark Slauter, Jo Good, Tina Nichols, Myca Arcangel, Chloe Nagle, Tasha Turner, Sheelagh Semper, B. Keith Dunn, Jude, Jennifer Berk, Hoose Family, Nirven, Terry Williams, Leah Webber, Katherine Matthews, ChillieBrick, Jennifer Robinson, Jaymie Larkey Maham, Ian M. Fowler, Martina W., Brenda Rezk, Céline Malgen, Jennifer Priester, Cory Williams, Brendan

Lonehawk, Tina Noe Good, Katherine Malloy, Margaret Bumby, Cheryl Losinger, andrew ahn and sin soracco, Pierre Gauthier, Susan Simko, Kate Barela, Colette Reap, Danan Bradley, Steve Lord, Götz Weinreich, Scott Raun, William Leisner, Scott Drummond, Julie Kovac, Kristine Smith, Michael Stearns, Veronica Kavanagh, Tim Jordan, Debbie Matsuura, Rick McKnight, Nick W, Josie Ryan, Cathy Green, A.Chatain, Toni Lichtenstein Bogolub, Brad Roberts, Stephen Ballentine, Melanie McCoy, Jamieson Cobleigh, Anne Burner, Lutz F. Krebs, Francesca, Jillian and Doug Zeigler, Peggy J, eric priehs, Christine Ethier, Patti Short, Colbey, R.J.H, Mary Alice Wuerz, Helen, Robert Claney, Gina Freed, K. Hodghead, Clariben Huntington, Ginger Field, Katrina Coll, Leila Qışın, Amanda Nixon, Tom Powers, Charles Budworth, RKBookman, Jenni P., Leonie Duane, Brian D Lambert, Dagmar Baumann, Gavran, Michele Hall, Graeme, C. L. Werner, Andrew J Clark IV, jjmcgaffey, Anne M. Rindfliesch, Gary Phillips, Stacey Kaye Manuel, Andrea Watson, Abby Kieser, Aysha Rehm, Angie Hogencamp, Elizabeth Klandrud, Annalise M., Taryn, Peter Thew, Mark Newman, Tim Jones, Donna Gaudet, Michael Kahan, Craig "Stevo" Stephenson, T.D. England, Mark Hirschman, Niall Gordon, Jerrie the filkferengi, Sheryl Ehrlich, Edward Ellis, A. Eddy, Elektra Hammond, Uncle Batman, Sean and Catherine Kane, Gail Morse, Sarah Klapper-Lehman, Erik T Johnson, Bonnie Stewart, Eleanor Russell, Amanda Hudson, Kerry aka Trouble, Stephanie Slavin, Kristin Coley, Rebecca M, Koen Andrews, Matthew Aronoff, Rachel Shell Vance, Evergreen Lee, Margaret St. John, Jonathan S. Chance, Mark Lukens, Jenn Whitworth, Yankton Robins, Carl Dershem, Erin Himrod, L. E. Doggett, Andrew Foxx, Ruth Duggan, Jonathan, Greg Vose, Danny Dyer, Beckey and Steve Sanchez, Shirley, Jesse N. Klein, Meg Fielding, Guy W. Thomas, Chantelle Wilson, Linda Pierce, Alexander Smith, Jason Tongier, Brenda Moon, Nathan Turner, Anthony R.

Cardno, Catherine Gross-Colten, SusanB, compiledwrong, SwordFire, Amelia Smith, Chris Brant, David Rowe, Michael Bernardi, Kayla Sinclair, Joe Stech, Ronald H. Miller, James Lucas, Barbara Matzner-Volfing, Natascha McGilvray, Louise Lowenspets, Mark Featherston, Deanna Harrison, Phillip Spencer, Susan Carlson, Liz Tuckwell, rissatoo, Brent Johnson, Duncan's Books and More, Chris Matosky, Matt Hope, Mervi Mustonen, Kerry Ebanks, Michelle Brenner, Karen the Griffmom, Sarina McKown-Goh, K. R. Smith, Gretchen Persbacker, Camille Lofters, Andrew and Kate Barton, Q Fortier, Sally Qwill Janin, Paul Alex Gray, Kitty Likes, Chris, Carol Mammano, Lisa Howard, Rolf Laun, H. Rasmussen, Sharan Volin, Lace, Elisabeth Bender, Frank Nissen, Steven Mentzel, William Hall, R. Hunter, Deirdre Murphy, Simba, Lisa Rich, Kathryn Haines, Mary Hargrove, Charissa Weaks, Marty Poling Tool, Dan R. Herrick, Chris McLaren, Curtis Frye, Nancy M. Tice, Elizabeth, Carla Hollar, Olivia Montoya, Paul McErlean, Sarah Eyermann, Amy Rogers, Deborah Torrance, Mark Manning, Barbara Silcox, C. Joshua Villines, NewGuyDave, Kevin Niemczyk, Max Kaehn, OgreM, Kixie K. Nowell, Ichino, Chloe Turner, Robby Thrasher, Yosen Lin, Tanya K., Daniel O., Caitlin Mininger, A.J. Abrao, Louisa Swann, Fred and Mimi Bailey, John H. Bookwalter Jr., Kevin Looney, Alex Shvartsman, Mom, Alyssa Hillary, Isaac 'Will It Work' Dansicker, Steven Howell Wilson, James McIntosh, Axisor, Olav Rokne, Michael M. Jones, Jason Palmatier, Belkis Marcillo, Elaine Costa, Jennifer Dunne, Mud Mymudes, Jules Jones, Melissa Shumake, laura robbins, Julie Holderman, Lizard L., Cliff Winnig, Rhiannon Raphael, Cherie Livingston, Amanda S., Tom B., D-Rock, Y. H. Lee, Kristin Evenson Hirst, Tibs, Linda, Keith E. Hartman, R Kirkpatrick, Yaron Davidson, H. Kriesel, Mike M, Elaine Tindill-Rohr, Kathryn Allen, Cat Rambo, Walter Prawak, Kayliealien, Crystal Sarakas, Elizabeth Gray, Lynn Kramer, Michelle Botwinick, Sharon

Sayegh, Becky Allyn Johnson, Tom Berrisford, Erin Penn, Taylor Alcantar, Shawn Blackhawk, Missy Katano